JACK OF ALL TRADES

JACK WELLS

LAST WALTZ PUBLISHING

PUBLICATION HISTORY

Riding the Ghost Train initially appeared in These Lingering Shadows, a gothic short story anthology published by **Last Waltz Publishing** on 10/5/2022, ISBN 979-8355229467.

The Stowaway initially appeared in Out of the Shadows, a drabble anthology in support of Mulligan's Manor, a home for at-risk LGTBQ+ teens, published by **Red Cape Publishing** on 12/17/2021, ASIN B09MV7CY3W.

The Sentimental Ending was submitted in answer to an open publication call for a short story of roughly 5000 words, and initially appeared in the periodical Stranger with Friction (Vol. 6), published by **St. Rooster Books** on 06/19/2022, ISBN 979-8837168550. It has been re-edited, with only minor corrections made to fix the most egregious of mistakes.

A Frontier Haunting, in its original form, was submitted in answer to an open publication call for a short story of roughly 5000 words, and initially appeared in the periodical Stranger with Friction (Vol. 4), published by **St. Rooster Books** on 12/13/2021, ISBN 979-8783959912. The version presented here is almost completely revamped, with significant changes made to the location, cast, and overall plot. At nearly three times the original word count, it is, for all intents and purposes, an entirely new tale.

CONTENTS

Dedication   1

Foreword - Monsters Among Us   3

Introduction   7

1. See No Evil (Overture)   11

2. Chapter I   13

3. Chapter II   19

4. Chapter III   27

5. Chapter IV   33

6. Chapter V   37

7. Chapter VI   41

8. Chapter VII   47

9. Chapter VIII   57

10. Her First Time   61

11. Psycho Killer   87

12. See No Evil (Chorus)	107
13. Chapter IX	109
14. Chapter X	117
15. Chapter XI	127
16. Chapter XII	133
17. Chapter XIII	139
18. Chapter XIV	147
19. Chapter XV	153
20. Chapter XVI	159
21. Riding the Ghost Train	167
22. The Stowaway	185
23. See No Evil (Cadenza)	187
24. Chapter XVII	189
25. Chapter XVIII	193
26. Chapter XIX	201
27. Chapter XX	207
28. Chapter XXI	213
29. Chapter XXII	217
30. Chapter XXIII	223
31. Chapter XXIV	233
32. The Sentimental Ending	239
33. A Frontier Haunting	257

34. See No Evil (Finale)   303

35. Chapter XXV   305

36. Chapter XXVI   313

37. Chapter XXVII   317

38. Chapter XXVIII   323

39. Chapter XXIX   333

Acknowledgements   343

Jack Wells   344

About the Author   345

Last Waltz Publishing   346

Free Story from LWP   347

FOREWORD - MONSTERS AMONG US

I'm going to start off by saying, when you read something by Jack Wells, you can trust he's taking you on a journey. Setting you down in a place and time, creating an immersive atmosphere that wraps its arms around you with a chilling embrace.

Monsters, as we have come to know them, take on many forms. They are the vampires that haunt the darkest corners, the ghosts in the attic, the goblin under the stairs, or the creature lurking beneath murky waters. But our perception of monsters extends beyond the bounds of imagination—it reaches into the realm of reality. They live amongst us, camouflaged in the ordinary, cloaked by the mundane. They wear the masks of our neighbors. Our friends. And even ourselves.

How often have we glimpsed into the eyes of another only to find a glint of darkness or uncertainty? How often have we looked in the mirror and found darkness staring back?

Our personal demons which we grapple with in our daily lives, those invisible shadows that haunt our thoughts, often wield a power more potent than any supernatural beast. These monsters are born from our insecurities, regrets, and unspoken desires, lurking within the dark recesses of our hearts. They gnaw at our resolve, testing the strength of our character and the boundaries of our compassion.

To acknowledge monsters is to acknowledge our own vulnerability, our fears and doubts, and ultimately, our shared humanity.

Dear reader, brace yourself as Jack Wells takes you on a journey that traverses the boundaries between reality and imagination, where monsters roam both within our minds and in the world around us.

See No Evil takes you into the pages of a penny dreadful and makes you feel the unsettling atmosphere creep all around you. The year is 1892, and detectives are on the hunt in the grim underbelly of London, searching for a serial killer leaving behind a trail of gruesome murders. Don't worry, Jack will let you breathe, unlike the monster in this tale. The story is broken into four parts, threaded throughout the collection like back alley stitchwork, so be patient as it seeps within and nestles into the back of your mind.

Her First Time is a sultry tale centered around a young woman in rural America who learns the potency of seduction.

Psycho Killer follows homicide detective Desmond Little as he is faced with his most baffling case yet. He is met with a scene of horror inside an ordinary diner—every patron is dead. There are no visible injuries, no blood, and no signs of a struggle. Then, his attention moves to the jukebox. Is it a clue? A warning? Or something worse?

Riding the Ghost Train is about one man's journey to recover from alcoholism in a secluded cabin. In this gripping tale, witness the relentless struggle to confront one's inner demons, as the line between sanity and madness becomes increasingly uncertain.

Stowaway is a drabble of dread for one unlucky hitchhiker who finds himself in churning waters.

The Sentimental Ending follows Roger Neiman who is taking an impromptu trip to Norway to tour the setting of a first-person survival-horror game. Roger prepares to visit the café where a virtual murder takes place, along with locations where many of the game's other iconic locations were filmed. However, as Roger steps into the real-world settings of his favorite digital pastime, the lines between reality and fantasy blur, and he finds himself trapped in a game of survival he never signed up for.

A Frontier Haunting is about a young girl who falls prey to a malevolent entity. To combat this spectral menace, former lawman and ghost hunter extraordinaire, Garrett Kayce, is summoned to the town. But before he can confront the spectral foe, he must first fight its sinister army of draugr. In this supernatural Western showdown between the living and the dead, Garrett must summon all of his courage to save the girl and banish the lingering evil once and for all.

As you turn these pages, I hope you embrace the profound truth that monsters, in their various forms, are a haunting reflection of the complexities that define what it means to be human.

Marie Lanza
09/13/2023

INTRODUCTION

Hello.

Thank you for letting me have the floor.

My name is Jack, and I have a problem.

My problem, dear reader, is that I cannot help but write oddball stories. I always gravitate towards ideas that are just slightly left (or right) of the center. The roads less traveled, as it were. Those darkened corners which receive minimal traffic and only the barest hints of illumination. M. Night Shyamalan has his requisite "twists", I have my bizarre little tales that don't always have a niche. Does it sometimes make my works difficult to market? Yes. Does it (potentially) make it harder for me to sell books? Also, yes. Am I likely to change my approach anytime soon? Nope.

I think there's an inherent beauty in strangeness, and a melancholic appeal to the things which exist on the edge of normality. In the periphery of our perception. Like a classic car concealed under a tarp, its stately lines and regal bearing hidden just out of view. I suppose, if nothing else, it is notions like these which fuel my creative process. That's not to say that I cannot, or will not, indulge in a straightforward story at times, I just prefer to be esoteric whenever possible. Call it a foible. A character flaw.

Not that there is anything wrong with the other aspects of horror story-telling. Shock, gore, splatter, smut, abstract, and classic monsters with new twists... it's all good. It all fills in the various nooks and crannies that keep the horror industry alive and airtight. As for me, I am perfectly content to leave those slices of spookiness to the professionals, those who weave such tales far better than ever I could. I will stick with my subtle dark fiction, thank you very much, and be perfectly content in doing so. A common thread across the indie writing community (and within the horror subset especially) is that there's plenty of audience to go around, which is an outlook I subscribe to wholeheartedly. There are still, comparatively, far more readers than writers, and each genre gets its time in the limelight—at this moment, extreme horror is all the rage, but those seas will shift soon enough. Perhaps subtle scares will get their moment to shine once more.

For those of you who don't know, I am still a relatively new author, with my first book having been published in January of 2022. I suppose you could say that I'm low mileage, still with that "new car smell" (to return to vehicle metaphors). As such, I am still trying to establish goals and a consistent cadence for my writing career. These, more than anything else, will be the adversaries standing in my way. I deeply admire writers who can set aside a chunk of time, plop down in front of their word processor of choice, and just hammer out thousands of words without pause. It's impressively productive, to say the least. It is also, however, something that I will never be able to do. My writing style has always hewed closer to small-scale skirmishes as opposed to large, protracted battles. Between work, kids, home improvement, needy cats, and my laughable attempts at a social life, I have to be willing to accept what little victories I can. Hit-and-run wordsmithing, adding a sentence here or a paragraph there as time permits. Oh, I'll win the war eventually—but only by way of heavy attrition and guerrilla tactics.

As such, many of the stories included within *Jack of all Trades* (and especially *See No Evil*) took quite a bit of effort to bring to life. Probably more than was strictly necessary. A perfectionist at heart, I agonized over a litany of factors: period-appropriate vernacular, researching factual details that had maybe half a second of page time, and when to use (or not use) alliteration and poetic passages. All of these considerations lengthened an already arduous writing process. And then there is the fact that, at roughly 87,000 words, *Jack of all Trades* is the largest book I have released thus far. That's a lot of words, my friends. A lot of opportunities for self-criticism.

I share these things with you not out of some misguided search for sympathy or in a veiled attempt to impress; merely to convey that I want you, the reader, to have the most well-written stories possible held in your hands. Even if it takes a ridiculously long time for me to get them there.

Some of the tales contained herein have already seen the light of day, having been written in response to open publishing calls, back while I was still working on the *Monochrome Noir* series. As per standard guidelines, these were shorter offerings, typically constrained to a max of 5000 words. *The Stowaway*, my one and only drabble, was (by definition) constrained to 100. Some of these stories might even be a little rough, indicative of where I was with establishing my narrative voice at the time. The rest of the works, however, are brand new creations targeted specifically for this collection, with the only limitations being my creativity and schedule.

Friend, publisher, and good human extraordinaire, Mr. Daemon Manx, has earned (and rightly so) the qualifier of writing "horror with a heart". His creations are frequently scary AND emotionally earnest, which is a wonderful combination. For me, I aspire to earn my own qualifier, hopefully establishing a legacy of being the author of "strange stories, beautifully told". Of course, whether or not that goal has been achieved is ultimately up to you, the reader. If nothing else, I just hope you were entertained and/or educated along the way to your decision, and I appreciate you giving my labor of love a chance.

With the utmost respect and a heaving helping of humbleness,

Jack "Always Doing it the Hard Way" Wells

SEE NO EVIL (OVERTURE)

Wherein ritual murders, somewhat similar to those of Jack the Ripper, are being committed against prostitutes in the dockyards of Victorian England.

Dramatis Personae

James Guthrie

An inspector with the London constabulary

Constance Wright

A prostitute in London's Poplar district

R.M. Müller

An unscrupulous man of science and medicine

Lady Ellington

A powerful Ministry official

Fiona McCarthy

A prostitute in London's Poplar district

Constable Higgins

A young policeman

JACK WELLS

Superintendent Barnhold
Guthrie's superior

CHAPTER 1

R.M. Müller
Undisclosed Location
Sept 11th, 1892
Research Journal Entry # 62
2:51 AM

Subject # 2 arrives several hours after the expected delivery time, an interminable delay which frustrates me to no end. I pace the length and breadth of the room whilst laborers unload the cargo, my footfalls heavy with displeasure, half-formed words of reprimand hovering on my lips. I find tardiness to be the very peak of unprofessional behaviour, not to mention a waste of my time. Such unbecoming conduct would <u>not</u> be tolerated were this a sanctioned medical procedure.

Given the illicit nature of the conveyance, however, I understand that there must be an allowable margin of error. Criminality is not an exact science. As for the individuals who engage in such activities, they can hardly be expected to observe proper etiquette, now can they? Still, these acknowledgments do little to quell my mounting impatience.

Constitutionally unflappable, the project's director stands to one side in silent observation, face half obscured by shadow. Deft eyes take in every detail, missing nothing. If I am criticized for my involuntary fretting, there is no visible indication.

Our makeshift base of operations is still undergoing construction. Within the main room—a space roughly forty feet by sixty—controlled chaos reigns, people and machinery scattered throughout seemingly at random. The oversized immersion tank, like an industrial version of a child's aquarium (albeit exponentially larger), was completed yesterday but has yet to be filled. Six sizeable oaken casks are stacked next to it, their mysterious contents safe from prying eyes. Near the stone stairway, specialists wearing cumbersome leather gloves unspool thick copper wire sheathed in oil-impregnated paper, the cable on each reel longer than several city blocks. Meanwhile, on the opposite side of the room, metalworkers toil away on three-inch-thick iron rods, constructing the gaol piece by piece, every blow of their hammers reverberating throughout the underground chamber. Masons have already drilled holes into the ceiling, roughly ten feet above our heads—all that remains is to affix the boxy ventilation machines and custom ducting. So much disparate work performed within a confined space has filled the air with a multitude of aromata and particulates.

My operating theatre is located in an adjacent room, separated from the main area by faded brick walls, and further cordoned off from the rest of the space by heavy curtains draped across the doorway. These serve to dampen some of the ambient noise while keeping my work hidden from the laborers. An unfriendly-looking individual stands outside the antechamber, guarding the entrance with all the charm of a gargoyle come to life. I am unaccustomed to such precautions, though I understand their necessity—only a hand-picked few have been made privy to our true efforts, as per the director's orders.

The overdue delivery lies inert upon an adjustable physician's table, withered but not yet decayed, colorless in the manner of things long buried. All scraps of fabric have already been cut away by my operating staff. The pine box in which our experiment arrived leans against the far wall, an earthen, loamy smell still clinging to it, firmly dispelling any illusions as to where this specimen was acquired.

As for the extra appendages, they arrived yesterday, and have been kept in a medical-grade icebox crafted specifically for just such a requirement.

{This seems an unnecessary precaution—the specimen is fresh from the earth, with all of the associated entropy, so why must we strive to keep the additional limbs from decaying?}

The tools and apparatus of my trade have been laid out in preparation, gleaming dully in the glow of gas lanterns. These lamps, liberated from various establishments throughout the city with little care given to their functionality, are mismatched and shoddy, haphazardly placed wherever space permits. Scarcely enough light to read by, let alone perform surgery with.

{My other collection of medical implements were sent, through an intermediary conversant in such dealings, to an address on the Isle of Dogs. They were remitted to an M.D., though I am unaware of any doctors practicing on the isthmus. I was loath to part with them but received assurance that it was in service of the cause.}

Question—can what I am about to do still be termed "surgery" if it is not in service of saving a life? If it is performed upon remains instead of a patient in dire straits? I suppose it could be construed as a different sort of postmortem. An interesting topic, to be sure, and one that I shall revisit later, if time permits.

Irrespective of our unorthodox methods, the director is sympathetic to my needs, exacting though they may be, and has provided a single bank of electric lights to aid with the procedure. Some manner of portable device provides power to the incandescent bulbs. An amazing contrivance, this harnessed electricity, proving useful in so many ways. Never before has my work been abetted by such brilliant illumination. Then again, never before have I attempted so complex a procedure. Alas, needs must when the devil drives, as the proverb goes.

Three assistants stand ready to support in whichever manner I require. I know precious little about the team which has been assembled, save that most of them are versed in the fields of either science or medicine (or occasionally both, like myself). I don't even know from which hospitals or laboratories they were poached. Such nescience is as much by design as due to my own proclivity. Our endeavour is a secretive affair, with compartmentalization being a key component. As such, why get overly familiar with them when many are here temporarily, filling their roles only as the situation demands?

Perhaps it is conceitedness or a sense of professional pride, but I do not plan on relying upon their aid unless absolutely necessary. I was selected for this project by virtue of my aptitude and achievements. Therefore, I feel it is only appropriate to validate the director's decision, to justify the esteem in which I am held.

Given the crudeness of my surroundings and the intricacy of my task, I anticipate the procedure will take most of the morning, and likely some of the afternoon as well. This dreary basement is far from ideal for connecting nerves and muscle tissue. Regrettably, when innovating beyond the margins of ethical propriety, we must work with the tools we have been given.

{That I am committed to the cause is beyond question. Even still, my mind wanders of its own accord, and I cannot help but allow myself a trice of fanciful reflection. In trading the bright lights of vaulted operating rooms and lectures at university for dimly lit rooms in the bowels of some crumbling edifice on the outskirts of Whitechapel, I seem to be emulating the infamous Doctor Faustus, making deals with fiends in exchange for forbidden

knowledge. But such was the price for standing at the forefront of scientific & medical breakthroughs, and I paid it willingly. Nevertheless, there is a part of me, small but insistent, which cannot help but feel affronted. The most complex medical procedure of our time, and nobody (aside from a few hirelings) is here to witness it.}

Any remaining annotations shall have to be revisited later—all remaining preparations have been made, and the director gives me a single nod of commencement.

My patient awaits.

CHAPTER 11

In the dimness of cheap candlelight reflected by a mirror that barely qualifies as such, the eyeliner is difficult to apply. Constance sighs and adjusts herself, angling for better light. The makeup is nearly depleted, a mere nub held between delicate fingers, used to the point of nothingness. She'll need to find a replacement within the next few days. Yet another expense to add to the never-diminishing list.

Blue eyes cast appraising glances at her reflection. Washboard flat and skinnier than a post, she is more boyish than some of the lads that call Pigott Street their home. Teased mercilessly in her youth by spiteful brothers, Constance cannot help but be censorious of her appearance. Many of the prostitutes she calls "friends" are no better, advising her to charge double for the buggerings she must undoubtedly receive. Infrequent meals only serve to exacerbate the issue.

Despite her lack of overt femininity, however, Constance is rarely hurting for clientele. There are plenty of randy men to be found in the factory and warehousing districts, if not within her neighbourhood proper. Some even seem to prefer her lanky appearance, forgoing the more curvaceous ladies entirely. As long as it brings in the shillings and pence, she doesn't care if they view her as a lad in their fantasies.

Income is far from guaranteed—sex work is just as susceptible to lulls and swells as any other business. When a dry spell (both figurative and literal) does occur, Constance is not without options. Possessing a boyish figure affords her the opportunity to dress accordingly, earning employment on the side in trades routinely unavailable to her gender. With but a hat to tame her blonde tresses, a liberal application of grime across her rosy cheeks, and a sideways set to her narrow chin, Constance can pass as a lad to all but the most observant of employers. She has performed a multitude of odd jobs while disguised: chimney sweep, rat catcher, and linklighter, to name a few. She has also, on rare occasions, served as day labor for the resident shipbuilders, running rigging lines and performing additional caulking deep within the bowels of half-finished sailing vessels.

None of the jobs pay as well as "taking a turn at Bushy Park," but she knows that beggars can't be choosers. A hungry belly cares not for the extra effort taken to fill the coffers. She also cannot deny that the honest work simply feels more gratifying, where being talented is more appreciated than being tawdry.

Her favorite is when the shipbuilders need extra riggers; high above the deck, shirtsleeves rolled up and salt-filled air caressing her lungs, Constance has never felt so unburdened. Being born in the dirt means the only way she can go is upwards. Atop the spars and masts, seafaring rope coarse against her smooth palms, she feels like she's already halfway there.

But such wistful thinking must be put on the shelf, at least for now. A fresh influx of youths from various parts of the city means clothed jobs are scarce. There is nowhere near enough work to go around. Streetside affrays are commonplace, small-scale skirmishes that leave broken bones and bloodied faces in their wake. Though she is stronger than her appearance suggests, and not afraid of resorting to fisticuffs against a single opponent, Constance cannot hope to prevail against gangs of boys twice her size. Much like the rest of the enterprising poor in Victoria's industrious England, she must make do with limited options.

Falling back to the world's oldest profession is simply the easiest avenue to take.

Behind her, half-glimpsed in the corner of the mirror, Fiona McCarthy adjusts her pale-green corset, fiddling with the laces in hopes of accentuating her cleavage. Not that the girl has much to work with. Another wisp of a woman, Fiona is only slightly more endowed than Constance. Her shock of red hair, emerald-green eyes, and charming Irish lilt, however, give her a leg up over the competition.

Constance, a Christian through and through, tarnished though her halo may be, bears no grudge against her roommate's good fortune. A touch of envy is all that surfaces, and that only rarely. It is a feeling she refuses to let linger. She and Fiona are far too good of friends for such pettiness, the red-headed lass filling in as the sister Constance never had. Alike in temperament and humour, the girls have been inseparable since their very first meeting.

Fiona, noticing her staring, calls out in a sing-song voice, "Peep all you want, Con, but we both know you can't afford me!"

"Considering how little sleep you got last night, you should be paying *me* just for looking, Fi. Those bags under your eyes are well and truly packed for a trip to the countryside."

"Aye!" Fiona responds with a smirk. "Packed full of all the coin I'll be raking in today."

Constance shakes her head, wagging a finger at her roommate in admonishment. "Better bite those coins first to make sure they're real. Hard to tell the difference between silver and tin when you're basking in the afterglow."

"Yours stick around for the afterglow?"

The girls stare at each other for a long moment before bursting into a fit of giggles. Such is their morning ritual—stolen moments of levity before the day begins in earnest. Though there exist many jokes at a whore's expense, not the least of which is that they're paid to lie down, it is far from the easiest of professions. Aggressive clients, rampant disease, increasingly depraved sexual acts, and the tumultuous nature of the streets all work in unison to ensure youthful prostitutes do not remain so for long. They must take their amusement when and where they can.

"Let's at least try to stagger our times today, yeah?" Constance offers, her tone indicating that she's only half joking. "It's hard for me to find a good rhythm when you're howling like a moggy in heat only an arm's length away."

Fiona shakes her head emphatically. "Guess you'll just need to stuff your ears with cotton. They pay extra when they think you're enjoying it and more still when you make them feel like the cock of the walk."

"Just as long as their cocks take a walk afterwards, they can think whatever they choose."

"Oy, you don't want them leaving you a little something to remember them by?"

"Oh, they have the 'little' part down pat," Constance says with a wink. "And what they leave behind is hardly what I want my bum lying in whilst I'm trying to sleep."

Both girls giggle again, the laughter echoing around their small quarters. It is a delightful moment, and Constance wishes she could stretch it out for all eternity. But the sounds of real life are intruding through their open window.

"Aye, and that's a fact. But fear not, my pet. Your eardrums shall be safe until the morrow. I'm heading down to Blackwall today, see if I can drum up some more business. Pickings here are getting slim. You'll have the whole flat to yourself."

Fiona has the right of it. Pigott Street is situated on the western edge of the hamlet of Poplar, a stone's throw north of the West India Docks. Theirs is a small neighbourhood, quiet and unassuming, relatively safe for a pair of young coquettes with only a single rusty stiletto for protection. Such safety has its drawbacks—local clientele is sparse, forcing the women to seek interested parties further afield.

The adjacent thoroughfares of Canton and Saracen Streets bring in much more business and increased visibility. Prostitution might be perfectly legal in London, but that doesn't stop the constables from cracking down over minor infractions, and Constance has no desire to run afoul of the bobbies. Even something as simple as public intoxication or brawling could result in a fine and prison time.

Far worse than prison, however, are the reformatories. Overseen by nuns of dubious piety and governed by routines a great deal stricter than those in actual jailhouses, an immoral woman could find herself confined within such a place for up to two years. Between recurring prayer sessions, studying the Good Book *ad nauseam*, and endless hours spent repenting for one's accumulated sins, those two years could end up feeling like twenty. Constance would rather die than abide by such draconian rules.

Even without the Town Police Clauses Act of 1847 (still in effect) hanging over the heads of the lower class, a statute which allows the police increased liberty to indict citizens for even minor infractions, leaving Poplar for greener pastures is still a risky gamble. Pimps and rival whores are not known for lenience when it comes to infringements upon their territory. Not that Constance hasn't taken the same risk from time to time. Expenses aren't in the habit of taking care of themselves. Between the lease, food, and supplies of the profession, both girls are scarcely eking out a living.

Their flat, such as it is, barely qualifies as actual lodging. At least the rent isn't completely outrageous. The space is just big enough for their two beds and a shared dresser/vanity, all of which have seen better days. But the door has a lock, and the smells from a nearby bakery help make their mornings tolerable.

And yet, Constance cannot halt a shiver of worry from dancing down her spine. Fiona is near and dear to her heart, as irreplaceable as a limb. She cannot imagine a life without her red-headed friend.

There is more to Constance's trepidation than mere territorial concerns. She has heard whispers, on street corners and amongst back alleys, of a most disturbing nature. Rumours of doxies murdered in and around Blackwall, as well as points further abroad, their bodies disfigured and discarded like refuse. Prostitutes, as a rule, have neither the time nor the energy for superstition. However, Constance cannot help but wonder if *that* most vicious of killers has returned, taking up his signature trade once again.

In spite of her reservations, she keeps her fears to herself. They need money, and soon. Fiona's belly grumbled throughout the night, causing Constance's stomach to protest painfully in commiseration, a grim reminder of the precariousness of their existence. They will need to pool their earnings later to procure a decent meal and a few sundries.

"Very well. I shall hold the fort whilst you caterwaul and moan your delight in the Yard."

Fiona smacks her lips and thrusts a hip to the side, one of her favorite poses. The green of her attire enhances the color of her eyes. Her freckles make her appear as if a child shamming at adulthood, unaware of the true cost accompanying such maturity. "Quite so. I'll give those seagulls a run for their money, eh?"

"Mmm hmm. Take the blade, if nothing else. I implore you."

"Nay. I shan't need it. Besides, it's more secure in your stockings. Mine are getting threadbare."

"As you say. Nonetheless, do try to avoid getting crushed by a horse-drawn carriage along the way, will you?" Constance pleads, her voice soft with unfeigned concern. "Or, heaven forbid, murdered by a madman."

"I shall endeavour to return in one piece, and only a titch despoiled."

Fiona flashes a smile, emerald eyes sparkling, then disappears through the doorway with a swish of her skirts. The room is suddenly quiet, as if all the air has vacated. A great exodus of vivacity. The space feels overlarge, impossibly cavernous. Constance cares neither for the silence nor the sensation that accompanies it.

"Just return," she whispers softy to the closing door.

CHAPTER III

Just before dawn, the body was discovered in Blackwall Yard, floating face down near the lower graving dock.

A waterborne corpse, in and of itself, could scarcely be considered an uncommon occurrence. R. & H. Green had assembled ships in that spot since 1843, and shipbuilding, a notoriously dangerous vocation hardly worth the pittance it paid, caused its fair share of deaths in any given year. Accidents do happen, after all.

No, what is newsworthy about this corpse is that it belongs to a woman. And a nude woman at that.

Logically, my first suspicion, upon being notified of the buoyant body, is that she must be a lady of the evening. Between its three West India docks, dogleg-shaped Millwall Dock, and the other, smaller quays and piers, the peninsula known as the Isle of Dogs is home to a rough-and-tumble crowd of dockworkers, their ranks comprised of former seamen, loafers, orphaned wharf rats, and petty criminals, many of whom have no qualms about paying for the company of a prostitute.

Considering the high volume of foreign traffic, the peninsula is a haven for all manner of illicit activities. Smuggling rings, opium dens, impromptu black markets, and dissolute gambling halls pop up like weeds, no matter how vigorously the constables crack down. The isthmus is, by proxy, certainly no place for the well-to-do or the delicate.

As such, the only females to be found by the docks are "ladies" by nighttime occupation rather than by birth, marriage, or upbringing. Naturally, only the English language could employ the same word to describe women on two very opposite ends of the social spectrum.

Alas, such is the British way. We never do anything by halves.

Awoken by Constable Higgins roughly an hour after the body's discovery, it took us nearly another full hour to traverse southwards through the Limehouse district on our way to the docks. Though well past daybreak by now, the sun remains hidden by a heavy fog permeating the air. Commonly referred to as a "pea-souper," the noxious blend of coal smoke and factory output is thick enough to make travel difficult (even dangerous, at times), and we engaged the services of a linklighter to hasten our journey. The urchin's face is all but smothered with accumulated soot and grime, but the torch he holds aloft provides decent enough illumination.

Though the fog is not always so dense, rarely a day passes when it is not present in some fashion. We are told that such is the price of modernization. The Industrial Revolution may be decades in the past, but its tendrils remain rooted in every facet of English society. This great city of London is the chorale that all other voices strive to emulate; the thrum and thump of industry is our constant accompaniment.

Guided by our torch-bearing pathfinder, we arrive at Blackwall without incident. I toss the lad a coin, and he scarpers off into the gloom, disappearing like an errant spectre, searching for the next pedestrian in need of illumination. With the murk as thick as it is, the boy will earn a decent wage today.

The Yard is, by and large, unremarkable in every way. Utilitarian and bereft of personality. This section is even worse—it is where the surfeit of work happens, resulting in a stretch of real estate as pallid and featureless as the fog in which it lies. Dim shadows pass by hither and thither, workers intent upon the various tasks of their station. Tasks that I am unable to identify. It is fair to admit that the vagaries of shipbuilding elude me; I am the son of a printing clerk, more at home with steam-powered cylinders and ink stains than carvel planking and barrels of oakum.

Here, where the burbling of the Thames is stifled by manmade locks and channels, the salty air is nearly stodgy enough to chew (despite the English Channel lying over two miles to the east), a briny tang which coats the tongue in a way that I have yet to become accustomed to. Gulls cry overhead with unceasing complaint, a sound that trickles down like incongruous quarrels to echo off soaring stone walls. The ubiquitous birds, much like cats, are never satisfied with their lot in life. They are simply better equipped to carp about it.

Whatever complaints are uttered by the constables cease upon my arrival. I am generally impartial to workplace grumblings, but the men respect my rank regardless. Several of the bobbies, assisted by a smattering of dockmasters and their apprentices, have already removed the woman from the water. She now lies on her back, covered by a ratty tarpaulin. One arm sticks out from under the covering, the skin ghostly pale.

By this time, gawkers and rumourmongers are out in force, though the thick London particular prevents anyone beyond arm's length from seeing anything of note. How someone managed to discover the body in the first place is beyond me.

The dispositions of the constables transform noticeably upon my arrival. These are men accustomed to breaking up the occasional pub fracas and arresting streetside hoodlums—a female corpse with goods and sundry visible to all is beyond their expertise, not to mention their disposition. With an inspector on the scene, they can revert to the simplicity of following orders. I designate various assignments—interviewing the men who discovered the body, establishing a cordon, and canvassing the area—and then send them on their way. Their relief is palpable.

Constable Higgins remains nearby, seeking to keep me company while I prepare for the grim task ahead. He's a good man, Higgins, and will most assuredly make a fine inspector after a few more years of patrolling. But I prefer to be unaccompanied whilst I work. I send him off to fetch a cart—the deceased must be moved in due course.

Now that I am alone with the body, I can begin my examination. In this, I am thankful for the haze. It will provide her a modicum of dignity, in death if not in life. Sadly, corpses are nothing new to me, female or otherwise. Having been an inspector for the Metropolitan Police Service for three years, and with the Isle of Dogs as my jurisdiction, I have seen Death in many of his forms.

She is also not the first girl to be murdered in my bailiwick recently. I have investigated the killings of three prostitutes within as many weeks, each with consistent physical traits, wounds, and methods of disfiguration. I suspect that our waterlogged woman will follow the same pattern.

Pulling back the canvas, I find my suppositions proven correct. The young victim, in her early twenties at most, would have been radiant when flushed with vigor. In death, she is anything but; her pale skin is akin to the bellies of dead fish that frequently wash up along the banks of the Thames. A fiery red mane frames an oval face dotted with freckles. With her petite frame, small bosom, and sparse pubic hair, she's more girl than woman. Not the traditional shapely seductress that one finds on most street corners. Which, I suppose, is part of the appeal.

The killer must prefer them childlike.

I examine the wounds next. Ligature marks on the victim's wrists show that she was restrained in some fashion. There is substantial bruising across her breasts and hips, similar to the previous women. Most revealingly, the discoloration above her décolletage indicates death by strangulation. I hold my fingers up to the wound, encircling the woman's neck as the killer had done, verifying what I already know: the murderer's hands are nearly twice the size of my own.

Like the previous victims, her torso is covered with other, less readily identifiable blemishes. The flesh in sensitive locations—inner thighs, nipples, buttocks, etc.—has been seared in some fashion, the gashes cracked and bumpy in a manner which I have never before seen. They are akin to burns, albeit not caused by fire or caustic chemicals. In addition, the front of her body is covered in tiny dots of discoloration, a hundred or so blisters that appear to have been imparted by a hot needle or similar tool. These lesions are only superficial, none having broken the skin. Nevertheless, they were undoubtedly painful in their own right.

The bruises I can understand—hallmarks of the traditional ways in which people inflict violence upon one another. Contrarywise, the lesions and strange burns are most perplexing. Are they a form of torture? That they have been present on each victim lends credence to the theory. Regrettably, they are also not the most telling of injuries. I let my gaze travel downwards, lingering on the appendage not concealed by the tarpaulin. I am unsurprised by what I find. Like the other victims, her little finger is missing, cleaved from the left hand by either a chisel or dull blade.

And yet, that is still not the ghastliest of the disfigurations. Not even close. Although I know what to expect, it takes me the span of a few heartbeats to ready myself. This next part is always the worst. Knowing what is coming next does not make it any less grotesque.

I try to soothe my ragged breathing to no avail. Unsteady hands seek out her face, my thumb lifting first one eyelid and then the other. Empty sockets stare back at me.

As expected, the orbs, like those of the other victims, have been taken.

CHAPTER IV

Why the eyes?

That is the question that plagues me before, during, and after examining each victim. Hounding my mind like a long-cast shadow, always in lockstep.

It is no easy feat, withdrawing the orbs from their sockets without utterly destroying them in the process. Or so medical professionals from London Hospital have told me. Being a man of methods instead of medicine, I must take them at their word. What I do know, however, is that if destruction were the goal, there are much easier ways to accomplish it.

No, a cold feeling in my gut tells me that their removal has a purpose. It is a sensation I've learned to trust over the years.

What adds to the strangeness is that the eye removal is done with precision and skill, while the separation of the finger appears almost amateur in nature. The skin is ripped, and the bone fractured, as if the tools hadn't seen the edge of a grindstone in some time. Surgical apparatus versus unsharpened implements. Why are the two methods so disparate? In this, I have my theories, though I have yet to utter them aloud. Without proof, my notions are merely vapor in search of form.

That the disfigurations were inflicted after expiry is scant comfort. Though her features have slackened in death, assisted in no small part by time spent in the water, those full lips still hold a grimace of pain and terror. Her passing was far from gentle.

My father has always maintained that any demise not occurring whilst one slumbers is a bad death. In this, if not much else, he appears to be quite correct.

Of course, London's East End is no stranger to bad deaths. Transpiring just four years ago, the Whitechapel Murderer had cut a violent swath through the slums over two months, dismembering doxies in the most gruesome ways. I had been a newly minted constable then, wet behind the ears and scared out of my wits. The whole affair had very nearly caused me to return to my family's printing business, tail between my legs like a chastened cur.

Public opinion at the time, which persists to this very day, is that the police had bungled the entire affair. In reality those accusations are not far from the truth.

It was a grim set of circumstances, the sort for which us bobbies had not been trained, but it had instilled in me, after the fact at least, a desire to mitigate future foibles. To that end, I applied myself as studiously as I could, learning tricks of the trade from my peers at every opportunity. I interviewed reformed criminals when such opportunities presented themselves, forming a baseline for their erstwhile felonious behaviour. A copy of Sir Arthur Conan Doyle's *A Study in Scarlet* was purchased, perused, and parsed, though any takeaways from said novel are impossible to quantify, and the book now collects dust on the edge of my desk. I even received mentorship from such august personages as Detective Inspectors Abberline and Andrews. In less than a year I had been promoted.

These new deaths are reminiscent enough of those committed by the Whitechapel Murderer that some of my peers wonder if he has returned. I have my doubts, but do not voice them. After all, if I had a shilling for every fresh sighting of the Hammersmith Ghost, Spring-Heel'd Jack, or the Lady Lovibond gliding into port, I would be a wealthy man indeed. Ultimately, whether it is the same killer or not changes nothing.

I must find this madman. I must stop him.

Naturally, I am not the only person who feels this way. Pressure is already mounting from above, and although we withhold the details from the public as much as possible, they are starting to take notice. This, to me, is the most disconcerting part. The masses are not ready for another macabre murderer stalking our streets.

London has many more experienced inspectors than I, grizzled old veterans who know her tired streets and loveless alleyways more intimately than the lines on their wives' faces. Seniority is an unwritten law within the constabulary, nearly as ironclad as jailhouse bars. Despite this fact, there is a reason that Higgins was sent to my door, although an ingrained sense of modesty prevents me from boasting. I'm told I have a knack for discerning the particulars of a crime, and I suppose the statement is true enough. I presume it stems from the numerous efforts which led to my promotion. The disparate elements play out in my head in a stream of images, much like the motion picture films now developed in France, my assumptions blending with established evidence to provide a rough order of events. Perhaps it is nothing more than an overactive imagination, but I sometimes believe that I can assume the mantle of these criminals for a short while, seeing the chain of events as if through their eyes.

There are even times when I reenact the method of murder, playacting as if I were the killer: retracing the steps, handling the weapons, and vacating the scene in the same manner. In those moments, the methods and motives are clear to me, as if I am inhabiting the very mind of the perpetrator.

Many other inspectors find my methods abnormal at best or downright heretical at worst, but my peculiarities have led me to no small amount of success within the Service. I make no apology for my methods; I intend to employ any and all tools in my repertoire to keep the public safe.

Because this particular body was obviously moved from wherever the murder occurred, there is no crime scene for me to unravel. My only recourse is to make suppositions about her final moments—the flashing of cleavage or a hint of thigh, the proposition and haggling over a price, the escalating violence during copulation, the asphyxiation during or after climax, and the removal of her eyes and finger postmortem.

Grisly trophies, to be sure. And now the killer has four sets of them.

CHAPTER V

Constance awakens to find Fiona's bed empty.

The absence of her roommate isn't necessarily cause for alarm. They aren't always on the same schedule, and morning visits to the privy are unavoidable. A few pre-dawn liaisons are known to crop up from time to time, necessitating an earlier-than-usual start to the day. It is also entirely possible that Fiona is off spending fresh coin on a few sumptuous delights from Smithfield's Bakery.

That her sheets and pillows are in the exact same state as the night before, however, is a different matter altogether.

Struggling to quell her mounting panic, Constance searches for any other signs that Fiona has come home, if even briefly. In such tight quarters, the rummaging takes only a few seconds and yields no fruitful results. Fi's clothing hasn't been touched. The penny dreadfuls resting on the nightstand, with lurid titles such as *Sold For Naught*, *The Nefarious Necromancer*, and *Butchery in the Berths*, have not been leafed through. Nothing within the flat appears to have been touched or moved.

Fiona hasn't returned from Blackwall Yard at all.

Utterly worried, Constance dresses hastily, throwing on a rough-spun tunic and practical woolen skirt. The stiletto finds its customary location on her inner thigh, held in place by the hem of a dirty stocking. She realizes that working herself into a lather won't help matters in the slightest, but she cannot keep her mind from racing. She tries to find some way, any possible way, with which to rationalize Fiona's absence.

It is not unheard of for prostitutes to find a patron during their illicit encounters. Some British gents want a well-bred woman, prim and proper, accompanied by some manner of dowry to sweeten the pot. These men get their seduction on the side, paying discreetly for perversions that their uptight wives would never deign to perform. Other men, however, simply want a woman to come home to. A companion. Someone who can cook, clean, and copulate as the situation warrants. As such, marriage proposals for young prostitutes are not quite as uncommon as one might expect.

Not that Constance expects to be on the receiving end of such an experience. Though she is skilled in all manner of carnal acts, and has plenty of experience cleaning up messes, she's never once stepped foot into an honest-to-God kitchen. Just attractive enough for a dalliance, she is far from the kind of woman gentlemen like to have on their arms. Certainly not the kind to be shown off to one's peers. And, it would go without saying, not the type of lady a man would see fit to introduce to his mother.

Fi, on the other hand, would thrive in such a circumstance. A former scullery maid and Lady's servant, Fiona has plenty of household experience to bring to the table. Not to mention her inherent Irish loveliness. Gifted with her mouth in more than just the expected ways, she possesses the kind of quick wit that could make even the surliest of individuals crack a smile.

But, even had Fiona received such a blessing, she would have returned home to share the good news. And to keep Constance from worrying. No, something is desperately amiss. Constance knows it with a certainty bordering on the supernatural. There is nothing for it but to make her way to the Yard and ask after a red-headed lass.

She heads for the door, but a sudden thought stops her cold. Even in plain attire, she will stick out like a sore thumb in Blackwall, a slip of a woman far removed from her element. Poking around the Isle of Dogs will be difficult enough without being unnecessarily conspicuous.

"Which simply will not do," she tells herself, speaking aloud just to fill the space with something other than her own breathing.

Mind made up, Constance shucks the feminine clothing and pulls her dockyard attire from a satchel underneath the bed. Nobody will spare her a second glance as long as she looks like she belongs. Just another wharf rat looking for employment. Smelling of yesterday's sex and cheap ale will substantiate her camouflage. The blade fits neatly into the inside cleft of her battered leather boot, its hilt covered by a torn pant leg. Her blonde locks take longer to hide, requiring several hair ties in order to fit under a moth-eaten casquette hat. As for the rest of the disguise, merely walking from Pigott to the dockyards will ensure she is thoroughly coated in soot and grime.

Masquerading as a linklighter would be ideal for reconnoitering the nooks and crannies of Blackwall, but as luck would have it, Constance is fresh out of torches. And the previous day was far from lucrative, bringing in barely enough money for a decent meal. Nowhere near enough to spare for a *flambeau* or two. Her small purse has never felt so light. Such meagre earnings just might be enough to convince a mum witness to share what they saw. If there are any observers to be found, that is.

Without money, and with her feminine wiles (such as they are) hidden away, she'll have to make do with sharp eyes and timid alacrity. Keeping on the move, never underfoot. A spectre in the smog. The irony is not lost on

Constance—her normal *modus operandi* is to be as visible as possible, and now she must attempt to achieve the opposite.

With nothing more than hope and a handful of coins to her name, she hurries into the early morning mist. It feels more like dusk than dawn, the thick fog reducing the sun's majesty to nearly an afterthought. It is in such moments that Constance misses the countryside. She doesn't recall much from her youth other than grueling farm work and cold nights spent in a rickety barn. Contrarywise, the food was abundant and flavorful. More than she could ever hope to eat. Her stomach twists painfully in remembrance, but Constance ignores it. Sustenance will have to wait, provided she still has any money left after locating Fi.

At a minimum, it will take her an hour to traverse the distance to Blackwall on foot. Determined strides leave Pigott Street behind in a matter of moments, familiar buildings and landmarks diminishing into the impenetrable haze. Southward, the docks await, no doubt already bustling with activity. Somewhere within the numerous causeways and channels lie answers to her roommate's whereabouts.

And Constance is determined to uncover them.

CHAPTER VI

R.M. Müller
Undisclosed Location
Sept 13th, 1892

Research Journal Entry # 87
9:27 AM

SUCCESS!

After nearly a year of preparation, several abortive attempts, two major setbacks, and one abject (not to mention messy) failure, our endeavour finally bears fruit.

The electric charge has not yet dissipated from the air; this is how quickly the transformation manifests. Several seconds at most.

{I must remember to bring a stopwatch next time. Do NOT forget!}

Shoulder to shoulder we stand, the team and I, some with mouths agape, as our creation rises from the tank, viscous fluid sloughing off its mottled flesh in sodden portions. I try to preserve the assorted emotions that I am feeling in that very moment, in the hope of jotting them down for future reference. Unfortunately, I am unable to find the words to accurately convey my state of being. Maybe I am too excited. Perhaps I cannot break from the confines of laboratory jargon. Or, quite possibly, suitable terms simply do not yet exist.

The building's improvised ventilation system struggles to keep pace with our endeavour; the smells of ozone, burnt hair, and boiled liquids are beyond pungent. Some of the team gag. The odour, however, does not bother me: this is not a boast, just a simple fact. I have endured much worse.

As for the fluid itself, it has its own scent, one that I cannot identify. Saccharine? Olive? Tallow? My olfactory senses are not up to the task of recognizing the constituent compounds.

{While such knowledge is not necessary for my role, I cannot help but wonder what makes it work. Our director trusts me with many facets of this project and has graciously imparted quite a few secrets. Yet the chemical composition of this mysterious solution is not one of them.}

One of the other scientists, who's name I haven't bothered to remember, bounds out of the room screaming "It's alive!" at the top of his lungs, showing a complete lack of scientific decorum. Thoroughly unacceptable behaviour, and I will surely mention it in my official report.

{Earnest? Edmund? I simply cannot recall. Bespectacled fellow with a hawkish nose and prominent bald spot—the director will know his name.}

The man's proclamation is also, I must note, quite incorrect. The thing before us is NOT alive. It moves, yes. Its head turns, its limbs shift, and its fingers flex, but no life clings to this creature. It is merely a husk. A simulacrum possessing no spark of vivacity. No soul. And yet, we had hypothesized months ago that if the project were successful, such a thing would also no longer be deceased.

Our creation is now, as our director had coined (at this project's inception), in a state of undeath.

{Unalive? Undead? Exanimate? Azoic? One of these words will come to define what we have wrought, entering into the public's vernacular for all

eternity. For my money, I'm leaning towards exanimate. It has an air of pragmatic certitude.}

Though the term "undeath" is somewhat morbid, not to mention unnecessarily dramatic, it is also unequivocally accurate. Are we, thusly, modern-day necromancers? Channeling black magic through the disciplined application of the scientific method? After all, if you think about it, I daresay that most feats of contemporary science and medicine would have been deemed witchcraft or thaumaturgy by our less enlightened forebears. Does that not make us some manner of sorcerers?

Short answer - yes. Through our toils, death has been undone.

Long answer – I'll save that for later. There are some underlying (or is it overarching?) philosophical precepts here which I should explore further.

For now, there is so much to do. And I have spent too long scribbling notes as it is.

10:32 AM

It still has the capacity to learn.

An hour has elapsed, and though it does not possess sight (eyes and other soft tissues, including genitalia, are some of the first things to decay upon expiry), our creation has already memorized the layout of its cage and the assorted obstacles within after only a few circuitous explorations. A truly astounding accomplishment. Deep within that desiccated brain, pathways are still in existence.

{I believe it was three times, but it could have been four. For the official record, I shall leave it at three.}

Locomotion is still spasmodic at best, but I anticipate that will change over time. All four arms function independently from each other. Legs seem sturdy, though it is hard to tell due to the creature's irregular movements. I shall have to reexamine them later to see if there is any improvement. Even *with the uncoordinated motions, it moves quietly for such a large brute, as silent as a shadow.*

Standing well over six feet, it towers over even the tallest member of the team, grotesque head nearly touching the top of the cage. The director had been quite serious about finding the largest specimen possible.

Unexpected discovery – there are sounds emanating from the thing's throat: guttural moans, soft bleats, and stuttering clicks. The latter is akin to a death rattle, which would make a certain sort of sense, except that no salivatory secretions remain in the creature's throat to cause such a resonance. Further research will be required.

Are these noises stemming from an effort to communicate? Or are they simply reflexive behaviours of which it is unaware and/or over which it has no control? Either way, with a thoroughly withered tongue (another thing that doesn't last long in corpses), the sounds are half-formed at best. They are not loud, merely of average volume, coming only intermittently. Still, this is not in keeping with the director's wishes (silence is key), so we will likely have to restrain the creature and remove the vocal cords entirely.

{This is fine with me. The noises it makes are beyond sinister, causing the hairs on my neck to stand on end. Perhaps this is what Hell sounds like, and if so, eternal damnation due to my actions is something I may wish to reconsider. I mention this with complete seriousness—an hour of such disturbing agitations has already seemed to age me significantly. Salvation must wait a while longer, however, as I am too invested in this project to walk away on the very cusp of triumph.}

The creature should have no want of sustenance or warmth. Nor do I foresee the necessity for bodily functions (there should be nothing within its belly or bowels to create urine/excrement). We also expect that it will require neither sleep nor moments of respite (though it is far too early in the process to validate those suppositions).

None of us have yet to enter the cage, as per strict orders. The director wishes to be here in person for the creature's first interaction with another living being. A sticking point that I am unable to argue against. I, for one, am rather excited for that momentous step, whenever it is to occur. For purely scientific reasons, of course.

In the interim, all the team and I can do is observe and annotate.

But, prior to anything else, I shall have to find some cotton to stuff into my ears. I cannot abide the dissonance emanating from the containment cage much longer.

CHAPTER VII

Instead of burning off as one would expect, the already dense fog is thickening, filthy byproducts of factories and shipyards contaminating the air as the workday begins in earnest. Nobody at street level will see the sun today.

I can't help but fret, just the slightest bit. Is it only I who imagines our city atmosphere is solid enough to choke on?

It is a concern I keep to myself. My mates would box my ears if they heard me disparaging London's great mechanical revolution. Worrying, they would say, is for women and well-diggers. And so, I carry on, outwardly unconcerned. Stiff upper lip, as is the British way.

My examination complete, I replace the tarpaulin, taking care to ensure the entire body is covered. There is nothing further to be gleaned here.

Knuckling my back, I make several circuits around the immediate area, clearing my head whilst stretching sore muscles. Three years off the beat, and I have begun to go soft. Not outwardly, thank heavens. Or at least not yet. But I can feel it within, telegraphed through aching joints and tingling extremities. Men of science and physiology claim that humans are living longer, improvements in both nutrition and lifestyle pushing old man

Death further down the road with each passing generation. Nevertheless, such advancements have seemingly bypassed policemen entirely. These days I feel as arthritic as the misers whiling away their days in London's overcrowded almshouses.

Higgins has returned with a slat-sided cart, likely appropriated under protest from a local fishmonger or the like. With his assistance, I manage to get the girl situated well enough for transport. She can't weigh much more than six stone but is an awkward burden due to her post-mortem stiffness. Wearing discomfort like a cloak, Higgins handles the body with obvious displeasure, a severe frown commandeering his ordinarily jovial face.

Gawkers have closed in during my examinations, curiosity drawing them forward until it feels like they are pressing down upon me. Cursing my distractedness, I set Higgins upon them like a guard dog. For such an unassuming fellow, he has been gifted with a voice that is both deep and commanding. His admonitions push the crowd back to a respectable distance.

All but one, that is.

The lad, a slight fellow dressed in patchwork hand-me-downs, stands stock still while the rest of the onlookers recede into the murk. Something about the boy's expression captures my attention. Perhaps it is the look of sheer torment which no person so young should have to wear. Mayhap it is something else entirely.

Whatever it is, I am positive that the lad knew the victim. My certainty on the matter is ironclad—as inarguable as arithmetic. I gesture to the boy, signaling him to approach. His gait is slow and wooden, the tread of someone suffering from a profound sense of shock. As if his body is moving of its own volition, with neither his knowledge nor contribution. A marionette tethered to uneven strings. I have seen the same mannerisms in family members of other deceased individuals; incredulity, incomprehension, anger, and above all, irreconcilable grief, all warring for dominance across a psyche unprepared for said onslaught.

The boy gestures to the cart with a trembling hand. "May I?" he asks, effeminate voice nearly buried by the ubiquitous racket.

Not a single whisker adorns an unlined face, making his age difficult to determine. But he can't be much older than the girl in the cart. Aside from comparable physical statures, I cannot discern any resemblance between the two, familial or otherwise. It is unlikely that they are siblings or cousins. A frequent customer, perhaps? A paramour? Whatever the boy's relation to the victim, the next few moments will not be pleasant.

"Allow me," I respond gently, pulling the corner of the canvas down a notch. Even in the half-light of the thick fog, the dead girl's pale face stands out like a beacon.

Despite a valiant attempt to the contrary, the lad is unable to contain a sharp cry of anguish from escaping his lips. A torrent of tears burst from sky-blue eyes, leaving unsoiled tracks along his sooty cheeks, like running mascara in inverse. Higgins appears from the gloom, drawn by the sound, fully prepared to drag the boy away. I stop the constable with an upturned hand. Though I am an officiant of the law, more concerned with catching the malefactor than the emotional aftermath of the crime, I am not without compassion. Call me a bleeding heart, but something about the boy's distress moves me.

"You have my condolences," I whisper, giving his bony shoulder a squeeze. There is nothing that I can do or say to ease his sorrow. The best I can do is give him a few moments with the dearly departed. "I'll step to the side, allow you to grieve in peace."

A minute passes. Maybe two. The boy's shoulders shake in time with his wracking sobs. Higgins and I pretend not to notice, studiously looking everywhere except in the direction of the cart, wishing we were elsewhere.

There's a quiet desperation to the British mentality, a stoicism of fortitude; public displays of emotion are infrequent and discomfiting.

Several more minutes pass, cumbersome and awkward. Just as I am about to return to the cart, I feel a presence at my side. I turn to face the boy. His cheeks still glisten, and his nose is running, but composure seems to have returned, in dribbles if not in droves. I hand him a handkerchief into which he blows daintily, almost prettily. His delicate mannerisms are peculiar, but I cannot identify why.

"Is it him? Has he returned?"

"Has who returned?" I respond, though I have a notion of whom he speaks. "The Whitechapel Murderer? No, lad, I do not believe so. I fear that this is the handiwork of someone else entirely. What is your name?"

"Cons... Connor," the boy stammers in response, still shell-shocked, it would seem.

I make to shake hands, but then remember that I've been handling a waterlogged corpse and think better of it. "Inspector Guthrie. I'm sorry our meeting had to be under such inauspicious circumstances. If it's not too much trouble, I would ask you some questions regarding the young lady. But first, I must excuse myself for a moment."

The boy simply nods, remaining in place, thoroughly dejected.

By this time, our contingent has grown. Several other inspectors are milling about, mere shadows in the murk. While I wash my hands in the Yard's brackish river water, I am approached by my superintendent, a portly man named Barnhold. He scarcely gives the body any attention, steering well clear of the cart almost by reflex, as if afraid the deceased might reach out and grab him. The man, who rarely leaves the comfort of his office, evidently waited until after breakfast before making an appearance.

Barnhold's attendance alone is noteworthy, but the woman at his side gives me pause. She is pretty in an austere fashion, taller than myself, thin where Barnhold is rotund. They couldn't be more dissimilar. A cold intelligence emanates from her eyes, which are the color of the ocean at dusk. My age or slightly older, the alabaster skin of her face and neck is flawless. She dresses in a fashion similar to a man—finely cut trousers and a tight-fitting tunic that do nothing to hide her gender. With nary a hair out of place, she looks positively alien in this proletarian environment.

Her presence and attire cause quite a stir with the rest of the men. For myself, she instills a peculiar nervousness. I have a nagging feeling that nothing good will come from this interloper's presence.

"A damnable start to a miserable day, wouldn't you agree, Guthrie?" Barnhold asks by way of greeting while brushing traces of soot from his shoulders with epicene motions.

We don't get on well, the superintendent and I. He believes I am slightly deranged. I maintain that his only sense of urgency is when tucking into a meal. I have heard through interoffice scuttlebutt that he feels somewhat threatened by my success and is actively thwarting my attempts at further advancement. For my part, I doubt he possesses the wherewithal for such clandestine underhandedness.

We have, fortunately, reached a wobbly stalemate, one where we address each other as infrequently as possible. It still takes effort for me to keep a civil tone. "That it is, sir."

"What's all this, then?" he asks, nodding in the direction of the lad.

"We, uh, commandeered his cart," I reply, not as smoothly as I had intended. Both Connor and Higgins turn to stare at me in surprise, but I shake my head slightly, praying that they remain silent. Neither opens their mouth to correct the intentional *faux pas*, much to my relief. "The boy will be, um, assisting with the transport of the body. It's quite a long way to travel, sir."

Barnhold does not seem to notice my sudden sheepishness. He simply barrels onwards, talking just to hear himself speak. The superintendent gestures to the woman at his side, the boy and the body swiftly forgotten. "Inspector Guthrie, allow me to introduce Lady Ellington, England's first female electrical engineer." He then glances at Lady Ellington and gestures to me. "Milady, this here is Inspector James Guthrie, one of our, uh, more unorthodox investigators."

Those are probably the kindest words he has ever spoken about me, undoubtedly intended to present a unified front for our distinguished guest.

Unlike many of my contemporaries, I have no qualms with members of the fairer sex holding positions of authority. It is, however, quite a rare occurrence indeed, save for the royal family. I was also unaware that Oxford is now granting degrees to women but I decide to keep my mouth shut on the subject. Antagonizing one of my social superiors will only result in career suicide. The class divide may instill in me a sense of loathing, but I am shrewd enough to play by its rules.

Unfortunately, there remain certain formalities which I am unable to ignore. Academic or no, a woman in attendance at an active investigation site, especially with a corpse still nearby, is unheard of. I turn to the superintendent, words of protestation bubbling from my lips. He stops me with an upturned hand.

"Your reservations are duly noted, Mr. Guthrie. They no doubt mirror my own concerns, which I have voiced most judiciously. However, I have been assured by our superiors that Lady Ellington is not easily ruffled. Her pursuits have led her to similar tableaux around the city, and we will extend to her *any and all* assistance that she requires. Is that understood?"

Similar crime scenes? This is news to me and wholly unwelcome information at that. If comparable crimes are being perpetrated in other districts, we have a far larger problem on our hands than I have been led to believe. One exacerbated by the fact that I am hesitant to impart certain theories to my colleagues.

There is, however, someone I can turn to. I maintain a regular correspondence with a friend of mine, epistles and memoranda which allow us to keep abreast of the happenings in each other's lives whilst also sharing our suppositions with an objective and like-minded audience. Purcell is an inspector in the Soho District, across the river Thames and a bit west of the Isle of Dogs. We came up together in the constabulary, newly minted bobbies walking the beat as a pair, and he possesses a keen mind for the inexplicable and the bizarre. His promotions have taken him far, and I am proud of the man he has become. And, if I am being completely forthcoming, a fair bit jealous as well. Whereas I am somewhat of an embarrassment to my division, Purcell is held in the highest esteem. It all comes down to the methods by which we solve crimes, I suppose. While I root around in the muck, reconstructing events in a thoroughly tactile manner, Purcell frequently needs only a few circuits around a crime scene to comprehend not only how something was accomplished but also the identity of the most likely perpetrator. Almost akin to Doyle's literary creation.

In all honesty, I should forgo a letter and simply stop by in person. I have been to Purcell's apartments several times over the years. He even entrusted me with a key to let myself in should I call upon him while he is away. If there have been similar murders in other districts, it is highly probable that he will already be knee-deep in his own investigations. And, like the good chap he is, perfectly willing to collaborate.

But such a visit shall have to wait. For now, I must deal with the inconvenience directly before me, and not fly off the handle in the process.

"What does she require, sir?" I manage, through no small miracle, to keep my misgivings to a minimum.

"Cooperation, Mr. Guthrie. Our full and unfettered assistance. Lady Ellington is here on behalf of the Ministry."

"And which Ministry is that, sir?" I ask, though I know he expects me to accept the news silently. But silence has never been one of my strongest characteristics.

Superintendent Barnhold harrumphs loudly, no doubt preparing to dress me down for my impertinence.

"The Ministry of Special Sciences," Lady Ellington responds, smoothly taking the reins from Barnhold without batting an eye. I can tell the superintendent is unhappy with the interruption, but he stifles his rebuttal with an audible swallow. The Lady continues unabated. "On special appointment from Parliament. I trust those are acceptable enough qualifications, inspector?"

Her posh accent, what we call Received English, falls in line with her dignified appearance. My own dialect, undeniably working-class, must sound lugubrious to her refined ears. The Ministry of Special Sciences must be a new one, as I have never before heard of it. This is not a surprise, considering a new Ministry seems to pop up with each moon cycle, and half of their overarching purposes confound the vast majority of England's citizens.

It is clear that Lady Ellington assumes I will be impressed. But her presence has me out of sorts, and I've never been one to grovel at the feet of my betters. As far as I'm concerned, the aristocracy can float belly-down on the Thames with silver spoon handles sticking out of their arses like masts on a sailing vessel.

The mental image is enough to make me chuckle, but I stifle it lest she assume I am mocking her appointment. There is a singular truth known to each and every British commoner nearly from birth—the aristocracy does not take kindly to being lampooned.

I tip my inspector's cap, burying my hesitations under a carefully constructed mask of genteel humility, publicly conceding defeat. The sooner I offer my assistance, the sooner I can be rid of this unwanted guest and return to Connor and the murdered girl.

"More than acceptable, Milady. I am at your service."

CHAPTER VIII

With her worst fears realized, Constance feels like a rudderless ship at sea, hopelessly adrift, bound to the whims of both wave and weather. Seeing Fi's lifeless body had been hard enough. Glimpsing the bruises around her neck and chest, not to mention the bloating from the water, was the stuff of nightmares. Her friend had suffered in those final moments, and Constance feels like an ice-cold pick has been stabbed right through her heart.

Other considerations flit across her mind in brief flashes: the impending silence of her living space, packing up Fi's meagre belongings, the clients she's already missed out on while snooping around Blackwall, and how she'll be able to afford rent on her own. But those are thoughts for later, when she has more time to be suitably worried about them.

Though she is loath to leave Fiona's side, Constance knows there is nothing further to be done. The police will need the body for their investigation, and she doesn't have nearly enough money to cover the cost of a proper burial. Despite the inspector coming across as a decent bloke, Constance feels nervous in the presence of the law, itching to be anywhere other than the docks.

But she has gotten herself well and truly trapped. Pressed into cart service, surrounded by a knot of constables and now the nobility, all she can do is stand idly by, trying not to fidget or draw any additional attention. She feels as ineffectual as a fork in a sugar bowl.

Constance cannot suppress a twinge of vexation. When she costumes herself as a lad, it's for survival, raw desperation forcing her hand. And yet, even under such a reasonable motivation, she would still catch hell if her ruse was discovered. Receiving a dressing down at best or a clout across the head and boot to the arse at worst. But when a lady of station does it, some refined peeress with wealth and power, nobody bats an eye or dares make a crosswise comment. The hypocrisy is galling.

Judging by Inspector Guthrie's body language, he is none too pleased to make the lady's acquaintance. A curious development, as most commoners try to ingratiate themselves with the nobility, hoping to enjoy some of their favor (and wealth) by proxy. Seeing Guthrie barely contain his displeasure raises him a notch in her esteem. He is still a member of the constabulary, and as such he makes her wary. But at least he's not a complete ponce.

In spite of the tragedy that has upended her entire existence, the world has not stopped turning. Normality exists everywhere except within her personal bubble. Constance wonders if this is how coal miners feel as once-safe tunnels collapse, crushing their cohorts under tons of rubble whilst the rest of the world goes about its business, blissfully unaware of the unfolding tragedy beneath their feet.

Such dangers seem to occur solely within the professions of commoners. Youthfulness notwithstanding, she is already intimately acquainted with the yawning chasm between the privileged and the working class. A span as desolate and inhospitable as the Sahara. A divide she will never be allowed to circumvent.

The stiletto presses hard against Constance's ankle, bringing her thoughts circling back to Fiona's corpse. Somewhere in the water-stained byways of Blackwall, hidden amongst the laborers, skivers, and drunkards, a killer lurks. While some whores may have nobody to mourn or miss them when they pass, the red-headed lass was beloved by the residents of Poplar. And none more so than her grieving roommate. Constance feels her anguish ebb like low tide, slowly being subsumed by an incandescent fury. A plan begins to take shape in her mind, the constituent parts coalescing like frost creeping across a windowpane, going from fleeting fancy to conviction in the span of several seconds.

Perhaps the killer prefers the diminutive lasses, those streetwalkers who appear more girl than woman, slight of frame and understated in their femininity. Mayhap it's their perceived innocence that excites him. And perhaps, of equal or greater import, they are the types of women who are too small to fight back.

As luck would have it, Constance knows of just such a girl—someone who has no problem acting as bait to draw the predator out. Someone who feels like she has nothing to lose and is unafraid to place her head within the lion's jaws.

"Hunting for a defenseless little plaything, are you?" she mutters under her breath, hand resting on the side of the cart in solemn fervor. She has never felt more focused than she does at that very moment. The blade nestled in her boot is suddenly icy against her skin as if it too thirsts for retribution. And why not? Even a streetside whore knows that revenge is a dish best served cold. And if said vengeance happens to be delivered by literal cold steel aimed right at the killer's heart, then that will be the very definition of poetic justice.

"So be it, you monstrous bastard. I shall give you the most tempting plaything you can imagine."

End Overture

HER FIRST TIME

There is a saying that, out of all the four seasons, autumn offers the most to man and requires the least of him in return.

An easy enough axiom to remember, to be sure, albeit not entirely accurate. Autumn can be just as insistent as any other season—spring does not necessarily have a monopoly on the busywork of new beginnings. Children return to school as the leaves begin to turn. Football season kicks off anew. Thankfulness swells, and Samhain is observed, a celebration of those pagan beliefs of old, at once ancient and yet unceasing, many of which have gradually insinuated themselves within the dominant religions of the era.

Despite misconceptions to the contrary, fall is just as pregnant with commencements as any other time of year; they are simply easier to overlook in the wake of collateral considerations.

For the town of Harper's Hollow, autumn is an especially busy time. Fields are tended and furrowed, livestock fattened, and mixt household repairs are completed, all in anticipation of winter's chill. Assuming, of course, that the expected snowfall truly arrives. The last few seasons have been drier than usual, summer droughts invariably following less-than-average midwinter precipitation. In a region where produce and animal meats are the prime exports, drastic changes in the weather can spell doom for the entire economy.

But it is not all grim faces and heavy hearts. The autumn equinox, Mabon, also known as the time of the second harvest, is in full swing. The days and nights are equal in length, bringing harmony and balance to the land. Even the nonbelievers, of which there are a few in Harper's Hollow, transplants from the big city as well as a smattering of foreigners, can't help but offer up wishes and entreaties to Mother Nature, hoping for a bountiful fall yield followed by a wet winter.

The Harpers, emigrees from England for whom the town is named, are foremost in their furtherance of Mabon.

Reclusive in a way that only the wealthy can achieve, the rarely glimpsed founding family graciously sponsors an annual fall festival for the whole county, replete with carnival rides and live entertainment. Though the Harpers never attend themselves, preferring to remain sequestered in their manses on the edge of the neighboring forest, the townsfolk and farmers of the Hollow (as it is affectionately known) help to make each festival an occasion to remember.

Much ballyhoo is made about the Harpers and their cloistered lifestyle, with rumors both prosaic and phantastic flying from the mouths of gossipers. Witches and warlocks, some of the residents maintain, perpetuating a myth that has been fooling the gullible for decades. Awkward albinos, assert others, claiming that the founding family cannot stand the light of day because of their rare physical condition. As if they are some manner of southern-gothic vampires turned undead by the great Albert Harper himself over a hundred and fifty years prior. Fanciful though they may be, none of the rumors are mean-spirited or spiteful—the people of the Hollow know better than to malign their enigmatic benefactors.

For Madeline, a slip of a girl just turned seventeen, such talk is a waste of both time and energy, meaningless speculation that serves no purpose. Boasting sharper hearing that most, she has stumbled upon her fair share of idle chatter while navigating the town. Having heard it all before, and more besides, she possesses enough knowledge on the subject to sift fact from fiction. Not that she is willing to share her secrets.

She has made her way, step by determined step, from her home on the outskirts of town to the festival grounds, white cane leading the way, tapping the ground before her in measured movements. Though her affliction did not happen recently, she will never quite grow accustomed to the blindness which dominates her life. It is a part of who she is now, though she refuses to be defined by it. Instead, she has learned to work with her infirmity, to twist and turn with it as if a leaf on river water.

And yet some days remain harder than others.

The town fair had seemed to spring up overnight, from empty fields to open for business in the span of a single day. Rarely one to linger too long within the city limits, Madeline makes a special exception for the festival. The barker, a bellowing gent who fills the same role each year, is kind enough to waive her admission fee. She makes her way past the stalls and attractions with cautious steps. The layout is never quite the same from year to year, and she must take care to (figuratively) watch her step. She is searching for the center of the festival, the common area where the noise is quieter and the press of bodies less prevalent. Where things are more manageable for a girl like her.

As if shuttered behind a closing door, the sounds of autumn gaiety recede into the background, but a dozen delightful odors linger in the air, invading her nostrils in pleasant waves; the subtle scent of fresh kettle corn, the sugary sweetness of fruit-topped funnel cakes, and a myriad of Dutch-oven masterpieces blending over low heat.

She breathes it all in, wishing to partake of each and every morsel on offer, but steadfastly refusing to give in to such temptations. Or to add to her waistline.

All around her, distant yet distinct, the carnival rides spin and swerve and stutter, providing thrills for young and old alike. Their calliope music rises and falls in staccato accompaniment, tempo keeping time with the mechanical motions. Madeline can barely remember what those rides looked like; all she can muster are vague impressions of gaudy colors and bright lights, abstract images of spinning machinery and metal supports. Imprints from another time. Another life.

Now it's just noise and the heady aroma of petrolatum.

She sits on a wooden bench in the middle of the green, eyes closed, simply absorbing the energy around her. As if merriment and satisfaction can be soaked up through her skin, like some form of social osmosis. She could partake of the rides if she wanted; the operators are unfailingly kind to a blind girl roughly their own age, treating her as though she is some fragile princess suddenly emerged from a popup storybook.

But though Madeline enjoys the way the rides tickle her stomach and hasten her heart, it is a different kind of thrill that calls to her tonight. A thrill which brings warmth to certain areas. Areas which, as dictated by social mores, a lady is expected not to acknowledge.

As if sensing her sudden flash of yearning, a man takes a seat next to her. She knows it is a "he" by the heavy footsteps of his approach, the dull tang of cheap aftershave, and the way in which he settles close to her, a proximity that is hardly necessary. The stranger is a heavyset fellow, judging by the way the bench sags and tilts her towards him. Remnants of slow-cooked chili cling to his breath, along with the scent of something else. Something distilled and drawn furtively from a secreted-away bottle or flask.

"Pardon me, miss," he begins, and Madeline curls her hands tighter around her cane. She hates the slow and pitying way in which strangers address her. As if she is dim-witted as well as blind. There is little that she despises more than the papercut stings of condescending benevolence. "I happened to see you sitting here and I..."

"I'm quite fine, thank you," she replies with a hint of finality. Her tone is not quite hostile, per se, but hovers somewhere in the neighborhood thereof. Madeline has learned, across countless identical interactions, that she must be firm up front. Show any hesitation and men like this one will take it as an invitation to continue with their advances.

The man harrumphs, stymied in his attempt at condolatory gentle-manliness. A flask uncorks and he takes a slug, swallowing loudly. To her attuned ears, the motions are more than obvious, as if emanating from a loudspeaker. An uncomfortable silence follows, settling between them like a physical barrier. But the torment is not yet over. It's as if Madeline can hear the gears turning in the man's head, the needle wavering between "no" and "maybe". She realizes that he is going to try again even before he does and can't keep from sighing to herself. Liquid courage is no kind of courage to be proud of.

He clears his throat, perhaps to inject a little more bass and bravado. Like some animalistic mating dance that she can't help but find pathetic. "Well, what I really wanted to say was..."

She turns her face towards the stranger, eyes fixated on where she assumes he is located. Years of experience have taught her that being regarded by the blind tends to be unsettling for most people. Unnatural and unnerving. She doesn't wish to be cruel, but he is leaving her little alternative. His presence has become odious. Tiresome.

"I will ask you to save it, good sir, for some other conciliatory conquest. You are occupying the seat of the very person I am waiting for, and he will be along presently. He will also not be pleased to find his date being harassed by an inebriate. I bid you good day."

The man remains there for a moment, either stunned or angered (she cares not which), before sniffing loudly in an attempt to conceal his wounded pride. The bench returns to level as he finally departs, stalking away with clomping footfalls. Her grip on the cane relaxes. Distractions from her goal are the last thing she needs tonight, especially from a man barely worthy of the moniker.

Alone with her thoughts once more, Madeline allows herself a moment of indulgence, giving her imagination over to the anticipation of the evening to come. To the clandestine events which will undoubtedly transpire. The very events which she has been building herself up to, for weeks on end.

Madeline has prepared as best she can. Much effort went into styling her hair, including a purposeful braid along one side that tickles her ear in reassurance, with one of her older sisters helping to apply just the right amount of makeup afterwards. Her clothing is appropriately enticing, a black dress that is moderately revealing without being overly scandalous. And hidden beneath her attire... something for *his* eyes only. Something which will undoubtedly draw his gaze and quicken his pulse.

"Spellbinding" is how her sisters described Madeline's appearance. She must take their word for it, obviously, but trusts that they would not steer her wrong. Not tonight. Not with the plans that she has made. In such cunning confidences they are united. Of single mind and intent.

No wonder the heavyset man sought her out. Spellbinding, indeed. Madeline chuckles at the notion, shaking her head in exasperation, but then expunges the thought entirely. It is not worthy of further contemplation.

She sits on the bench, anxious and excited, forcefully quelling her body's desire to fidget. The heat in her belly refuses to listen. An intensity, pulsing even lower on her body, threatens to spread like wildfire. Madeline rests a hand on her stomach, willing it to settle. If not for the public setting, her fingers might have been tempted to stray downwards, soft and surreptitious, as they are sometimes wont to do in the silent sanctuary of her bedroom.

Nevertheless, such immoderations can wait. It is highly probable that her date will help to placate those particular fancies.

Of all the countless things that changed once Madeline lost her sight, being untethered from the constraints of time is one of the few adjustments she genuinely enjoys.

One of the earliest lessons taught by her sightlessness is that blind people are never early or late. Timetables simply adjust themselves in her presence, for how can one be accused of (and punished for) tardiness when they cannot see the minute and second hands, the lengthening of shadows, or the sun's position in the sky?

Existing in perpetual darkness has given her a rare sense of freedom that sighted people simply cannot fathom. Yes, the old grandfather clock within her family's home counts out the phases of the day, bell tolling each hour with antique solemnity. Once free from the confines of her residence, however, it is as if she is no longer beholden to the tick-tock measure of mankind's existence. Whether wandering the woods, strolling through the Hollow, or simply settled on the back porch in a wicker chair, Madeline is unbound and unburdened.

As such, she is unable to gauge whether Joel has arrived at the appointed time or not. She simply senses his presence, from absent to present in the blink of an eye—a blaze of vivid red within the inky veil of her perception. Her heart does a pitter-patter of nervous excitement while butterflies whirl and tumble within her belly, animatedly aflutter. She is doubly thankful for avoiding the temptation of food.

Not everyone possesses a color, she has ascertained over the years. The vast majority of strangers are simply voices to her, blank slates identifiable solely by their tones, timbres, and enunciations. Only a few of the towns-folk shine, for reasons she has yet to discover. Her family, on the other hand, blaze with an incandescent fury to rival that of the sun. Not one of their colors is the same, their hues as varied as their dispositions. And those individuals which they've cast their gazes upon glow as well. A crimson radiance that is almost physical in its manifestation.

Joel, for reasons that have not yet been made clear to him, has captured their interest quite handily. And Madeline's most of all.

The bench judders as he sits down, much nearer than the odious man was. Closer than would be strictly appropriate, had she a chaperone keep-ing watchful eyes upon them. He smells of fallen leaves and tilled earth, of well water and woodsmoke. He wears the scents of autumn like a cologne. She even detects a trace of leather and sweat, conspicuous but not unpleas-ant, undoubtedly stemming from his after-school football practice.

"Hey, Maddy. I wasn't sure that you'd show," Joel breathes, his voice hovering somewhere between innocence and responsibility.

"Hey, yourself," she replies in husky tones. She cannot rely on the bed-room eyes that most girls her age can cast at will; she must use the other tools at her disposal. "Well, you asked me here, and I said yes. It would be quite unseemly to turn coward after making such a pact, don't you agree, Joel Hartigan?"

The slight hesitation in his voice signifies that he is still figuring out her nuances. That, or he is staring at her *décolletage*, which she has never allowed to be quite so exposed before. Either option is fine with her.

"I... suppose that's true. It just seems a strange choice for you, that's all."

Madeline snorts, a rather unladylike response. Not that she cares overmuch. "As opposed to what? Remaining isolated in my darkness, viewing the world through the reflections of my memories, like some inverse adaptation of Tennyson's Lady of Shalott?"

"I don't know what you mean," he replies carefully. In her mind, Joel is scratching his head in confusion as the words tumble from his mouth.

"They don't teach you Tennyson in English class?"

"If they did, I must have missed it. I apologize, Maddy. I didn't mean to offend."

"Don't worry about it," she says, waving a dismissive hand. "It happens all the time. Even to people who should know better."

His fingers touch the braid lightly, hesitantly. "I love what you've done with your hair."

"Thank you. I had help, of course, but felt it would be a nice touch."

They have been courting for the past several weeks, during the random intervals in which she finds herself within the city limits. It is a strange wooing—stolen moments behind the Woolworth's, quick treks through the moonlit woods, casual conversations out front of the soda shop. What physical contact they've had has been fleeting and somewhat chaste, with no articles of clothing yet removed. Her peers call it "heavy petting". Apart from making out and permitting him a healthy dose of over-the-clothing fondling, Madeline has, as the situation demands, been playing hard to get.

But she knows that Joel wants more. One does not need eyes to behold the obvious.

Even through the various layers of her apparel, Joel's touch is consistently firm. Insistent. Demanding in a way that is exclusive to teenage boys. He claims to have little carnal experience, but Madeline isn't fooled. So far, his fingers have managed to discover her most intimate and sensual of spots with minimal effort, regardless of whichever fabrics might be acting as a bulwark.

There is no virginal innocence where Joel Hartigan is concerned.

Though her date is not lacking for confidence, it was Madeline who initiated the courtship, in outright defiance of expected conventions. But her family has never allowed themselves to be bound by the usual societal traditions. Still, she knows that she must be careful. Overzealousness could throw her carefully laid plans into disarray. Fortunately, their "accidental" run-ins were far easier to pull off owing to her blindness. Madeline has been quite adept at planting the seeds for this evening's rendezvous. So adept, in fact, that Joel undoubtedly believes it was his idea to begin with.

Madeline slides across the wooden slats, closing the remaining distance between them in one smooth motion, their thighs touching with insistent pressure. She can feel the body heat radiating from him like a country stove. His color grows even brighter, filling the entirety of her "vision". It is now more burgundy than blood-red, an extraordinary tint that she has never experienced before.

"Have I given you any reason not to trust my word or intentions?"

He stammers a quick response, thoroughly flustered. "No, of course not!"

She continues her verbal advance, unwilling to cede the high ground she has so thoroughly captured. Injecting a hint of pout in her voice is as easy as breathing. "Are you having second thoughts about us? About me?"

Rough hands grasp hers; even at a young age, callouses from hard labor have begun to form on his fingers. Whether from plow, mattock, or shovel,

Madeline cannot be sure. She has lived a sheltered life in comparison to the majority of the county's residents, for whom toiling from sunup to sundown is all they've ever known. The vagaries of farm work are as elusive to her as a kite in a stiff breeze.

"Oh, Maddy," Joel murmurs, giving her fingers a squeeze. He even manages to sound sincere. "That's not it at all. I've never been more certain about anything in my whole life. It just seems a little unfair that you know more about me than I do about you."

He is not wrong. Madeline has been guarded, parceling out details with a miser's reluctance. What facts she *has* revealed have been obfuscated by half-truths and misdirection. Her vagueness is a curated thing—instilled at a young age by her family, moderated across the years of maturation, and further exacerbated by her loss of vision.

Courting Joel has been a balancing act of furor and intent, with Madeline baiting the hook, tugging the line, and flashing the lure, all from the emotional safety of dry land. Reeling him in has been deliberately paced—too much slack, or too little, and he's bound to slip away.

Though she is loath to acknowledge the correlation, she realizes that her strategy, like football, is a game of inches. And sometimes, a trick play is needed to win the game.

"Feeling at a disadvantage, are you?" she asks playfully, carefully assailing his male ego. It did not take her long to realize that Joel, like most of his gender, can't help but view everything through the lens of competition. "Though I cannot really argue with your logic. Ok, handsome, what is weighing upon that mind of yours?"

To his credit, he genuinely seems to have put thought into his concerns. She finds herself mildly surprised. "Well, I don't even know where you live. You don't go to the high school, so you're either from another town, or you do your studies at home. Everybody knows 'of' you, but nobody actually 'knows' much at all about a girl named Madeline. You know the combination to my locker, yet I don't even know your last name. You're like a ghost."

"Would a ghost be able to do *this*!?", Madeline asks, nudging him hard with her shoulder. He gasps in surprise before barking out a laugh, caught off guard.

"You hit harder than some of the guys on the team," Joel responds, returning the gesture, albeit with less force. "You could show them a thing or two."

"I'd gladly show *you* a thing or two," she mumbles under her breath. The words are barely louder than a whisper, but she knows that he heard them. Which, of course, was her intent. Before he can draw a breath for a response, she continues. "Very well. If it will help set your mind at ease, my full name is Madeline Elizabeth Harper."

"Wait, Harper? As in, like, our town? One of *the* Harpers?"

"Well, that would be a treat for both of us, now, wouldn't it?" she responds cryptically.

Joel sucks in a breath. Madeline can sense that he's about to pull away, this new mystery suddenly commanding the lion's share of his attention. An understandable reaction. And one of the many reasons she prefers to keep the name to herself. Why, in fact, her entire family does, no matter the circumstances or company. The Harpers. Always so careful with their secrets.

For the briefest of moments, Madeline's thoughts turn to Delilah, her dearly departed sister. Of all the myriad glows in their household, Delilah's was always the brightest. The warmest. She had been Madeline's closest confidant. Her best friend. Her favorite mentor. The most captivating of their family in spite of, or possibly due to, her endearing awkwardness.

Siblings in pact if not in blood, they were as unalike as two women could be, both in appearance and disposition. Where Madeline has always possessed a gilded tongue, Delilah had to forge her thoughts, and the words that followed, from the rawest of materials—much toil and travail in order to produce a finished product. And yet, when conversing of Joel, she spoke eloquently. Fervently. With an unexpected poetry that belied her quiet nature.

Delilah Harper. Both exceptionally quiet and exceptionally beautiful. She was good at so many things—baking, needlework, and even keeping the family's secrets, even though she was trusting of everyone around her.

Too trusting, as it had turned out.

Madeline realizes that she is drifting, getting ahead of herself. Stepping outside of the established order of things. She knows, through many a lesson in the dead of night, that cycles must be adhered to. That there is power in sequence and succession, in pattern and in preparation. Such things are of no small consequence.

But there is power in other things as well. In more... primal practices. Delilah, may she rest in peace, can wait for just a little longer. Madeline isn't quite ready to resolve that aenigma. Not yet. There is another knot that requires untangling first.

She shifts forward, leaning her face in close to Joel's. The warmth of his breath washes across her lips, the urge to act threatening to overwhelm her right then and there.

"So, now that we're here, what is the plan?"

"I don't know," he replies, focused solely on her once more. "What would you like to do?"

She reaches out, finding his thigh, resting her palm well north of his knee. His muscles tighten in a most enticing way. She has a sudden desire to do more, to slide her hand upwards, grazing him in a manner that will rob him of his senses completely. But, as ribald as she is feeling, the green is far too public a place for what she has in store. Such forwardness must wait until later.

For now, innuendo-laden answers will have to suffice.

"Why, Joel, I would like to do *everything*."

Hours later, the sun has become a distant memory. Though Madeline cannot see it, she feels the absence of light from her skin, like bedsheets that have slipped away overnight.

Despite the growing chill, she has been enjoying herself. Yielding to the merriment of the moment. They have gone on most of the rides, partaking of several sugary confections afterwards while waiting for their dizziness to subside. Joel is both well-known and well-liked, continually greeted by classmates and neighbors. Madeline remains silent and aloof, rarely joining in the friendly conversation, perfectly willing to be seen and not heard. For the time being, at least.

His friends, for the most part, seem content to allow Madeline her indifference. They are courteous and careful, studiously avoiding the words "seeing" and "watching", but even in this they stumble. Her blindness makes them wary. Their pity grazes her armor but does not penetrate.

Not that she is impervious to sorrow. Acceptance of her condition does not preclude her from missing certain sights: the undulating dance of firelight from the wood-burning stove, the shifting shades of autumn leaves, the smiles borne upon the faces of her family.

No, these things will always leave her wanting.

Throughout the mental tit-for-tat, Delilah's face hovers in the back of Madeline's awareness like an apparition, a constant reminder of what is to come. As if Madeline would ever let herself forget. There is no judgement upon her sibling's visage, only an implacable impatience for events yet to transpire.

The erstwhile entertainment of the fair, however, has been a welcome distraction. A rare treat during eventful times. Each ride and attraction are thrilling in their own way, their own manner of foreplay, instilling a giddiness that transcends mere physical sensation.

Joel is just as enraptured by the evening as she is permitting herself to be—she hears it in his genuine laughter and can feel it when goosebumps appear on his skin. As the hours slip by, he is questioning less and conceding more. With the crowds thinning out and the lines for the attractions getting shorter, Joel grows ever bolder with his affections. Nestled together in a metal carriage, slowly winding through the festival's requisite haunted ride and free from prying eyes, Madeline is practically in his lap, arms wrapped around his neck. Their kissing has been growing more passionate by the minute, lips sticky and sweet from a shared caramel apple.

Amongst the smell of chain grease and the prerecorded screeches and howls playing over cheap loudspeakers, she has never felt so alive. So unshackled from herself.

The fluttering butterflies have returned, and in far greater numbers—Joel's hand steadily creeps along her bare clavicle, masked by the pull of the twisting carriage. She has never let him feel beneath her clothing before. But this time, in the secluded chaos of the spook alley, Madeline allows his hand to wander. Warm fingers glide across her skin, slow and steady, slipping under the dress and soft lace of her underthings, finding the engorged bud at the tip of her breast and pinching softly.

His skill is evident, and she can't help but comment, breathlessness coating each syllable. "So much for not being very experienced... you are *far* too good at this."

"I think you're overthinking it," he replies with a whisper before taking her earlobe between his lips and sucking softly.

"And *I* think you should kiss me proper, Joel Hartigan."

As his tongue darts between her teeth, his fingers twist and flick, the illicit contact sending pulses of pleasure throughout her entire body. Intimate touches are always better when imparted by someone other than herself. Madeline's moans are lost amidst the clanking of the drive chain and the playful shrieks of riders further ahead. But Joel can hear them perfectly, and his touch becomes more insistent in response. Shameless desire threatens to overwhelm her, the patience of the past few weeks evaporating under his assured ministrations.

Madeline has heard, in snippets of whispered conversations, that creative lovers often sneak into the dark confines of the spook alley to do the deed. Almost as a rite of passage. The vast majority of such tales, she knows, are unquestionably false, excitable adolescents spinning yarns with which to impress their friends. But more than a few have carried the weight of truth.

The location leaves much to be desired in terms of romance, but she cannot deny that it is uniquely suited to her needs. The machinery will mask any untoward noises if nothing else.

Though she is certain that Joel has been reduced to putty in her hands, Madeline is unwilling to take any chances. She knows exactly what needs to be done. Her fingers trail down his chest and past his belt, searching for, and finding, evidence of his arousal. His entire body tenses at her touch, and she gives his manhood a firm squeeze. Joel spasms in response, the reaction empowering in a way she would be hard-pressed to describe.

It's been too long since she felt such control.

"You're no shrinking violet, yourself," he groans, voice strained with arousal. With their bodies pressed so tightly together, she can feel the excited rise and fall of his chest, like the breathing of large bellows at a blacksmith's forge. The thrumming of his heart is very nearly perceptible to her attuned ears.

She squeezes again, slowly this time, a lingering pressure that makes him squirm. He is hot beneath her fingers. "I'm a quick study."

As Joel follows her lead, moving his hand to her thigh and slowly parting her stocking-clad legs, the hem of her skirt hiking further and further upwards, she knows that there will never be a better time. If she is to get what she is after, it must happen now.

"I'm ready, Joel. For you. Find me a safe place to get out."

He is quiet for a moment, undoubtedly perplexed, but then seems to grasp what she is insinuating. She hears his breath catch even through the din.

"What about me?"

She leans in close, lips against his ear. The lust in her voice is unfiltered. Unfeigned. The hint of coyness that nearly registers as a giggle, however, is pure pretense. "Get off the ride and make like you're heading home. Be seen by your friends, be seen by everyone. And then, when nobody is looking, find a way to sneak back in here, just as quick as you can. Don't get caught! I'll be waiting... with nary a stitch to keep me warm. That part, I leave up to you."

Joel gulps audibly, his limbs suddenly shaking with excitement.

"I just hope you realize that I'm not like the women in your father's Playboy magazines."

"And that's ok," he responds, voice hoarse with fervency. "I like a real girl. In fact, I think you're the most beautiful woman I've ever seen."

They are enchanting words, spoken with the soft tinge of sincerity, and a part of her desperately wants to believe him. To lose herself in such a fantasy. But they are words he has spoken before, not so long ago. And very nearly verbatim.

Joel is many things, but much to her disapproval, sincere is not one of them.

He takes Madeline's hand and helps her stand. The motion of the carriage causes her to sway, but his strong grip keeps her upright. She has no idea how far into the ride they have travelled, not that it really matters. She'll be able to find her way out, later, when all is said and done. Of that she has no doubt.

"Step out here," he urges, assisting her with the effort. "It's a graveyard scene with a big plaster mausoleum. I've heard that it's hollow on the other side, and we should fit with room to spare. I'll be back as quick as I can!"

Madeline has heard of the recess in the back of the mausoleum as well, and the various dalliances that have taken place within. The notion is stimulating in a slightly uncomfortable way. But needs must when the devil drives, as the saying goes.

Joel plants a kiss on her hand and then releases his hold, masquerading as the perfect gentleman. A trace of moisture lingers above her knuckles like a promise. Madeline steps back several paces, feeling her way with carefully placed footfalls, holding the cane against her chest. Nobody had been in line behind them; she'll have a good window of time to get situated.

She allows herself an indulgent smile—it won't be long now. Hovering in the shadows, her presence the merest intimation of a whisper, Delilah's specter wears a similar expression, the corners of her lips arched wickedly. Like a cat that caught the canary.

Madeline's grasping hand finds the edge of the structure. The plaster is coarse against her flesh, rough and sturdy. Satisfied that she can maneuver safely, she calls after him in a muted voice, certain that she is still audible.

"Don't dawdle, or I might just start without you."

Joel's color betrays his arrival long before Madeline hears him traversing the faux graveyard.

As before, she holds no real concept of how long she's been waiting. Hidden away inside the mausoleum, cloistered within her own pocket of implacable purpose, time is as elastic as rubber. As fleeting as foxes. With no other distractions vying for her attention, Madeline is acutely aware of the sharp pang of lasciviousness winding within her, taut like a compressed spring. That, and the all-encompassing impatience which threatens to drown her.

Serenity was easy to achieve when surrounded by townspeople and carnies. When vices of the flesh were hampered by the inscrutable judgment of acceptable behavior. Regardless, now that she is free from prying eyes, her ardor is fighting for control, threatening to leave Madeline a mere spectator in her own body.

From the shrouded veil that looms between the living and the dead, Delilah looks on, pleased with her sister's resolve.

Though the air beyond the confines of the ride carries the bite of autumn's chill, the interior of the spook alley is comfortably warm. True to her word, Madeline has removed her dress along with her unmentionables, the abrupt nudity far more exhilarating than any of the carnival's rides or games managed to be. She folds her clothing with leisurely precision—the soft fabric will serve nicely as a makeshift pillow.

She has prepared for their tryst with meticulous deliberation: red hibiscus from her family's garden sprinkled around the corners of the structure, an aquamarine ring (which once was Delilah's) adorning her right heart finger, and cinnamon perfume applied to her wrists, neck, and bosom.

The rest of her accoutrements lie nestled beneath the fabric. Foremost amongst them is her family's athamé, the ceremonial implement older than all of her living relatives put together.

Vivid red engulfs her awareness as Joel clambers into the hollow, shoes scuffing against the wooden floor. Not a single word is spoken in acknowledgment. He simply stands motionless for the span of several heartbeats, drinking in Madeline's nakedness with voyeuristic silence before colliding against her like an avalanche, mouth seeking her own, suckling her lower lip with immoral abandon.

Despite her fervor, she cannot help but feel a prick of annoyance. Not a single remark about her bareness? No gentlemanly appreciation of her exposed state? Not that she is surprised. So close to the finish line, bereft of any opposition, all he can see is the reward. A failing of the male gender, it would seem.

Joel undresses with fumbling awkwardness, the small recess of the mausoleum hampering his efforts. Madeline helps as best she can. Her seeking hands roam each freshly exposed part of his body, fingernails scratching along his flesh enticingly. Delilah had told her all about his physical features, late at night while the rest of the household slumbered; with her infirmity, these things matter far less to Madeline than other girls her age.

And yet, she cannot help but explore, "seeing" with the pads of her fingers. His body is trim and toned, as is befitting of someone so vigorous. Her questing hands examine each groove and channel defined by muscle and bone. Joel shivers under her touch, breath coming in ragged gasps.

"Oh, Maddy. I've been wanting this for so long."

"As have I, my darling," she coos, fingers trailing downwards, inching ever closer to the advent of his desire.

Finding what she seeks, she claims it for her own, Joel quaking uncontrollably as she fondles his girth. He is rock-hard in her hand, a stiffness that must surely be of some discomfort.

"You poor thing," she purrs, stroking the length of him. "So much tension, just aching to be released."

"Oh. My. God." His words are muted, forced through gritted teeth.

In that moment he is as blind as she, dumbstruck by the pleasure of her caress. Outside of this very moment, Joel holds every advantage: bigger, faster, sighted. Possessing a strength Madeline could not hope to overcome. But here, in the delirious dark, a slave to his own lust, he is powerless before her.

Fingers encircling him, she draws him forward and down, guiding his erection straight to her sex. Shivers caper along her entire body—she has never before been so wet. So wantonly willing. The anticipation is like electricity, running along her nerves and muscles in a closed circuit, heightening every sensation to the point of anguish.

A playful shriek emerges from one of the passing carriages, the sound masking Madeline's cry as Joel's hips thrust forward, his manhood impaling her with exquisite agony. They are both motionless for a trice, desperate to prolong such an unparalleled feeling. Finally, with a grunt and a groan, he increases the tempo, finding a rhythm that elicits a shuddering growl deep within her throat.

Joel's firm hands roam her body like questing fingers across a newly-acquired roadmap, his touch tracing along byways and lingering on points of interest with eager intensity. Calloused digits slide and seek, never truly relinquishing their hold, a pressure as unyielding as iron, as if she is an object he owns. As if she is now *his*. She doesn't need eyes to know that the look upon his face would prove her suppositions correct—he masks his motives with a camouflage that is gossamer thin and twice as sheer.

Madeline surrenders to the moment, relinquishing all control to the most secret of ceremonials. The most revered of rituals. Joel's breath is hot on her neck, as fiery as the place where their bodies are joined. Minutes stretch interminably, each one that passes carrying her closer to the edge. None of her previous experiences have ever felt quite like this. Though there is power in passion, making love to Joel exceeds all that has come before, bringing her to the precipice in a way that previous lovers, as well as her own fingers, have yet to achieve.

Joel, of course, assumes that she is a virgin. That he is her first. And he is—just not in the way he expects.

That lingering thought is enough to push her over the brink. A scant few seconds later, Madeline climaxes with a muffled shout, hips bucking violently, the dizzying eruption sending her fingernails scratching down Joel's back. There is no thought, only the mental static of sweet release.

It takes several seconds for her senses to return. By the steadily increasing tempo, she can tell that Joel is approaching his own threshold. Like a furtive sigh, Delilah's voice slinks into Madeline's ear, more a thought than anything else. *"It is time, dear sister."*

"Maddy," Joel sputters, thrusting with reckless abandon. "You feel so damn good!"

"Better than anything you've ever felt?" she asks, baiting the trap.

"Yes," he replies, drawing out the word mindlessly as if summoning a serpent.

Madeline wraps her legs around his backside, drawing him close. He is too lost in lust, hips futilely trying to push, but she refuses to release him. She has abandoned the huskiness entirely; her words are said in a sing-song, mocking tone. "Is it love, Joel? Have you never felt anything like this before? Do you think you could be mine forever?"

"I...what?"

"Isn't that what you told her? Delilah? The night that you seduced her, deflowered her, were those not the very words that you used?"

She is unable to see the look of confusion that washes over Joel's features. But she hears it in his voice, and feels it too, as his member softens inside her. "Who? Delilah? You mean that blonde girl?"

Hearing her sister reduced to simply being "that blonde girl" is like a shot through Madeline's heart. She squeezes her legs tighter, locking him in place, clawed fingers grabbing a handful of hair and pulling his face close. He yelps in pain and surprise.

"She was my sister, you thoughtless prick! You awoke something within her with your promises and your platitudes. You gave her hope. And then, as so many of your gender do, you took away her purity without a second thought. She believed she had found love! But all that you brought her was devastation and an early grave. It is only right that you be given the same."

While she is speaking, Madeline's other hand slides beneath her folded clothes, grasping at what she secreted away. Joel finally manages to overpower her, breaking her hold and pushing himself away. Before he can escape, Madeline swipes at his midsection, quick as lightning. The sharpened blade of the athamé slices through the flesh of his stomach like warm butter. Warmth spills across her belly in spurts, a completely different kind of release than what he was imagining. She strikes again before he can cry out, the knife stabbing into the soft tissue under his chin, its tip penetrating all the way into his brain.

"A life for a life," she intones as Joel's limp body crumples to the side, twitching several times before lying still. The words echo faintly in the enclosed space. "Delilah wasn't the only one who was too trusting."

And, just like that, it is over. A great weight lifts from her shoulders, and she wipes away a solitary tear. Joel's color seeps into shadow, disappearing without a trace. The circle has been closed. "I wish you hadn't given up,

Li," Madeline whispers, Delilah's nickname thick on her tongue. "He wasn't worth it."

Her sister remains silent and motionless, aspect shimmering with scintillating hues, wavering at the very ingress to infinity. As if hesitant to succumb to the pull.

"It is done. Go, my love. Seek Summerland, and I shall find you there in due course. Will you guide me, when my time has come?"

Delilah, her freckled face pale and half-hidden by golden tresses, nods once, a sad smile playing across her lips. And then her spirit is gone as well, fading from Madeline's mind like yesterday's wind.

Madeline stays prone for a long moment, the vestiges of pleasure and emotion draining away. The scent of their exertions still lingers in the air. That, and the coppery tang of blood, a visceral commemoration of her first kill. It was a messy affair, but Joel won't be the last person to run afoul of the Harpers. She'll have plenty of opportunities to practice.

The taking of a life is no simple matter, or so she has been told. However, despite the expectation of sickness, or shock if nothing else, Madeline finds herself strangely dizzy, as if intoxicated on pilfered wine.

She does not believe in heaven, at least not in the way that most residents of Harper's Hollow do. Her tenets have a more natural bent, hewing closer to the pagan deities of earth, moon, and the myriad far-flung celestial bodies. A lifestyle predicated on the balance of karma and the potency of intent. The very same beliefs passed down by her earliest ancestors.

Those considerations aside, she suspects that, were it indeed real, a Christian hereafter would impart the same sense of empyrean ecstasy which she is currently feeling.

Using Joel's clothing to wipe away the blood, Madeline makes sure she is free of any telltale signs of his murder. She dresses slowly, casually, returning the knife to her stocking while listening to the carriages that trundle by. The majority of them sound empty. She'll be able to exit the ride without being seen.

As for Joel, the carnies will find and hide the body; the last thing the fair operators want is any sort of scandal impacting their business.

Her sightlessness, a desideratum which affects one member of her family every generation, is all but forgotten. Madeline has proven herself worthy of her surname, and therefore worthy of what shall follow. The primacy that is soon to come. She will no longer view her malady as a hindrance. It is an equitable exchange, a covenant made long before she was born, one to which she is eternally bound. The loss of one sense for command over another.

Eager to return home and share the news of her success, Madeline's mind cannot help but return to one the region's most popular sayings: out of all the four seasons, autumn offers the most to man and requires the least of him in return. That is, of course, unless he earns the ire of the Harper coven, in which case autumn offers only one thing.

A certain death.

PSYCHO KILLER

I n the entirety of his seventeen years of marriage, Homicide Detective Desmond Little had never once been dishonest with his wife.

As he saw it, matrimony required enough work as it was, and he found no value in complicating matters by adding falsehoods to the mix. Not that he had much to hide. Desmond was as faithful as a hound and possessed not a single vice that would have necessitated deception. The only things that might have required filtering were the grittier aspects of his job. Or the ways in which they affected him, both mentally and emotionally.

But no, Wanda got all the details—or all the details he was allowed to share, at least.

And yet, as he stood in the doorway of Dante's Diner, taking in the macabre scene before him, he realized he might be telling his wife a few little white lies before the day was over.

Thirteen bodies were arrayed throughout the restaurant in various poses which, under nearly any other circumstances, might have been innocuous. Most were seated in booths, either slumped over their tables or leaning sideways across the seats. A waitress lay face down on the tile floor, standard-issue pen and notepad scattered several inches away from her curled fingers. The cashier's legs were visible from where she'd fallen behind the register's podium. And, somewhere behind the saloon-style doors that led to the kitchen, as discovered by the first responding officers, would be the body of a busboy, also prone.

There were no injuries immediately visible on any of the bodies. The other expected telltale signs of a homicide were curiously absent as well; no blood spatters from gunshot or knife wounds, no signs of a struggle, and not one of the victims seemed to have been trying to escape a dangerous situation. In fact, each of them looked, for all intents and purposes, as if they had simply fallen asleep where they were.

Over a career spanning thirteen years—thirteen again, maybe it really was an unlucky number—Desmond had experienced far more gruesome crime scenes. But so many dead in such a confined space, with no clear indication of how they had perished, was more than a little unnerving. And also, more than a little perplexing.

Bloodless and unbruised did not usually fit into the homicide equation.

Though he'd seen death in many of its forms, and was far from a superstitious man, there was still something eerie about the bodies, some indefinable element that had his hackles up. It was as though he had suddenly stepped into a dread-inducing horror film. He kept expecting one of the corpses to move, to rise in exaggerated, herky-jerky motions. He wasn't quite sure how he'd react if one actually did. Probably not well, he conceded.

And then, of course, there was the song.

Issuing from a jukebox sitting in the far corner, the Talking Heads song "Psycho Killer" was running on repeat, the driving baseline and off-kilter vocal delivery adding sinister undertones to an already bizarre tableau. The track had looped twice while he stood in the doorway taking in the details, playing nonstop since the initial patrolmen responded to the 911 call. If

Desmond knew anything, he knew this: there was not a chance in hell that the song choice was coincidental.

There had been exactly one survivor of the...incident. The line cook, after witnessing his coworkers and customers falling dead through the serving window, had hightailed it out the back door, dialing emergency services from a payphone down the street. First responders arrived less than four minutes later. Desmond and company were a scant fifteen minutes behind them.

Questioning the man, one Demetrius Dante Jr., had yielded precious few facts. The victims were all regulars, frequently arriving right as the diner opened. Despite spending most of his time in the kitchen, Dante still knew their names, faces, and even their favorite meals. Shortly after serving coffees and other beverages, Mindy, the waitress, a six-year veteran of Dante's and always a bundle of energy, complained of a sudden sense of lethargy. A few of the customers grew visibly weary as well. And then Hector, the busboy, just collapsed, falling like a sack of potatoes while pushing his cart. Mindy crumpled to the ground only a few moments later. And that, the cook said, had been that.

Dante was now on his way to AC General to get checked out by medical professionals, just as a precaution. Survivor's guilt had already been weighing heavily on the man, and Desmond felt for the guy. He had looked positively devastated.

Desmond had plenty of double-homicides under his belt, as well as a few gang-related drive-by shootings with multiple casualties. He had, in fact, come across roughly ten dead during the prior year's Color Killer showdown. But thirteen bodies all in one go? That was a distressingly high number. A new high score.

He had no idea what to tell Wanda, or where to even begin. But that bridge, as the saying went, would get crossed later. For now, he had bigger fish to fry.

Worried about the potential for toxic fumes or a deadly gas of some kind, Desmond was waiting for the patrolmen to be checked out before he allowed any of his own guys to enter the building. Of course, if there was such a danger, he had already been exposed just by being in the open entryway. But there was nothing to be done about that now.

As if on cue, the precinct's paramedic gave him the thumbs-up: the first responders were fine. All clear.

"Alright, folks, let's get in there and get to work," Desmond grumbled, his basso voice easily audible amidst the din. "And tell the forensics team that they're welcome to join us. Plenty of room to go around."

"Sir!" one of his junior detectives acknowledged, running off towards the CSI van.

"Well, that's a crap deal," Pete Donaldson, the unit's newest member, said ruefully. "This was actually a really good place to eat. But, looking at those bodies, I sure as shit won't be coming back here, and that's a fact."

Desmond couldn't fault the man in the slightest.

It was just after nine in the morning in Angel City, prime time for the breakfast crowd, but late in the day for the early risers. An oppressive late-August heat was already making itself known, promising a scorcher of a Wednesday. Desmond could feel perspiration beading on the dark skin of his forehead. It might have even been from the warmth.

Police tape and sawhorses had been erected before his arrival per his radioed request, cordoning off the diner entirely. Beyond the temporary barricade, a fair number of onlookers were milling about, drawn to the heavy police presence like moths to flame.

Inside, the temperature was cool, refreshing. Deceptive in its normalcy. The same, however, could not be said of the smell. Even without the tang of blood and other aromas of violence, the dead frequently lost control of their bodily functions as their muscles relaxed. That, coupled with the unmistakable reek of burning meat emanating from the kitchen, resulted in a miasma of foul, sickening odors.

He pointed to the swinging doors with a sharp motion. "Pete, get in there and turn off the burners. The last thing we need is a fire adding to our troubles."

The junior detective nodded, heading for the kitchen at a quick march.

Slipping on a pair of latex gloves, Desmond started by doing a quick once-over of each of the victims, looking for any telltale signs of what had caused their demise. Against a backdrop of white tile, light gray vinyl, and bright light from the diner's fashionable fixtures, anything amiss should have stood out like a sore thumb. But there was nothing readily apparent. Just dead eyes staring out of slack faces; not a single look of horror or dismay to be found. As if they had just been...switched off, like a television set.

The other detectives fell into the rhythm of their individual tasks, fanning out with professional precision. Commandeering one corner of the diner, the forensics team began setting up their equipment as well, their photographer already snapping preliminary pictures.

And still the song played on, a surreal soundtrack accompanying the teams as they worked. Typically unfazed by ambient distractions, it was beginning to get under Desmond's skin, his jaw clenching uncontrollably.

"Ok, I can't take it anymore. I'll get the jukebox," Andrea Fleming stated, as if reading his mind. She was the only female detective on his team, hair straight and long where his was wiry and short, her extremely pale skin a stark contrast to his darker tones. Never one to judge someone's abilities by their appearance, Desmond knew Andrea's cool beauty was dwarfed by her deeply analytical mind. She ran circles around some of the other detectives with minimal effort.

Desmond nodded in appreciation. "Please and thank you. That song is giving me the heebie-jeebies."

Approaching the waitress, he noticed a small puddle of blood pooled around her face. His heartrate quickened, but upon looking closer, he realized the blood originated from her nose, which had smashed against the floor as she fell. A purely accidental wound, one not caused by a perpetrator at all. Which put Desmond back to square one, with no initial clues to go on. He couldn't help but sigh.

Twenty feet away, Detective Fleming gave a grunt as she pulled the juke-box away from the wall, kneeling and grabbing the cord with well-manicured fingers. Less than a second later, she was uttering a string of curses, starting quietly, but with mounting volume and intensity after each word, almost drowning out the still-playing music.

"What is it?" Desmond asked, instantly alarmed by the change in her voice.

Shaking her head, she threw a worried look his way. "Uh...I really think you need to come and see for yourself, boss."

A sinking feeling took root in his gut. Andrea was as cool as a cucumber, so if something had ruffled her feathers, then it was undoubtedly going to make his day a whole lot worse.

She scrambled out of the way so he could take her place behind the jukebox. Desmond was by no means a small man, despite his surname, and his linebacker frame could barely fit in the tight space. What he saw made his stomach do cartwheels. A section of the machine's back panel had been cut away, exposing its inner workings. Inside, a jury-rigged wiring harness was attached to the existing control panel, various cables snaking around the embedded circuit boards. Usually, when there were aftermarket cables like those, it could mean only one thing.

For the briefest moment he was unable to breathe. The room suddenly felt a thousand degrees too hot. He broke out in a cold sweat. Tunnel vision crept in to where all he could see was the harness in front of him. But, as he forced his initial panic aside and scanned the interior of the machine once again, he let out a sigh of relief. Desmond was no electrician, but he'd been around the block enough to know that whatever the cabling was for, an explosive device wasn't on the list. In fact, the wiring looked like nothing more than an overly complicated bridge across circuits. Probably to force the machine to keep looping the same track. An inventive workaround, but far from dangerous.

But it wasn't just the cables which had caused Detective Fleming's reaction. Nestled within the circuitry, held aloft by a creative angling of several wires, was an off-white envelope adorned with thick letters in neat, uncluttered handwriting. Just six words, each of the letters capitalized, but they made him want to swear as well, despite his prevailing aversion to profanity. He read the two sentences several times, letting the gravity of the situation sink in.

HELLO POLICE. LET'S PLAY A GAME.

The sinking feeling in his gut returned, more pronounced than before. "Son of a..." Desmond muttered, unwilling to commit to finishing the thought. He grabbed the envelope with tentative fingers, pinching it as if it were diseased.

Detective Fleming clicked her tongue. "Yeah, my sentiments exactly. And here I got out of bed thinking today was going to be a good day."

"That's what you get for thinking."

"Uh huh. So, what do you want to do here, boss?"

Desmond contemplated that question for a few seconds, weighing the options, planning out his next moves. He tried not to keep glancing at the envelope but failed spectacularly. There was at least a full day's worth of work to be done within the diner, even with his full complement of staff. Doing a job right meant doing it at a reasonable pace. The forensics crew might be finished before dusk, but his own team would be there until well after sundown.

Plus, he still needed to open the envelope. To see what manner of taunting or disturbing paraphernalia it contained. Despite how things were portrayed the movies, letters and calling cards left at the scene of a crime were quite rare. Across thirteen years of service, Desmond had only experienced one other such instance. Its mere existence made him anxious.

"For now," he replied, deep voice sounding like two boulders grinding together, "we do what we do best. And we do it by the book, no mistakes."

"You wanna see what goodies the killer left for us?"

He nodded, though it was noncommittal at best. He knew opening the envelope would be akin to taking the lid off Pandora's Box—once unsealed, there'd be no shutting it again until the psycho quit or was caught. But such were the rules of the game, simply how it was played, and Desmond was a consummate veteran. He would meet the challenge head-on. "Get Pete over here, would you? Let's have one more set of eyes on it right up front."

Once the junior detective joined them, Desmond carefully opened the flap of the envelope, his gloved fingers necessitating extra effort. Within was a folded sheet of college-ruled paper, the kind found in virtually any supermarket and office supply store. Far too plain to trace a sale. Behind the lined sheet was a photograph, four-by-six inches.

Desmond retrieved the photo first, turning it over slowly, afraid of what he might find. But instead of some grisly or horrific image, the picture appeared to be of a metallic structure of some kind. Almost like a cargo container or boxcar, but with what appeared to be tubes and ducting attached to one side. The details were blurry, as if the photographer had deliberately moved the camera right as the photo was taken. He would have to scrutinize it later, when he had more time and better lighting. Desmond handed the picture to Andrea and returned his fingers to the envelope.

Unfolding the lined sheet, Desmond let out a long sigh as he read the words printed upon it. They were in the same neat handwriting, deliberately spaced, not a single word misspelled or out of place. Considering that most notes from killers contained botched grammar and missing punctuation, the correctness of the letter meant they were dealing with someone with at least a moderate level of scholastic education. And, as all cops knew, a smart criminal was a dangerous criminal.

The game is simple. It is the basis for almost all problem solving (speaking of...this many dead is a BIG problem for you guys), and consists of the following words: who, what, where, when, and why. I have provided the WHERE, and now it's up to you to find out WHAT I plan to do there and WHEN it will happen. Figure those out, and maybe you'll start to understand WHY. Which might even lead you to WHO. Good luck.

Pete swore silently, while Andrea's stoicism was marred by a grimace. She gave the letter another once over, shaking her head the entire time. "Is this guy serious? The five W's? Good thing I'm single, cuz it looks like we're in for another circus. Fucking Angel City. I swear, between the Night Stalker, the Color Killer, and now this yahoo, there must be something in the water. Right, boss?"

Desmond was once again thinking of Wanda, and how she would probably be having dinner alone for the next few nights. Such were the downsides of being married to a detective, and Wanda was more than understanding and supportive, but he felt guilty regardless. Not even a full year had gone by since his last sensational case. Too soon, he thought to himself. Too soon. It was always the innocents who suffered in situations like this, a fact that didn't pertain to just the victims.

"It's a circus alright, which must be why they pay us in peanuts," Desmond stated, his voice dropping an octave as he yanked the jukebox's power cord from the socket. The music slowed as the record wound down, a quarter-speed dissonance that set his teeth on edge before it died out completely. Only the soothing patois of professionals hard at work remained.

"Now, all we need to do is catch this clown."

Ernest Brickman, Brick to his coworkers and Ernie to his friends (which were admittedly few and far between), was an impatient man, shifting his weight from his heels to toes and back again with nervous energy. Beyond the diner's glass windows, his job awaited. A veritable cornucopia of images just waiting, begging even, to be captured on film. So close, and yet so far away. Being stuck outside in the morning heat was beginning to wear thin.

He was itching to get to work.

Standing nearly six feet tall, with a blocky physique that had earned him his nickname, Ernie more than stood out amongst his peers. As such, when the detective came and told the CSI crew they were good to go, it was Ernie the man addressed.

"It's clear, Brick. Desmond says you guys can get started."

The senior investigators were the first to enter, which was to be expected. He watched them go; Desmond with his bulky frame, short and squat

Pete, and the alluring Andrea with her height and unmistakably feminine curves.

The CSI crew was hot on their heels. Ernie let the rest of the team enter first, bringing up the rear with a forced casualness that was difficult to maintain. Though the detectives and assorted patrolmen gagged and made faces at the smell which permeated the air, Ernie hardly noticed the stench. It had been a long wait for such a delightful opportunity, and nothing was going to ruin it for him. Not even emptied bowels.

Dante's Diner was a midsized establishment, with ten booths and six tables, but it seemed much smaller crowded with bodies—both living and dead—taking up space. Ernie carefully navigated the environment, searching for the best locations from which to start photographing.

As the strains of "Psycho Killer" washed over him, he couldn't help but smile. Though the song had been released ten years prior, Ernie had only recently given it a fair listen, slowly becoming obsessed with it. The lyrics, the music, the overall *feel* of it. The entire four minute and twenty-one second track just...spoke to him.

While the rest of CSI team were busy setting up their forensic equipment in a corner, Ernie began snapping pictures. He got the obligatory ones out of the way first: the establishing interior wide-angle shots, followed by mid-range photos of each of the victims, both in relation to each other as well as their positioning within the diner itself. For Ernie, they were the busywork shots, the mundane and mindless portion of his occupation. So simple a one-armed baby could do it, as his father used to say.

Ernie made sure to keep his peers out of the photographs as much as possible, as per standard operating procedure. Most of the detectives knew the drill, politely moving out of the way, giving him space in which to work. As he made his way around the space, he couldn't help but overhear snippets of conversations. Some were technical and authoritative, while others were of a less professional nature.

"Just what Angel City needs, another serial killer," complained one of the detectives to his partner. Ernie was only passingly familiar with both men, unable to recall either of their names.

Ernie, rarely one to initiate conversation unless spoken to first, couldn't help but interject. He had a thing for details, and it irked him when people got them wrong. "Mass murderer, you mean. Not serial killer."

"Huh? Whatever, man. It's just a different term for the same thing."

"Hardly!" Ernie retorted, heat beginning to creep up his neck. "Serial killers murder over a long period of time, while…"

A hand on his shoulder stopped him cold. "Easy, Brick. Just stick to the photographs, yeah?" Detective Fleming's voice washed over him like a cool breeze, electricity lancing out from where she was touching him, shooting across his entire body, its current both thrilling and debilitating.

He tried to respond, but a frog had suddenly taken up residence in his throat. All he could manage was a croak and a nod.

"And, for the record, Brick's right. Know the difference, boys." Her admonishment was only slightly scathing, but to Ernie, she might as well have been dressing them down with the fervor of an angry drill instructor. "It's part of the job."

Was he dreaming, or had Andrea Fleming just defended him? He turned to thank her, but she was already in motion, focused on a task of her own. A woman on a mission. He figured he'd have to revisit that moment, later on, when he had more time. Tumble it around in his head for a while.

Moving away from the men, Ernie segued into the part of the job he loved the most: photographing the dead. There was something about their peaceful repose that stimulated him. Each picture taken sent a pulse of pleasure through his body, tiny throbs of torment and titillation. Humming along with the song on the jukebox, he moved from body to body, snapping images of their faces, clothing, and distinguishing characteristics. Had anyone been paying close attention, they might have realized he was taking far more pictures than were strictly required. But nobody really gave the CSI crew much notice. If anyone on the force did look through his negatives, they'd simply discover that he was very thorough in his work.

And if some of the film canisters never made it back to the precinct's dark room, who would know? Photography was an art form, not an exact science. Sometimes shots didn't turn out as intended. Entire rolls occasionally had to be...discarded. In addition, Ernie was responsible for ordering all supplies for his department. What little oversight that existed was incredibly nonchalant. If he burned through fifty canisters in a day, nobody would know or care.

That those "unusable" rolls frequently made their way to his own darkroom, the developed prints added to his private collection, was one of his carefully guarded secrets. That the bodies in the diner had been his doing was another.

There was, he supposed, a natural progression to his craft. Up until Dante's, he had only ever caused the deaths of individual victims. Lone fatalities, easy to pull off, and even easier to keep clean. Free of discoverable evidence. But something had changed in him last year, at the Bonaventure Hotel, where the Color Killer left a swath of bodies in his wake.

Yes, the top floor of the hotel had been a burnt-out husk, the accidental fire consuming everything of interest, leaving nothing stimulating to capture on film, not even the corpse of the murderer himself. But the bodies in the lobby? That had been a different story entirely; a mix of gruesome and innocuous deaths nearly poetic in their randomness. Artful in their execution. And they had instilled in Ernie a profound sense of purpose. A desire to broaden his horizons. Single victim images no longer held his interest. Yes, the violent streetside gang deaths scratched the itch in their own way, but he had grown more interested in unique fatalities. The inexplicable and the distinctive. They possessed more subtlety, more finesse.

They were also far too scarce. If no one out there was going to give him another cornucopia of brilliant deaths to document, he'd just have to do it himself.

And, so, over the course of several months, Ernie had prepared and plotted and schemed. Built out his plan with the precision of a Swiss timepiece. Being so embedded with law enforcement would be a double-edged sword, naturally, but he knew how to be careful. He knew what his peers and coworkers would be looking for, and he knew how to throw them off his trail.

Picking a location had been the easy part. The real challenge had been figuring out the how. And, in conjunction, just what kind of images he wanted to add to his collection. Serene? Horrific? The options had weighed heavily for a time, but, in the end, he had opted for the hard to find; a quiet and relaxed parting from the mortal coil. And his victims had played their parts perfectly.

The poison had been of his own making, a concoction of various compounds which, when combined, would result in a quick and painless passing. Odorless and tasteless, he'd coated the interior of Dante's drinking glasses and coffee mugs with the substance. Breaking in proved to be a cinch, while applying the poison to each and every cup had been a multi-hour endeavor. As a purely synthetic mixture, the poison had a shelf life of roughly twelve hours, sixteen at the most, after which its chemical components would begin to break down, rendering it inert. And, as a byproduct, incredibly difficult to identify and isolate. Not a bad bit of chemistry, if he did say so himself.

Of course, it hadn't been a perfectly executed plan—what with the cook miraculously surviving and all. Apparently, the man didn't drink from the diner's cups while on duty. Hell, maybe he just sipped from the industrial faucet instead, or kept a flask in his back pocket. It didn't matter. The man had been down the street on the payphone when Ernie had slipped in and did his thing with the jukebox. He'd remained undetected.

"Psycho Killer" played on, and he was pleased with his choice. Perhaps it was the juxtaposition between the upbeat tempo and the dark lyrics, but Ernie felt that it set the tone perfectly. He knew that, ultimately, most of the nuance would be lost on his colleagues, but there was little he could do about that.

His letter, on the other hand, was sure to stir up the hornet's nest. Initially, he hadn't intended to be so dramatic. But as he composed the words in his head, he couldn't help but let the melodrama flow.

"Ok, I can't take it anymore. I'll get the jukebox."

Detective Fleming's words caused a shiver of excitement to course through Ernie's entire body. He had more than enough images to satisfy his short-term cravings. Now he could sit back and watch the figurative bombshell explode.

The fallout was not disappointing in the slightest. Detective Little, usually so stoic and unaffected, had nearly had a meltdown. Ernie's only regret was that Andrea had been the one to discover the wiring and the envelope. He had no desire to cause her undue stress.

The photo of his next location would have them scratching their heads. It was of a hypobaric chamber, also referred to as an altitude chamber, designed to test the effects of hypoxia and hypobaria. Airtight and made from thick metal, roughly the size of a large moving truck, with oxygen supplied by external tanks, the chambers were also used in selective surgeries. They were uncommon enough structures that he was certain none of his colleagues had ever seen one. In addition, his intentionally blurry photo completely obscured most of the telltale features. It looked more like a shipping container than anything else.

While the diner's patrons had succumbed to an almost dignified death, Ernie wanted to see his next victims in a different light, after he locked the chamber from the outside and closed the valves to their oxygen supply. After his next victims perished from asphyxiation, he wanted to capture their expressions of horrified and breathless bewilderment, freezing their suffering onto a canvas of barium sulfate-coated paper for all eternity.

In only a few weeks' time, barring any unforeseen breakthroughs by the detectives, he would make that desire a reality.

For now, however, he had to return to his duties. He'd stalled long enough—any longer and someone might notice. In the middle of his own killing grounds, surrounded by criminal-catching professionals, was decidedly *not* a good time to be drawing any undue attention upon himself. Peering through the viewfinder once more, he returned to snapping close-up shots of the markers and numbered evidence placards arranged by his colleagues.

As the music slowed to a stop, Ernie kept humming the tune, quietly so only he could hear. Between the corpses and Detective Fleming's unexpected rescue, he felt like he was on top of the world. That things would continue to go his way from that point forward.

Life, as the saying went, was pretty damn good.

Hours later, Desmond was making the rounds throughout the diner, checking in with the various support teams onsite. Doing his "due diligence" as he liked to say.

He'd already called Wanda from Dante's payphone, explaining the situation without going into the grislier details. Those would have to wait until they were face-to-face. Some things, he knew, simply couldn't be discussed properly through plastic handsets. He might not be able to disclose all the finer details or specifics, but she deserved to know why her husband wouldn't be home most nights. Especially since years of experience had taught him that a case like this was going to drag on and on.

It felt strange, surreal even, to have so many people in the restaurant without a lick of food being prepared or served. Would Dante's survive the stigma of today's events? Desmond couldn't begin to guess. The place did seem like it would have been a great place to dine. But, as Pete had mentioned, even if the diner remained in business, Desmond doubted he'd be eating there anytime soon.

But those were thoughts for another day. He was still on the clock, and he needed to comport himself accordingly. Andrea was out making a coffee run somewhere farther down the block, and Pete had gone outside for a smoke. The rest of his team were finishing up with their individual tasks. The forensics crew had done all they could and were packing up for the evening, stowing their gear and samples. Brick, the hulking photographer, was loading his film canisters into the small plastic cylinders used to protect the negatives.

"Good job tonight," Desmond said, meeting each of their gazes firmly with unfeigned gratitude. He believed in treating his teammates with respect, even if he didn't necessarily know all their names. He did know Brick, however. Everyone knew Brick. "I hope you all have a good evening."

He approached the photographer and gave him a clap on the shoulder. "Catch you later, Brick."

The big man seemed to stiffen for a moment, as if pierced by a sudden jolt of nervousness. Desmond, who knew all about Brick's social awkwardness, chalked it up to nothing more than the man's bubble being unexpectedly breached. He would need to remember to not violate certain people's personal space in the future.

"Yep. You have a good evening as well, detective," Ernie eventually responded, throwing a wave over his shoulder before heading out the door and into the night. He sounded far more chipper than Desmond felt. "See you at the next murder spree!"

It was, on the face of it, a very "Brick" thing to say. Desmond loved his job, even with all of the inherent ugliness that came with it. The recurring loss of faith in humanity, the occasional danger to himself or his team, and many long nights spent away from home—they were all acceptable speedbumps on the road to ridding the streets of bad people. A worthwhile profession that he was honored to be a part of.

And yet he had never met someone quite so enamored with their craft as Brick. The big man truly loved what he did, to the point of occasional giddiness. A man could excel at anything, Desmond knew, and photographers were a specialized bunch, largely content to view the world from afar, telephoto lenses keeping them safely removed from the vagaries of daily interactions. For Brick to be so dedicated to his job, Desmond figured that the guy must also enjoy snapping pictures outside of work as well. Hell, he probably had a pretty extensive collection of well-composed and stunning shots littered around his residence—amazing work without an audience.

It was a tenuous thread, but Desmond figured he should probably get to know Brick a little better. Possibly stop by the guy's place with a six-pack and a few hours to kill. Hobby talk was a great way to break the ice. Wanda was a budding photographer herself, and maybe Brick would be willing to impart a few professional tips to help her improve. Provided Desmond could get past the social awkwardness, of course. But the big man was one of the team, and Desmond didn't want anyone feeling left out or underappreciated. Every person contributed to the squad. Everyone mattered, strange or not.

At worst, the endeavor would be a waste of time and beer. On the other hand, perhaps Desmond could help break the big man out of his shell and support his wife's hobby in the process, bringing home some useful insider know-how. Mind made up, Desmond vowed to set aside some time in the next few days to pay the quiet photographer a friendly visit.

After all, what did he really stand to lose?

SEE NO EVIL (CHORUS)

Wherein we meet the full cast of characters, bizarre clues are discovered, and a horrifying creation is ascending.

Dramatis Personae

James Guthrie

An inspector with the London constabulary

Constance Wright

A prostitute in London's Poplar district

R.M. Müller

An unscrupulous man of science and medicine

Lady Ellington

A powerful Ministry official

Constable Higgins

A young policeman

Doctor Bixby

A doctor employed by London Hospital

Milton Dinsmore

JACK WELLS

An inventor and craftsman
Schaffer
A metalworker and tradesman

CHAPTER IX

The way in which Lady Ellington examines the eyeless body is both clinical and efficient. It is evident that she has been around corpses before, behaving more like a surgeon than a woman of science. The men look on, no doubt shamed by her fearlessness.

I try my damnedest not to stare. Outside of cabaret shows and the occasional masquerade ball, seeing a woman dressed thusly, and in full view of the community no less, is shocking in a way that borders on scandalous. The gentlemanly part of my personality, as institutionalized within my psyche as our dour English perseverance, itches to throw my overcoat across her shoulders to shield her from any lascivious glances. Considering that I could not help but notice her pert backside the moment she knelt next to the corpse, I must, shamefully, include myself in the register of guilty parties.

However, despite my best efforts at being displeased and discomfited by the unwelcome intrusion, I cannot help but be somewhat fascinated by her pluckiness. Does she possess a medical background that has been hitherto unmentioned?

Unless I wish to query her directly, I have lost my only other source of information—Superintendent Barnhold has long since departed. I suspect he will visit at least one dining establishment on his way back to the precinct. The man is nothing if not perpetually peckish. By default, his cowardly retreat has officially made me the lady's chaperone. Silently cursing all mid-level leadership, I plaster on my most tolerant expression.

Lady Ellington straightens, wiping her hands on her trousers distastefully. "Well, I suppose that's one way to avoid paying the bill."

"Hardly the method I would choose, milady," I offer hesitantly, unsure whether her statement was directed at me or herself. A few heartbeats later, I realize my attempt at a good-natured agreement has led me down a most slippery slope.

Any hope that she misheard me is dashed when she arches a perfectly formed eyebrow in my direction. I feel my ears turning red. My tongue chooses that very moment to become glued to the roof of my mouth, rendering me unable to come to my own defense. And this, among several other reasons I prefer not to dwell upon, is why I am still a bachelor.

"Oh? Docking with the doxies in your spare time, inspector? Stiffening the mainmast, as it were? Would that not equate to a conflict of interest?"

"Not at all, ma'am," I manage to stutter, sounding like an imbecile. "I apologize. That did not come out as intended."

"Very well," she replies, waving my apology away. Is it my imagination, or did the corner of her lip arch up into a spectre of a smile? "Walk with me."

It is not a request.

I fall into step alongside Lady Ellington, but not before casting a meaningful glance at Higgins and the boy. A gaze that strongly suggests they stay put. The lady, intent on her destination, does not notice. Her stride is long and self-assured, forcing me to exert some effort to keep pace. We leave the knot of constables behind, moving further into the bustle of the Blackwall shipyards. Peals of clanking, sawing, and hammering surround us. Boisterous curses accompany the toil—sailors have no exclusivity to salty tongues. The wharf is a most incongruous place for a woman of standing, but as a location for conversing privately, it is unparalleled. The fog renders us invisible to prying eyes, and our words are swallowed in the din.

As she draws to a stop, she rests her hand on my shoulder. The uncommonly intimate gesture fills me with a sense of confusion and dread. The behaviour of women, even in the most innocuous of settings, confounds me to no end. And this is by no means the most innocuous of settings. I suddenly feel like a pheasant about to be flushed by the hounds, an impending sense of dread overwhelming every other response. Lady Ellington smiles broadly, though I can't help but wonder if the showing of teeth belies a predatory nature.

"Now that the Great Balloonship has made swift his exit, we can speak plainly. I have heard your name mentioned in circles as a man who gets results. I would hear your thoughts on these gruesome murders. Yours, mind you, not those of your superiors nor the expected party rhetoric."

In what possible circles might my name warrant mention where the nobility has heard of it? Sensing a trap, I do not respond right away. But I notice that my mouth is agog and close it with a snap. Did she just refer to the superintendent as a...

"Hop to it, man. I am not partial to waiting, and I refuse to repeat myself."

"Yes, milady," I gulp. I may have no love for the nobility, but drawing the ire of a representative of Parliament is the first step towards ruination. "From what I can gather, the eyes appear to be the motivation. Judging by the precision with which they are removed, they must serve some purpose.

Though, to what that could possibly be, I cannot begin to surmise. I believe that the intercourse prior is simply to satisfy the killer's carnal cravings. As to why the bodies are left in places where they can be found, I can only hypothesize that, like the Whitechapel Murderer, this killer is taunting us."

She taps a finger on her chin, measuring my responses against some internal counterweight. "And the removal of the *digitus minimus*?"

I am now balancing upon a knife's edge. The points I have presented thus far, while still conjecture at this point, are still based upon sound reasoning. Likely to be supported by anyone within the constabulary. Nevertheless, these next bits are nothing more than my own inferences. They could be taken at face value or make me a pariah amongst my peers. All concerns aside, I cannot deny that a part of me has been aching to bring someone into my confidence.

"I haven't the faintest idea. At least, not yet." The words are true, but I cannot fully hide the trace of presumption in my voice. My hidden hypotheses bloom within the void of nescience. Curse me for a fool, but I am like a dog with a bone when it comes to the mysterious and bizarre.

With a nod, she bids me to continue. "And yet you have pondered it, have you not? Finding some semblance of an answer, regardless of how far-fetched it might be?"

"A fanciful notion, nothing more, milady. Hardly worthy of consideration."

"I would hear it just the same." Again, it is not a request so much as a command. A command I am powerless to disobey.

"Very well. I cannot help but wonder, with the removal methods so different, if the fingers aren't taken by someone else entirely."

She purses her lips in thought. "A second party? Partners in crime?"

"Like I said, a fantastic conjecture," I reply, knowing how foolish it must sound. "Incredibly unlikely, to say the least. Whoever heard of repetitious killers working in pairs?"

"Why, we both have, inspector. One need look no further than the Burke and Hare murders at the start of this very century for proof of homicidal collaboration." Is the hint of disappointment in her voice real, or am I simply imagining it?

I tip my cap in acknowledgment. "Point to you, milady. Not sure how such a detail escaped my recollection."

"You're forgiven just this once. It *is* an interesting theory, killers working in tandem. One could conceivably be the muscle, whilst the other fills the role of the... artisan, as it were. Some manner of mutually beneficial relationship."

Realization dawns on me suddenly, a certitude that I cannot help but voice. "You've been thinking along the same lines this whole time, haven't you? The superintendent said you've been privy to other crime scenes. You've been examining the clues and coming up with your own theories."

"And the point returns to you, inspector," Lady Ellington responds demurely. "Well played. Yes, I have seen what you have seen and appear to be drawing much the same conclusions. Is there anything else you've considered? Anything else you'd care to impart, regardless of how unbelievable it may be?"

There is, as a matter of fact. But it all boils down to how much I feel like sharing. And, by extension, how much I trust this woman of station. Which, given my aversion to people of privilege, is no further than I can throw her. And yet I feel that she will discern any attempt at deception. As if some preternatural ability will alert her to my reticence. I have no other choice than to forge ahead.

"One more uncertainty, I suppose, peculiar though it may be: is the removal of the finger possibly done later, after the killer absconds with the eyes? Perhaps the first party is unaware of the second party's proclivities."

Lady Ellington stares at me for an indeterminate amount of time as if weighing my merit upon some internal scale. Beads of sweat appear along my hairline. I do not know whether to continue talking, in some desperate attempt to explicate my theory, or remain silent and await her scorn. Before I can open my mouth, a smile graces her lips.

"We are of a similar nature, it would seem. I have also pondered that possibility. Very well, that settles it. Inspector James Guthrie, regarding this matter, you shall henceforth be my direct liaison within the constabulary. Consider yourself commissioned into the Ministry of Special Sciences for the foreseeable future. You are under my purview and will report to me alone. I shall have a letter of temporary reassignment drafted posthaste."

A mere inspector at the beck and call of the nobility, completely outside of the chain of command? That simply does not happen. I am unable to contain my surprise, and my mouth drops open yet again.

"But is the superintendent not your consultant for these proceedings?"

"Consultant? Ha!" she remarks with genuine mirth. "Hardly. Barnhold is a buffoon, though even buffoons have their uses from time to time. No inspector, I go where I please. Your superintendent was merely trying to curry favor. He even failed to ask the obvious question. You, I gather, are not so short-sighted, and have been contemplating one discrepancy above all others since my arrival."

She is not wrong. Though a myriad of suppositions and assumptions have run rampant in my head, a singular mystery has indeed remained at the forefront of my thoughts. The neighbouring district of Whitechapel has only this year received electricity through the Sixth Electric Confirmation Act of 1892. The Limehouse district, including the Isle of Dogs (wherein Blackwall lies), is not slated to receive voltage for at least half a decade. As such, even if the dead doxie is somehow tangentially related, Lady Ellington should still have no legitimate business in my bailiwick.

"Why is an electrical engineer interested in the death of a prostitute on the Isle?" I ask, growing bolder with every word.

"Clever chap. That *is* the question, now, isn't it? And one that I may deign to answer. In due time."

"And said answer is dependent upon?"

"Upon you, of course," she responds with a lilt as if nothing could be more obvious. "Or, more specifically, your acumen."

Realization dawns, and I feel a rush of heat gather in my ears. I do not enjoy the thought of dancing to the tune of some noble's fife. However, I am also in no position to deny her. "So, it is to be a test, then?"

"It is to be a test," she confirms, fathomless eyes giving nothing away. The words that follow are nearly subsumed by the dock whistle signaling elevenses. Not many on the Isle have the means, nor the manners, for a pre-afternoon cup of tea, save for perhaps the shipmaster himself. "But first, a question. Is there a Mrs. Guthrie who shall be jealous when I insist that you meet me tomorrow at this very hour for a spot of Earl Grey? I always think better with a steaming cup in my hands. Meet me on the morrow, let us natter over related and tangential details, and I shall then reassess where we stand."

"What fate awaits me, should I pass this test of yours?"

"Is the answer to that question not exceedingly obvious? You get to spend more time with me, naturally, unraveling this most bizarre of mysteries."

Being saddled with a member of the aristocracy is far from my idea of a reward, curves notwithstanding. It's more akin to punishment, if I'm being honest. The smile plastered to my face slips a bit before I can fix it.

"And who wouldn't want that?" I reply, masking my disappointment behind a small cough. But what other choice do I have? "Very well, tea it is. Where shall we convene?"

CHAPTER X

Transporting her bezzie's body across town to London Hospital is the most awkwardly informative experience of Constance's young life. The wooden cart is not large, and Fiona was a mere slip of a girl in life, hardly weighing anything at all. Just the same, the trek is far more arduous than it should be. London's cobblestone and granite sett streets are certainly not conducive to smooth travel. The slight incline away from the riverside, only noticeable when traveling uphill, is more impactful than one would expect. There also exists no direct route to the hospital from Blackwall, requiring multiple turns, which increases the overall distance with each jog to the left or right. It is, however, the figurative encumbrance which wears Constance down the most. The emotional heft of heartbreak and ire. She feels as though she is dragging boulders, with fresh stones added every few minutes.

Instead of being removed from the effort, Inspector Guthrie and Constable Higgins take turns pulling the slat-sided wain, spelling Constance at regular intervals, giving her sore arms a respite. She is glad for the reprieve; her body has long since abandoned any traces of farm-bred fortitude, rendering her scrawnier than she'd care to admit. She is accustomed to exertions of a different sort, and it shows. The unexpected generosity makes her chary and grateful in equal measure.

She has already shared Fiona's particulars with the men, following Guthrie's return from his private discussion with Lady Ellington. The only altered details were those regarding the nature of their cohabitation and Constance's gender. Deceptions borne of habit more than intentional subterfuge. For everything else, Constance remained as truthful as possible.

Her gnawing hunger has returned, stomach grumbling vociferously, the noise masked only by the cart's creaking wheels and axle. Locating Fi took some doing, as Constance was far less familiar with the Isle than her departed friend. The majority of her coins were exchanged for information of questionable veracity, provided by individuals of suspect character. Information which led her from thoroughfare to thoroughfare, and alleyway to alleyway, with nothing to show for it other than aching feet and a nearly empty purse. She actually stumbled upon Fiona's resting place quite by accident, surreptitiously tailing several bobbies who were moving with a purpose. As for the subsequent events, they are what lead to her current predicament.

A predicament predicated on her rumbling belly, blistered hands, and the most unlikely of traveling companions. Relegating her ravenousness to an inflexible inevitability, she does her best to ignore it. She chooses instead to focus on her unusual entourage. If she must be conscripted into manual labor, heading northwest at what feels like a snail's pace, she is determined to make the most of her assignment.

The lawmen talk openly amongst themselves, being neither secretive nor voluble. Theirs is the discourse of familiarity, of colleagues who've spent countless hours in each other's company. Constance listens with attentive ears, learning much about the constabulary's inner workings in general and Guthrie's investigative process in particular along the way. While the inherent layers of police bureaucracy are enough to make her head spin, she still gleans a few useful tidbits.

Judging by the way in which he lays out facts and suppositions, Inspector Guthrie is a thorough man who clearly has a knack for the idiosyncrasies of policework. There is no bluster behind his words, simply a fatalistic professionalism she can't help but respect. He is a man for whom murder is an expertly prepared main course, to be devoured in measured strides whilst the essential ingredients are individually identified and pontificated over at length. Those assorted lesser crimes that came across his desk, burglary, larceny, sabotage, and the like, serve only to whet his appetite, each functioning as an *amuse-bouche* of sorts.

For him, being a policeman is less a job and more a calling, what he was born to do. Constance feels a slight twinge of jealousy at that. She doesn't have the faintest notion about what her true vocation is supposed to be; she only knows that making a living on her back (or knees, or even belly) isn't it. If not for her gender, she would have a spate of options laid out before her.

Constable Higgins is far less verbose, seemingly content to glean what he can from his superior. The man rarely interpolates, usually for clarification of some obtuse point or other, his behaviour unfailingly polite. Deferential even. Nevertheless, his restraint is not for lack of intelligence; she can tell that Higgins is by no means a dullard. He is simply behaving in the manner that a good subordinate should.

While the more gruesome details are hard for Constance to swallow, she nonetheless keeps her ears open. Though not as sensational as the eviscerations done by the self-titled Jack the Ripper, there is still some surgical skill employed with the theft of the eyes, though she, like Guthrie, cannot fathom the whyfors of their removal. But four victims in as many weeks is, in a word, distressing.

The ways in which the killer has disposed of the bodies sound familiar, but due to her distraught state, Constance is unable to recall where from. Surprisingly literate compared to her peers, she feels certain that she has read about something similar. She'll have to give the source more thought when less preoccupied.

Other facts are learned as well. Specifics that may be somewhat perplexing to the police, but speak volumes to someone in Constance's line of work. While a man with large hands and a penchant for violent copulation is far from a rarity, it does help to narrow the field quite a bit. Coupled with his evident preference for youthful girls and perhaps even an unusual fixation with hands or fingers, she feels certain the killer's identity can be gleaned through idle gossip with other whores. If one thing is for certain, it's that prostitutes are not shy when it comes to conversing about the men they have serviced.

But, even if only provided with a possible suspect or a short list of possibilities, she'll at least have a better idea of where to place herself as bait. And a much clearer notion of who to look out for. For this, if for no other reason, she is obliged for her current dilemma.

It is only when Guthrie mentions the possibility of related murders in other districts that Constance dares to interject in the discussion. "I've heard rumours of the same," she says offhandedly, joining the conversation with little by way of tact. "More than just the killings in Blackwall, that is."

"Gossip travels at speeds which can beggar belief," the inspector acknowledges, tipping his cap in her direction. "From the lips of libertines to the ears of earls. Pray tell, where else have you heard of such misdeeds occurring?"

Now that she is the center of attention, Constance feels suddenly reticent. How much longer can she maintain the "Connor" ruse? At some point, she will either inadvertently slip or Guthrie, as canny as a dockside cat, will catch wise. But she was the one who opened her mouth. All she can do now is forge ahead and try to allay their suspicions.

"Fiona mentioned a murdered doxie in Soho, and I've heard tell of another in Southwark."

"Soho, you say?" Guthrie muses, thoughtfully rubbing his chin with pale fingers. "I know an inspector in Soho. I have been keeping him apprised of these mysterious killings, sharing with him my thoughts whilst receiving his in return. I have every intention of paying him a visit in the coming days, and it would appear we will have much to discuss."

"Purcell, sir?" Higgins asks. The name means nothing to Constance, but something in the constable's voice indicates a slight sense of reverence.

Guthrie acknowledges the question but remains otherwise reserved. "The same."

The rest of the trek is made in contemplative, if not quite companionable, silence. The constable seems reluctant to intrude upon Guthrie's tacit thoughtfulness. Constance is content to keep her peace and leave the men to theirs. The trio's arrival meets with little fanfare; when none of the staff come out to greet them, Higgins is sent inside in search of orderlies. Guthrie explains that, under normal circumstances, the body would have been taken to the Limehouse morgue to be studied by the police department's resident surgeon. But because these killings are reminiscent of those committed by the Whitechapel Murderer, aka Jack the Ripper, the better-trained hospital staff will perform more thorough examinations. Thus, the trio's trek of several miles.

London Hospital itself is rather stately in a restrained way. The stonework, tall multi-paned windows, and recessed archways are serviceable, if not remarkable. A large clockface is set into the building's gabled façade, centered under a peaked roof. Even in the mid-afternoon, the fog remains thick enough that the hands of the clock are nearly impossible to make out.

"So, what will be done with Fiona's body?"

Guthrie doffs his cap and runs his fingers through brown, unruly hair. "A fair question. While I possess rudimentary knowledge of anatomy and physiology, I am by no means educated in said fields. One of the resident surgeons will perform a much more in-depth examination. There may be particulars which, in my ignorance, I might have overlooked. If so, they could provide additional insight into the person responsible. From there, unless she has family to claim her, the hospital will likely opt for cremation. Do you know of any such relations, whether in the city or beyond?"

"No," Constance says, her words coated with sadness. "She doesn't have anyone. I'm the closest thing she had to a sis...sibling."

"Then, once again, I am sorry for your loss. Would you prefer to handle the burial instead?"

Constance shakes her head slowly, lower lip trembling. Though it pains her to no end, she is bereft of options. "Nothing would please me more, but I am without the means to do so." She gestures to the hospital. "If I may beg your indulgence, please ensure that they treat her with dignity. I'm afraid that all I can offer in return is my gratitude."

"On my honour," Inspector Guthrie replies, dipping his chin in solemn acknowledgment.

"What about the cart?"

"Higgins will get it sorted out. You've more than done your part, and I shall detain you no further. In fact, if you are returning home, I can summon a carriage if you'd like, a recompense for your assistance. You've no small distance to travel—Pigott Street is even further from here than my residence on Ash Grove."

That she and Guthrie are practically neighbours comes as a surprise. She would have expected such a steadfast gendarme to live somewhere nicer, perhaps in Whitechapel or Southwark. Shacked up in a home large enough for a family. But no wedding ring adorns his finger, and considering the runt-sized houses on Ash Grove, he is likely a bachelor. Not that she checked to see if he was married; women in her profession simply noticed such things right from the start.

Given that Poplar and Limehouse are adjoining districts, both nestled just north of the Isle of Dogs, she is well acquainted with the street where he lives. Being in such proximity to one another, she has likely crossed paths with Guthrie whilst flaunting the goods. She might have even propositioned him a time or two. It is an amusing thought, so much so that it causes no residual embarrassment.

With her feet already tender, and nothing but an empty room awaiting her, the interminable trek home seems daunting indeed. A part of her, small but insistent, longs to take him up on his offer and travel in style for once. Admittedly, a doxie benefitting from the ignorant charity of the constabulary would be the very definition of irony. Something she and Fi would have shared a good laugh over. Nevertheless, for several nebulous reasons, she is unable to accept.

"I appreciate your generosity," she replies, shaking her head slowly. "But I think a walk will do me some good."

In all honesty, the distance Constance must traverse is not what worries her. Far less appealing is that she must break the news of Fi's murder to their mutual acquaintances. The thought terrifies her to no end. Constance's only source of comfort, such as it is, comes from the slow, simmering anger hiding just beneath the skin. A heat that invigorates her resolve if not her dampened spirits. All she needs is rest, and then her hunt can commence.

Although, judging by the expression on the inspector's face, she is going to have competition on that front. The way he keeps glancing at the cart indicates his thirst for judicial punishment. Constance might have the streetside grapevine on her side, in addition to the physical attributes which will gather the right attention. But Guthrie is backed by the might of the constabulary and his deductive skills, not to mention his prevailing sense of justice.

"You're determined to catch this man at all costs, aren't you?" She already knows the answer but still feels a need to hear it from his mouth. To gauge the conviction in his voice.

He nods once, eyes boring into hers. She feels picked apart, section by section, strand by strand. As if the tangled knot of her motivations and deceptions has been expertly undone, the various threads segregated and evaluated. Weighed and measured. While she has undressed in the company of countless men, this is the first time she has ever felt so bare. So entirely exposed. It is a feeling she cares not for in the slightest.

"Indeed. I will not rest until he is brought before the magistrate, clapped in irons and pleading for his life. And, although it goes without saying, I would be quite... displeased... if anyone were to hinder my efforts toward that end. I hope I am making myself clear, lad."

"Quite clear," Constance responds, though not without a hint of steel in her words. She is not afraid of Guthrie. Intimidated? To be sure. Respectful of his authority? Beyond any doubt. But frightened? Not remotely.

The implication is unmistakable, however. Guthrie has picked up on her undercurrents of vengeance. How he managed such a feat eludes her, and she does not yet know how he intends to use said knowledge. Regardless, with the fat boiled away, what remains in the pot is one simple truth: it will to be a race to see who can get to Fi's murderer first. A mad sprint to the finish line. Given how level the playing field is, Constance isn't willing to bet for or against herself. But one thing is certain—by hook or by crook, the killer is going to pay for what he's done.

"Oh, and Connor..." Inspector Guthrie flips a coin her way with a perfect end-over-end spin. Constance snatches it from the air with deft fingers. The weight and color of the denomination surprises her; a full gold sovereign bearing Queen Victoria's likeness on one side, the gilt as lustrous as the day it was minted. And worth far more than she would make on any given day, regardless of how vigorously she applied herself. She doesn't even feel the need to test it with her teeth.

"Your stomach has been grumbling for hours, lad. Don't think I didn't notice. Fetch yourself a decent meal or two."

CHAPTER XI

London Hospital is, through no fault of its own, quite an anomalous setting, its existence seemingly divorced from the established tenets of reality. A nucleus of homeopathic incongruities in a perpetual state of flux. Behind the unassuming façade, hidden from the awareness of the general populace, a war of sorts is being waged. One in which orthodox procedures and philosophies from the past clash with new medical processes and unconventional theories from around the globe. Archaic therapeutic machines share space with the latest in surgical apparatus, and curmudgeonly old physicians deride the younger generation of up-and-coming surgeons. Not even within the police headquarters itself have I witnessed such professional discord.

Unceremoniously caught in the middle, the assorted nurse and orderly contingents keep their heads down and their steps quick, remaining far removed from the internal politics of doctors and registrars. Irrespective of which school of thought is responsible for the healing, they stay focused on that which is most important—the care of the patients themselves.

Though it lies more towards the western side of Whitechapel, a respectable distance to travel on foot even without pulling a cart, I have visited the hospital frequently over the course of my investigations, both old and new. As such, I am no stranger to its myriad (and mismatched) corridors, lecture halls, and operating rooms. In point of fact, I feel that I have become almost *too* familiar.

Such things, however, are not within my control. I simply go where the job sends me.

The smell of astringents, disinfectants, and less pleasant aromata is omnipresent, a miasma exclusive to infirmaries, hospices, and field triage tents. I have smelled far worse in my line of work, yet I still pinch my nose at certain points. Familiarity doesn't make the experience any less unpleasant.

Two orderlies transport the prostitute's body to an examination room near the back of the building. I follow at their heels, mind adrift in the phenomena of the past. Though London Hospital did not play much of a role in the Whitechapel murders of 1888, it was still where half of a preserved kidney thought to belong to the Ripper's fourth victim, Catherine Eddowes, was sent to be studied by Dr. Openshaw. The so-called "From Hell" letter, initially mailed (along with the kidney) to the Chairman of the Whitechapel Vigilance Committee, accompanied the bisected organ. Another such letter was posted to the hospital two weeks later, addressed to Openshaw himself. This second bit of correspondence claimed that more innards would soon follow. Thankfully, such barbarism did not come to pass, and there were no further related murders.

Four long years have already slipped by, but the Ripper killings skulk in my memory even so. Even now, the dread that gripped the city still tends to manifest across my cognizance, like a phantom pain which lingers long after the associated injury has healed. The putrid odours that accompanied those dead women are almost tangible. As if the stench of dried blood, excrement, sweat, and less easily identifiable bodily fluids have crossed the oceans of time to assail my nostrils once more. I maintain that they are the defining scents of primordial fear itself.

Why do these past events torment me so? Why am I unable to rid myself of such melancholic sentiments? I have oft searched for answers to those questions, but none have yet presented themselves. If I cannot be free of my disquiet, I pray for some modicum of tolerance, lest I eventually be driven barmy. Lord, grant me the strength to accept the things I cannot change.

Though they weigh heaviest upon my mind, grievous injuries and taunts from a madman are not the only events for which the hospital is known. Infamous medical enigma Joseph Merrick, better known as The Elephant Man, was admitted here in 1886. He spent the remainder of his days in converted rooms in the structure's basement. I actually had the honour of meeting Mr. Merrick several times, not long after my promotion. Despite his difficulty communicating, once I became familiar with his manner of speech, I found him quite an engaging conversationalist. He seemed especially fascinated by the peculiarities of policework, chiefly those techniques which were investigative in nature. Though I cannot claim we were friends, I became quite fond of the Elephant Man, and was saddened by his passing.

Merrick's former surgeon, the renowned Frederick Treves, is still in residence at London Hospital, though his proficiency is far too valuable to waste on a lowly inspector and dead doxie. No, for my particular case, I have been assigned a less vital personage. Which is not to say that Dr. Edward Bixby is without talent. Keen of intellect and blessed with the steadiest of hands, one could not accuse the fellow of being in the wrong profession. He is simply... odd. In every sense of the word.

A vaguely mousy gent with wide eyes and untamed hair, Dr. Bixby possesses mannerisms that are best described as fiddle-footed. As if he is teeming with an abundance of energy that his body cannot properly dispel. I almost pity the bloke, for aside from performing complex medical procedures, he seems utterly incapable of keeping still. Being governed by such a manic disposition must be tiresome. He is also rather socially inept, as though normal human interactions bewilder him. I can only surmise that he perceives the world differently than most people. Perhaps his acuity is inverted, rendering gruesome things beautiful and showing light where others see only darkness.

Through snatches of conversations with the man, and bolstered by my own silent observations, I have concluded that Dr. Bixby is, despite his obvious skill, somewhat of an embarrassment to his colleagues. A circumstance of which he seems perfectly aware. Whilst the other surgeons are afforded every opportunity to improve their craft and impress their peers, Bixby is handed the least desirable of patients and protocols. The castoffs that nobody else wants. The lost causes. As the resident pariah within my department, I can't help but feel a sort of kinship with the strange doctor.

"Back again, eh, inspector?" he says by way of greeting, entering the examination room as if a king appearing before his subjects. Such is his way—straight to work, forgoing the usual pleasantries entirely.

"Indeed. I might as well set up a secondary office adjacent to yours," I reply, trying to complement his eccentric humour. "It would appear that this is a city-wide dilemma."

He nods in response, laying out the tools of his trade in a frenetic but orderly fashion. Yet another way in which the doctor and I are similar: we both find ourselves driven to the point of distraction by our vocations, consumed by, and slaves to, the formulae of solving the mysteries laid before us. It is not until everything is arranged that he can be bothered to answer.

"And this one was clearly submerged. First time we've seen that, isn't it? It's as if the chap can't quite make up his mind. Almost like he's just grabbing at straws."

His sentiment mirrors my recurring thoughts. While the victims may be of similar stature and professions, the locations of their corpses have been quite varied. The girl prior to Fiona, her name as of yet unknown, was found hanging upside-down in a dockside warehouse. The rope tied around her ankles had been fastened with a bowline knot, a common loop used by sailors the world over. Gravity drained nearly all of the blood from her body. The one before her had been stuffed, along with copious amounts of straw, into a small shipping crate in a well-traveled staging area. Most of her bones had been broken to facilitate the snug fit.

"Never the same place or posture twice," I confirm. "Or at least not yet." I do not fear sharing details with Dr. Bixby; his discretion is all but guaranteed. "He could be testing methods of disposal, trying to find one that suits him best, though I am disinclined to believe that theory. Things do seem a little *too* haphazard, don't they? And unnecessarily sensational."

"Suspiciously so. I daresay they border on the theatrical. Still, whether sham or strategy, his actions undoubtedly serve some sort of design."

"An opinion that I share. In my experience, criminals rarely do anything without an underlying cause. Alas, making sense of it all will certainly prove difficult. At least until we catch the man responsible."

As he inspects the damaged finger, his eyes flit to me for a heartbeat. "I presume that means you have no suspects as of yet. Still no closer to solving this mystery?"

"None whatsoever. The Isle is quite large, and though some corroborative evidence suggests a nautical background, there is no guarantee that our killer resides there. Or even operates in the vicinity. Blackwall may just be a convenient dumping ground."

"Perhaps he is merely trying to confound. To keep you lot running in circles."

"I have entertained that very notion myself."

What I don't impart is that, should confusion and misdirection be the killer's goal, he is achieving it most handily. Speculation and fanciful theories are all I possess. Staged deaths, stolen eyes, and lopped-off fingers—we are running in circles, indeed. And then there's the fact that some of my peers are not overly troubled by the deaths. As far as they're concerned, fewer whores roaming the streets is a boon. Like a malignancy cut from the flesh of respectable society.

I find no merit in such rationalization. Quite the opposite, in fact. In what society is violent murder a lesser aggrievance than streetwalking? Is not a woman's body hers to do with as she pleases? In addition, what's to stop this man from targeting someone else next? The peerage? The elderly? Or, God forbid, a child?

Murder is murder, plain and simple. As distasteful as some people may find their profession, even prostitutes have people who love them. People who want and deserve some measure of closure.

And I shall bring it to them.

CHAPTER XII

"Toil and trouble," says the first voice, high-pitched and raspy, as if its owner has held back a cough for far longer than is healthy.

"Bither and bother," replies the second voice, a deep rumble that sounds like stones grinding together in slow motion.

The door to the workshop shuts with a clang, a sound that reverberates throughout the enclosed space like a cannonade. Although it is fairly large, the room gives the impression of being cramped, much of the floorspace taken up by mills and lathes of various proportions. The lighting in the room is quite bright, amber-colored lamplight augmented by brilliant electric-powered incandescent bulbs, the latter emitting a low hum as they shine. Since electricity has not yet come to this part of London, the lightbulbs are powered by something their patron calls a DOVE, short for "diesel-operated voltaic emitter," a bulky-yet-portable internal combustion engine of elaborate design. Like its feathered namesake, the generator is both messy and fragile. How it functions is something that neither man can explain. All they know is that the machine is governed by sciences well outside their areas of expertise, and though it burns through fuel at an incredible rate, the electricity it produces allows them to work well into the night. The generated current also lends itself to other applications, far less savory in nature.

The owner of the first voice, a wiry man with thinning hair and a slight hunch, lowers the double-barrel shotgun trained at the door. It is an archaic firearm, more rust than unblemished metal. But such weapons were made to endure, and the man doesn't doubt that it will function as needed. If anyone other than his compatriot had emerged through the door, especially without uttering the counter-phrase, the man would have opened up with both barrels, sending them to meet their maker quite expediently.

Having their little workshop discovered so close to the completion of the project would be the epitome of bad timing. Much easier to blast any gatecrasher into smithereens and then ask the hard questions later.

"Did you see what's what, then?"

"Aye," the deep voice responds. The second man is much larger, like a mythological giant come to life. He ruffles the lapels of his dull-gray overcoat, the garment made from enough fabric to double as a maritime studding sail, sending a veritable explosion of soot and filth in all directions. "Them coppers are in a right tizzy, they are. Runnin' all over the Yard with bees in their bonnets. But ain't nobody knowin' a thing, and that's a fact."

The wiry man's voice raises an octave, words of admonishment spilling out even while he lowers the shotgun, leaning it against a large workbench that dominates the center of the room. "They ought not to be up in arms at all, yes?"

"Ain't nobody in Blackwall gonna rat us out to the bobbies, Milt. The Isle looks after its own."

"Perhaps. But all it takes is one overly observant person with a con-science. I've said it before, and it bears repeating—your theatrics are going to cause us no end of trouble."

"And yer harpin' is gonna get yer neck wrung, little man. Just because you ain't got a cunny don't mean I won't enjoy choking the life out of ya."

The smaller man raises his arms in submission, work gloves slick with viscera. "I'm not looking to make a thing of it. I have no qualms about you bringing the women here for your... amusement. Makes things easier for everyone, it does. Besides, it can't be repudiated that I like to watch you give them what for. I'm just saying, when we are done with them, is it too much to ask for you to dump the bodies properly? Or, if nothing else, why not take them to that loopy dame, Mrs. Lovett, over on Fleet Street? She'd make them disappear right quick. No fuss, no muss. And likely provide you some extra coin in recompence."

"I was to dispose of them however I saw fit. That's wot the boss said," the big man states, taking several steps forward until he is looming over his counterpart. His tone is petulant, like a child experiencing a pique of rage, albeit a child who happens to be worryingly strong. Bull-sized nostrils flare with each choleric exhalation. "And you know it—you was there when them words was uttered. The boss also said fear is a necessary part of great change. I'm just gettin' the fear started early, is all. Greasin' the gears, so to speak. Allowin' them whores to serve one last purpose. Sides, twixt you and me, being ground up for meat pies is too good for cut-rate hussies." He raises a clenched fist in the other man's face, the appendage larger than a ham hock. "Wot you got to say to that, then, Milt?"

The smaller man, one Milton Dinsmore, flinches noticeably, eyes widening in surprise. The duo are not friends, despite his best efforts to the contrary. The big man seems disinterested in anything other than women, metal work, and a handful of disparate leisurely pursuits. He is also not the most even-keeled of individuals. Milton shifts towards the shotgun ever so slightly, a motion that is more instinctual than intentional. Several moments pass before he can comport himself, and he rests one hand on the other man's forearm in a visible display of fortitude, glove squelching as it makes contact. Violet-green fluid splatters over the clothing of both men, making haphazard stains that will be difficult to remove. The big fellow either does not notice or does not care.

"I do believe the boss's actual words were 'necessary *preemptor* to great change,' but I'll not belabour the point. Oratorial exactitude notwithstanding, old chum, there are moments when you are full of surprises. Greasing the gears, indeed. Who am I to argue against such a logical and marvelous rationalization?"

The big man chuffs but does not otherwise respond, uncertain if his diminutive partner is clowning. Which is an understandable dilemma. The words Milton uses are frequently oversized, a wholly intentional behaviour. Derided for his slight frame all his life, he feels obliged to compensate by plumbing the lonesome pages of dusty dictionaries. He may not tower over any of his peers in height, but he can certainly overwhelm them with a sophisticated lexicon. He must also admit to himself, if nobody else, that he has relied upon such phrases for so long that he is now incapable of skimping on syllables.

Silence reigns for a handful of seconds before Milton removes his hand and returns to his stool, wiping sweat from his brow with the back of his arm. Being so close to imminent violence has made him even more paranoid than he already was. Thankfully, there is solace to be found in the repetition of toil, and he has much yet to do.

Spread across the workbench in front of him are a multitude of incongruous items: thin filaments of silver wire on a spool, assorted medical implements, a leather-and-steel band currently wrapped around a wooden mannequin head, and a stone bowl containing four sets of intact eyeballs afloat within a violet-green fluid. Not quite the work Milton had in mind when he took the job, but he knows better than to look a gift horse in the mouth.

"I've got nothing for you to cut down at present, so take a well-earned breather," he calls out absentmindedly, attention already returned to his commissioned work. The band is more harness than anything, a narrow channel of machined steel fronted by thin glass. The contraption encircles the wooden head completely, affixed directly over where a person's eyes and ears would be. Like some wraparound visor of sorts. As for the leather, it serves as a type of apron, conforming to the contours of the mannequin's face like a second skin. "The yoke is as waterproof as I can make it. I need to perform a few alterations for fitment, but we are getting close. Your millwork is second-to-none, old chum."

Milton's cohort shrugs his shoulders in acknowledgment, ire fading as rapidly as it had appeared. The big man, like anyone, seems to relish complements. "Twasn't nuffin' special."

He moves off to one side, further away from the DOVE, where a makeshift nook has been erected for periods of relaxation. It may not constitute an actual home, but it does contain a few of the creature comforts thereof. A large blue plaid chair dominates the space, well-worn and moth-eaten. Next to it, a stack of reading material lies atop a rickety end table: books, penny dreadfuls, and assorted flyers from around the city. Though he may be wanting in the vocabulary department, the big man is, surprisingly, quite literate, voraciously devouring the written word at every opportunity. A rather innocent pastime for such a brutish individual, in Milton's opinion.

But it is not the periodicals which draw his partner's attention. Situated near the back of the nook, a pair of sawhorses topped with a wooden plank form an improvised table, upon which rests a glass tank. The aquarium is moderate in size, filled to the halfway point with the same violet-green liquid as the bowl. Instead of eyeballs, however, the tank is home to four severed fingers, each of which has been neatly preserved. The digits are completely submerged, metacarpal and phalanx bones making them too heavy to float.

An electric rotor with a hand-crank sits beside the tank, silver wires running from the device directly into the fluid. Turning the reel spins the flywheel, the motion producing a low-voltage output. Similar, in theory, to the DOVE generator, only on a much smaller scale. The device provides nowhere near enough electricity to power the lightbulbs, but its meagre output is more than sufficient for the big man's needs.

While Milton watches, his partner gives in to another of his favorite diversions—cycling the crank with a gentleness that belies his imposing stature. Within the aquarium, stimulated by the voltaic current, the fingers begin to stir, stretching and curling like earthworms, inching their way across the glass bottom of the tank in reflexive mobility. Much more alive than dead flesh has any right to be. The reanimation process, as the duo's mysterious patron has dubbed it, presents a strange tableau, divorced from any of the congruent laws of nature.

Then again, Milton concedes, the world is a strange place, and jolly old England more than most. He's borne witness to similar phenomena and has learned to check his doubts at the door. A little bit of mystery helps to add spice to his life. Moreover, if it keeps the big man entertained, then so much the better.

After all, a bored giant is a dangerous giant.

CHAPTER XIII

Small talk with Bixby is akin to learning the steps to a new dance, both awkward and exhilarating. At times, he regales me with medical tidbits which run the homeopathic spectrum gamut, vacillating between fascinating and ghoulish, his words tumbling out like a bushel of spilt apples. Conversely, we seem to lose the thread of every conversation quite easily, rendering us both quietly uncomfortable.

After several such starts and stops, as well as a few moments of silent deliberation, the good doctor returns to his examination of the body. He flits around the table with nearly reckless abandon, as if an excitable child with a new toy. Various noises escape his lips—a "hmm" here, an "aha" there, and a soft susurrus of what I can only assume are questions asked of the corpse. Considering how unusual some of my methods are, I cannot criticize the doctor for his. The best I can do is stay quiet and allow him to work.

It is only when he spends an inordinate amount of time at the victim's feet that my curiosity becomes piqued. "What have you found?" I ask, joining him at the end of the table.

"Metal shavings," he replies, holding a pair of tweezers up to the light. The curled flake gripped between the teeth is tiny, no more than a sliver, almost imperceptible to the naked eye. It is akin to a corkscrew, only in miniature. "Just under the skin between her toes, and more under the pads of her feet and heels. Some are larger than others, but they are all very minuscule. I very nearly missed them."

The metal is dull silver, probably steel. While iron is still the most common alloy used in sailing vessels, plentiful in supply and relatively easy to work, it is slowly losing favor over steel, which is both stronger and lighter. It is also more expensive, meaning the vast majority of the merchant vessels coming out of Blackwall remain iron-hulled as a means of reducing costs. Dr. Bixby removes several more shavings, each with some degree of curl or curve. There is something familiar about their shape. But, despite my best efforts to the contrary, I am unable to conjure up anything meaningful in that moment.

"Did our other victims from Blackwall have them as well?"

The chagrined expression that creeps across the doctor's face answers my question long before he opens his mouth. "It is entirely possible, but I'll admit that I wasn't looking too closely. I must offer my apologies. It is not something I should have overlooked."

I wave his contrition away; there is nothing to be done for it now. To be fair, I never gave any of the victims' feet more than a cursory glance myself, so I must shoulder some of the blame. After all, who would think to look between their toes? It is an error I shan't make again. And yet, the shape of the iron shavings haunts my subconscious.

"And the rest?" I ask instead, returning to familiar ground. It was an honest mistake, and I refuse to hold it over his head.

"The same as the others," he answers with palpable relief. "Cause of death was asphyxiation. Removal of the finger was postmortem, as we suspected. The small pinhole burns, though superficial, are consistent with the other women. As are the larger, blistery gashes, which I am beginning to suspect are electrical burns. I recently observed treatment given to a fellow who suffered an accident at the power plant, and his wounds looked nearly identical, though far more severe."

Astonishment makes my words sound harsher than intended. "Excuse me? Are you suggesting that these women were harmed by an electric current?"

"It would appear that way, yes."

I let the ramifications rattle around in my head for a trice. If the injuries were caused by electricity, in whatever manner such a thing could occur, it would help explain Lady Ellington's interest in examining the corpse. Especially since Blackwall has yet to be modernized in such a fashion. One mystery solved whilst several others have taken its place. A lamentably all too common occurrence with police work.

"Considering their locations on the bodies, primarily in the more, ah, intimate areas, I'm inclined to believe it is done intentionally."

"As am I," Bixby replies, a grimace contorting his features. "Which is a distressing thought. However, the theft of the eyeballs still concerns me the most. Given the rough treatment these women have received, I would expect their faces to be in ruins. And yet there is no damage to the orbital bones themselves. Not on any of the victims thus far. Very little bruising of the surrounding skin and no damage to the eyelids."

He pauses for a long beat as if organizing his thoughts into a coherent stream. These are more words than he has ever before uttered in one instance.

"To cleanly sever the optic nerve inside the victim's cranium? All the way down to where it ends at the optic chiasm? That is no easy feat. The killer would need to boast some shrewd knowledge of cranial anatomy and have access to something beyond the usual implements found in commonplace labor. Some sort of specialized surgical tool, quite minuscule in design. Like thin, long-bladed shears angled ninety degrees near the tip, the better to perform surgical cuts in small cavities. We have similar apparatus here within the hospital. But for a pair be found in the hands of mere street rabble? Unlikely."

"How long is the optic nerve?"

"Roughly two inches in a full-grown adult."

I can't help but circle back to my recurring question: Why the eyes? And more specifically, why keep the optic nerve intact? As difficult as it must be to sever, it seems too much trouble. Keeping the orbs as trophies, as ghastly an idea as it may be, is at least something I can understand. Inasmuch as any of these events are understandable. I can reconcile that killers sometimes like to revisit their crimes, with trophies serving as a sort of vicarious manner of doing so. And eyes, as windows to the soul, must be especially appealing to someone with an unsound mental state. But why the added difficulty of surgical exactness?

A thought occurs to me, and I feel compelled to voice it, diplomacy be damned. "Have any such tools gone missing from this facility, perchance?"

Dr. Bixby affixes me with a queer look, visibly uncomfortable with where my question is leading. "I cannot begin to say. But, due to the influx of new personnel and processes, not to mention frequent internal renovations, a full accounting of our surgical inventory would be nearly impossible to accomplish. Surely, you're not suggesting someone from this institution could be the culprit?"

"I am suggesting no such thing, doctor. Merely hypothesizing. Nevertheless, irrespective of how remote a possibility it may be, I cannot discount the notion entirely. Lest you forget, many experts still believe the Whitechapel Murderer had some manner of medical training."

The snort that emanates from Bixby makes his feelings plain on that particular subject. "That popular theory is utter rubbish. It is much more likely that he was a butcher or at least apprenticed to one. Bah! I would have an easier time believing the Ripper to have been a metalworker than a man of medicine."

No sooner has the doctor made his statement than my mind realizes what the steel shavings are. I return to the tray in which they were deposited, moving the assorted spirals and flakes of metal (some longer than others) around with my finger. I have seen these shapes before. Such shavings are actually called turnings, also known as swarf, and emanate from a machinist's table whilst cutting down larger metal product into smaller sizes. The smaller the objects, the finer the cutting blade. The finer the blade, the more minuscule the swarf. Due to the precision components used by my father's printing press machines, he employs several millwrights to repair or remanufacture the various specialized gears and rollers required by the presses. I have seen turnings much like these on the floor of our workshop, unavoidable byproducts of fine metal work. The swarf from my father's machinists is larger than these shavings, meaning whatever is worked on within this unknown shop is even more delicate or lilliputian.

Another truth hits me just as suddenly, ancillary but no less vital.

"I know what the pinhole burns are from," I state confidently, pulling Bixby's attention back to me.

His thirst for knowledge, even outside of his dedicated field, is palpable.

"Do tell."

"Sparks," I say, and the word carries the weight of fact. It is the only answer that fits.

The doctor nods in agreement.

"Sparks cast from some kind of metal-working machine or process," I continue. "Could be expelled from a blacksmith's hammer and anvil, a grindstone, or maybe a mill. Which gets us no closer to the 'why.' Perhaps they are a form of torture or used to generate fear? Maybe they serve to excite him further as a bizarre sexual fixation or ritual. It is impossible to know for sure. But sparks caused those markings. I'd stake my career on it."

My certitude is nearly a physical thing, encircling me with the insistent pressure of deep water. Shivers dance along my spine. The killer's large hands were too broad in scope to be a helpful clue. This new information, however, has given me much more to work with. It may even allow me to be preemptive for a change, instead of several steps behind. One thing is abundantly clear—he is taking his victims to, or through, an operational machine shop before murdering them. One where raw metal is throwing sparks as it is worked. But, more importantly, one where steel, far from a common commodity, is milled or machined for small, intricate projects. Fiona, and most likely the other women, trod on the shavings during their ordeal.

Which means the perpetrator is likely a millwright or machinist himself. Given his apparent size, it is a profession that makes sense.

A glimmer of hope appears through the gloom, and I am optimistic for the first time since these killings began. There can only be a smattering of such locations in lower London, and the vast majority of them will be on the Isle. Reconnoitering them won't prove overly difficult. In fact, if it keeps me away from headquarters, Barnhold will unquestionably approve any suggestion I place before him. His dislike of me makes him both pre-dictable and malleable, which suits me just fine. I prefer to operate without oversight or underlings getting in the way, and I can easily maneuver the superintendent into allowing me my freedom.

There is still the manner of tea with Lady Ellington on the morrow, but that is only a small hurdle. I suspect that she will be pleased by my findings. Perhaps I shall be rid of her quicker than I had initially hoped.

I feel my heart rate increase, and my fingers twitch involuntarily. I can now begin my search in earnest.

145

CHAPTER XIV

R.M. Müller
Undisclosed Location
Sept 13th, 1892
Research Journal Entry # 94
6:17 PM

There is a stink that clings to the creature like barnacles to a ship's hull.
Foul odours emanating from a corpse, from the initial point of expiration
and throughout the decomposition process, is a well-known occurrence and
also scientifically explicable. Putrefaction may not be pretty, but it's complete-
ly natural. This stench, however, is something stronger. And far, far worse.
I have heard, through the small talk of my subordinates who have been on
safari in South America, that certain peccary pigs have an unbearable stink
that is used to mark their territory. The scent is supposedly strong enough to
cause nausea in humans. These odours are quite similar, and I'm unsure
what steps we must employ to mask them.

{Lye? Carbolic acid? Urine? Some combination thereof?}

Hosing it down did not seem to make a noticeable difference. On the other hand, the process had the unexpected side-effect of aggravating the creature to the point of belligerence. It stomped and stumbled around the cage in a near frenzy, moaning and clicking like a thing possessed, lashing out at the bars with enough force to bend some of them. Which is a point of consternation. If containment protocols fail, the creature's odour will be the least of our problems.

As expected, our creation is showing no signs of lethargy or exhaustion. It has made no attempts at sitting or going prone, and it never completely ceases its movements, like a jittery child with toys or baubles just out of reach.

Unfortunately, until we add variables to the formula, there is precious little additional datum to make note of. I would like to add obstacles to the cage in order to gauge how quickly the creature adapts to changes in its environment. I would also like to test, through various methods and means we have been devising, if it still has use of its olfactory and auditory senses. But strict orders to the contrary keep us on the periphery, ready for the next steps yet unable to take them.

{It frustrates me that science must be beholden to those in authority, but alas, such is the way of the world. Power before progress.}

A few members of the team, myself included, have discussed an odd coincidence, and I feel it prudent to expand upon that debate here.

In her novel "Frankenstein," Mary Shelley fictitiously prophesized the reanimation of a corpse through the application of chemistry, still widely referred to as alchemy at that time. The methods described were vague at best, which worked well enough for the illusory nature of her narrative. Her pseudoscience does make for great reading. And yet, almost a century later, we have proven her suppositions largely correct, save for the application of electricity in an industrial/medical setting (which was unthinkable in 1818) to galvanize our confidential reanimation compound.

That we have done Mrs. Shelley one better is only a matter of course. Mankind's understanding of the vagaries of the human body has grown by leaps and bounds since her great work was first published. Grafting additional limbs was tedious but hardly impossible. Such an enhancement to the creature was the director's brainchild, an endeavour that has proven far more successful than we could have anticipated.

{She is quite the visionary, our superior, and I am honoured to have been hand-selected for this project. I am not ashamed to admit that her intellect surpasses my own, and her ambition is compelling in its scope. Great change is coming: our creation will be both herald and executor. If Victor Frankenstein was the modern Prometheus, does that make our director the modern Shelley? I, for one, say yes.}

I must wrap up this section; the director has arrived and wishes to test the creature's reaction to a living thing invading its space. It is a moment that the team and I have awaited with barely disguised impatience. Such an experiment should start small, of course, to establish a baseline.

As such, for this first trial, I believe I shall select a lamb.

More to follow.

6:43 PM

What a mess. If the stench was bad before, it is nigh unbearable now. The odour of the creature mixing with the reek of entrails and bloody tendrils of raw mutton has created a sickeningly rich miasma. It has saturated the very fabric of my clothing, which will be heading for the incinerator once removed.

As for the lamb, it barely had time to bleat out a scream before it was summarily ripped apart. In this, the creature's four arms are remarkably effective. In fact, it behaves as if they have always been a part of its anatomy, thoroughly efficient and well-coordinated. What a remarkable outcome to such a radical procedure. Each hand grabbed one of the lamb's legs and...

Well, the rest happened almost too quickly to see. The gory results, however, were more than evident. Several of the scientists became instantly ill as a result, their meals coming up quite forcefully. This only added to the sickening brume permeating the air.

The director, on the other hand, was completely unfazed by any of it. I don't know how she managed to remain so clinically detached, but such a feat is both impressive and terrifying.

{And yet, that is far from the most worrisome part. As much as I dread documenting my concerns—my fingers shake even now—I must do so, for the sake of science. And posterity.}

While the rest of us stood stock-still, dazed by the sheer violence of our creation, the director made her way to the edge of the cage without preamble. Despite being well within grasping distance, she exhibited no signs of fear. The creature could sense her presence, for it turned its head towards her as surely as if it still had eyes. However, the moment it began to approach her, she spoke slowly but firmly, commanding it to halt.

And, though I cannot fathom the how or why of it, the creature did as it was bidden, coming to a complete stop like a hunting bitch at its master's heel. An impossible occurrence, but it transpired all the same. She then ordered it to retreat to the far end of the cage, and again, the creature complied.

At least we know that it still possesses aural capacity. My suppositions were that the creature would be able to hear, though whether or not it would retain its sense of smell and touch was speculative at best. These aspects remain unknown at this time.

One more thing to ponder: if it has no sense of touch, it will likely be unable to feel pain as well. And if it feels no pain, it will surely know no fear.

But those are minor factors contrasted against the larger consideration—how does it know to heed her directives? Does it recognize the voice of its progenitor? Is it something about how she modulates her speech, akin to how a flute can entrance cobras?

{Or is there more to it than I'm seeing? I've been involved with this project since its inception but have not been privy to all of the director's comings and goings. Did she perform some other procedure when I was otherwise indisposed? I don't know what I don't know, and that is the most troublesome part of all. I am beginning to feel like I'm a smaller cog than I initially thought. Or perhaps the wheel is simply far larger than I'd ever imagined. With no way to know for sure, all I can do is shove those concerns to the side and focus upon my tasks. I must see this through.}

Against our protests, the director then removed the lock to the cage and let herself in, leaving the door open behind her. At that moment, I was certain that our creation would escape, that it would somehow know that freedom was merely a few strides away. And though the creature's head swiveled back and forth, and its fingers twitched and flexed ominously, it remained otherwise stationary.

This has answered one of the questions lingering in the back of my mind since the beginning: How will we control this beautiful and ghastly thing we have wrought?

{I suppose the true response to that question is relatively unambiguous. <u>We</u> won't control it. <u>She</u> will.}

CHAPTER XV

The walk back to Poplar seems to take twice as long as it should.

Following the same zigzagging route back, Constance loses herself in the late afternoon crowd. With a staggeringly large population of 5.5 million, London is positively teeming with pedestrians as evening sets in. A veritable mishmash of end-of-shifters, gentlemen enjoying a pre-supper constitutional, and even the occasional foreigner flooding the streets and thoroughfares. Horse-drawn carriages travel a little slower during this congested time of day, wary of the increased foot traffic.

Restaurants and bakeries have their doors open wide, enticing passersby with assorted scrumptious offerings. Newsboys hawk their wares, shouting out the most sensational of headlines, desperate to be rid of the last of their periodicals and earn the maximum wage. It is another of the many professions that she has dabbled in while disguised. The pay is rarely commensurate with the effort, however.

Constance barely takes notice of the journey, as her gaze is turned inward in remorse. An easterly breeze does its best to thin out the smoky haze, carrying a chill which reddens her cheeks, though the sensation is not unpleasant. The wind is not the only wintry thing—Constance's simmering anger has been smothered by exhaustion, hate's embers left to cool under the harsh reality of fatigue. And not just of her body but of her spirits. The omnipresent London particular is very nearly a mirror of her soul—murky and desolate, leeched of all color. She should never have let Fi leave for the docks. She should have tried harder to earn coin, to have done more to improve their lot.

Fi, bless her Irish heart, never once complained. She'd possessed the inherent stoicism of a true Londoner, if not the accompanying grimness. The red-headed lass had carried on with moxie, and nobody could claim otherwise. But it hadn't been enough. The city had chewed her up and spit her out like so much grist, and Constance cannot help but focus on the things she could have done differently. All the ways in which she let Fiona down.

She knows self-recrimination is part of grieving, but awareness of that fact makes the process no less painful. The heaviness of her heart is matched only by the weight of the sovereign nestled in her purse, which seems to tug at her belt with impossible heft. More compensation than Constance would earn over the course of several days, and for what? Some manner of piteous succor for the friend left to wallow in the turbulence of grief? An appurtenance that could be held between fingers as barter for someone who filled a room with their presence? Inspector Guthrie was only being generous, so why does Constance feel such overwhelming bitterness for his act of charity? She is half tempted to toss the coin in the river, but the painful twisting of her stomach prevents such folly. She cannot avenge Fi while suffering from starvation. Lashing out at the blameless is also not going to help anything, and Constance forces herself to abandon the misguided castigation. The resurgence of her ire is a welcome thing, lending strength to her weary limbs and quickening her step, but Guthrie is not the man to whom it should be directed. The sleuthhound genuinely seemed to want to help.

Although it has proven useful, Constance is also ready to be done with the Connor disguise. She cannot deny that men's clothing is perfectly comfortable compared to most feminine attire. Nevertheless, keeping up the dockworker pretense is wearying in its own right. The walk. The talk. The trenchant posture. Such subterfuge takes a toll that is far from visible to the naked eye.

A streetcorner barker catches her attention whilst promoting a new magic act at the nearby Carnaby Theatre that very night. His rich baritone breaks through her fugue with the force of a hammer, well-enunciated words audible amidst the incessant din of conversation and clatter of horseshoes—a *man's* voice if she's ever heard one. The barker is handing out flyers, cheap yellowed paper awash with large garish text. Constance grabs one as she walks past. The advertisement promises a magic act like no other, featuring the Great Danton performing his "New Transported Man" as the show's climax. Real magic on display for the low cost of only ten shillings. She has never heard of Danton, only a middle-class illusionist called The Professor who has held several exhibitions close to Poplar. Not that Constance could have afforded to attend such a performance, *bourgeois* or not. The closest she's ever been to magic was trading sex for entertainment, occasionally subjecting herself to the lecherous attentions of Samuel Slip-Fingers, a back-alley prestidigitator of parlor tricks and sleight-of-hand. Bargains where Samuel certainly came out ahead.

Despite being denounced by the dominant religions of the country, mysticism and the occult are hot-ticket items for both wealthy and poor alike. Newfound belief in the supernatural is spreading like rats in a tenement. Mesmerists, mediums, and magicians are all the rage, *en vogue* in a way that other trends cannot emulate or capitalize on. Given its geographical location and sizeable populace, London is a veritable mecca for all manner of spirituality.

Constance finds the paranormal utterly fascinating, though she has no personal experience with ghosts or spells. There is something about the unearthly and uncanny which ignites her imagination and sets fire to her soul. Instead of being fearful, she often finds herself wishing for a brush with the inexplicable, even if only once. Just the slightest peek beyond the veil. An integer to vindicate her belief in the paranormal and distract her from the harshness of reality. The penny dreadfuls she shared with Fiona only served to fuel that particular fire. Mysticism and the supernatural are frequent topics of the cheap periodicals: vampires, ghosts, warlocks, and other, far more imaginative phenomena.

In light of her sudden prosperity, Constance could afford a ticket to Danton's show if she desired, though there'd be precious little left for food. Given her current attire, she would also have to sit in the cheap seats. It's a momentary consideration, nothing more, but shame still wells up within her, warring with her sense of longing. She finally has enough coin to spoil herself, and yet her circumstances simply won't allow it. Nor will her guilt.

Alas, such is the lot of an underprivileged commoner. Fragments of a better life perpetually out of reach, either because of money or morals. Although, in Constance's experience, it is frequently both simultaneously.

The sun is setting by the time she reaches Poplar. Streetlamps are aglow, the fog has mostly dissipated, and warm light exudes from behind the drapes and curtains of her neighbours' windows. The peace of her surroundings is in juxtaposition to the heaviness of her heart. Although Constance has no desire to burden anyone with such awful tidings right before supper, Fi would have wanted their friends and acquaintances to know of her fate immediately. The girl was nothing if not considerate. After all, the sooner everyone heard the news, the sooner they could work through their shock and grief.

Instead of remaining alone with her sorrow, hoarding the pain of loss like a pinchpenny, Constance will allow herself one night to share in the bereavement. One night to commiserate with friends, divvying up drinks and anecdotes at backstreet pubs in lieu of a church-held service. One night to gather her strength and resolve, awash in the glow of communal reminiscence. And then she will hunt that murdering bastard down.

Silence reigns in the apartment, oppressive and sad. As melancholic as an interment. Constance changes clothing in a wearied inertia—she is relieved to be free of Connor for now but is having difficulty keeping her mind attentive. A halfhearted effort is made to ensure she is presentable, touching up her hair and applying minimal makeup, stifling frequent yawns the entire time. She can't help but glance in the corner of the mirror, hoping to catch sight of her friend. Even just a hint of a ghostly presence. She can think of no better initial encounter with the supernatural than to be visited by Fiona's spirit, as in the Dickens story. The ghost of friendship past, as it were.

But the mirror remains free of phantoms, instructive or otherwise. With a sigh, Constance rises with difficulty, bracing herself for the emotional tumult to come. It is going to be a very long night.

CHAPTER XVI

Midnight has come and gone when Milton declares the workday finished, a circumstance which comes as no great surprise. Outside of his preambulatory commute to and from home, and occasional trips to the lavatory a few buildings over, the need for secrecy keeps him inside the millworks almost continuously. A lack of windows or skylights causes the days and evenings to blend together into a dreary haze. When was the last time Milt saw the sunset? A week ago? Maybe two? He is unable to recollect. Being so insulated from the outside world has made time stagnant, as immobile as a fossil.

It doesn't help that their working environment is cramped, hot, and odourous. Perfect for keeping their activities confidential, but very much on the wrong side of hospitable. That Milt has labored in far more draconian conditions is scant comfort; a sixteen-hour workday is still a sixteen-hour workday, and their tittle of improvised extravagances does little to ease that onus. Situated off the beaten path, the workshop is not easy to find and well enough removed from neighbouring establishments that the odds of accidental discovery are slim. But slim does not mean impossible. As such, he has been extra vigilant, simply as a matter of course.

Better safe than sorry, as the saying goes.

Of course, Milt has no influence over Schaffer's schedule whatsoever; the big man comes and goes as he pleases, usually with nary a word edgewise. Along with hardly any attempt at being surreptitious. Then again, Schaffer is not in possession of a physique which would lend itself to concealment and, as such, likely wouldn't recognize clandestine behaviour if it bit him on the nose.

There is also the fact that Schaffer occasionally returns to the workshop without providing any sort of warning or advisory beforehand, accompanied by doe-eyed and unsuspecting donors. How can Milt be prepared if not provided advance notice? Yet another factor beyond his control.

Such women are invariably youthful in appearance and mannerisms, the expected curves of their gender conspicuously absent—certainly not the kind of ladies Milton would seek out. But he doesn't mind. Considering how fixated he can get on his creations, Milt is more than content to let his gargantuan companion do the heavy lifting, both literally and figuratively. Because they were given *carte blanche* with how they harvested the eyes, Schaffer has been satiating his physical needs while finding suitable candidates. Girls, he has asserted on multiple occasions, who will not be missed.

A reasonable enough contention as far as Milt is concerned.

And, if he is being honest, indulging his voyeuristic tendencies while Schaffer "entertains" the women is an unexpected, but not unwelcome, bonus. A little break from the tediousness of the harness fabrication. Rarely one to mix business with pleasure, Milton has (several times over) grudgingly conceded that the big man's methodology, while a bit on the theatrical side, is not entirely without merit.

As for the prostitutes, they are a means to an end, nothing more. As disposable as gutted candles. Their individual characteristics are already forgotten, leaving only indistinct fragments that flit across his mind in random intervals—images of flesh and blood. Of titillation and torture. It is the noises they make that he is unable to forget: cries of pleasure and pain which, after hours of unending degradation and torment, tend to blend into a single animalistic keening. A banshee wail of pure suffering.

Milt may have a cruel streak a mile wide, but something about those sounds causes his stomach to twist uncomfortably. Perhaps he's growing soft in his later years.

And it isn't just the noise but the smells as well. Try as they might, the men cannot completely rid the workshop of the pungent scent of bodily functions, which seem to have soaked straight into the foundation. Schaffer doesn't seem perturbed in the slightest, but Milton is beginning to find the stench untenable.

The DOVE has been switched off, no longer filling their workspace with its exhaust and motorized racket. The pervading silence is almost dense enough to grasp. Milt's pocket watch has the time—a little after midnight—which is earlier than they usually finish. But, looking at the provided schematics, coupled with an issue that has been lurking in the back of his mind, he can progress no further with the supplies he has on hand. He'll need to send Schaffer on one more excursion.

Resting on the table like some sort of relic, the harness itself is finally complete. Leather treatment has been liberally applied to the apron, rendering it supple and shiny, while the metal fasteners and hinges glisten with oil. He has certainly manufactured far more intricate contraptions in his time, but there is still something special about this one. Its bizarre trappings set it apart from his other creations. It may not be his *pièce de résistance*, but the harness is certainly unique.

No longer fascinated by his macabre finger collection, Schaffer hovers over Milton's shoulder like a stringent schoolmarm, far too close for comfort. The big man seems even larger in low light, as if festering anger and sexual sadism have somehow added mass to his already hulking frame.

"Will it do wot it's sposed to?" Schaffer asks, eyeing the contraption dubiously.

A legitimate question despite his doggerel manner of speech.

"Well, the glass fitting is the finest I've ever done, and the frame you've built is precise. From a mechanical perspective, I see no deficiencies with the design. I don't know the first thing about the fluid we've been provided, of course, and I'm not ashamed to admit that I cannot comprehend exactly *how* the apparatus will function on a physiological level. Those considerations notwithstanding, yes, the harness should do the trick."

Milton sucks in a breath before continuing. "However, having said that, we are still not quite finished. I believe the second lass you picked up was rather nearsighted. I don't know about you, but I have no desire to deliver a partially defective finished product. So, the more I consider it, the more I think we should replace her set with another pair of eyes. That will require us to change up our timetable a bit, but it can't be helped. Think you're up for another snatch and grab?"

"Aye. But them constables will be as thick as flies on fish guts until sunrise. I'll let the heat die down a titch and then nab us a fresh one in the evening."

"Good. On the morrow it is. I can't speak for you, but I require some rest. Oh, and this last donor must be a rush job, my good fellow. This little cockup will already put us right up against the agreed-upon delivery schedule, and I shall have to explain the unplanned extension to our patron. As such, you probably shouldn't spend as much time with this last girl as you usually do."

The big man chuckles without humour, causing Milt's hackles to rise. "Just gotta dial up the hurt early then. Ain't nuffin' to it."

"As you say, friend. As you say. Still, right hand to God, you are a true artist at inflicting pain. Your talents are wasted here in the Yard; you should be on the monarchy's payroll. The Queen's royal torturer, even. Enemies of the state would divulge their deepest secrets before you even got started on them."

"I'd still break them all the same, even after they spilt the beans."

"My point exactly," Milt replies, suppressing the urge to roll his eyes in exasperation. "A posting like that would be in the best interest of all parties involved. Save for those getting tortured, that is."

"Wot 'bout you? You ain't keen on getting' yer hands dirty, but you ain't no stranger to death neither. Other than a stiff one, wot you get out of it?"

Another unexpectedly esoteric question, and Milt once again finds himself taken aback. He has pondered the topic frequently and with great fervidness in the still of the night, when no other distractions are at hand. Why is he so enthralled by the transition between life and death? While he has uncovered numerous valid reasons, one always rises to the top of the heap. The one that renders him nearly stupefied in his fascination. Even now, he finds himself giddy at the thought. Nevertheless, this will be the first time he has spoken his reasoning aloud.

"It's quite straightforward, really. If you look closely, right at the point of expiration, there are times when you can see a person's soul rise up from their body."

Schaffer sniffs loudly, shaking his head in doubt. "Now you're just pullin' my leg. I've kilt plenty of people but ain't never seen no soul poppin' out of 'em."

"Observed it with my own eyes, mate," Milt rejoins, reedy voice full of conviction. His statement is neither bluster nor fabrication—he has truly witnessed such an occurrence on two separate occasions. It is nothing that can be verified, of course, but as far as Milt is concerned, both episodes are unequivocal proof of some manner of afterlife. Whether other people believe him or not doesn't make it any less true.

"Then I'll be lookin' with the next one. See if you's speakin' honest."

"Very well," Milt concedes, stifling a yawn. "We'll see what's in store for us two days hence, yes? But first, a question: Can we maybe avoid the showmanship with this final corpse?"

Schaffer holds his breath briefly, and Milt can feel the big man bristling, a dam precipitously buckling under mounting pressure. The charge of imminent violence fills the air, like lightning that has somehow become trapped indoors. Such a shame. They had been so close to sharing a moment.

"For a brainy fella, you sure is dumb," Schaffer growls, a perilously feral sound, their rapport from moments ago instantly forgotten. Milt has to force himself not to shrink away in fear. This time, the shotgun is too far away to be of any assistance. "Wot did I already tell you about that? I gots my reasons. And I ain't partial to repeating myself, little man. You keep blithering on about shite that don't concern you, and what follows won't be to yer liking."

This is ground they have tread and retread to a nearly farcical degree during their time together. Comment, threaten, cower, and repeat. There is no changing who a person is on the inside, Milt concedes. He can't help but utter snide comments, and Schaffer is unable to be any less of a brute, the same way a tiger is unable to change its stripes. They simply are who they are. But just because the dance is familiar doesn't mean the danger is any less potent.

"My mistake, chum. I found myself a little distracted is all. Won't happen again."

Schaffer leans down until they are eye to eye. His bovine face makes him look comically slow, but Milt is no longer fooled. An evil intelligence lurks behind the big man's lumbering façade. Schaffer's breath is fetid, a hot wash of foul air nearly as sickening as the evacuations of the women. He jabs a finger into Milt's chest with all the subtlety of a sledgehammer.

"See that it don't. Just cuz we get paid by the same person don't make us friends, Milt. And ain't nobody said that all them eyes need to come from whores."

End Chorus

RIDING THE GHOST TRAIN

What is it about slipping into middle age that suddenly instills in a man the predilection for self-reflection? Why must we wait until our bodies begin to complain before we take stock of both ourselves and our deeds? How are we so ignorant of the harm we perpetrate upon those we love? That men survive the impetuousness of youth, not to mention the folly, is both astounding and incomprehensible.

These are the thoughts that accompany me as I step into the horse-drawn carriage that awaits outside of my home. The shame I carry is burden enough that my shoulders seem to ache, and I furtively glance from side to side, hoping that none of my peers are watching.

I do not wish for them to see me in this wretched state.

That I am the subject of gossip within the community is not unknown to me. No stranger to the bottom of a bottle, I have mistaken my neighbors' front door for my own on several occasions and am known to be argumentative when deep in my cups. There are many kinds of drunkards, from happy to morose; I am of the unfriendly variety.

But the haze of alcohol also served as a suit of armor, and I endured the stigma with inebriated indifference, like a stone statue unfazed by decades of inclement weather. The stares and whispers never penetrated.

Sticks and stones, as they say.

And yet, just this previous night, I crossed a threshold that had been hitherto unimaginable. In a pique of rage, I became the vilest of suburban habitants. There is a new stigma attached to me now; a new title that I will bear until the end of my days.

Abuser of women.

Was it merely the alcohol? Or has my incessant drinking unlocked some part of me that has always existed, coiled tight and waiting to strike? I would like to blame my actions solely upon the liquor-induced stupor; but that is not where the culpability lies. That I only lashed out once makes no difference. Drunk or not, I struck my wife in front of our children, and in doing so, I have created a new and fractured reality that we must all learn to live in.

She said she forgave me. As I poured the contents of each and every bottle down the drain, self-loathing pounding me like heavy waves, she swore that we could move past it. I promised that it would not, under any circumstances, happen again. That I could change. That I *wanted* to change. I made a vow to never touch another drop. And though she has every reason to distrust my words, I could tell that she believed me.

But nothing is ever as straightforward as we anticipate. Forgiveness does not equate to *tabula rasa,* and one does not harm an angel without repercussions.

And, so, I am taking a sabbatical, from work, from home. From the murmurs of the rumor mill. And from the discoloration that mars my wife's cheek. I must let the poison run its course and remove myself from any means of acquiring more. I must abscond somewhere remote.

As fate would have it, there exists such a place.

The cabin has been in my family for generations, though I have rarely had cause to visit. No great outdoorsman, I derive considerable gratification from the hustle and bustle of the city, where creature comforts are within walking distance. Being so far removed from kith and kin holds no appeal for me. Nor does the structure's singularly remote location, nestled deep within the Appalachian Mountains.

And yet, my promise lingers like a phantom, always on the periphery of my waking mind. If I am to face my devils, if I am to wrest my life from their clutches, then I must do so alone. My family has suffered enough. I cannot ask them to walk through this particular hell with me.

I *will* not.

My journey up the mountainside is uneventful; the carriage's spring-and-leaf suspension bouncing me as if I were a babe on my mother's knee; the clopping of hooves like some organic metronome, lulling me into a fitful doze with their measured meter. The din of the city fades. Even my regrets fade, if only temporarily. In that null hour between lucidity and dream-state, all of my failures cease to exist. I am no longer *that* man. He is below me now, sinking like the city is sinking, dispersing into the depths while I rise above, looking down upon my submerged self as if beholding a stranger.

My mistakes seem so small from this height. So inconsequential.

I awaken some hours later, the driver's knock against the carriage roof startling me back into mindfulness. Never have I slept so soundly when not occupying my own bed. I peer out the window, though night has fallen, and details are scarce. But the outline of the cabin is perceptible against a backlight of stars, the silhouette eerie and ominous to my cosmopolitan inclinations.

Exiting the buggy on stiff legs, I knuckle the small of my back, coaxing feeling back into my extremities. The driver has already offloaded my luggage, such as it is. Just two meagre trunks contain everything I expect to need for a week in the backwoods. Before me, my erstwhile abode beckons.

It is a single-story affair, clad in clapboard and fading paint. The front of the structure had always resembled a face in my youthful imagination. That appearance has somehow perpetuated into adulthood, and now, with the porch sagging and the windows half-shuttered, the resulting visage is both forlorn and frightening. As though the place is unhappy to see me. A single Tulip tree towers over one corner of the roof, a stalwart sentinel ever watchful through the seasons. Its pointy limbs drape the edifice in a jagged embrace, while yellow leaves cling desperately, swaying in the evening breeze with a susurrus of sound.

The cabin. I haven't been here since I was a young man, and the memories are far from pleasant. Fragments return unbidden; my father arguing with his brother, nearly coming to blows; my mother's pleading voice; the children, myself included, waiting on the porch, neglected in the wake of perplexing adult matters. I never did learn what the row was about. I just know that it must have been a matter of some significance, creating a rift in our family that has yet to be mended.

But such remembrances are best left undisturbed. I push the thoughts from my mind and fish the wrought-iron key from my pocket. The carriage and horses have long since departed, and I feel strangely exposed on the stoop, a lone man hemmed in by endless acres of foreboding back country. The hairs on my neck tingle, as if a thousand eyes watch me from the darkness.

Suddenly spooked, goose pimples appearing on my arms, I unlock the door with haste, escaping into the safe confines of my manmade dwelling.

No longer abetted by clear starlight, it takes some time for my eyes to adjust to the cabin's murky interior.

For holding such a spot of intense repugnance in my memory, my temporary lodgings are, in reality, quite discouraging. The place is smaller than I remember; a ceiling low enough to touch; cluttered furniture encroaching upon narrow walkways; the wood burning stove that has appropriated an entire corner as its domain. Everything, from the furnishings to the assorted bric-a-brac, are flanked by walls that feel closer than they should.

Lighting the cabin's lanterns is a test of both my ability and my patience. Electricity is still relatively new in Pittsfield, yet I have already grown accustomed to its convenience. Cold fingers fumble through the unfamiliar motions of filling oil reservoirs and saturating wicks. I eventually manage, though not without uttering a few blasphemies. Flickering flames cast serrated shadows hither and thither, untethered darkness that capers across the walls and ceiling like grotesque goblins.

A storm is blustering in from the east, the wind whistling through the cracks and gaps in the framing. My nostrils are filled with a chilly tang, the promise of snowfall made manifest. In my haste, I had failed to consider potential changes in climate. A quick accounting of the cabin's stores sets my mind at ease; one of my estranged relatives has left the place well-stocked with firewood and canned goods.

My visit may be less cozy than expected, but I am in no discernible danger.

I go about the business of settling in, fluffing pillows and dusting surfaces. For such a large monstrosity, the cast-iron stove is ponderous in its heating, although I have filled its belly with plenty of fuel.

The busywork keeps my mind from revisiting that which brought me here. I am grateful for the mental respite. And yet, not everything is going in my favor. I sense a chill across my flesh as I work, one that has nothing to do with the temperature. Again, I perceive that I am being observed.

The source of my unease is obvious upon further inspection; the flat eyes of dead animals seem to follow my every move. A wolf resides near one wall, killed mid-snarl, its hateful expression still affixed even in death. Above it, on a dusty bookshelf, roosts a northern barred owl. Like most members of the strix genus, this bird's eyes are beady and devious. But it is the animal closest to the door which produces within me the most dreadful unease.

Mounted on a plaque the size of my wife's vanity mirror, the elk's neck and head are stupendous, topped by antlers that are fearsome in their abundance. The creature must have weighed more than a thousand pounds when it was felled. Though it lacks a body, the elk still gives the impression of powerful vivacity, as if the rest of it will come crashing through the wall at any moment.

Whichever taxidermist was utilized certainly knew his craft.

I tear my gaze away from the stuffed trophies, returning to the task of making the cabin habitable. While I toil, the first pangs of hunger gnaw from within, and I give the small dining table my undivided attention. A thought occurs to me then, bringing with it no small amount of shock: tonight's supper shall be the first one not accompanied by a drink in more than a decade.

It is a notion that is both exhilarating and terrifying.

My sleep is fitful; filled with both dreams and cravings, both which haunt me through the night.

I am shivering when I awaken, my breath visible in the air. The source of the cold is immediately apparent; somehow, the front door came open during the night, though I am certain I had latched it prior to climbing into bed. Through the doorway, a white wonderland is visible. As expected, the evening storm brought several feet of snow, a large quantity of which is spilling across the threshold.

And yet, it is not the nippy air that chills the blood in my veins, but instead the tracks that lead into the cabin from outside. The continuing snowfall has mostly obscured their finer details, and whatever scant knowledge I possess of fauna escapes me; I cannot tell what sort of animal created them.

Or whether it was an animal at all.

Despite my overactive imagination, however, the odds of the tracks belonging to a human are slim. For a start, they do not appear large enough. In addition, the carriage driver is not set to return for six more days, and there are no other lodges within walking distance.

The cabin is not large, and I rummage through it in a panic, searching for whatever interloper has invaded my solitude. Nothing seems to have been disturbed. The only creatures to be found are the dead ones already in residence, and I discover no other oddities, save for the wet spots on the floor, leading from the doorway to the side of the bed.

I shiver anew, terror causing my entire body to shake; whatever it was, it had stood over me while I slept.

With the door re-latched and the fire stoked, I hurriedly poke through every nook and cranny. My search bears fruit; a double-barrel shotgun is hidden in one of the linen chests, well-oiled and sturdy. The only shells I am able to find are birdshot, but they are better than nothing.

Perpetually on guard, my muscles ache from unreleased tension. I stalk the cabin like a night watchman, stomping to and fro, unable to quell my nervous fidgeting.

I try to eat, but the dry rations taste like ash in my mouth, and my stomach roils in protest. Water is the only palatable option. Yet no matter how much I drink, that revolting flavor clings to my teeth. The toothbrush I brought feels strange in my hand, but I am desperate to be free of the pasty residue. It is only when a sharp pain lances across my gums that I realize I am, against all reason, gripping my safety razor instead. Shock and agony wage war across my senses. Hours pass before I am able to stem the flow of blood; in this, at least, the copious snow proves useful.

Though it has been lingering in the back of my mind nearly this entire time, the desire for a drink is suddenly overpowering, a compulsion that assails my self-control with the force of battering rams striking a portcullis. The dull glow of alcohol would steady more than just my nerves. However, the cabin is bereft of spirits; not even a bottle of laudanum or paregoric can be found.

Cursing my weakness, I settle in by the stove, cradling the shotgun in my hands. The promise I made weighs heavy upon my heart, shame eating at my belly like a feral rat. Only one day in and I'm desperate for hooch. I truly am a wretch of a man.

How did I fool myself into thinking this would be easy?

The dreams of the previous night still linger, refusing to dwindle into the unlit depths of reminiscence. Their tendrils run deep, infecting every long hour, pervading my every thought. They were violent and hateful; I may not remember them with perfect clarity, but that much remains.

I curse my crumbling fortitude and the stubbornness which has led me here. My conceit is nearly a physical thing—an active fault line that compromises the mantle of my wishes and intentions, undermining my every action.

If I am to prevail against my base urges, I must be stronger than this. And I shall be. But, alas, not tonight. I am too out of sorts to enact any alterations to my temperament. Mayhap tomorrow will be kinder.

Despising my very existence, I stumble to bed, bleary-eyed and desolate.

My second morning starts out much the same; door ajar, wet prints on the floor, the air deathly cold.

These new tracks appear different, more pronounced in both size and depth. I still cannot fathom their origin, but whatever made them must be colossal in stature. How I managed to sleep through such heavy footfalls is truly a mystery.

The prints, in and of themselves, are most disquieting, but they are not the sole inconsistency within the cabin. Both the wolf and the owl have been moved from their original positions. The owl now roosts on my nightstand, far too close for comfort. The wolf, for all intents and purposes, appears to be guarding the door, incursive snowdrifts pooled around its paws. It faces the bed, rictus snarl seemingly more pronounced than before.

Even more ominously, the elk is no longer simply a head and a neck; its broad chest and long forelegs now adorn the placard as though they had always been there. The sheer size of the shaggy brute makes my knees buckle. Am I misremembering the trivial particulars within my refuge? Are my anxieties eroding my sanity?

I once again search high and low, finding nothing. What has done this? What *could* do this? Perhaps this place is cursed, insomuch as any physical exemplar can exceed the maledictions which we inflict unto our own hearts and minds.

A profound terror grips me, and I yearn to plunge through the doorway and escape the strange tableau, just as swift as my legs can carry me. A fool's errand, to be sure. I have not the appropriate attire for traipsing through a blizzard. Mother Nature also opposes me; the snow is now higher than the doorframe, as if the very elements conspire against me. Digging out would be no easy feat.

There is but one recourse available to me, and that is to hunker down and ride out the storm.

Not content to trust in the latch, I have stacked two linen chests against the door. Their combined weight should prove an immovable obstruction. The windows I have blocked with wooden shelving. No fortress, to be sure, yet it shall have to suffice.

But though I can barricade every ingress and arm myself against physical threats, I am defenseless against the machinations of my own mind. In the dark disquiet of solitary thought, each facet of my existence is magnified to gargantuan proportions, with my mistakes looming largest of all.

I keep the shotgun close, both barrels loaded, cold hands gripping it like a lifeline. My arms shake like unsecured railway tracks. The sweat dripping from my brow, in spite of the frigid air, is indicative of a fever.

Some rational part of my brain recognizes the symptoms, providing a name for my ailments. Riding the ghost train. Barrel-fever. Both exist as saloon vernacular for *delirium tremens*, itself merely a fancy appellation for one's detoxification from liquor dependency. That I am suffering the effects so soon is disconcerting. I had hoped to hold out longer.

A face takes root in my mind, that of my wife. The bruise is purpling, standing in stark relief against alabaster skin, her expression one of astonishment and hatred. Darkened skin around her eye calls to mind the black orbs of the owl. Was this how she looked at me, in that snatch of time after my fist connected? I am unable to recall. But if she did, one could hardly blame her. Attempting further recollections yields no clarity; my dishonor has colored each memory, painting them in a patina of negativity, replacing certitude with nagging doubts. I knew there would be repercussions for my malicious deed; perhaps I am living through them now.

Through the miasma of withdrawal, I sense an awakening of other senses. As if I alone can somehow unravel the mysterious threads of the unknown and unknowable.

All the while, the dead animals regard me with eyes that seem animated. Perhaps they've been watching me from the start.

In my burgeoning delirium, I begin to ascribe characteristics to each of the creatures. The owl, forever a symbol of wisdom and veracity, undoubtedly represents my pride. My temper is handily embodied by the snarling wolf. And the elk, that majestic and terrifying beast which dwarfs the others, is the physical incarnation of my regret. Such thoughts are truly the ravings of a madman, but rarely is the truth an easy pill to swallow. Deep down, in my heart of hearts, I know that I have touched upon something factual.

How many hours have passed since the morning? With the snowpack higher than the cabin, a gloomy darkness prevails, interfering with my circadian rhythm. Time stretches like glue, distended and delicate.

Lamp oil cans seem to mutate into whiskey bottles before my eyes, but after several instances of coughing up the vile substance, I no longer fall prey to that illusion. Fool me once...

Who, who? Whether the enquiry comes from the owl or my own imaginings is trivial compared to what is being asked. Who indeed?

I'm afraid the answer is quite simple; there is only myself to blame.

My belly rumbles, aching to be filled. But these are hunger pangs like I've never known. The truth is more than evident; it is not food my body is craving, but an altogether different form of sustenance. I realize, in this very moment, that I would sell my very soul for even the cheapest of bathtub gins.

And yet my exhaustion is greater than my appetite; my eyes growing heavier with each exhalation. I do not wish to sleep, to be so undeniably exposed, but my body and resolve are powerless to prevent it. The shotgun barrel thumps against the floor and my eyelids make good their betrayal.

Slumber overtakes me.

Does there exist a more enigmatic phase in life than when one realizes they are dreaming, and yet are utterly incapable of waking from said dream?

In my nocturnal reverie, I have been transported home, to some undefined time in the future. My children are older, taller, no longer clinging to their mother's skirts. I welcome the change. Being able to speak to my progeny without simplifying the topic is, in a word, liberating.

But that sword is sharp on both ends; they are old enough now to see through pretenses. There is judgement within their eyes, and maybe hatred as well.

My wife, too, has changed. Gone are her carefree disposition, gentle smile, and kind expression. The lines in her face have deepened, carving into angular planes which once were rounded. Hair that was formerly as golden as summer wheat has turned pale. In my dream, she is nearly a stranger.

No great deductive reasoning is required to understand this future; the bottle clasped in my hand lays bare the origin of their altered behavior. My choices have led to this, as inexorably as the setting of the sun. The fault lies with me, as it frequently does. *Mea culpa.*

And yet I do not relinquish the liquor.

The dream shifts, morphing into another scene entirely. My wife stands firm in front of our children, blood trickling from her nostrils, while I rave and rant about, spittle flying from cracked lips. What I am angry about is unclear. But in my stupor, it matters not. Anger begets anger, and the letter opener held in my wife's hand like a weapon ignites within me an incandescent fury. How dare she threaten me, as if I am some lunatic who has unexpectedly barged into her home?

I now comprehend that the dream is, instead, a nightmare, one from which I am desperate to awaken. I know what transpires next and have no desire to experience it. But my dream persists; there is no stopping.

In an instant, my hands are wrapped around her throat. The blade is lost in the commotion, and our children beat at my arms and face in desperation, their fists ineffective in the face of my wrath. I will *not* be deterred. My wife glares at me in defiance. Gasps escape her lips, and the thrum of her heartbeat pulses against my palms. I squeeze tighter, and then tighter still. The spark of life fades from her eyes, her limp body crumpling to the floor.

And still my rage has not been quenched. I turn to my children next. Their footfalls as they flee sound louder than cannons, the noise strangely out of sync with their motions.

The cacophony jolts me from my torpor, igniting my every nerve; it is not coming from my dream.

It is originating from within the cabin itself.

I jump to my feet in a flash. My weary arms can barely manage to lift the shotgun. A lingering horror clings to my conscience; the atrocities committed in my dream went beyond the pale, and they have hounded me into wakefulness. Such a twisted future cannot be allowed to take place.

Nevertheless, in this moment, I have more pressing concerns.

In the faint glow of the stove's smoldering embers, I witness a sight that nearly stops my heart. The elk has almost broken free of its confinement, most of its body now emerging through the wall. The front hooves beat a deafening staccato against the wood, and an ear-shattering bugling escapes its mouth, interspersed with raspy grunts as it attempts to extricate itself.

Meanwhile, the wolf is returned to life as well, and has withdrawn into the shadows, growling and snarling with unmistakable menace. The owl screeches by overheard, close enough that I feel the beating of its wings. Sharp talons brush my hair; I duck down in just the nick of time.

Despite clasping the shotgun, I do not feel that I can prevail. These creatures hold every advantage in the low light. My only recourse is to flee, to dig myself out somehow, blizzard be damned. Furniture blocks my way as I scrabble towards the door, only to find that it is gone; stacked chests guarding nothing. The windows have vanished as well, unbroken surfaces where they once were situated. Whatever fell magic has brought the animals to life has also stolen away all manner of egress.

I am trapped with my demons.

As if my very thought has summoned it, the wolf snares my pant leg betwixt its teeth, yanking me from my feet. I land bodily upon my weapon. Within moments, the wolf's jaw has latched onto my ankle, biting deep. I scream in torment, trying to bring the shotgun to bear while it savages my flesh: ripping, wrenching, tearing. The pain is like nothing I've ever felt, hot and acrid like lava.

The creature relinquishes its hold, drawing back for a lunge, and I finally manage to bring my weapon to bear. I pull both triggers just as the wolf pounces, the deafening roar is like music to my ears. A veritable torrent of birdshot strikes the animal full in the chest, mere inches from the barrels, sending it careering backwards, its lifeless husk thumping to the ground in a most satisfying manner.

From the darkness, the owl screeches in remonstration, and the elk seems to double its efforts; the pounding of hooves is ceaseless, as if it possesses dozens of feet, each drubbing against the wall in a frenzy. The room seems lighter now, as if lit by braziers that are just out of view. My mangled leg makes standing difficult, yet I manage it all the same. In the corner, that which embodied my temper lies dead, fur still smoking from the point-blank impact.

Optimism wells within for the first time since my arrival; a lone vessel of hope atop a dark sea of despair. If I can kill my ire, then I can vanquish my other sinister aspects as well. The latch on the breach slides easily; I load two more shells into the gun while searching for the strix.

But the devil bird is faster than I. It swoops in from behind, sharp talons grazing painfully across my scalp as it soars past. I turn, tracking its flight with the gun. However, it is far too fast, my lameness slowing my motions considerably. The blood trickling into my eyes is also proving a hindrance. Several seconds pass, the beating of my heart competing with the elk's hooves, each thumping impossibly loud. The beast is almost free; hindquarters pulling through, forelegs stamping on the floor. I will need to contend with him shortly.

First, however, the owl. My pride.

I sweep the weapon from side to side, not knowing where to aim. I can sense my foe, however, somewhere in the clutter, beady eyes surveilling, stalking me as surely as a predator in tall grass. It will strike while my attention is diverted, as conceit is wont to do. Of this, I am certain.

The elk steals my attention for a trice, and some preternatural impulse warns me of the bird at my back. My ploy has proven successful. I kneel down as the owl sails overhead, directly into my line of fire. Thunder once again fills the air. My opponent, vitiated by a salvo of small steel, bursts into a flurry of bloody feathers that drift to the ground in silent defeat.

I have overcome both my anger and my pride; my shoulders already feel less burdened. The room is brighter as well, as though the sun itself has been contained within the cabin's walls, burning away shadow and distress with fiery intensity. For the briefest of moments, I see my wife's face, filled with the vibrant vitality of which I am familiar. She smiles at me, the warmth of her expression heating my skin, scintillating radiance igniting my each and every nerve.

Such a vision can mean only one thing; that terrible future glimpsed in my dream need not come to pass. My downfall can be avoided. So long as I remain steadfast, I can...

Before my mind can finish the thought, a sharp agony flares across my back, white-hot and debilitating. I need not even glance down; the antlers piercing through my chest extend for several feet in front of me, dripping with ichor.

My wife's aspect dissipates, drifting apart as if a dandelion on a breeze. The light tapers as well. I am back in the cabin, door and windows obstructed, gloominess ubiquitous and stifling. My wound steams in the cold air; that my tomb is glacial seems fitting. The beast steps back, extracting its horns from my rent flesh. What little strength I have fails, unresponsive limbs spilling the shotgun to the floor with an impotent clatter. My body follows shortly thereafter. I cannot inhale no matter how I struggle.

We stare at each other for several minutes, my remorse and I, while my very lifeblood stains the floor beneath me. Compunction seeps out with it. What a buffoon I was, believing that I could subdue my regret by running away. By facing it alone in some godforsaken wilderness. I should have known such an act would lead only to folly.

But it is now, and shall forever remain, far too late.

THE STOWAWAY

The stowaway shivered slightly, sequestered secretly within the sailing ship's storage. The scow seesawed across salty surf; cargo creaking; seamen swearing.

Suddenly, the ship slammed against some shrouded shoal, shuddering and splintering. Shrieking sailors splashed into the sea. The vessel veered violently, capsizing quickly. Seawater swept in through the shattered side, snatching at the stowaway, wrenching him within the windswept waves.

He swam towards shelter, a single slab of safety seen. But the slab was scaly; serpentine; squirming. The very villain who had vitiated the vessel. A stupendous sea snake, swimming sinuously towards him, swallowing. Swiftly silencing the stowaway's screams.

SEE NO EVIL (CADENZA)

Wherein secrets and revelations are shared, a dangerous hunt begins, and the ultimate evil is let loose.

Dramatis Personae

James Guthrie
An inspector with the London constabulary

Constance Wright
A prostitute in London's Poplar district

R.M. Müller
An unscrupulous man of science and medicine

Lady Ellington
A powerful Ministry official

Constable Higgins
A young policeman

Milton Dinsmore
An inventor and craftsman

Schaffer

JACK WELLS

A metalworker and tradesman
The Director
A mysterious figure with an agenda

CHAPTER XVII

R.M. Müller
Undisclosed Location
Sept 14th, 1892
Research Journal Entry # 107
4:23 AM

The director has concluded the initial portion of the project to be complete, and we have begun the laborious process of dismantling the base of operations. All the laboratory and experimental equipment is being carefully wrapped and boxed in due fashion. The cage will be cut down and rendered into scrap, though I do not know what will become of the raw materials. I have not received much information, only that we are moving to a larger facility. Phase two, as I have come to understand, will involve applying what we have learned here to an assignment broader in capacity.

I, of course, have my suppositions. Though I do not know the particulars of what the director has dubbed "the think tank," she has confided in me its ultimate objective, and there are only so many ways in which we can make it a reality. In addition, now that we have proven the feasibility of both the reanimation process and the physical alterations to a test subject, it would only make sense to use such knowledge to improve the procedures and methodologies thereof. To build a better beast, as it were.

{But I would be fooling myself to think that this initial creation is to be our only one. No, the director's plan is far too ambitious for a single "disciple," as she has begun calling it.}

{Also, I cannot help but find the religious connotation disquieting. Is her choice of moniker intentional? Or does it simply sound fitting? Either way, I do not care for it in the slightest. Even a God-fearing man such as myself can understand the vital importance of keeping church and science separate. A collision of religious zeal and scientific fervor is unlikely to end in anything other than catastrophe.}

As for the creature itself, it was moved (under the director's careful guidance) to a specially designed carriage, a metal-reinforced monstrosity which requires four Clydesdales to pull. Aside from the occasional clicks and mewls, our creation was almost docile in its movements. The same cannot be said for the horses, all of whom became uneasy in the creature's presence, snorting and stamping their disapproval most emphatically.

Is it the stench that dismays them so, or some other, more heightened sensory input we humans do not possess? I have heard of dogs and cats behaving warily around mentally defective or psychotic persons. Occasionally, even, to the point of attacking said individuals, a feral side emerging as some sort of innate defense mechanism. Perhaps horses have the same level of instinctual intuition? If our creation, in its undeath, elicits such reactions in animals, that information will be useful. I am already thinking of the myriad variables—distance, exposure, type of animal, etc.

{NOTE – discuss this with the director at earliest convenience.}

On that note, I must also annotate that I have overheard several of the assistants discussing an aura that emanates from our creation. An invisible cloud, insidious and pervasive, like echoes of loathsome emotions. Emotions which have somehow bridged the veil of the afterlife. I have not experienced these phenomena myself, and such melodramatic descriptions make me question the veracity of their statements. Still, judging by the horses' reactions, I feel further study may be warranted.

Where the director is taking the creature, I cannot say. The only thing she will tell me is that a trial awaits. To say that I am dismayed would be an understatement. There are still so many factors we have yet to assess. There are too many unknowns. Too many ways in which control could be lost.

{A field test this early is not only bad science but also, quite frankly, a grave mistake. I can appreciate that the director is remaining heavily involved with the program instead of the endless delegating and pointless intermediaries which most people in power choose to employ. But, that said, I still feel the potential dangers outweigh any possible benefits. I keep my reservations unvoiced, however. It is not my place to question my betters.}

Nevertheless, there are questions I feel compelled to ask. Especially when it comes to how the creature will navigate. All of this effort to produce a being incapable of even the most basic directional functions, including pathfinding around unfamiliar locations and obstacles, seems like a gross oversight. Unbridled strength is next to useless if it cannot be aimed. The director assures me that a third party is handling a method for providing sight, and my expertise will soon be required in installing the optical implement that was fabricated.

{Exactly who is performing this additional work is not shared with me, and I know better than to inquire. I also cannot help but wonder what the ophthalmic design will entail. I do not doubt that the reality will be far different from what my imagination has conjured.}

It is a strange sight—the director riding atop the dickey box alongside the coachman, her face obscured from view by a dark veil. Unafraid to be in the thick of things—an impressive attribute. But she has her responsibilities, and I have mine. I return to the busywork of packing up our equipment (save for my operating theatre, which will be utilized again today) whilst the carriage, along with its fiendish cargo, disappears into the pre-dawn gloom. The echoing staccato of horseshoes is an ominous rhythm that reverberates deep within my bones. A funeral march played at double time.

{I am not ashamed to admit that our handiwork fills me with terror and pride in equal measure. There is no disgrace in such an admission. To fear one's own creation must surely be the apotheosis of creative science—a portent that arriving at the zenith of man's great intellect will likely be the very catalyst of his downfall. Whether now or a thousand years hence, we will surely be the architects of our own extinction. Our own worst enemy. A self-fulfilling prophecy. Such thoughts send me traipsing along endless roads of conjecture. Some related, some tangential. Far too many contemplations to list, though one train of thought reigns supreme.

Can that which is unalive be rendered dead again, should the need arise?

And, if such a feat is possible, by what methods could it be accomplished? Decapitation? Immolation? Trauma to the brain? More ambiguities and assumptions to be added to the ever-growing list. I do not like how many unknowns we still face (a side-effect of my atelophobia). But scientific progress is a messy enterprise, as competitive as any sport and oftentimes violent. Eggs and omelets, as the saying goes.}

{As to the matter of what will transpire when the carriage reaches its destination, I am endeavouring not to dwell upon it. For what can come from such a secretive test other than wreckage and pain?}

CHAPTER XVIII

The sun has not yet risen as Milton makes his way back to the workshop. Perpetually up before dawn, Milt has discovered the older he gets the less sleep he requires. Even a handful of hours seems enough for his old bones. *One of the only upsides to aging,* he thinks wryly.

Of course, there are plenty of downsides as well, not the least of which is the gout forming in his knees and feet, which, aside from frequent periods of pain, also produces a hitch in his step. It has gotten bad enough to require the use of a cane for any lengthy constitutionals. But even with the discomfort, Milt doesn't mind the walk. It gives him time alone with his thoughts, and he rather enjoys how rakish he looks with the custom walking stick, as though he were some dauntless aristocrat lifted straight from the pages of a gentleman's periodical. Plus, any time away from Schaffer's bellicose presence is a good thing. Even a paltry six hours of separation from the big man and the workshop has done wonders for Milt's spirits.

While waiting for Schaffer to retrieve their final donor, Milton will spend the day performing cleanup duties, removing all traces of their activities from the workshop. Personal knick-knacks will be segregated and placed into valises. Any scrap pieces of metal, glass, and leather are bound for the forge to be melted down or incinerated as per their composition. Packing up all of his fine tooling, including the specialized medical implements recently delivered, will take the longest, as each piece must be arranged with care. But Milt doesn't mind the effort. On the contrary—it is punctilious in a way that soothes his methodical mind.

There is nary a soul in sight as he trudges along the back streets of the Yard, warehouse exteriors dark and uninviting, the air as still as held breath. Even in the early hours, some fog is present, though not so thick as to hinder his progress. But something feels off. There is a strange murmur in the mist, a charge not unlike what is generated by the DOVE, though Milt cannot ascertain the source. A rotten tang assails his nostrils as if sewage has spilled out onto the cobblestones. Milt glances around for the source of his disquiet, to no avail. The only thing that appears out of the ordinary is a large, unadorned carriage parked near the workshop, similar in style to those used for transporting prisoners, with four imposing stallions harnessed to the yoke. The driver is nowhere to be seen. A predawn delivery to one of the neighbouring mills, perhaps? The fellow could very well be lost—it is easy enough to get turned around within Blackwall's winding avenues, even for locals. Whatever it is, however, it surely has nothing to do with him or the hidden millwork, so Milt pushes it from his mind.

It is only when he approaches the workshop and notices that the door is ajar that he suspects something is amiss. An inky blackness lingers just beyond the portal, a gloom as impenetrable as the ocean depths. He strains for a moment, listening intently. Silence is all that greets him. The smell is also far stronger, and Milt realizes it is emanating from within the shop itself. It is rare for him to experience any hesitancy, but he feels it now, one foot still suspended midstride.

The door was latched and secured when they left, of that he is certain. The deadbolt, crude in design but sturdy in craftsmanship, would be unlikely to fail without vigorous assistance, nor would such a heavy iron door be able to swing open of its own accord. Furthermore, in spite of his many faults, Schaffer wasn't one to overlook closing up after his comings and goings, especially if he had brought another doxie back in the small hours. Given the pitch-black conditions within, nobody boasting credible intentions was liable to be toiling away on a borrowed lathe. No, the only explanation is that someone had forced their way inside for a more mendacious purpose. It is also possible that they are still haunting the premises.

A chill which has nothing to do with the autumn season races down his spine. Never one to be unprepared, Milton twists the handle on his cane, the thin blade hidden within its shaft springing free with a satisfying rasp. Three feet long and razor-sharp, such a rapier is deadly in the right hands. Milton is more than passingly familiar with the weapon—his best years may reside in the past, but he is not so gammy as to be incapable of giving a thieving wharf rat what for. Provided they didn't choose to employ his own shotgun against him.

Stepping within the workshop's interior is akin to entering a slaughter-house, only much fouler. The air lies thick with rancid humidity, and Milt feels his gorge rising, the bile of half-digested breakfast searing his esophagus. That feeling of wrongness intensifies, a cold sweat slicking his skin in response. Darkness reigns. Every sound seems muffled and amplified at the same time. Refusing to be mastered by his fear, Milt navigates further inside by memory, rapier held at the ready.

"I admit that I was expecting a rather different welcome, Mr. Dinsmore, all things considered," calls a familiar voice from the gloom. The woman's dulcet tenor, soft but firm, startles him so thoroughly that the sword nearly slips from his fingers. "Do you intend on running me through?"

"No, madam, not at all. My apologies," Milt replies, letting out a long breath of relief. He returns the blade to its sheath with a click. He knew his patron would be arriving today but did not expect her so early, nor did he expect to find her lurking in the dark like a dodgy cutpurse. Standing near the workbench, her silhouette is barely visible, no more than the vaguest hint of corporeality. A shade amongst shadows.

His patron has never offered her name, and he has never asked. Over the course of several meetings, he has only gleaned she is clever, impatient, and authoritative. Whatever her background and whatever her intentions, he neither knows nor cares. One does not last long in the commerce of disreputable dealings by getting chummy with the clientele.

"I see that my special requisition has yet to be completed, despite the very specific deadline. A deadline which has come and gone. Is there a problem with the instructions you received?"

Milt is not sure how she is managing to see anything in the darkened room, nor does he understand how the smell isn't overwhelming her feminine sensibilities, but he keeps his thoughts unvoiced. Patronizing Schaffer is one thing—being antagonistic towards the boss would be ill-advised, to say the least. He swallows hard before answering.

"No, ma'am, that's not it at all. We, ah, ran into a slight impediment. An unexpected delay, nothing more."

"A delay," she responds, drawing out the last syllable long enough to change the question into an accusation. The disapproval in her voice is more than evident. "Would you care to explain?"

Milt swallows again, harder this time. His throat has gone bone dry. "It was the eyes, madam. The second set, to be precise. I, ah, deemed them to be defective, so I took the liberty of disposing of them. Schaffer will acquire a new pair tonight."

She makes no response, which seems even worse than a dressing down. Perhaps she is waiting for more clarification?

"The second lass was nearsighted, I believe, so I felt it prudent to find a better candidate. To furnish you with the best possible product, of course."

There is a long pause before she answers. "Of course. I suppose it couldn't be helped. But let us talk about your commission. Have you drawn up any diagrams or plans, anything that provides detail for the harness' design?"

"No, madam," he replies, shaking his head. "Mental schematics only, with measurements and adjustments verbally communicated. No annotations. We wrote nothing down, per your request."

"Very good. Your work is quite exceptional considering you were forced to work without references. Quite exceptional, indeed. More's the pity that we won't be working together in the future."

A putrid draft washes over him from behind, as rank and vile as a midden heap mixed with a latrine. The stench forces him to gag uncontrollably. Before Milt can react further, four hands grab him by the shoulders and forearms, squeezing hard. He tries to struggle, to break free, but cannot match their strength. The assailants' fingers are like iron, smooth and unyielding. As cold as the grave. Old bones creak agonizingly under the powerful grip, causing Milt to hiss in pain. Whoever is accosting him, he never heard them approach. He can't even hear them breathing. But there's something about their positioning that doesn't seem right. As if it's only one person flanking him instead of two.

Their footfalls may have been silent, but one lets out a keening moan every few moments, making his skin crawl. Even more unsettling, however, is the malignant pall that accompanies the hands. It's as if a shroud of pure evil has enveloped him, rife with the inescapability of quiet decay, smothering Milt's senses like a heavy blanket. Even the big man, with his finger collection and torturer's heart, did not command so revolting an aura.

Milt longs to turn his head, to see just what is causing such an unearthly disturbance. But he refuses to give this woman the satisfaction. If intimidation is to be her game, then Milt is determined to face such a tactic with bravery. As much as he can muster, at least.

His patron speaks again, utterly calm, a sharp contrast to the distress that he currently feels. He gets the impression she is an old hand at navigating unpleasant situations. "I admire your prudence, Mr. Dinsmore. Truly, I do. Such proactiveness is hard to find. Unfortunately, I have my own deadlines to meet, and the harness is needed now. As such, I am forced to acquire the last set of eyes forthwith. And yours seem to function flawlessly."

Milt's stomach drops like a stone, testicles clenching painfully. So much for his attempt at bravery. Schaffer's threat reverberates through his skull, eerily prophetic. As if the big man had somehow foreseen this very moment. "No!" Milt cries, struggling anew. It cannot end like this. Not here, not now. But it is no use. The hands are far too strong. He may as well be fighting a statue.

"What about Schaffer, that hulking gobshite!?" Milt hates the quaver in his voice, but panic has set in, a push for survival as raw and desperate as any animal instinct. Now is not the time to be worried about humiliation. Now is the time to grasp at any and all straws. "That ogre's antics have surely caused no end of trouble. But I... I was careful! I followed your instructions to the letter! I only did as I was asked!"

"You did, and you have my gratitude. As for Schaffer, I'll admit that he has been a tad... judicious in executing the plan. And yet, such methods are not without their allure. He may be nothing more than a blunt instrument, but using the DOVE in such a fashion was surprisingly imaginative. No, despite his imperfections, Schaffer still has his uses. You, on the other hand, have regrettably outlived yours. This is where we part ways, Mr. Dinsmore. On behalf of the cause, I thank you."

She takes several steps backwards, disappearing completely into the darkness like a phantom. Milton's struggles become less and less vigorous as his strength fails. In spite of all of his thrashing, he hasn't been able to budge an inch. Warm urine flows down his leg as his bladder turns traitor, and he can't help but feel a sudden kinship with the dead prostitutes, each one pissing herself out of fear while Milt leered and salivated and shuddered with voyeuristic ecstasy. If that isn't poetic justice, then he doesn't know what is. A profound weariness settles upon him, spreading from the inside out, turning his insides to jelly. He now understands what utter defeat feels like. And, more importantly, what Schaffer's victims endured during their final moments when Death came for them with outstretched arms and a black-toothed grin.

Will he be able to witness his own soul escape as he dies? The thought blooms unbidden across his psyche, the sole intelligible cognition to emerge from his mind's frantic churn. A wholly trite reflection for such a dire moment, yet perfectly in character.

"I require the head only," the woman states, sounding as if she is suddenly leagues away. Her voice is dispassionate. Indifferent. As clinical as that of a sawbones performing battlefield triage. "Do what you will with the rest."

No response comes from behind him, but something shifts in the ether. An abrupt change in the malevolent force pervading the room. Two hands move to his skull, cupping under his chin and behind his neck, pulling upwards with all the might of a cargo hoist. The other two remain on his shoulders, holding his body in place. Milt's fear gives way to blinding agony as his jaw crumples under the pressure, the bone snapping like kindling.

His spine soon follows, the vertebrae separating like an accordion's bellows, each popping as though overtaxed rivets. The scream erupting from his lips turns into a wet gargle as his vocal cords rip and tear. Inconceivable pressure mounts and mounts, and it only takes a few more seconds for the hands to separate his head and body with a glutinous pop.

And then Milton Dinsmore, craftsman of the bizarre and purveyor of perversions, is no more.

CHAPTER XIX

I arrive at headquarters early, determined to jot down some notes and get Higgins up to speed before my appointment with Lady Ellington. I cannot think of it as anything else. Ours is certainly not a social engagement, nor, heaven forbid, a personal coquetry. It is a debrief and a sharing of information, nothing more.

Much to my dismay, most of my finery was nowhere near nonpareil enough for rubbing elbows with the nobility, obliging me to settle for a suit at least a decade out of fashion. Ridding the garments of their mothball scent was a chore unto itself, the effort of which has left me in an irritable mood. I am a working man with a utilitarian mindset—strutting around in a dandy's wardrobe makes me feel as though I am playacting, as puffed-up and self-important as a peacock.

At least my face is cleanshaven and my wild hair tamed with pomade. My features favor those of my father: strong jaw offset by deep-set eyes, a narrow nose with a bridge straighter than a ruler, thin eyebrows that make me look perpetually troubled. My rowdy shock of thick brown hair, however, was inherited from my mother. Of course, it looks far better on her than it does me. I will never claim to be handsome, but I manage to clean up nicely.

London's back alleys are not the only place where rumours travel at speed; news of my temporary reassignment has already made the rounds through the rank and file of the Limehouse constabulary, prompting a multitude of reactions. Some of my colleagues appear genuinely happy about my change of scenery. Others appraise me through fresh eyes, openly reassessing me and my place within the department's tacit hierarchy, not yet ready to abandon their neutrality but open to the possibility. As for my detractors, this changeup (and my attire) has only strengthened their already low opinion of me. I know they believe I am intentionally hobnobbing with the nobility to advance my career. Nothing could be further from the truth, of course, but any protestations to the contrary would only fall on deaf ears.

That *they* would hobnob if they were in my shoes isn't worth dwelling upon. Fighting hypocrisy with further hypocrisy is a recipe for failure, and if my mother has taught me anything, it is this: if you behave no better, then you are no better.

Even still, there are days when the high road seems rather difficult to traverse.

True to form, Barnhold can't even be bothered to inform me of my new duties in person. Instead, a hastily typewritten memorandum was left on my desk, detailing the particulars of my reassignment, his scorn evident despite the formal language used. Which is fine—he can remain holed up in his office for all I care. I am in no mood to deal with his bureaucratic bumbling today. He has his function, I have mine, and we are under no obligation to meet in the middle as friends.

Nor is his letter the only new paraphernalia to be found on my blotter; a wrinkled flyer has also mysteriously appeared, some cheaply manufactured epistle on onion-thin paper, warning that the supposed Werewolf of London has been overheard in Mayfair. The accompanying artwork of the beast itself is ridiculously exaggerated and rather disproportionate. *He'll rip your lungs out, Jim!* is scrawled across the flyer in large, flowing script.

Another of England's ubiquitous folktales, the werewolf has been spotted or heard in nearly every district for the past several decades. The incidents are invariably similar—a citizen will report hearing howls and snarls of a particularly ferocious nature, far more stentorian than those of a common cur. Some will even claim to have spied the beast, larger (of course) than even the largest of men. Flyers will be printed, the constabulary will investigate (finding nothing, naturally), and nothing further will come from it.

This constant cycle does nothing to dissuade public belief, however. A copious number of grisly murders have been blamed on the creature, as well as the disappearances of innumerable women, children, pets, and livestock. Inspector Francis Aberline of Scotland Yard (no relation to Inspector Frederick Abberline of the London Metropolitan Police—my mentor and the lead investigator in the Ripper case) claimed to have personally encountered the werewolf in 1891, first in the guise of a man (famed Shakespeare actor Lawrence Talbot) and then again in wolf form on several occasions shortly afterwards. He further attests that it perished, from a silver bullet no less, in the woods on the outskirts of the Talbot family estate. Such proclamations were met with much derision within the force. Ultimately, the powers that be chalked the incident up to nothing more than an especially violent case of psychosis, primarily due to Mr. Talbot being aggrieved by the sudden death of his twin brother months earlier. A woman was also purported to have been involved, though her identity was never officially disclosed. The contradictive rumours surrounding Lawrence Talbot were nearly comical in their abundance. The constabulary were left with egg on their face (Scotland Yard in particular), with backlash by the aristocracy being especially severe. Inspector Aberline was summarily dismissed, and the incident was quietly swept under the rug.

Regardless of whether Aberline was telling the truth or not, reports of werewolf sightings in and around London have continued unabated. My personal opinion is that the entire incident was, and is, a load of hogwash. Despite having witnessed many a strange or inexplicable occurrence throughout my career, I do not believe in supernatural monsters or occult happenings. Every crime I have investigated, even those that appeared impossibly baffling at the outset, was eventually distilled down to human ingenuity and iniquity.

I may have let slip, early on in my career, that I would like to use deductive reasoning to debunk the werewolf myth once and for all. It was an honest proclamation, albeit somewhat naïve. Naturally, my colleagues took my statement and ran with it, and now, whenever news of the beast resurfaces, they are quick to have fun at my expense. Given that I will meet Lady Ellington in that general vicinity, they must have found the timing quite comical indeed.

Unfortunately, I am unable to join them for a much-needed chuckle; the time is rapidly approaching for said appointment, and I'll be damned if I am going to blemish the station's reputation by being tardy. The social club where I am to meet her is a good distance away, situated between the districts of Mayfair and Soho. Further than the walk I took with Higgins and Connor. As such, though I am loath to be anywhere near horses, an aversion which stems from a childhood incident best left undisclosed, I must enlist the services of a hansom cab.

I check my suit once more, making sure no chalk dust has blemished the elbows and that the shoulders and collar are free of ash. It is the same care with which I attend to my uniform, though that is more a matter of pride than appearance. It's not enough to act the part; one must also look the part. It is a rare occasion indeed when I am not bedecked in the attire of my station, during the daylight hours at least, and the absence of my uniform, cap, and truncheon is keenly felt.

With nothing left do to within the station, I make my way to the street, flagging down a cab with only the slightest twinge of trepidation. That I am perfectly willing to chase after an alleged monster and yet remain utterly terrified of domesticated equine is the very pinnacle of irony.

Nevertheless, I have investigated far more equestrian-related deaths than those purportedly caused by a moon-obsessed, shapeshifting lupine beast, so I stand by my assertion.

Horses are, beyond any doubt, the deadlier creatures by far.

CHAPTER XX

Illumined by morning's cold light and girt by the deafening silence of solitude, Constance lies motionless, comfortably swaddled within second-hand bedsheets, Fi's pillow still clutched in her arms. Dried tears dig painfully at the corners of puffy eyes. Time seems viscous, advancing slower than should be possible. The last vestiges of sleep linger with quiet defiance, clinging to her mind like anxious children to the skirts of hovering mothers.

After the late night devoted to breaking the news around Poplar, revisiting the pain each time, she was altogether spent. The sorrow that filled her heart was its own manner of exhaustion, pressing down with the weight of rain-sodden clothing, rendering her physically and emotionally numb. As muddled as an opium addict. The bevy of beverages hadn't helped. By the time Constance finally crawled into bed, drunk and dizzy, she was almost completely incoherent.

Despite sleeping like the dead, no apparitions came to visit her in the night. No red-headed ghost hovering by the bedside whilst imparting strange tidings. The only things to haunt her were dreams, transitory visions that vacillated between whimsical and terrifying, flowing from one to the other with little rhyme or reason. Fiona was present, radiant as always. Inspector Guthrie made several appearances as well. Despite her belief in the paranormal, Constance isn't quite sold on the idea that dreams are portents or pathways to the netherworld. Enigmatic though it may be, the brain is, as far as she's concerned, simply a mechanism that never rests, much like the heart. Albeit one which occasionally behaves in the most inexplicable of manners.

Again, much like the heart.

Not that Constance allows herself to dwell on sentimentality overmuch. The daily grind of the working class allows for no other outlook than stoic practicality. Consequently, there exist several proverbs by which she lives her life. Truisms which have become ingrained upon her psyche, day by arduous day, until they are practically instinctive.

First and foremost is that no good deed goes unpunished. If there was a singular law by which the lives of the poor were governed, that would be it. Second, and no less significant, is that both fish and unexpected visitors begin to smell after three days. The third is that there is no rest for the wicked. Given the means by which Constance puts bread on the table (or nightstand, since there is no room for actual dining furniture), she is considered very wicked indeed.

And yet, despite her wanton impiety, she is more refreshed now than she's been in months. The wicked might not get much rest—unfortunate souls suffering from fatigue were another matter entirely. Constance cannot recall the last time she slept so deeply.

That her repose was abetted by a full belly is only a matter of course. The gold sovereign spent easily enough, disappearing like greased lightning into the coin purse of a streetside produce merchant, even though his remaining wares had begun to spoil. Some of the leftover change paid for assorted canapés from The Blackened Biscuit, Poplar's least reputable pub. Food enough for three meals, and yet Constance hadn't left so much as a single crumb for the dormice. Small wonder that London's wealthy seemed so lethargic and soft; a stocked larder and live-in cook would ensure that she remained abed from dawn to dusk. And her undergarments could even stay on. It's a nice reverie, but one upon which she cannot allow herself to dwell. The need to find Fiona's killer supersedes Constance's torpor, an insistent pressure that refuses to be ignored. The body's hunger has been mollified—slaking her thirst for vengeance is all that remains.

There is nothing for it but to rise and get dressed. At least she can be herself again, tarted up and feminine, dirty wharf rat clothing stashed under the bed once more. She dons her most eye-catching dress. The eyeliner runs out right at the end, spread as far as it could go. Even her hair receives extra attention. She's never known a good method for marching towards certain danger, but Constance is determined to look comely regardless.

She does, however, forgo a brassiere entirely. Normally, she would try to heighten her femininity, augmenting her curves through any and all means. Cleavage is almost always a sure bet in her profession or any other. But, for her plan to succeed, she must appear childlike. As smooth as a rail.

Imparting bad news and gorging herself were not the only activities with which Constance occupied her day. She had also interrogated several other whores about a pugnacious man with big hands. One who favored scrawny girls. While several johns fit the bill, most of the women agreed that the culprit sounded like a man named Schaffer, an itinerant tradesman of the Isle. The kind of dodgy fellow who enjoyed forcing doxies to perform acts with which they weren't comfortable, with invariably painful and bloody results. His name had cropped up along the grapevine with enough regularity to not seem like a coincidence.

Schaffer. Hardly a name befitting a monster. But such is the way of the world. People were more than happy to create fanciful stories of grotesque creatures—the more sinister the better—ascribing all manner of violent and reprehensible behaviour to them. The penny dreadfuls stacked beside the bed bear testimony to the fact.

But one needn't look much further than their peers and neighbours to understand that the worst fiends are far from imaginary.

Along with his name, she was also provided with Schaffer's particulars, a rudimentary description which should nevertheless enable her to recognize him with ease. Most tradesmen only owned a couple of outfits, and even then, they were complemented with the same basic accessories. This man preferred suspenders and a tattered scarf secured with a false knot. Contrary to popular fashion, he also favored leaving his head bare. Armed with such information, she feels confident that picking him out of a crowd won't prove difficult.

She can't help but think of Guthrie and the irony of their situation. If Constance finds the killer first, removing him from life's mortal coil by whichever method is most expedient (preferably a dagger in the gullet), the inspector will come after her instead. Murdering a murderer might make for great headlines, but vigilante justice is still illegal. And Guthrie isn't the type of bobby to look the other way, justification be damned. The law is ironclad for men like him. Inviolate. Of course, he'll be searching for Connor, but that temporary disguise will only slow him down. Everyone in Poplar knows where Fiona lived. Everyone knows who her roommate really was. From those details alone, the inspector would undoubtedly put two and two together with relative ease.

Constance must also concede that she might not survive her encounter with Schaffer. The man is adept at taking lives, after all, and much larger than she. Her paltry blade may not be enough to fell someone of that size and ferocity. But one thing is certain—if Constance is to go down, she has no intention of going quietly. She'll make him work for it, kicking and screaming the entire way, creating enough of a ruckus to be heard all the way to Buckingham Palace.

Perhaps it is anguish which instills a fatalistic indifference inside her heart, but Constance is, strangely enough, at peace with either outcome. Due to both profession and social standing, peril has never been far from her doorstep. The mortality rate amongst the poor is certainly not low. Not that she wishes for death. She still has her youth, and, for now, her health. There is always the slim hope of something better coming her way. Even so, she won't be able to move on until she confronts the killer and hopefully delivers his comeuppance in the process.

Makeup applied and stiletto secreted in her stocking, Constance takes one last wistful look around the room. It is possible that she won't be returning home after today. Not that it's much of a home without Fi. Memories and a few inexpensive trinkets cannot fill in the gaps, and recollections don't make for the best of ghosts. Much better to be haunted by the real thing.

"We'll get him, Fi," she vows, voice quiet but steady. "One way or another. Either I will, or I'll soften him up enough so the bobbies can finish the job. I miss you, lass, with an ardor I didn't think possible. And I suspect that shall always be the case."

CHAPTER XXI

R.M. Müller
Undisclosed Location
Sept 14th, 1892
Research Journal Entry # 113
9:22 AM

The director returned several hours ago, while I enjoyed a few moments of much-needed rest. Even with the discomfort of a hard cot and thin pillow, I must have been in the deepest of slumbers not to have heard the carriage arrive.

{I am slightly chagrined to have been asleep when she returned, as if a guard caught napping at his post. But the relentless pace of this project has been grueling, and I am no longer as spry as I once was. I must allow myself a catnap or two when time allows, or I will surely topple over. Even if all I have at hand is this damnable army bunk.}

Despite my fears, she assures me the field test went as well as could be expected. I cannot help my inquisitive mind from wanting to learn more of the particulars, including what went flawlessly and the places where things fell short, but prudence dictates that I keep my mouth shut. I must trust that I will learn what I need to in due course.

{Except for the eyes. There is no need for me to know where they came from, nor do I have any particular desire to be informed. In this regard, if nothing else, ignorance is bliss. Conversely—the lingering question of what my other set of surgical implements was needed for has been answered.}

Though I am not easily impressed, the optical harness she has brought me is a rather remarkable manufacturing feat. While the principal design is relatively simple, rarely have I seen such precise metalwork outside of scientific and surgical apparatus. Using a cured leather apron to mitigate leakage while ensuring a snug fitment, no doubt a trick devised by a shipwright or seasoned dock worker, was an inspired idea. It also adds to the overall durability of the construction, as does the steel used in the eye channels. The fact that the harness will allow our creation vision at four opposing points, ergo a full 360 degrees, is nothing short of genius.

If there is anywhere the piece could fail or be compromised, it is the thin glass of the channels themselves. And that is through no fault of the engineered design so much as the inherent fragility of glass in general. This is but a minor concern, however, and cannot be helped.

{Now that I understand how our creation will perceive the world, and therefore just how effective it could be in the right circumstances, I am starting to realize the depth of the director's commitment to her intricate web of revolution. I have always known she had vision, but now I am truly witnessing the full force of her drive. The lengths to which she will go in order to succeed. With but a handful of such "disciples", she can accomplish what Guy Fawkes and his thirty-six barrels of gunpowder could not.}

{On that topic—I do not know the sequence of events which have caused her to become so disenchanted with England's government in general, and the aristocracy in particular. We all have our motivations for turning to

treasonous behaviour. For some, it's money. For others, it's a chance to be a part of something new. Something powerful. Whatever the director's reasons, I have no doubt they are equally as justified as my own.}

As for her immediate plan, everything seems to be running smoothly. The entirety of this location has been vacated by all personnel and emptied of all equipment, save for the antechamber with my surgical paraphernalia. The rest of the required tools and sundry have been set on a cart. I review them one final time to ensure nothing is missing:

One sealed bucket of reanimation fluid.

One small spindle of fine silver filament, roughly twenty feet's worth.

{Far more than I'll need, but it won't hurt to have extra, just in case.}

One canister of tree resin (waterproofing sealant for the glass and optical wiring).

Two horsehair paintbrushes for resin application.

Electric soldering iron (of experimental design).

One canister of solder.

Four sets of eyeballs, with optical nerves intact. One blue pair, two sets of brown, and one green pair.

{Although it serves no scientific purpose, I am compelled to catalogue them all the same.}

Our creation is already within the operating theatre, lying atop the physician's table once more, completely motionless. How the director convinced it to go prone is anyone's guess. I also cannot begin to estimate how long this procedure will take. Since I am not tampering with the fundamentals of human physiology and seeing as I possess a fair amount of ophthalmic knowledge, I would imagine only a handful of hours at most. Unlike grafting nerves, muscle, and bone to places where they technically have no business being, embedding the silver filament into the optic tract should be relatively straightforward.

As for whether it will have the desired outcome or not, that remains to be seen.

{Pun intended.}

Once again, the director has pressing matters to attend to, so I will perform this procedure unaccompanied. Lethargy is making my eyes and joints ache. I will need proper rest soon, or I'll be of no use to anyone. Possibly even a detriment. As for the director, she is as unfazed as ever—with as busy as her schedule is, I don't know how (or when) she finds time for sleep.

{Perhaps the intrigue fuels her, like some dark conspiratorial energy source. An inverse photosynthesis, assimilating shadow and whisper whilst the city sleeps, refining them in the crucible of her scorned heart until naught remains but hate. Or maybe it's merely the vigor of youth. Either way, she is more than welcome to her Machiavellian schemes; I am simply happy to create.}

Speaking of creation, I find the green eyes alluring in a way I cannot explain. I do believe that I shall put them in front.

CHAPTER XXII

Discomfort notwithstanding, I must admit that the horse-drawn carriage is remarkably efficient. London's fog is thinner than usual, and the driver makes excellent time across town, with nary a near-miss of a single pedestrian. In fact, I arrive at my destination almost a quarter of an hour early. Which gives me ample time to make sure I am presentable, not to mention a few moments to take stock of the location Lady Ellington has chosen.

I have heard of the New Somerville Club only in passing—the idle banter between my peers which I cannot help but overhear. It is, by all accounts, a very feminine-forward establishment, one of many such progressive businesses becoming increasingly popular with members of the fairer sex.

The social club is located directly above an Aerated Bread Company tearoom, yet another liberal enterprise that has proven quite lucrative. Men may have their billiards halls and smoking parlours (plus, admittedly, plenty of other options), but women are slowly gaining their own communal salons, locales where they can be free of chaperones and societal expectations. The ABC tearooms are just such a location, the bread and tea they serve being secondary considerations to the freedoms contained within their four walls. A place where ladies of all social stations can, quite literally, let their hair down.

I do not get any odd looks as I make my way through the ABC lounge. Female-centric though the locations might be, men are certainly not prohibited from partaking in their self-serve tea options. As a matter of fact, there are several other fellows dotted throughout the establishment, alone or seated close to their ladies, reading newspapers or other such periodicals. Each of them appears perfectly at ease.

Upstairs, however, is another matter entirely.

The New Somerville Club's hostess, a rather imposing woman who looks like she wrestles bulls for sport, greets me with a reception cool enough to cause frostbite. She may be dressed in the traditional waitstaff attire, but there is no mistaking her true function—the Somerville's equivalent of a bouncer. It goes without saying that she could likely knock my block clean off.

The woman intercepts me well before I have crossed the foyer. "No men," she practically growls, raising her hand with fingers splayed as if to stop me by force. Her gruff tone brooks no quarter. She takes one look at the badge held in my hand (which I have removed from my inspector's cap for this very purpose) and scoffs loudly. "Not even coppers. Unless by special invite."

I find myself somewhat fascinated by this sudden turn of events, a fascination which quickly turns to vexation. I have never before been rebuked due to my gender, let alone rebuffed despite being an officiant of the law. Quite a dramatic turning of the tables, I must admit. But, after I give the circumstances a moment's consideration, I find myself reevaluating my opinion. If I maintain that others could benefit from spending time in my shoes, it stands to reason that I should hold myself to the same standard. To maybe try and understand how things affect others for a change.

Truly, these impressions of frustration and incredulity must be how women feel when facing a "Gentlemen Only, Ladies Forbidden" placard. Second-class citizens, for all intents and purposes. Galling is the only word that seems to fit.

Stymied and unsure how to proceed, I tip my top hat in her direction. "Good morning, ma'am. Inspector Guthrie of the Limehouse Constabulary, here to meet Lady Ellington. I am, uh, expected."

The hostess' demeanor transforms only slightly, going from inhospitable to merely tolerant. I hesitate to think about how I would have been received had I not uttered Ellington's name. "Ah, very good, sir. You are, indeed, on the list. If you'll follow me."

She leads me into the Somerville's well-lit and cheery lounge. Its muted colors, soft edges, and numerous indoor plants are completely at odds with the inherently masculine equivalents to which I am accustomed. Instead of the aroma of tobacco and coffee, the air is filled with the cloying scent of spring: flowers, herbs, lemon, honey, and orange rind, to name a few. Never before have I experienced a more thoroughly gardenlike atmosphere contained within four walls.

The lounge itself is quite large, teeming with decorations and furniture without feeling cluttered. A cursory glance confirms that I am the only male in attendance, a fact which does not go unnoticed by the club's other occupants. A bevy of well-to-do ladies, many with handmaids in attendance, watch me as I pass, regarding me with unfeigned curiosity. As though I am the newest animal on display at the London Zoo. Or a prisoner enduring the long walk to face a magistrate. I can feel the women taking my measure, though whether I have been found wanting or not is anyone's guess. Their inscrutable expressions betray nothing.

Murderers, lunatics, and anarchists; I have had dealings with all manner of dangerous persons, in various settings. And yet, here amongst the upper crust of London society, in the presence of some of England's wealthiest and most powerful women, clad only in an antiquated suit, I feel hopelessly imperiled. If Lady Ellington's intent was to throw me off-kilter, she has succeeded quite admirably.

I cannot recall a single time when I have felt more at a disadvantage.

Situated near the rear of the establishment, seated on a divan ornate enough for a palace, my benefactor is barely recognizable. Gone are the tight trousers and economical tunic. Dressed in what I presume to be the latest in Parisian fashion, Lady Ellington commands attention with effortless grace. She was fetching before, in spite of her contentious ensemble—materializing from the gloom like a galvanizing apparition, challenging the mores of the era, and showing up the constables. But today she is stunning, every inch the Lady that her marriage to Viscount Atticus Ellington has made her.

That I researched my new boss prior to our follow-on meeting is only a matter of course; I prefer not to walk blindly into a thorny state of affairs whenever possible. Or at all, if I had my druthers, which I do not. Ergo, if I am to be a conditional puppet to the Ministry of Special Sciences, I felt that I should at least know a few details regarding the person pulling the strings.

Unfortunately (though not unexpectedly), the entire situation surrounding England's first female electrical engineer is, if I am being frank, quite unusual. Precious little is known about Amelia Ellington, née Griffiths, other than that she was considered a child prodigy in mathematics and several related—albeit undocumented—fields and had no title before being wedded to the Viscount at nineteen. Whilst it is not unheard of for the nobility to marry someone below their station, it occurs infrequently enough to attract attention. From commoner to a member of the peerage overnight—a daydream of many a British citizen, male and female alike.

After their much-publicized nuptials in 1887, details were harder to uncover. In spite of the many charitable events which London's elite were expected to support, from a sense of *noblesse oblige* if nothing else, the newly minted Lady Ellington was rarely in attendance, becoming somewhat of a recluse. Rumours abounded, as they are wont to do, with many insinuating she was in poor health or suffering from a fragile mental state. As such, news of her appointment to the Ministry came as quite a shock to both political pundits and idle gossipers alike.

Regarding her formal education, there was even less to unearth. That she is truly a graduate of Oxford is indisputable. This fact was verified by more than a few folks who would indeed possess knowledge of such an occurrence. Nevertheless, it is the how of it that remains a mystery. I maintain a tentative thread of hope that the topic will come up during our dialog.

But first, I must somehow hold my own within a veritable lioness' den.

"Milady, your invitee has arrived," the hostess announces as we halt beside the divan. An unnecessary announcement, as I am clearly visible, but such are the rules of England's damnable social etiquette. I make to hand the stout woman my coat and cap, which is evidently a New Somerville *faux pas*, for the scowl she shoots my way could strip rust off of a derelict's hull. Any goodwill I might have earned through the Viscount's name has thoroughly evaporated. "You can see to your own attire, good sir. You are a guest only, receiving no special privileges. Is that understood?"

By my side, Lady Ellington stifles a snort with the back of her hand. Judging by the tittering from the other ladies present, it is evident that the hostess' voice carried throughout the entire establishment. Heat crawls up my ears and the back of my neck, making me squirm uncomfortably—I do not handle embarrassment well on the best of days, and, like nearly every other fellow, nothing makes me feel quite so inadequate as the derision of pretty women.

"Sit down before you fall down, James," Lady Ellington says through a perfect smile, picking up on my discomfort.

She gestures to a nearby chair, the motions demure and graceful, far from the clinically trenchant efficiency she displayed at the dockside crime scene. Even her voice has changed; it was authoritative but pleasant during our first encounter, yet now it is full of the imperiousness of station. As haughty as a spoilt princess.

I find myself wary. Skittish even. My dislike of the nobility aside, the ease by which she has adopted a different façade is unsettling. She seems to be a different person entirely, as though deception were a skill she mastered long ago. It is not unheard of for certain predators to camouflage themselves, blending in with their surroundings to better trap their prey. And, as every commoner knows, the aristocracy is comprised of some of the most dangerous predators in Europe. Some are certainly not above toying with the working class for sport.

But is that what is happening here? And which persona is her true self? The arrogant woman of station? The intrepid scholar who defies the rules? Or someone else entirely?

Perhaps I'll manage to stave off embarrassment long enough to find out.

CHAPTER XXIII

To say Lady Ellington is well-versed in a myriad of topics, the vast majority of which are deemed "unbecoming" of a lady of station, would be an understatement. Her breadth of knowledge is both truly shocking and strangely intriguing.

She is also the single most gregariously aggressive person I have ever met—and completely unafraid to be so. Is it her wealth which enables her boldness? Her beauty? Her prestige? Or has she always been unconcerned about the way the world perceives her?

I am not one of those men who believes women are intellectually inferior. One needn't look very hard to see that the deck is stacked against them. Whether through deliberate efforts or as an unintentional, albeit passively accepted, byproduct of our rigid social hierarchy, they are barred from bettering themselves, limited in what constitutes appropriate discourse, and generally confined to modest occupations of minimal threat. Seen but not heard.

The suffragette movement, spearheaded by the National Society for Women's Suffrage, is steadily making grounds in that department, working tirelessly to swing public opinion to the side of greater rights for women.

But it is a slow process, as change usually is. For my part, I hope they find success sooner rather than later.

As delightful as the tea and biscuits are, which is to say better than I have ever had, the conversation is even more enjoyable. Perhaps it is the open atmosphere of the New Somerville itself. Or maybe it is the way we leapfrog between topics with ease, especially the subjects I find enjoyable. I am still leery of her political and social eminence, but am doing my best not to let distrust colour my opinion. Or my behaviour. I am even managing, through no small effort, to disregard her occasional condescension, which comes across as incidental instead of intentional.

It is only when we inevitably shift to the topic of the dead doxie, one Fiona McCarthy, that the mood turns serious. She has already heard my theory about there being two malefactors and how I believe the eyes serve an unknown purpose. All that remains is to share what I learned whilst examining the body with Dr. Bixby.

"New discoveries, you say?" she asks, visibly intrigued.

I set my teacup down before replying, folding my hands in my lap. I must navigate these waters most cautiously. "Yes, milady. Several all at once, as a matter of fact."

"Do tell. And you can forgo the 'milady' for the time being. It hinders our ability to converse properly. My name is Amelia; you may address me as such."

"Very well, Amelia. The pinhole burns across her torso and legs are from sparks. Sparks cast across her body deliberately, I surmise. That, coupled with the fine steel shavings we found embedded in her feet, led me to believe that the killer hails from somewhere within Blackwall. It is only an assumption, but I believe him to be a metalworker or craftsman, luring the women to an isolated workshop of some sort. The bruising on her neck indicates that his hands are quite large, which means we are looking for a fellow of significant stature. Considering that transporting bodies from another location greatly enhances the risk of being caught, it stands to reason that he would choose to remain local. All of these points combined should narrow the aperture of my search considerably."

She takes it all in without interrupting, forefinger tapping her cheek in quiet contemplation. I cannot tell if she approves of my suppositions or not. The silence between us stretches long enough to become *gauche*, but as I begin to speak, she stops me with an upturned finger.

"A moment, James." Her tone is not unkind but still retains a hint of dominance. I close my mouth at once, teeth clicking together painfully. "If you'll allow me a tangent?"

All I can do is nod—one does not tell a member of the peerage no. In every sense, even pertaining to legal matters, her authority exceeds mine.

"Do you know what consumes most of the Ministry's resources? When you strip away all of the bureaucracy and peer beyond the formality, do you know what the main thrust of Special Sciences is? I can tell you what it isn't. It is not research, and it is certainly not the development of new machines and methodologies."

"Then I'm afraid I don't, milady. I would have assumed that most Special Sciences personnel would be toiling away in laboratories and testing facilities. Doing what, I cannot begin to presume. However, given that you are an electrical engineer, much like Nikola Tesla, I would have thought that many of your peers would come from a similar background."

"A fair assumption. And not without merit. Whilst we have scientists, theoreticians, and engineers on the payroll, those positions are few and far between. And Mr. Tesla now resides in America, far beyond our grasp."

I find myself lost, uncertain as to where this thread of conversation is leading. It is not often that a person's motives elude me. But Amelia

Ellington has changed tack abruptly—I am forced to do the same or risk being left behind.

"What we are primarily about," she continues, locking her eyes on mine, "is investigation. Policework, if you will. Or near enough to it. We are chiefly interested in making sure new inventions, large and small, do not fall into the wrong hands. Or are not used in a questionable or unsafe fashion. Most of our duties consist of fieldwork, mine included."

I tilt my head to the side, confused. "Forgive my impertinence, but you seem a little high-ranking to be spending your time scouring hovels for purloined novelties and apprehending ne'er-do-wells. What brings you, specifically, out into the field?"

Her broad smile indicates that I am not failing her test. Or at least not at the moment.

"A very good question, James. One with a remarkably easy answer. I spend the majority of my time investigating the unsanctioned pilfering of electricity, including the means by which it is redistributed from an established main line to an unmetered source through a splice or a shunt, thereby avoiding the hourly ampere charge."

Amps and ohms. Current and voltage. Splices and shunts. These things may be child's play to Tesla and evidently to Lady Ellington as well, but they are proving difficult for me to grasp. The basic science of electrical current is fundamentally sound. Straightforward even. But the finer details, terminology, and how it all interconnects slip through my brain like water through a sieve.

"I'm not sure I follow."

"Thievery, James. I'm talking about thievery. Electrical espionage, as it were. Turn anything into a commodity, and eventually some imaginative ragamuffin will find a way to filch it, whether in dribbles or droves. Electricity is no different. In most cases, the thieves tap into one of the main lines, somewhere between the power plant and the metering boxes. By doing so, they bypass the meters entirely, which is our only means of measuring usage. These criminals can siphon off as much power as they want, and we're none the wiser. After all, how do you track down something that cannot be seen? We are rapidly approaching a new century, James, and electricity will be a key contributor to London's prosperity and strength. We cannot afford to have that future undermined by vagabonds and miscreants."

I nod in agreement, outwardly mollified, but my mind is awhirl with activity. Everything she is saying makes sense. It's all perfectly logical, packaged and presented in such a way as to be easily consumed and digested. The kind of explanation that most people would take at face value. The kind that Barnhold undoubtedly lapped up like a cat with cream. Nevertheless, something isn't adding up. I get the feeling she is deliberately leading me off-topic, providing too much tangential information in an attempt at distraction. For all the enjoyment of our conversation up until now, we have oscillated from cordial to circumspect. And just when I was beginning to rethink my stance on certain members of the peerage. Must the nobility always be so damn inscrutable?

Fortunately, I have dealt with such tactics, and refuse to be baited by them. There is one remaining card to play. One which will, hopefully, put us back on track. It is a gamble, prodding an aristocrat in such a fashion. But nothing ventured, nothing gained.

"Be that as it may, electricity theft is not what brought you to Blackwall yesterday. Not with the interest with which you studied Miss McCarthy's corpse. Not with how you were unsurprised by anything you saw. No, I think you were far more concerned with the electrical burns and where they might have come from."

There is no noticeable shift in her expression, but a sudden change falls over the table, a hush of wariness that wasn't there before. All remaining traces of cordiality have vanished. I feel like a stranger who has inadvertently stumbled upon a private family gathering, overly conspicuous and distrustfully scrutinized. An unknown quantity.

"What makes you so certain they were caused by electricity?" There is naught in her tone to suggest that anything is amiss, but I am certain that, behind those oceanic eyes, I am being reevaluated. A new set of weights and measures has been introduced, which suits me just fine. The peers of the realm have a habit of underestimating we commoners, and I have no qualms whatsoever about proving them wrong.

"Three things," I reply, holding up my thumb and forefinger to show the count. "First, I've been policing many of London's coarsest neighbourhoods for quite a while. Places which are positively teeming with unscrupulous people making terrible decisions. As such, I've seen burns of all sorts, accidental or otherwise. The wounds on our doxies are quite unlike anything I've experienced thus far."

Lady Ellington nods, conceding the point. I take a deep breath before continuing.

"Second, a doctor at London Hospital, who is far more conversant in such particulars than I, all but confirmed their origin as electrical in nature. I have every confidence in his perceptiveness and integrity. Third, as stated before, your very presence. There can be no other logical explanation."

Another stretch of silence reigns, pregnant with wariness. My gambit seems to have worked, for Lady Ellington is gazing at me intently, unblinking eyes boring into my own, as if her every thought is bent towards assessing the very composition of my soul. When she speaks, her voice is quiet. Contemplative. Almost distracted. Though her stare never wavers.

"I do believe that brain of yours is wasted in the constabulary, James. Tell me, if you would be so kind—what made you want to become a policeman? Familial tradition? The steady pay and guaranteed pension? Or were you motivated by something more... chivalrous? Perhaps a desire to be of service to Queen and country?"

I wave her comment away. For reasons I cannot discern, my tongue has become less guarded. I feel free to speak my mind without fear of reprisal. "Nothing so gallant, I assure you. It was an escape from a life of menial drudgery. No more, no less. The constabulary offered second-rate pay compared to some professions but was more honest than most. Which I believed, then and now, to be important. That I had a knack for investigation was unknown to me until after the fact. And, no offense intended, but I don't give a fig for the royal family. I'm a servant of the masses, not the monarchy."

Lady Ellington raps a knuckle on the tabletop as if in confirmation. "I suspected as much, and your candor is appreciated. Most people tell me what they think I *want* to hear instead of what I *need* to hear. That you avoid doing so is rather refreshing."

"I've never been one to mince words, Amelia, and I see no reason to start now. Speaking of candor... in reference to Miss McCarthy's wounds, I'm onto something, aren't I?"

"You are, indeed," she replies slowly, as if choosing her words with care. "But they originated from a lower voltage source, not a main power line. The current carried on a main line would have charred her beyond recognition."

"And yet, how is that possible if there is no electricity on the Isle?"

"That is the question, now, isn't it? How, indeed? Perhaps between the two of us we can figure it out."

Something about her tone suggests our *tête-à-tête* is coming to an end, and my suspicions are confirmed when she leans back into the divan, hands folded in her lap with an air of finality. She has returned to the lightheartedness of earlier, as though our recent bout of discord did not happen at all.

"Well, James, this has been a singularly enlightening conversation. Most informative, truly. I would love to stay and chat, but other matters demand my attention. Please return to your office forthwith and type up everything we've discussed. All the facts and your suppositions. I would like to present our findings to my superiors. In person. With you in attendance, naturally."

I swallow hard to mask my disappointment. I have more questions now than when we started, but it is evident that no additional answers are forthcoming. "So, that's all?"

"For now, yes. But I am more than impressed—everything about our time together has reaffirmed my decision. Welcome to Special Sciences, Inspector Guthrie. We are fortunate to have you collaborating with us, and I look forward to our next meeting."

I know a dismissal when I hear one; in this instance, she sounds remarkably similar to Superintendent Barnhold. His condescension is somehow less appealing than Lady Ellington's, but I still find it irksome, regardless of the origin. Classism may be a cornerstone of British society, but nobody likes reminders that they are the lesser party. Even so, there is nothing for it but to swallow my pride and depart, like a gentleman caller rebuffed at a lover's back door, perplexed and unfulfilled.

No sooner have I risen than the stout hostess appears at my side, materializing as if by magic. She makes no effort to disguise her pleasure in escorting me from the premises. The Somerville's other patrons take notice of my departure, openly intrigued, wildcat eyes tracking me all the way to the door. I may not be escaping with my dignity, but I am, miraculously, still in one piece.

And sometimes that is enough.

CHAPTER XXIV

Though Constance has plenty of experience trolling boulevards and byways in search of customers, scouring the streets of Blackwall Yard for Fi's murderer has given a new meaning to "being on the prowl."

The dockyard is a bustling place at midday, throngs of people going about their business amidst the clang and clatter of oceanic industry. In a rather ironic twist, she finds herself actively discouraging the attentions of men eager for a tumble, frostily turning down several propositions as she makes her way southwest. Never before has she felt so apathetic towards her occupation. But, then again, what use is coin to the dead or incarcerated? Besides, in her current frame of mind, with all her thoughts bent on slitting Schaffer's throat, carnality isn't even a consideration, and she's liable to stab anyone who lays a finger upon her. She holds no particular apathy towards men in general but is in no mood to suffer their advances. She eventually adopts a determined scowl that seems to serve as a ward, with no further intimations coming her way.

Rested and nourished but with a heart as callous as a bigamist penning wedding vows, Constance is patient in her hunt, allowing nothing to encroach upon her task. The bustle, the noise, the myriad smells of the

Yard all fade to the periphery. Even the towering masts of half-assembled ships fail to distract her. She moves at a leisurely pace, traversing every street with measured steps. There is no rush, after all. She has nothing but time. She will remain in Blackwall for as long as it takes, irrespective of her wants and needs.

Revenge is all that matters—an entire existence narrowed into a single point of focused intent as unwavering as her name.

That she and Schaffer will cross paths today is a certainty. Either she'll glimpse him, or he'll observe her, and the rest will be up to chance. The how of it is far from consequential; it's simply a question of when. And, even more importantly, what will come after. Whether it is to be his undoing or hers. To that end, Constance walks. And searches. And doesn't cease in her efforts, not even as her stomach rumbles and the blisters on her feet begin to bleed.

Afternoon has come and gone, shadows growing long and crowds getting thin. Constance has made the same circuitous route at least three times, passing by shop owners and fruit sellers often enough that several of their faces are becoming familiar. A few eye her with curiosity or indifference. The rest, with naked suspicion, as though she is a thief seeking an easy score, flaunting her own wares, such as they are, as a means of distraction.

Not that Constance expected anything different. This isn't her turf, and these aren't her people. She will find no allies here. No sympathy. The tradesmen, day laborers, wharf rats, and salty dockside whores of the Isle of Dogs are very nearly their own insular family, bound together by hardscrabble conditions and their proximity to the Thames. A country within a country. The Connor disguise blended in with relative ease, giving her the appearance of malnourished prepubescence. Just another grubby urchin looking for work. But now, with her unlined face, soft hands, and lithesome girlishness, Constance is very obviously an outsider. It comes as no surprise that the locals are apprehensive of her lurking around their businesses.

Despair has only just begun to creep in when she finally spots Schaffer, hardly fifteen feet away, his massive shape exiting a pub so ramshackle it doesn't even sport a sign. Given his size, she can't help but compare him to a troll emerging from its lair. Scarf. Suspenders. No cap. Block-shaped face marred by a cruel scowl. Exactly as he had been described.

Her heart skips a beat, a sudden thrill of danger causing her fingers to tingle. All Schaffer needs to do is turn his head, and he'll be looking straight at her. Her muscles coil and tighten in anticipation like a cat preparing to pounce. A part of her longs to brandish the stiletto and hurl herself straight at him while he's distracted, even without tangible proof of his guilt. To gamble everything on chance. A fool's errand, to be sure, but the white-hot rage climbing up her limbs and throat aches for immediate satisfaction. The roar filling her ears is as deafening as the churn of the sea. Her hand seems to move of its own accord, inching ever downwards, reaching for the hidden blade.

It is only through a twist of fate that he pivots to the right, the opposite direction from where she stands. He leaves the pub behind with heavy steps, heading deeper into the industrial area. The motion breaks through her fugue of impulsive retribution. She snatches her hand away from the blade as if scalded, hoping nobody noticed such peculiar behaviour. Constance has no compunction about killing Schaffer, but that doesn't mean she can't be smart about it. Attempting murder in broad daylight, surrounded by people liable to defend one of their own, would be the very definition of imprudence.

While she wrestles with strategy, Schaffer's determined stride carries him out of view. Vanishing just as quickly as he was found. With no other recourse but pursuit, Constance tamps down on her anger and follows in his wake, dodging around pedestrians with quick strides. She didn't realize that such a big man would be so easy to lose track of. With any luck, he is sozzled after a long day of work, heading home to sleep it off like any respectable drunkard. All she has to do is catch up with him.

But making that happen is proving more difficult than expected. She is still unaccustomed to the Yard's topography—winding avenues, dead-end alleys, and buildings that jut out at odd intervals, many established out of necessity rather than according to a grand infrastructural plan. She keeps losing sight of him at junctures and bends, where he turns corners seemingly at random, disappearing for long stretches at a time. It doesn't help that the thoroughfares and backstreets look virtually identical when shrouded in afternoon fog.

Schaffer finally slips from view entirely after ducking down a nondescript side street. Constance is out of breath, huffing painfully, practically having sprinted to keep up with the big man's strides. She pauses at the entrance to the alley, weighing her options. The buildings within are monotonous, bereft of ornamentation and discernable function, each one more unremarkable than the last. Schaffer could have disappeared into any of them.

Only a single structure is conspicuous, as evidenced by the open doorway that draws her gaze, a yawning chasm cleaving an otherwise featureless façade. The space beyond is pitch-black, its unknowable recesses strangely forbidding. She approaches the ingress slowly. Warily. All of her senses straining to penetrate the gloom before her. Constance wavers at the threshold, unable to push herself further. An ingot of intense dread has taken root in her chest, expanding outwards in pulsing waves, raising goose pimples along her arms and neck. The shadowy interior repels her for some inexplicable reason, as if the terminus of all existence lies within. A hollow where the very fabric of reality could unravel. Such an absurd fear, and yet her muscles remain defiant.

Before Constance can convince her legs to obey, a large hand grabs her by the arm, forcibly spinning her around. A cry of alarm escapes her lips as she is unexpectedly face to face with her quarry. Schaffer is even more formidable up close, looming over her like a folklore giant. Calculating eyes rake across her body, weighing and measuring in the span of a heartbeat, reducing her to little more than gristle in a grinder. The sneer on his face is ominously lascivious.

She had assumed that he would be a dullard. An ox in human form, possessed of rheumy eye and plodding movements, as dim-witted as defectives in a sanatorium. The cleverness with which he regards her puts paid to that notion. How could she have underestimated him so thoroughly?

"Well, 'ello, poppet," he says, voice thick with insinuation.

Trapped between the instinct to flee and the desire to fight, Constance's insides turn to liquid. A scream builds in her throat as she grabs for the stiletto, hand darting downwards like a striking serpent. But Schaffer is quicker. His right fist lashes out with surprising dexterity, the punch catching her directly on the temple, snapping her head sideways with such force that she collides with the doorjamb. Her faculties dissolve in an explosion of agony.

She is dimly aware that the ground is somehow rushing up to meet her, as if gravity has gone barmy, and then darkness consumes her.

End Cadenza

THE SENTIMENTAL ENDING

For the first time in his twenty years of life, Roger Neiman was taking a plane ride.

This in itself should not have been big news, except for the fact that Rog was not a fan of travel. Was ardently against it, in point of fact. He had never even left Idaho before. He'd gotten close a few times, when his family would take trips to City of Rocks, a national reserve near the Utah border. Rog's dad, always a spiteful man, had refused to cross over into what he had dubbed "Momo territory".

But that had been just fine with Rog. Everything he needed was within the space of a few square miles, so why bother going anywhere else?

Technically, it being his first time flying, Rog should have been at least a little terrified. But as the plane began to level off at cruising altitude and the ground became hidden under a dense layer of clouds, he felt a thrill of exhilaration shoot through him.

He was finally going on an adventure.

And not just any stateside jaunt but an honest-to-God overseas excursion. His newly minted passport was snug and safe in his laptop bag, still smelling faintly of vinyl and ink.

Rog knew that he was behind the curve when compared to his peers. Most of his friends had taken senior class trips to Mexico, and the French students had even gone to Paris one summer. But he had politely yet firmly declined such distractions, having been far too content to spend time nestled behind gaming monitors, eschewing real adventures for digital ones.

Which was why, when Rog had announced to his group of friends, both real and online, that he was taking an impromptu trip to Norway, they had collectively lost their shit.

But while the trip itself might have come as a shock, the location had been a surprise to exactly none of them. Not only was he a huge symphonic metal fan, which Norway was practically the official home of, but Rog had been talking about the game *Menace in the Mountains* to anyone who would listen (and even a few who wouldn't) for months. The game's multiple cutscenes had been filmed, guerilla-style, in various small hamlets around Lillehammer, a mountain-encircled town a couple of hours north of Oslo.

The game's American development team, Gather 'Round Studios, was a small one, with less than ten people on the payroll. As such, their first-person survival-horror offering was much more of a labor of love than most of its big-budget brethren. *MitM* was a somewhat grounded tale, centered on character development and actual plot, letting the traditional bombast and melodrama offered by AAA studios remain a secondary consideration. It didn't have the best graphics, the soundtrack wasn't conducted by an A-lister, and it had only garnered middling reviews from most of the respected gaming websites. Nevertheless, it was one of Rog's favorite games.

He couldn't speak for other gamers, and none of his friends had been more than passingly interested in it, but Rog had beaten *MitM* multiple times. His first playthrough had simply been to enjoy the tale. All subsequent replays had been more focused affairs, aimed at 100% map completion, fully upgrading the arsenal of weapons, or experiencing all of the multiple endings.

In fact, *MitM* had roughly thirty different resolutions, with most of them considered "bad" endings. Where the protagonist, Eric Walters, died in some gruesome and over-the-top fashion. Typical survival-horror gorefests, nothing more and nothing less.

There was one resolution, however, that had really impacted Rog when he had first experienced it. It was one of the most difficult ones to get, which the limited online fanbase had dubbed "the sentimental ending". The one where Eric died not by the hands of some menacing creature but instead by duplicitous townsfolk. A literal knife through the back.

It was a death that was aided and abetted by a fetching young lass whom, due to misdirection from the official gameplay trailers, had been teased to be Eric's blossoming love-interest. Indeed, up until the moment of her betrayal, and depending on choices made by the player, she and Eric would trade veiled innuendos and flirtatious stares, solidifying their "ship" status. Despite most video games' laughable handling of such subject matter, Gather 'Round had injected genuine pathos into the proceedings.

However, courting Inga was not mandatory during a *MitM* playthrough. Players could choose to be cold or indifferent to her advances as they saw fit, responses which would result in completely different outcomes for her involvement in the storyline. Just one of the many ways in which the game encouraged player agency.

On the flipside, Inga was a cute and perky blonde, with expressive eyes and an endearing accent. Perfect in the way that only animated (digitally or otherwise) characters could be. Rog had been smitten immediately during his first playthrough. Through the time-honored tradition of save scumming, video gaming's equivalent of a safety net, he had made sure to select the appropriate prompted responses from Eric in order to foster their emerging digital romance.

To say that Inga's involvement in Eric's death had come as a surprise to the gaming community was an understatement. It had dropped like a proverbial A-bomb (while eliciting plenty of f-bombs), and from that point forward the ending had been given the "sentimental" moniker.

And now Rog was well on his way to visiting the very café where that scene had been filmed. And not only the café, but multiple other real-life locales which had inspired some the game's best levels and environments. Gather 'Round had digitized the footage they'd recorded, of both actors and scenery, in order to amp up the "game" factor (and avoid possible litigation), but the cutscenes were still based on actual locations and people.

Locations that Rog felt drawn to, as if pulled by an invisible thread... compelled to visit them in person. To experience them with his own senses.

But, regardless of his reasons, the flight to Oslo was going to be a long one, with several layovers along the way. And yet Rog didn't mind. For the first time in his life he was excited to go somewhere new. Breaking free of his self-imposed prison. What were a few more hours in the grand scheme of things?

Plus, his excitement far outweighed any sense of discomfort. He was travelling light, with only a carryon full of clothes and his beloved laptop. Getting to connecting gates would be a breeze.

It was the perfect start to what would undoubtedly be an amazing vacation.

Not that he had a whole lot to compare it to, but the Oslo Gardermoen Airport was both ridiculously clean and amazingly efficient. Like an IKEA catalogue writ large. Going through customs was a breeze, and the baggage claim process was quick and easy.

Before he knew it, Rog was seated on the Vy high-speed train, heading north at speeds exceeding 100 mph. He had never taken public transportation before. In fact, his only exposure to the vagaries of trains and buses had come from movies, but he was duly impressed with the Vy. Even the coach car was quiet and comfortable, albeit in a distinctly foreign way.

The latest album from symphonic metal pioneers Sirenia was pulsing through his earbuds, and Rog was replaying an older save file (another benefit to save scumming) from *Menace in the Mountains,* going through the motions to earn the sentimental ending once again. For whatever reason, it never got old watching avatar Eric getting impaled through his back by a large knife, the surprise on his face fading as his lifeblood drained out. All while Inga observed, feigned shock giving way to a deceitful smile of pure wickedness.

The two hours to Lillehammer went by in the blink of an eye. Rog found himself standing in the train station's parking lot, staring at scenery that wouldn't have been out of place on a postcard. It was about as far removed from the uniform flatness of Idaho as one could get.

The ski resort town possessed a majestic beauty that Rog had only ever seen in big-budget films. The kind of classic-cum-modern architecture that seemed to only work in Europe, while in America the mashup of old and new buildings generally looked hideous and half-assed.

He stood stock still for a long moment, letting his senses acclimate to the new surroundings. The entrancing cadences of foreign dialects. The captivating smells of exotic foods. There was a cool crispness to the air that felt almost painful—a cleanliness that he had never before experienced. Perhaps he was too accustomed to the pollution of downtown Boise. Or maybe it was the altitude. Whatever the reason, it was wonderful just to breathe it all in.

In his head, Rog heard the line from The Lord of the Rings, the one where Samwise the Hobbit said he'd never been so far from home. It was a sentiment that had never resonated with him before now, and Rog couldn't help but chuckle.

Once the new location "magic" had worn off, Rog dutifully snapped pictures of the gorgeous backdrops, sending them out to both friends and family via text and posts on his social media accounts. Very few people had believed that he was actually taking an overseas vacation.

He was only too happy to prove them wrong.

As antsy as he was to get started on his adventure, evening was fast approaching, and the long flight had been surprisingly wearying. He had already pre-booked a room in downtown Lillehammer for just the one night. The hotel was small but charming, picturesque in a sort of "ye olde world" way. It was also within walking distance of the train station.

He would get a bite, a shower, and some shut eye, and then hit the outlying hamlets early the next day.

Even though he was not a morning person, Roger was up and active before his alarm went off. He was suffering from a serious case of jet lag but it was not enough to keep his excitement in check.

After all, this was the day that his adventure truly began.

He enjoyed a quick breakfast and coffee while waiting for a taxi, making sure his phone and laptop were fully charged using the requisite converters for his power adapters.

Rog had picked up a map of the local area from the hotel's lobby the night before, circling the "must visit" locations and doing kilometer-to-mile conversions with the help of his smartphone, gauging times and distances. There were eleven total sites where Gather 'Round had done their initial filming. Some were nothing more than remote locations with a memorable natural feature, while others were decent-sized villages and townships.

Outside of flight time, Rog had given himself three days to tour the Lillehammer countryside, which included the hamlet of Eksisterer Ikke, as well as Består Innsjø, a secluded lake high in the mountains. Naturally, the village of Falsktsted held the most appeal, since that was where *Menace in the Mountain's* sentimental ending had been filmed. But he would work his way through the less important areas initially, like a child eating their least favorite dinner morsels first before moving on to the good stuff. Once the secondary places were out of the way, Rog would finish strong, spending his entire last day in Falsktsted.

With little in the way of amenities, Består Innsjø seemed the best place to begin. He might as well visit the least comfortable location first so he could get it behind him.

"I think you are not here for the skiing," Roger's taxi driver mentioned, in thick but perfectly understandable English, after getting Rog situated in the back of the car. The taxi was a black & chrome Mercedes, much nicer than the squat economy cars favored by the Uber drivers that prowled Boise's roadways.

The driver's comment was an understatement. While many people around Lillehammer were sporting the latest fashionable snow gear and oversized name-brand travel bags for their skis, Rog looked rather incongruous in the meager cold-weather attire he had picked up from Ross and Kohls. The muted colors and bargain styles more than stood out.

"Yeah, I'm not much of a skier," Rog confirmed. He had, in fact, never held much love for snow activities of any kind, except for sledding when he was younger. "Just here to take in the sights of the surrounding area. Exploring the countryside. Can you take me here?" he asked, pointing at Består Innsjø on the map. He was unsure how to pronounce it and didn't want to sound like an idiot.

The taxi driver, an older gentleman with gray thinning hair and untamed whiskers, eyed the location dubiously.

"I know it. But I think you will find yourself disappointed, young man. It is very remote, with little to see. And even colder than here. It could be dangerous since your winter outfit is so shabby. Are you certain that is the place you wish to go?"

Remote or not, there was no way Rog was going to skip the lake. It was the location of the game's first big jump scare, where a frightening tentacle creature would attack without warning from the shoreline. If a player was unable to input the on-screen button prompts in time, Eric would be bludgeoned and snared by the beast's many appendages and then dragged, bloody and screaming, into the icy depths.

"Yep, I'm sure," Rog said, giving the driver a nod. "I won't be up there long. Just want to see the lake in person and get a few pictures. I'll be ok."

The driver started the car while shaking his head, muttering under his breath the whole time in his native tongue. Rog was pretty sure the man was lamenting the stupidity of American tourists.

But Rog hadn't flown halfway around the world to be deterred at the last minute. He would visit the lake and then warm back up in the taxi on the way to the next location.

He had it all planned out.

The first two days of exploring went by in a blur.

Består Innsjø had been even more remote than Rog had initially suspected, and he was surprised by how well the Mercedes traversed the ice-capped roads.

There had been no tentacle monster residing the lake, of course, but Rog had still been attacked by a biting wind that his clothing had been unable to mitigate. The taxi driver might have thought that his customer was an idiot, but he had still given Rog an extra snow coat that had been stowed in the taxi's trunk. The coat was old but serviceable, and Rog was moved by the unexpected generosity.

The driver, Henrik, had simply smiled and said something about how a frozen tourist wouldn't make anyone happy. Rog had been unable to argue.

The various locations on the itinerary were all uniformly beautiful, each one more interesting than the last. Består Innsjø's lake had been instantly recognizable, as had a few of the other locales. The Gather 'Round art team had done very little in the way of alterations for those more remote locations.

Eksisterer Ikke, on the other hand, was vastly different in real life than how it had been portrayed in *MitM*. In the game it was a nameless village, decrepit and ominous, completely isolated from outside influence. And completely devoid of living inhabitants. Dead ones, however, populated the village in abundance. The shambling corpses were the game's equivalent of zombies. *MitM's* design team, undoubtedly comprised of fans of The Walking Dead television series, had intentionally made the in-game streets and alleys smaller, resulting in close-quarters creature encounters that, if failed, would lead to several more gruesome deaths for Eric. As an unabashed zombie fan, they were also some of Rog's favorite segments in the game.

Unlike the creatures infesting the unnamed digital village, the real-life inhabitants of Eksisterer Ikke had proven a welcoming bunch. They were hardy folk, taciturn in a rough-living sort of way, all broad shoulders and weathered features.

Due to their hospitality, Rog had spent most of this second day in their company, forgoing several of the other stops altogether. The hamlet itself was quaint and quiet, with homes in good repair and well-swept streets.

The village's inhabitants remembered the *MitM* film crew, though they had little else to say on the matter. It was the only subject they were reticent on.

Rog had snapped several hundred pictures during first two days in the countryside. Some were to show off on social media, but the vast majority were for him alone. Tokens of his time spent on the other side of the world.

And then there was that strange compulsion, the one that had started him on his journey in the first place. It had grown ever stronger since he'd arrived in Norway. It was like a blanket, encompassing and comforting. Even when trekking in the unpopulated expanses, Rog never felt unsafe.

It was as if he was meant to be there. Like something was waiting for him.

There were no inns to speak of in the town, but the owner of the solitary pub bad been willing to let out one of his rooms, hostel style, for just a little extra cash. Rog, who had scrimped and saved in order to afford the trip in the first place, was more than happy to conserve a little money by staying in the cramped but cozy guest room.

Despite a hot meal and even hotter shower, Rog still hadn't completely warmed up from two days spent in the Lillehammer outskirts. But the perpetual cold did nothing to dampen his spirits. He had much to look forward to.

The next day he would be in Falsktsted, visiting the café where *MitM's* sentimental ending had been filmed. He wasn't sure exactly how faithful the design team had stayed to the source material, but he imagined it would look pretty similar.

Not that Inga would be there. She had been played by a Norwegian actress living in New York and digitally inserted into the game environment.

But beggars couldn't be choosers, and Rog was like a little kid on Christmas eve.

The taxi arrived the next morning at daybreak. Rog had barely slept, practically bouncing on his feet. His nervous energy threatened to spill over at any moment.

Henrik and his black Mercedes had, through accident or design, become Roger's unofficial chauffeurs. The man was no doubt happy with the guaranteed fare from the extra mileage, and had also opened up a bit while driving Rog from place to place, providing historical tidbits to the locations around them.

However, Henrik was just as tight-lipped as the Eksisterer Ikke villagers when it came to the subject of *Menace in the Mountains.* He knew of the game and had explained that it was a sore subject for many in the Lillehammer area, claiming that it cast the residents in a derogatory manner.

Apparently there had even been a petition going around Lillehammer to stop the game's release. Rog hadn't been aware of that particular bit of information but doubted that Henrik would lie to him about such a thing. Rog wouldn't call them friends, exactly, but they had formed a certain rapport, a shared friendliness that helped take the edge off of the solitary adventure.

As such, Rog found himself more than a little surprised that, when he mentioned Falsktsted as their final destination, Henrik's mood turned dour.

"Is something wrong?" Rog asked, more curious than anything.

"Falsktsted is truly an inspiring location," Henrik said solemnly, "old homes in an even older village. It has grandeur, to be sure, but I must advise you not to go there. Unlike the villagers in Eksisterer Ikke, the residents of Falsktsted are not very welcoming of foreigners. The community is, how do you say, close-knit?"

Though he didn't think Henrik was pulling his leg, Rog would not be dissuaded. He could deal with a few harsh people. After all, it couldn't be any worse than what he'd dealt with in high school or the online gaming community.

"That may be, but I'm still going," Rog asserted, standing his ground in a rare moment of stubbornness. "Falsktsted is the main place I wanted to visit. The café there is the reason for this whole trip."

Henrik shook his head. "It would be wise, my young friend, to not bring up that game to the people there."

They bickered back and forth for a few minutes. Ultimately, Rog managed to persuade Henrik to take him. The driver was visibly unhappy with the arrangement, but eventually conceded defeat, so long as Rog was careful around the townsfolk. They drove most the way in awkward silence.

Rog's flight home departed early the next morning, so he had to be back in Lillehammer with enough time to catch the train back to Oslo. Henrik sullenly agreed to return to Falsktsted for a pickup once the sun began to set.

Rog put the worried taxi driver from his mind. He would have all day to explore and was determined to enjoy every second of it.

Two hours later, however, he found himself conceding that maybe Henrik had been correct after all.

The town of Falsktsted was, in a word, breathtaking. Rog could see why the crew from Gather 'Round had chosen it as a principal filming location. There was a rustic charm to the village, which seemed frozen in time, possessing architecture and style that the rest of the world had left behind decades ago.

The myriad buildings and homes were instantly recognizable, nearly identical to their in-game counterparts. The colors might have been altered, or the house numbers deliberately obscured, but everything else was surprisingly unchanged.

It was a beautiful location, peaceful and serene, with an inviting atmosphere. The same, however, could not be said about the townspeople.

No sooner had he stepped out of the taxi than he was met with frosty stares and deep scowls. Conversations stopped once he was within earshot, and none of the residents responded to him when he called out a greeting, most turning their backs on him in a huff. He eventually stopped trying to say hello altogether.

Even the proprietors of the general stores were openly disdainful, grudgingly taking Rog's money when he bought a few mementos. He almost didn't want to give them his business, but he'd be damned if he was going to go home empty-handed.

Still, the hostility of the townspeople was beginning to wear on him, and sunset was a long way off. The welcoming aura of Falsktsted had completely evaporated. A couple of the villagers started tailing him after he left the second store, rough looking men with dark expressions. An ominous feeling settled onto Rog's neck and shoulders, and he felt his nervousness spiking.

Having no remaining options, and growing more and more fearful with every step, Rog headed to the café, hoping to salvage something from his last day. He picked up his pace and the rough men followed suit. He had the growing suspicion that he was about to get jumped. Rog wasn't one of the stereotypical gamers that people used as cautionary tales, the overweight incel types that still lived in their moms' basements, but he wasn't terribly strong either, and his fight-or-flight instinct was permanently stuck on the retreat setting.

The café was, thankfully, right where he knew it would be, and suddenly Rog felt as if he had stepped out of reality and straight into *Menace in the Mountains*. The tables, chairs, and decorations were exactly how they had been depicted in the game. In fact, outside a few color alterations, the café was the spitting image of its digital counterpart. Even the menu board looked identical, although the meal and drink selections were different.

Rog felt a slight twinge of déjà vu as he stepped under the awning. He had navigated Eric through the same motions numerous times in the game world; it felt surreal to be experiencing it himself.

There were only a few patrons in the café, all of whom studiously ignored him. Rog glanced back the way he had come, but his surly shadows were nowhere to be seen. Maybe the café was, unlike in the game, a safe haven.

He exhaled with relief, and then found his spirits lifted further when he noticed that the table where Eric would sit when he met his doom was unoccupied. Rog claimed it without a second thought.

The ominous feeling dissipated, fading like the sun at dusk. Here he was, at the real-life location of his favorite video game cutscene. While other people might not have cared much, to Rog it felt like the achievement of a lifetime. The money, miles, and even the enmity of the townsfolk had all been worth it.

Considering the unwelcoming reception he had received up until that point, he wasn't sure that he would even be served. He figured he'd have to amuse himself with gaming until Henrik returned. But as soon as he pulled out his laptop, a young woman in an apron appeared from the kitchen area and made her way over.

The waitress wore a smile, unlike the rest of the townsfolk, and Rog felt a sudden wave of relief crash over him. Maybe the day could still be salvaged. She was more than cute, with prominent cheekbones and bright blue eyes.

"You are not from around here," she stated in halting but passable English, the smile never leaving her lips. Rog gauged her to be his age, maybe slightly older, though her voice still possessed traces of girlhood.

"Tell me about it," Rog responded, trying to sound nonchalant. "I was beginning to think I'd get run out of town before long."

The waitress laughed, sharp and clear, and Rog thought it was the loveliest sound he'd heard in quite some time. He found himself chuckling along with her. "The day is young, good sir. That may still happen."

"I mean, I was told that the residents here don't like foreigners, but it was starting to get a little ridiculous."

She waved away his comment. "As a rule, we do not. But put it from your mind. This town, and its people, are old. Set in their ways. Which is no fault of yours."

"And what about you?" he asked hesitantly. "What are your thoughts on the matter?"

"I too am set in my ways, and an old soul. But you are here, and I am not so wicked as to turn away a customer."

It was a strange choice of words, but Rog played along. "Wicked can be good sometimes."

"Truly," she agreed, a mischievous grin taking over her expression. "My name is Signe. What is yours?"

Rog held out his hand, and they shook gently. "I'm Roger. It's nice to meet you."

Rog spent the rest of the day in the café, the hours flying by like minutes. Though there was a slight language barrier, he and Signe shared a natural affinity. A bond of youthful exuberance and similar senses of humor.

Patrons rotated in and out, though if they had a problem with the conversation between Rog and the waitress, they kept it to themselves. The men that had been shadowing him earlier returned, taking a table in the back corner of the café, making no efforts to disguise their watchful gazes. Rog watched as Signe gave them a brief shake of her head. Whatever it was, and whatever it meant, the men seemed content to stay at their table.

He should have been worried, but he was enjoying himself too much to focus on anything else. It was as if he was Eric, she was Inga, and they were reenacting the good scenes in *MitM,* the meet-cute moments prior to Eric's death. It was everything Rog could have hoped for.

By late afternoon, business in the café had picked up, and Signe had to divide her time between Rog's table and the other patrons. The susurrus of muted conversations surrounded him, though he had no idea what anyone was talking about.

Lost in the clouds, Rog figured that he could fill the in-between moments by replaying the sentimental ending one more time. And why not? He was in *the* café, after all. He had only just logged in to the laptop when Signe returned, however, a carafe of water in her hands.

"What are you playing, Roger? You are a gamer, yes?"

Rog nodded and turned the laptop so she could see the display. The *MitM* logo on the loading screen was unmistakable with its red hues and angular font.

"*Menace in the Mountains,*" he replied cautiously, not wanting to stumble across something that would anger her. But she *had* asked, and he didn't want to lie. "Some of the scenes from the game were filmed here. Do you know it?"

Every side conversation in the café stopped at once, the patrons all turning to face him in near unison. Rog felt the hairs on his arms and neck stand on end. If the stares from the villagers had been hostile before, they were murderous now, and he suddenly felt more afraid than he had ever been in his life.

"Yes, I know it," Signe replied, her eyes fixed on the laptop's screen. Her expression had become grim and there was sadness in her voice. Sadness, and something else... something darker. "You should not have brought that game here, Roger."

Roger stammered, closing the laptop quickly. "I, uh, yeah, you're right. I'm sorry, Signe. I wasn't thinking. I'll just leave, get out of everyone's hair."

"Oh, Roger," she sighed in resignation. "It is far too late for that now."

Before Rog could formulate a response, the two men from earlier were at his side, grabbing his arms and pinning him down in the chair. Though he struggled and fought, he was no match for the both of them. The rest of the patrons stood and approached, forming a circle around Rog's table.

It was eerily similar to the fate that had befallen Eric in the game.

"Get your fucking hands off me," Rog screamed, but the men only clamped down harder.

Signe stood before him, all traces of compassion and sadness gone. She gazed down at him with imperious eyes. In that moment she could have been Inga personified, duplicitous and vengeful.

"We know you were told to stay away. You should have listened to Henrik—he was only trying to save you. And yet, not only did you refuse to listen, but you had to flaunt that game in our faces. Just like the other travelers before you, bringing our town into your fantasies. Making us out to be the monsters, yes? You Americans never listen. Never learn."

"I'm sorry," Rog blubbered, tears flowing freely down his face. "I'm so, so sorry. It doesn't have to be this way."

"But it does, Roger," Signe replied vehemently. "It does. You wanted menace, and so menace you shall have."

Before Rog could reply, he felt a sharp pain shoot through his torso, and watched in horror as a long and bloody blade emerged from his chest. Stabbed in the back, just like in the sentimental ending. There would be no save files to reload from, no system reset that could undo his mistake—he was going to die as Eric had died.

The game had become real.

A FRONTIER HAUNTING

Part 01 – Footsteps in the Snow

Callie was deep in a vivid dream, riding a well-mannered palomino through tall strands of wheat, laughing at something unheard. Warm rays of sun caressed her cheeks and shoulders, a buffer against the crisp autumn air. Beneath her black leather saddle, the stallion ambled at a steady canter, gentle and responsive. There were no chores that needed doing—she had an entire day to spend at her leisure. Just her, the horse, and an endless expanse of prairie as far as the eye could see.

It was Callie's favorite recurring reverie, full of freedom and promise and the spirit of adventure. But, like most other things in her life, it was not meant to last.

She had just urged the horse to a gallop, gripping the reins with excitement, when a rough hand shook her awake. Callie had to stifle a gasp—her father's face was close, half hidden in the gloom. His bushy beard, a scraggly tangle of salt and pepper hair as coarse as a scrubbing stone, made him seem more creature than man.

"Callie," he said, voice firm but not unkind, "get your coat and boots on. Your brother has taken sick, and we need you to fetch cold water from the river."

She sat up slowly, rubbing sleep from her eyes. "Where's ma?"

"She's tending to your brother, and I'm tending to her. Come on, now. Let's not dawdle."

With the words spoken and obedience expected, her father turned on his heel and departed the bedroom, leaving her alone. Stifling a yawn, Callie threw off the thick quilted covers. Samuel's side of the bed had long since gone cold. She was still drowsy and sluggish, but awareness was gradually returning. The cold air helped hasten the process.

It was almost fully dark in the room, which meant it was still nighttime. She felt a knot of worry form in her stomach, a swift and unwelcome arrival, which she ignored with willful determination. Regardless of her concerns, Callie had been raised to heed her parents without dithering. Such was the way of things—adults spoke, children listened. She pulled a heavy coat from the rack, draping it over her long cotton shift. Scuffed leather boots followed. She could hear Samuel coughing in the common room, followed by her mother's lilting speech, soft and soothing. It was a voice that exuded assurance. Her mother was, if nothing else, the very definition of unwavering.

That same trait could not be applied to Callie. Effervescent and curious, she was cavalier in a way that confounded her parents, perpetually being distracted by the wonderful world around her. But she also fretted about things beyond her control. Such worries frequently led her straight to trouble, as sure as sunrise. Though she longed to stop at her brother's side, offering whatever words of encouragement she could muster, her father would assume that she was stalling. And he wouldn't necessarily be wrong;

remnants of the dream still lingered, the thrumming of hooves lulling her with their aching rhythm.

There was more to it, of course. Callie was a tough girl, a typical trait of frontier settlers, as accustomed to wrangling hogs as she was hanging garments on a clothesline. It took a lot to unsettle her. The nighttime, however, was the single, insidious exception. When the sun had set, and the world was still, other things were apt to be out causing mischief. Or worse.

Regardless of her qualms, loafing would not be tolerated by either of her parents, and she feared a stern word from them far more than any ephemeral spooks in the night. She exited the house quickly, making sure to grab the water bucket from the porch.

Winter had been kind for early December, with only a light dusting of snow blanketing the landscape. A few flakes were still falling slowly. Precipitation may have been unseasonably lax, but the cold was the same as it always was, creeping through the soft edges of her shift to nip at the flesh underneath. The last vestiges of sleep slipped away, banished by the chill. Breath frosting with each exhalation, Callie thumped down the steps, squeezing her toes back and forth to keep them warm.

A half-moon hung low in the sky, illuminating the landscape around her in a pale glow, barely enough light to see by. Not that she needed visibility. The river was close, and she had made the journey so often that she could have done it blindfolded. It was running strong despite the onset of winter, rushing over rocks to create a ceaseless murmuring. She had grown to cherish the soothing susurrus of the stream. If there was a more calming sound in all of nature, Callie certainly didn't know of it.

Her boots crunched in the snow as she made her way, the wet sound echoing across her homestead's yard. It sounded far too loud in the stillness. Putting on a brave face for her father had been easy; being alone in the darkness was anything but. Especially considering the tittle-tattles that some of the girls from neighboring homesteads had been spreading. The dread she had felt earlier was returning, and she quickened her stride.

Even laden with a full pail, the trip wouldn't take more than a few minutes. She would be out of the darkness soon, safe and warm back in her bed.

Step and scrape—the noises of her progress resounded around her. Was it her imagination, or did the echoes suddenly sound different? As if other footfalls had joined her own. Callie felt a surge of fright and stopped abruptly. The wet crunching continued for a moment, until it too faded. It sounded like it was coming from...

She spun quickly, so fast as to crick her neck, casting a fearful glance back the way she had come. She could have sworn that the footfalls had been originating from behind her. But there was nothing to be seen. Only her house, and a single line of boot prints in the snow.

Had she not fully awoken after all? Was that why things sounded so strange?

She tried to brush the concern from her mind. Samuel needed cold water, and here she was idling in the snow. Jumping at shadows like a girl in pigtails. She was too old to feel affright over some ridiculous ghostly yarns. And her parents would be cross if she delayed any further.

She turned back to the river, pushing herself to a jog. But unbidden thoughts blossomed in her mind despite her newfound resolution. Snippets of stories told by Abigail and Henrietta, local girls roughly Callie's own age. Things they had spoken of in hushed tones. Stories of being watched at night. Of being touched in the darkness. Henrietta had even sworn upon her mother's grave that someone had pulled her hair while she was washing for supper, only to find that she was perfectly alone. Fibs, to be sure, but still effective enough to scare the curls out of a girl's tresses in the dead of night.

Ghost stories were part and parcel for any frontier township, of course, and especially so with Harper's Hollow. Callie had told a few spooky tales of her own, from time to time. Usually at the expense of one of the willowy Harper girls. But something was off about tonight. The sounds around here were all distorted, warped as wood in water, as soured as curdled milk. The crunching behind her intensified, and she felt her hackles rise.

There came a tickling sensation in her hair, as if fingers had brushed the ends, almost grabbing a handful. Callie yipped and willed her legs to move faster. She was sprinting now, approaching the river at a breakneck pace, fear making her breath come in ragged puffs. The bucket slammed against her thigh with every swing of her arm. Glancing behind every few seconds but never breaking stride. And still there was nothing to see.

The bank of the river loomed in front of her before she knew it, and she dug in her heels, nearly pitching headfirst into the water. It was running steadily, breaking over a few rocks that were located mid-stream. Callie dunked the bucket as fast as she could, the brisk water causing her to gasp out loud. It was cold enough to make her hand instantly numb.

She began to pull the bucket out, grunting against the extra weight, when suddenly she felt a pair of hands grip her shoulders. A chill seeped across her neck, spreading to her arms with alacrity. As if the hands were as cold as the river itself.

Before she could even conjure a scream, the hands pushed her forward and down, straight into the water. The chill snatched Callie's breath away. Her entire body seemed to lose sensation. She struggled against the grip on her shoulders, numbed hands scrabbling for purchase in the riverbed, trying to push herself up, but to no avail. Her attacker was as strong as an ox.

She began to panic, limbs flailing wildly, fighting against the hands holding her. Though she tried to keep her mouth shut, her exertions allowed the river in, icy water seeping down her throat. Flailing turned into convulsions as she began to choke.

Vision and strength fading, Callie came to the jarring realization that she was going to die. She continued to fight, but it was almost a reflex at this point. She knew that she had no chance of escaping. Her motions became sluggish and halfhearted.

But, just as suddenly as they had thrust her forward, the hands began to pull her backwards. She had very nearly given up, making a strange sort of peace with dying, yet began to struggle anew. Surely drowning in the river was preferable to whatever fate her attacker had in store. She kicked and squirmed, lunging forward, fighting to stay underwater. Desperate to avoid an even more grisly fate. But her attacker was unyielding. She breached the water screaming, cursing at the hands that held her. Words that she had only ever heard from rough men escaped her lips without thought, tumbling over each other in her panic.

"Callie!" yelled a voice, hazy through her dulled senses. There was an air of familiarity about it. But why would the assailant be hollering her name? And why did it sound like a voice she knew?

"Blast it, Caledonia Anne Ferguson, quit yer struggling!" came the voice again. This time, however, she recognized it. Especially since nobody else would be using her given name. "What in the blazes has gotten into you?"

The voice belonged to her father.

Clarity blossomed in her mind like a cloudless sunrise. Her father had driven off whoever, or *whatever*, had assaulted her, and was coming to her rescue. Yanking her from the water like the world's largest fish. He continued dragging her backwards until they were back on dry land, at which point they both collapsed onto the riverbank.

Callie vomited water, a seemingly never-ending stream. Once it was over, she was able to breathe in gulps of air, occasionally broken up by wracking coughs. Her father had released his hold on her as soon as she started throwing up.

"Did you...?" she asked, wheezing and sputtering. "Did you see it?"

Her father was sitting up next to her, looking at her strangely, bushy eyebrows were knitted together. A large scowl, rife with future reprimands, was nearly lost within his beard.

"See what?" Concern laced his words. Anger as well, a harshness she was unused to hearing. Callie was an obedient girl, rarely needing to be scolded. "The only thing I saw was my damn fool daughter trying to drown herself!"

Callie tried to come up with a rebuttal but was at a loss. Her father would have certainly observed her attacker, had there been something to see. The other girl's tall tales came rushing back in her mind, sounding not so tall anymore. Invisible aggressors indeed! She needed to tell someone what had transpired. Her father probably wouldn't listen to her, especially not at that particular moment. Ma Ferguson was a dubious prospect as well. She was kind in her own way, quick with a salve or bandage, but had little patience for anything that wasn't practical or tangible.

The Harper women, with their mournful apparel and calculating eyes, cloistered in that big house on the hill, were another story entirely. They unsettled Callie—she couldn't even begin to deny it. But they seemed wise as well, versed in the things that never saw sunlight.

Her father rose and pulled her up with a proffered hand. "Come on, girl. Let's retrieve that bucket and get you back to the house. I'm not keen on telling your ma about them curses you were screaming, though she's liable to have heard them regardless. Either way, I'd best not hear you spittin' venom like that ever again, or she and I will be taking turns at yer hide with the thickest switch in the county. Are you hearin' me, girl?"

The only response Callie could manage was a weak nod. Her shock had worn off, and she was shivering from head to toe. The warmth of their house, and from the hearth in particular, sounded like heaven. Pa Ferguson had grabbed the bucket and filled it, since Callie's fingers were too numb to function. Together they began their trek home.

Callie kept looking around, fearful even in the presence of her father. But there were no spooks or haunts hiding in the background. No menacing spirits following close at heel. Even the sense of dread she had felt earlier had vanished. Could she have been mistaken? She felt more than a little abashed at the thought.

And yet, glancing backwards one last time, she couldn't help but notice that closer to the riverbank, there appeared to be three sets of footprints.

Part 02 – The Hunter

The sun was beginning its descent, shadows cast by storefronts growing long across a dusty street that hadn't seen water in several days. Daylight's warmth receded before the dusk in grudging acquiescence. A westerly breeze wended through main street, snatching at bowlers and bonnets alike, swirling dust devils left in its wake.

As was customary when night was approaching, the Spinning Spur saloon was filled with the raucous din of men at leisure, though the turnout was smaller than usual. The few who attended were extra boisterous, as if making up for their absent cohorts. In one corner, a piano player hammered out honky-tonk with a moderate appreciation of tempo. The enjoyment for the evening consisted of card games, jawing over glasses of whiskey and gin, with even a friendly game of billiards being played in one corner.

Not everyone in the saloon was partaking of the social atmosphere, however. Garrett Kayce, infamous ghost hunter and erstwhile U.S. Marshal, sat at the end of the bar in a pocket of space all his own. A bottle of whiskey rested on the countertop in front of him, cozied up next to a half-filled tumbler. As a visitor in Harper's Hollow, his solitude was far from unexpected. Given the town's current woes, a stranger, even one personally invited, was simply one strange thing too many.

Of course, owing to his unique profession, Garrett did not exude a welcoming mien regardless.

On a cloudy day, and with a good bit of distance from the viewer, he could have been mistaken for a cowboy. Or a lawman, owing to the way in which he carried himself. He had the requisite duster, gunbelt, and five-gallon hat associated with either profession. But that was where the similarities ended. The rest of his accoutrements were a mix of the bizarre and esoteric.

For one, a large sword hung from the opposite hip as his revolver. But he was no soldier, and it was certainly no cavalry weapon. There was a decidedly foreign look about the weapon. He also had a large leather bookcase slung over his back. It was rugged and bulky, like something a courier might carry, the leather faded to an nondescript color. Garrett appeared for all the world like a strange mix of trail-rider and scribe.

Iron charms were woven into his long beard, mixing in with streaks of gray. He was of indeterminate age, but the weathered lines around his eyes and ramrod posture gave him a distinguished air. Clad in clothing of a finer cut than most, his gunbelt and boots chased with silver, he enjoyed a nearly contradictory façade, an appearance that the country folks around him would call highfalutin. Apart from the unique attire, his black hair meant that Garrett certainly stood out amongst the dusky locals.

Those same locals kept stealing glances his way. Everyone knew why he was in town, what with the dead livestock, scratch marks on barn doors, and all the unexplained happenings out at the Ferguson ranch. Even in a rustic such as the Hollow, rumors travelled faster than a stone from a slingshot, and folks were whispering that it had been the Harpers, not the town's sheriff, who had summoned him. For that association alone, if for no other reason, the townsfolk viewed him with distrustful eyes.

A necessary evil.

Garrett continued to drink his whiskey, content with being left alone. Ghost hunting was an unusual business, and that which was unusual was also feared and misunderstood. Or occasionally, depending on who he was dealing with, outright hated. Ostracization was simply a natural byproduct of the profession, a fundamental inevitability. He had made peace with that fact years ago.

Of course, Garrett Kayce was never truly unaccompanied. Had any of the townsfolk been in close proximity, they would have felt the strangest of chills, as if a cool breeze was wafting across their very souls. They might have even remarked that they felt like someone had "walked over their grave."

They wouldn't have been too far off. A ghostly figure hovered next to Garrett, incorporeal and phantasmic, invisible to the men in the saloon. She could have made her presence known, had she wished. Tangibility was well within her ability. Nevertheless, she generally preferred to remain undetected, a silent spectator, largely indifferent to the mortals around her. She couldn't completely mask her presence, however. Anyone moving through the space she occupied would have felt inexplicable goose-pimples, a chill, or maybe even a sudden sense of foreboding.

But she was no malevolent specter, no whirlwind of evil infiltrating their town. She was Garrett's constant companion. His spectral ally.

"They come," the ghost said, her voice hazy and obfuscated, as faint as if heard from great distance, inaudible to all but him.

A few moments later, the saloon's swinging doors parted, admitting the town's sheriff and a myriad of deputies. They were heavily armed, shotguns and rifles slung over shoulders or across the crooks of their arms. Pistols of various sizes and calibers hung at their hips. Each man wore a serious expression, stoic in the face of what was to come.

The saloon's ambiance changed in the blink of an eye. Patrons quickly finished their drinks, slamming empty glasses down with alacrity. Chairs were scooted back, winnings haphazardly gathered up, and pool cues were returned to their racks. Not a single word was spoken, nor a crosswise sound made—never before had the establishment experienced such an orderly retreat. In less than a minute, the Spur was bereft of customers. Only the bartender remained, cleaning a single corner of the countertop with exaggerated intensity, studiously ignoring everyone in attendance.

"Well, Kayce," the sheriff said, his voice raspy, cheroot clenched between gritted teeth. "I can't say as I was excited about hearing you was in town, but I suppose your brand of help will have to do. I'm Sheriff Lindström, by the by."

Unwilling to partake in needless power struggles, Garrett simply tipped his hat in response. A pissing contest would only be a waste of time.

Seeing that he wasn't going to get the rise he was hoping for, the sheriff changed tack, focusing on business. "Nothing personal, but it wasn't my call to bring you in. When the Harpers say jump, we jump, and that's just how it is. I'm assuming they gave you the basics in their missive, and that you have a plan for how this will go down? We've got a bit of time on our hands, as the phantom, creature, or whatever the hell it is won't show up until the witching hour, as sure as Hades is hot."

"Fell deeds after dark, for they retreat to their lairs during the day," Garrett answered, voice a higher octave than what his stature might have suggested.

"Feeling theatrical tonight, are we?" his ethereal partner queried, acerbity lacing her words.

"Just playing the part," he replied under his breath. "Adding to the mystique."

Her only response was a very unladylike snort, which he found boundlessly amusing.

"It's probably just the ghost of one of those damned Indians," the youngest of the deputies growled, sending a wad of spittle and tobacco into the spittoon, metal ringing loudly with the impact. The brashness of youth made manifest. "Maybe we're too close to one of their so-called 'sacred' burial grounds. A curse on the cowardly lot of them!"

"No, deputy," Garrett responded with a sigh, moment of humor forgotten. His tone was brusque, exasperated, as though he were addressing a particularly vexing child. He had certainly encountered worse, but none of these men looked to be paragons of the law. Then again, so long as they could shoot straight, their principles didn't matter much. "That's not how a haunting like this works. And even if it were, would you seek to draw more ire by speaking ill of the dead?"

The deputy shook his head, crimson creeping up his neck and ears, embarrassed at being scolded in front of his peers. "But what else could it be? Maybe they're trying to starve us out, and the animals make for easy targets. Playing the long game... just seems like the kind of disturbance they'd resort to."

"Given this some thought, have you? Sorry to say, but you're wrong. Spirits, apparitions, specters, and the like typically only haunt their own kind. They rarely have anything to do with livestock or other fauna—ghosts cannot generate the same kind of lingering dread in beasts that they can in humans. And fear is that which sustains them. Attacks on animals are largely a hallmark of the risen dead, for their hunger is a maddening thing, a thousand times again as tempting as drink to a drunkard. A ravenousness that they can never truly sate. So, no, I do not believe that it is an Indian spirit. But, I do applaud your gumption."

Giving his man the side-eye, the sheriff cuffed him upside the head and then took a seat at the bar, fixing to converse with Garrett one-on-one. "Pay them no heed, Kayce. They're just skittish. So, something risen from the grave, then? What are we dealing with, exactly?"

"I'm surprised you have to ask."

"This isn't my area of expertise, hunter. That's why you're here. I'm all ears."

"Fair enough," Garrett said, getting comfortable. He pointed at the deputies and then gestured to the town in general. "This is a European town, with a largely English and Scottish population, but also a decent smattering of Scandinavians as well. Primarily Swedes if I'm not mistaken?"

Sheriff Lindström nodded once, conceding the point.

"And does Harper's Hollow have a history of these kinds of hauntings? Is this a recurring problem, a cycle of strangeness that the citizens have simply grown accustomed to?"

The sheriff stroked his chin thoughtfully. "I am obliged to say no. The Hollow is an eccentric town, full of inexplicable goings-on, but I've neither seen nor heard of anything quite like these happenings. But how does that discount native involvement?"

"Well, as a rule, hauntings don't manifest on their own. They're something we bring with us, something we cause. Do you have any Indians living here in town, or maybe on the outskirts?"

"Not a one."

"Any white folk who have renounced their own faith for that of the indigenous population, or maybe a mixed-race child?"

"In or around Harper's Hollow? No, sir, I would surely know if there was. We have nothing like that within a hundred miles, I should think."

"Well, then, there you have it," Garrett said, smacking his palm on the bar, the impact loud in the noiseless barroom. Several of the deputies jumped at the sound. "Native spirits cannot just manifest out of nothingness in your town, because nobody here shares the Indian beliefs in the supernatural, nor the afterlife, and have no immersion whatsoever in their folklore. Only the spirits of your own heritage can manifest around you. Your own legends, and those you have accepted as fact by proxy. You seed the land with your own superstitions, and then they flourish according to the fears and choices of your own making."

"I'm not so sure I buy that."

"Believe what you will, doesn't make it any less true," Garrett retorted, crossing his arms. "But think about it. What did your families bring with them when they emigrated to America? I'm not talking about belongings or hopes and dreams—what interstitial things did they carry with them across the Atlantic?"

The sheriff shrugged his shoulders, and looked over to his men to see if they had an answer. But they were just as perplexed as he was.

"Religious beliefs, that's what. Prayers and offerings, burial rites, the various superstitions of your homelands. Of your forebears—in your case Swedish tradition. Flowers and candy if you're Lutheran, shamanic customs if you descend from, or make allowances for, Sámi culture. These restless spirits, these hauntings, they weren't here waiting to be discovered; you brought them with you. Now, once manifested, a supernatural creature can haunt a site indefinitely, becoming a danger to everyone, regardless of beliefs. But first they have to manifest. To be brought to life... in a manner to speaking. However, with no Indians residing in or around Harper's Hollow, it is nothing of theirs that has invaded your town. And, by your own admission, it isn't anything that has been here for years, cropping up to cause you misery. A collective communal belief is what brought this into being. While it's not completely unheard of, hauntings aren't something we typically just walk into."

"Except in your case, you mean," Garrett's companion retorted, a tinge of contrition in her voice. She would know, to be sure, considering how their own fates had become haphazardly entangled.

Though Garrett preferred to speak to her aloud, he could communicate telepathically across their connection if he so desired. It was an ability which had come in handy on more than one occasion. *"Yeah, lucky me."*

"Fair enough," Lindström responded, nodding slowly, oblivious to the side conversation taking place before him. The sheriff still seemed unconvinced. If he even understood all of it to begin with. "But that still doesn't answer *what* it is. What evil heritage have we brought with us to the Hollow?"

Waiting a few moments for added effect, Garrett made sure to speak loud enough that the deputies could hear. He didn't want to have to repeat himself.

"A draugr."

Each of the deputies drew in a shocked breath, and the sheriff's eyes grew impossibly big. As if Garrett had just uttered the most blasphemous of blasphemies. Everyone of Scandinavian descent knew about the draugr, or the draugen as they were commonly referred to. Knew of them... and knew to fear them. Reanimated corpses of particularly greedy or odious people, who had either died upright or had not received a proper burial, they were as nasty in death as they had been in life.

As was typical with the risen dead, they were not terribly intelligent. Easily thwarted by locked doors and shut windows. Even ladders proved too difficult for them to climb, though they could manage stairs well enough. Out in the open, however, the draugen were dangerous foes indeed. Faster than most men and inhumanly strong. They hated all living things, attacking people and animals with equal ferocity.

The sheriff contemplated the news for several moments, chewing on his cheroot with renewed vigor. The entire atmosphere of the room had changed. Going from steadfast confidence to abject fear in an instant. The deputies were whispering amongst each other, shuffling restlessly.

Garrett couldn't blame them. Draugr were vicious opponents, notoriously difficult to overcome. It took a lot of lead to bring one down. Unfortunately, that wasn't the worst of the news he had to impart. But the men needed to hear it all. Every man deserved to know what he was up against, especially when the supernatural was involved.

"And not just one. From the accounts I was given, I do believe you're plagued by at least two, possibly three."

The dread permeating the room could have been cut with a knife. Their bravery already a tenuous thing, the lawmen were visibly wavering, a war between duty and self-preservation being waged within their hearts. Garrett had seen stouter men break under lesser conditions. Nevertheless, facing three draugen alone would be a difficult prospect—Garrett would need their assistance to guarantee success. And, it went without saying, his survival.

"Steady yourselves, men. It's a dangerous situation, but far from impossible. I have a plan."

"Well, then, let's hear it," Lindström eventually replied, trying to put on a brave face for his deputies. He was only partially successful.

"It's relatively straightforward," Garrett declared, looking at each man in turn. Meeting their eyes with his. Projecting confidence he wasn't truly feeling. "My horse and I will act as bait, drawing them into the town square. An irresistible target. You lot will line the rooftops of the adjacent buildings, shooting downwards as they pass. They'll whip into a frenzy as soon as they're hit, murderous as all get out, and will fixate on the easiest target they can sense, ignoring you altogether. Every round that hits will weaken them, and depending on your accuracy, might even kill them before they reach me. However, should they get within arm's length, I'll finish them off the old-fashioned way." He said the last part while patting the weapons at his hip.

"We'll finish them off, you mean," the ghost said frostily. He silenced her with a thought.

The sheriff swallowed loudly, his Adam's apple bobbing. "So, you'll be facing them head-on while we provide covering fire?"

"That is correct. They will be unable to reach you on the rooftops. In order for this to work, we'll need to control the engagement, funnel them into shooting lanes where we have clear line of sight. Pick them off one by one."

Assurance washed over the sheriff's features, and he breathed a sigh of relief. Knowing that both he and his men wouldn't be directly in the fight had restored some of his confidence. He stood a little taller, the very image of false bravado.

"Alright, then. That'll resolve what's getting at the animals. What about the hauntings out at the Ferguson's, the thing that was after little Callie? That sure don't sound like no draugr to me."

At Garrett's side, his ghostly companion closed her eyes and lifted her chin, as if sniffing the air. It might have been a subconscious mannerism carried over from life, or perhaps it had something to do with the realm of the dead. Garrett hunted the supernatural for a living, and counted a ghost as a friend, but there was still so much that was unknown about the afterlife.

"It's not," Garrett conceded. He had been wondering when they'd get to the meat of the matter and was honestly surprised that it had taken so long. "That is something else entirely. Something for the Harpers and I to resolve."

"They did say to bring you up to the house when we were done here."

Garrett stood, downing the last of the whiskey before grabbing his belongings.

"Perfect. Lead on, sheriff."

Part 03 – Of Dynasty and Diablerie

Callie's dreams were no longer things of happiness.

The carefree girl had withdrawn within herself, warding away the outside world with a bitter defensiveness at odds with her youth. She was skittish now, jumpy and worrisome, as nervous as a saddle-shy yearling. Not even Samuel could break through the icy veil with which she surrounded herself.

After her encounter by the river, things had only gotten worse. Her parents, as a matter of course, had pestered and pried for the reasoning behind her uncharacteristic behavior, but she was unable to tell them the truth. They would think her hysterical. Teched in some irrational way. She'd wanted to visit the Harpers straightaway, but the daily rigors of homestead living could not be ignored. In spite of her terror, shirking her duties was anathema; Callie was possessed of a giving personality, taught to put the needs of the family ahead of her own. In hindsight, she should have sought help from the Harper family the very first night.

Where before she had dreamt of the joys of girlhood, silly infatuations and majestic animals, dark and debased visions were the only things that occupied her sleeping mind anymore. Self-doubt had subsumed confidence, internal criticisms overtaking conviction.

Locked in a restless repose from which she could not awaken, Callie was forced to revisit the violation of the previous evening. When everything had gone sideways.

Samuel was still sick, nestled between the adults for added warmth, leaving Callie alone in their shared bed. It had been three nights since her father had yanked her from the water. Three long nights of whispered imputations. Of half-seen movement in her periphery, visions of a skeletal creature hovering just out of focus. A visage of death himself. Willing it away did nothing and invoking the Lord's name seemed to do no more than amuse the apparition. Her parents were less than twenty feet away, but with their attention given to her brother's malaise, they might as well have been on the other side of the mountains.

Callie had finally fallen asleep, lassitude forcing her body into an involuntary slumber. Her eyes might have only closed for a moment, or she could have been under for hours—time had long since lost definition and shape, an amorphous concept untethered to any recognizable principles.

She awoke to the feeling of pressure, of weight bearing down upon her body. Similar to when she and Samuel would tussle playfully. Only, there was no merry mischief to be found in the sensation, only a sickening trepidation. A certainty that something was very, very wrong. The bedsheets had been pulled away while she slept, leaving her exposed to the evening air, flimsy cotton shift her only coverture. Coldness had affixed itself to her skin, a chill that had nothing to do with the winter climate. She tried to move, to rise, but her body was held fast, arms and legs pinned by an unseen force. A coerced paralysis of wicked intent.

It was then that her shift began to rise, hiking up her thighs in jerky motions as if yanked by impatient hands. She tried to scream, to call out for help, but that same force had clamped her jaw shut like a vise. The only sound she could make was a weak moan. It was barely loud enough to be heard by her own ears, let alone the rest of the household.

The mood of the preternatural visitor had shifted since the first encounter, mutating from malevolent to licentious. It was an impression she was familiar with—Callie had perceived the immoderation of some of the men in town as she matured. Had seen how they leered at her body, denuding her with their eyes. As though she were a prize instead of a person. She knew to stay away from those men, lest they try to trap her in a compromising situation. The aura exuding from whatever grappled her was akin to those sensations, albeit a hundred times worse. Wintry, invisible fingers found the spot just above where her legs met, and a shudder of revulsion passed through her.

She felt certain that the being intended to deflower her right then and there.

It was that thought alone which lent her strength. She thrashed and writhed, bucking like a wild bronco, struggling to regain the use of her limbs, terror at the thought of defilement emboldening her muscles. It had been just enough free her from the apparition's grasp.

Her defiance angered the spirit, and agony lanced out from her abdomen as spectral claws raked across her belly. Warm blood erupted from the wound. Never before had she felt such lancing pain. Callie's voice returned to her in that moment, and she screamed for all she was worth, the sound deafening in the close confines of her room.

Through the wall, she could hear her father stumbling out of bed, coming to her aid on unsteady legs. The apparition remained until the last possible moment, unwilling to admit defeat. It was not quite finished with her yet. She felt a single, icy finger, as cold as the grave, come to rest right upon her...

Callie jolted awake, sitting upright with a tormented gasp.

"It's ok, sweetling," came a voice, soft and soothing, curiously beautiful, commiserative in a way that implied personal experience. "It's over now. You're safe, for he cannot reach you here. Not with a thousand of his thralls could he breach our wards."

The owner of the mellifluous tones, a miss Lucinda Harper, sat by the bedside in a small wooden chair. She was more outline than indelible shape, feminine contours obscured by the dusk. It was Lucinda who answered the door when Callie first arrived, breathless and whimpering, blood slick on her belly and thighs, babbling unintelligibly about the near rape. The Harper girl had let her in without hesitation, acting as a constant shadow ever since. A few years older than Callie, Lucinda exuded quiet competence. An aegis borne of implicit ability. In command of a bespoke power that was predicated on, but not beholden to, the underlying laws of nature.

With the memory fading, the pounding of Callie's hummingbird heart began to lessen, slowly returning to its normal rhythm. Just being in the presence of someone who understood was freeing in a way she could not explain. But there was guilt to be had as well. To her shame, she recalled how Lucinda had been the brunt of several disparaging remarks uttered from between Callie's own lips, belittlements stemming from a place of snobbish ignorance. She turned to face the girl, apology bubbling to the surface. Lucinda placed a hand on Callie's shoulder, stopping the words before they formed.

"Let it alone. There was no lasting harm done, and I forgive you."

Lying back, Callie allowed her muscles to unwind. The pain in her belly withdrew as well, reduced to a low throbbing. She had very nearly forgotten about the wound—it had been tended by one of the older Harper women, salved and stitched with the greatest of care. She touched the gashes with tentative fingers, but there was no fresh blood. The stitches had held.

Lucinda spoke again, hand reaching out gently, fingers brushing against Callie's forehead. "No fever, thankfully. And no frostbite on your feet, I'll have you know. Which was lucky. As for those lacerations, Avery does good work—it would take quite a tumble to rip open the sutures. Not that I recommend the attempt, mind you. We'll both get a tongue lashing if you undo all her hard work."

Memories flashed through Callie's mind, choppy and distorted. Dodging past her father in the half-light. Samuel peering at her from behind her parent's doorway with fearful eyes, as though she were a stranger rampaging through the house. Fleeing into the night on bare feet. She had run all the way to town without realizing it, heading straight for the Harper estate bereft of conscious thought, the phantom's touch loitering on her skin like a libidinous promise.

Sudden worry erupted in her mind, and she gasped aloud. "Oh! Ma and pa, and Samuel too, they must be frettin' something fierce!"

"Indeed," Lucinda acknowledged with a humorless chuckle, "but we have assuaged their fears as best we could. Your father was ready to smash our door to splinters, hollering loud enough for the whole town to hear. Charlotte chased him away with stern words and a healthy dose of the evil eye. She did, however, promise to let him know when you were recovered enough for visitations."

"I reckon he didn't care for that overmuch."

"Not one bit."

Callie let out a sigh. "I didn't know what to do, or where to go, and then suddenly I was here. Like my feet just took over. I hope I wasn't too much of a disturbance for your kin."

"Oh, the whole family knew of your arrival, sweetling. You shine like the first rays of dawn after a long night," Lucinda replied cryptically.

"How long have I been asleep?"

"Almost a full day. The sun has already retreated, and I will be needed elsewhere for a spell, but not for a few hours yet."

"I'm sorry. I don't mean to be an imposition. Although, I must ask, what is to become of me if I'm not safe outside of your home?" The question had been hovering at the back of Callie's mind since waking. She hated the quaver in her voice but was unable to prevent it.

A change had come over Lucinda's speech, deeper tones coloring her words, lending them a sense of gravitas. She sounded pensive. Uncertain.

"Well, if you're feeling up to a short stroll, you can accompany me downstairs. My family will be negotiating over that very matter in just a few moments."

Perhaps it was the way she said it, or possibly the words she used, but Callie couldn't help but feel a sense of trepidation at the girl's statement. "Negotiating?"

"You'll see," replied Lucinda, suddenly enigmatic. "Us Harpers have a certain... reputation beyond this town's borders. A legacy if you will. Or an infamy, depending upon whom you ask. We may aid those in need when the occasion warrants such intervention, but not everyone is keen to return the favor."

"Oh." It was all Callie could come up with. She had heard plenty of rumors about the Harpers—some folks painted them as practitioners of herbal medicines, while others felt certain they had traded their souls in exchange for dark powers. Callie had simply thought them strange. Aloof in a way that bordered on absurdity. Easy targets for derision, but only from a respectable distance. She had never seen them at worship and had no knowledge of them holding any sort of profession. Nevertheless, her feet had led her straight to their doorstep. But who were the Harpers, really? A family in league with the Devil, or gentle folk of nature?

She would soon come to learn that, as was the case with most aspects of life, the truth about their pedigree lay somewhere in the middle.

Part 04 — A Compact with the Coterie

After several weeks of subsisting on trail rations, the lingering scent of supper from the Harpers' dining room caused Garrett's stomach to complain. He masked it as best he could, leaning back in his chair so that it creaked, hoping that none of the assembly noticed.

It was a diverse bunch that sat across from him, women of all shapes and sizes, with a full representation of ages as well. As motley as they were, most had similar enough traits to be of relations. There were a handful of men included as well—dapper gents with long, well-maintained hair and neatly trimmed beards. Not the sort of fellas who were used to long days in the saddle.

Garrett couldn't tell if the entire household had turned out for the meeting, but it certainly seemed that way. If the numbers arrayed before him was a show of strength, it was working, even though not a single one of them was packing iron. But the Harpers didn't need firearms to cause a man grief.

For the moment, however, they were on their best behavior, as cordial as criminals in court.

Which was a relief, as their wards were powerful enough to prevent Moira from passing through them. He lost all perception of her the moment he crossed the threshold, their connection severed in an instant. It was almost like losing one of his primary senses.

In the several years since they had become intrinsically linked, they had never been truly separated from one another. Moira was prone to coming and going according to her own wont at times, fading into the hereafter at arbitrary intervals, intent upon matters of her own. What those undertakings were, she would not say. He had eventually learned to stop asking. But regardless of how long she was gone, his awareness of her always remained. Like a hum in the back of his mind. And now the hum was gone. Seated across from the most notorious coterie in the northern territories, exposed and essentially defenseless, he felt her absence strongly.

"It is fortunate that you were in the state, Mr. Kayce."

The speaker, situated in the middle of the group, commanded attention in a way that stage actors could only hope for. British ancestry coated her speech like a gilt varnish. Stark white hair topped a diminutive head, snowy strands that had seen more seasons than some of the neighboring townships. For all her apparent age, her face was nearly unlined, possessed of an agelessness which bordered on uncanny. She might have been all of five feet tall, smaller than even some of the younger girls flanking the chair in which she sat. And yet it was her milky eyes which marked her as separate from the rest.

Garrett was only partially familiar with the particulars of witchcraft, commonly referred to as sorcery in the New Testament. He was even less conversant with the framework of covens. Or sabbaths, as they were sometimes called, a distinction heavily influenced upon where in the country one found themselves. But he knew enough to be wary of the high priestess. Witches, especially sightless ones, did not live to a ripe old age by being weak or easily taken advantage of. He did not need to understand the significance of the woman's blindness to grasp that it did not hinder her in the slightest.

"Lucky indeed," he replied with a neutral tone. "Seems to me you've a bit of a spirit problem on your hands."

"That is one way to put it," the white-haired witch acknowledged.

"And the one is compounding the other. Multiple draugen in such close proximity is rare, as they tend to keep clear of each other. They were greedy in life, a trait which follows them into death—they do not like sharing their hunting grounds. Your other entity is stirring them up like angry hornets. Bending them to his will."

"The family concurs. And if it was just a draugr or two on their own, we would deal with them accordingly. Without the assistance of an... outsider. No offense intended, of course."

Garrett inclined his head, though his eyes never strayed from the high priestess. "None taken."

A pair of women slipped into the great room while Garrett replied, hovering on the edge of the group. One, a blonde, was on the cusp of womanhood, and would blossom into the kind of lady who turned heads without trying. She was also not a part of the coven; aside from her obvious discomfort and lighter hair, her features were softer, cheekbones and nose less severe, rugged in stature where the Harpers were willowy. That she was of Scottish descent was plain to see.

And yet it was the woman accompanying her who monopolized his attention. Dark and lithesome, as divided from the blonde as night from day, she moved with the sinuous grace of a water serpent. Her skin was fair and unblemished, unacquainted with both sun and strain. Black hair framed an elfin face, wavy tresses that appeared to trap the light, wrenching it towards her with impossible force. Her pale brown eyes seemed to pierce straight into his soul. She might have been a slip of a thing, half of Garrett's weight at most, but was easily the most intimidating person in the room outside of the matriarch.

The presence of the blonde answered a handful of unanswered questions, and Garrett returned his attention to the blind witch, letting out a low whistle that echoed throughout the large house.

"Ahhh... so it's a wraith. A Highlander spirit."

"Yes, a wraith. Soul stealer," the high priestess uttered, mouth twisting as though she wanted to spit. "A parasite in its worst form."

Garrett pointed to the blonde newcomer. "With her as the quarry." It was not a question.

"You are, unfortunately, quite correct. Caledonia is a Ferguson, her ancestors hailing from northern Scotland. Perhaps that is what has drawn his attention. He is strong, this spirit. Angrier than most. But his perversions are even worse, violence shifting to lecherousness in mere days. He has grown in potency, sweeping through the outlying homesteads, preying upon young girls when they are alone. And now he has fixated upon Callie's innocence like a leech. He wants to seduce her, to slough away her virtue fraction by fraction, and ultimately claim her entirely. Should she leave this house and the layers of protection we have woven around it, the wraith will come for her without hesitation. Like a wolf stalking the weakest lamb."

At the mention of her name, and the words which came after, the girl went as pale as a sheet. The captivating witch rested a hand on Callie's shoulder, whispering something into her ear. Whatever she murmured calmed the girl to a degree.

"Covetousness. That's good. We can use that, draw him out with jealousy." Garrett didn't mean for his words to come out quite so callous, but it was too late to take them back. "Your local law enforcement and I have a plan to deal with the draugen. A good, old-fashioned case of lead poisoning, but done on our terms. Aside from my fee, what assistance are you prepared to offer?"

The high priestess leaned towards him, fingers clasped together tightly, milky eyes almost flashing with enthusiasm. "Spellwork, for one. Our magic may not be able to kill the wraith, but we can help bring him out of hiding, perhaps even weaken him somewhat."

The lissome witch stepped forward, catching him off guard. Every member of the coven glanced her way, as surprised as Garrett, but none seemed keen on interrupting her.

"And I shall accompany you," she stated, her euphonious voice making the words sound musical. "We may be witches, Mr. Kayce, but that does not preclude us from being warriors as well. An extra rifle surely won't go amiss with the draugen, and I will lend what aid I can against the wraith as well."

Garrett eyed her dubiously, uncertain whether she was speaking from a place of bravery or foolishness.

The blind witch gave voice to his thoughts. "Lucinda has taken Callie under our protection, and every so often said protection needs to be of the more... hands-on variety. And thus it shall be. Besides, she's a better shot than most of those Svealander deputies. Of that I can assure you."

"As you say. This is, of course, your town. Your people. Far be it for me to deny her inclusion in the posse."

"Smart man," the high priestess said, leaning back once more. Her voice had taken on a contemplative air. "Then our business here is concluded. However, before you depart, I do have one more thing to offer you."

"I've been told, on more than one occasion, to be wary of witches offering gifts," Garrett remarked, wariness making him testy.

"That is a true enough statement, although not pertinent in this case, when the gift is given freely. Besides, it is more warning than benefaction.

One that I hope you will heed. Most ghosts are stagnant, as you know. Forever locked in a cycle that they are neither aware of nor capable of changing. But your companion is another matter entirely."

Interest piqued, it was Garrett's turn to lean forward. "Yeah? And what do you know if it? Of her?"

"More than you'd suspect, hunter. You're not the only one who has dealings with the dead. She too was bedeviled by a wraith, like our Callie here, was she not? Hounded, assaulted, and then killed? Most wraiths were practitioners of black magic in life. Did you know that? But, in certain instances, they can arise from a particularly violent or perverse demise. Such is the case with your spirit. She is not trapped in an endless cycle like others of her kind. Quite the opposite, in fact. She is on a very specific trajectory. The torment of her death will grow and fester, as rust on metal, warping her into the very thing which killed her. It is only a matter of time." Though Garrett's expression eluded her, the high priestess was evidently not blind to his aura. "But you already knew this, didn't you?"

"I've suspected it," Garrett admitted reluctantly. It was not a subject he was interested in discussing, especially with someone who genuinely had insight into his unique circumstance. It made him atypically uncomfortable. As did the eyes of the coven, the entire assembly regarding him with tremulant pity. "And perhaps you're right. But nothing is set in stone—she might surprise us both. Either way, I'll cross that bridge when I get to it."

The blind witch barked a single, humorless laugh. "So be it. For your sake, Garrett Kayce, I hope you don't drown when that bridge gives way beneath your feet."

Part 05 – Ghouls and Gun Smoke

The sun had long since set on Harper's Hollow, and the town was eerily quiet. It had been several days since the last snowfall, any lingering traces of moisture swallowed up by the parched soil, leaving only barren hardpan as a byproduct. Nothing moved in the stillness.

Garrett knelt in the dirt next to his horse, a snowflake Appaloosa named Epona. The mare, his companion for over ten years, had been christened after the Gaulish goddess of the same name. A protector of horses and other pack animals, Epona was the only deity of Celtic origin to be worshiped by the Romans, who had rarely recognized any religions outside of their own interpretations of Greek legendry. As for the horse, she was more reliable than well-oiled iron. As trusty a mount as could be asked for.

He had lain her down in the middle of town, right at the crossroads of both major thoroughfares. Epona was even calmer than Garrett, content to rest her legs while he brushed her mane—this was far from the mare's first rodeo. She would remain prone, unpanicked and out of the line of fire, regardless of what monstrosity was hurtling towards them.

Hunter and mount were only partly illuminated by the light of a vagrant moon, its pale silver face peering over the rooftops with ill intent. Not that the undead relied upon eyes to see. Whatever otherworldly force compelled them to rise also imbued them with uncanny perception, allowing them to sense and locate the living in the darkest of conditions, homing in on a being's lifeforce with unerring accuracy.

Lacking even rudimentary aptitude, the draugen would be unlikely to enter any homes or businesses, but the townsfolk were taking no chances. Lights had been extinguished, doors locked and barricaded. The residents had fortified themselves the best they could. Putting the dead back into the earth would be up to Garrett and a handful of frightened men.

And his spectral companion, of course.

Moira stood a few feet to his left, barely visible in the dim moonlight. Unlike the living, who fidgeted or made small motions unconsciously, she was perfectly stationary. Even her hair and clothing seemed frozen in mid-flutter. There were times when they would flap due to some phantasmal breeze, but it was not happening at that moment. The lack of movement was almost more eerie than her ghostly presence.

She was tinged in a soft blue glow, which in his experience was commonplace for most ghosts and apparitions. Garrett had long grown accustomed to it, and rarely gave it a second thought. She was a part of his life. A haunting of his very own.

Or, at least for the time being. The high priestess' words hovered in the back of his mind, refusing to be ignored. As reclusive as she could be, Moira had never given him a reason to doubt her, but he had to admit that her behavior, at times, had been worrisome. Changed from when she had first become tethered to his soul. More aggressive. Prone to misanthropic episodes. It was a conversation they would need to have at some point down the road, if he could draw it out of her. Which might require its own kind of augury.

As far as magic was concerned, he preferred to leave that to the adepts. Prior to leaving the Harper house, Lucinda had snipped a finger's width of hair from Callie's head, braiding it into a circular charm. Bolstered by spells, it was supposed to serve as a lure. An interlaced enchantment, shining into the hereafter like a lighthouse beacon. Holding the locket in one hand, Garrett ran his thumb along the woven strands, Caledonia's face filling his mind. He kept his thoughts vague, generalities and notions of no real substance—the process was all that mattered, not the particulars. Such rituals were trivial in the land of the living, insignificant idiosyncrasies when held against the unpredictable tribulations of daily life, yet they would reverberate across Moira's realm like the thunder of hooves in a narrow canyon.

A clarion call to the envious dead.

Much like a battlefield general, the wraith was sure to send the draugen in first, foot soldiers in service of their dark master. Exanimate infantry. It was a sound tactic, achieving two results at once. Not only would their attack be a test of Garrett's defenses, to gauge just what kind of threat he presented, but they would also be wearing him down, causing him to expend energy and concentration. Which in turn would make him an easier target for when their master joined the fray. A chess match between the living and the dead, with survival as the stakes.

He had checked his firearms several times already and resisted the urge to do so again. Too much tinkering could spell bad luck, and bad luck on such a dangerous night would be most unwelcome indeed. Every gun brought to bear against the risen dead increased the odds of survival, and the ones he carried most of all. Traditional logic dictated that most supernatural creatures could not be harmed by conventional weaponry, owing to their incorporeal forms. But the draugen were not intangible. They were reanimated corpses, perfectly capable of being struck, and possibly returned to death once more, by any conceivable implement.

Conversely, they were also more than capable of striking back. And did so with considerable might and ferocity.

Garrett's Colt New Model revolving rifle would open the exchange, striking out at distance. With six bullets in the rotating cylinder, the rifle would go a long way towards evening the odds. Its .56 caliber rounds had considerable stopping power and very little drop-off. Though its revolving cylinder design had been replaced by the more popular lever action weapons favored by cowboys and ranch-hands, Garrett's rifle was a mainstay of his armament. Mystical runes and depictions had been engraved upon every inch of metal, with additional carvings featured on the wooden stock. The rifle itself was powerful; its engravings made it doubly so against paranormal creatures.

The Colt Walker revolver at his hip was another big bore firearm, a .44 caliber behemoth that was as heavy as it was handsome. Like the rifle, Garrett's pistol was adorned with engravings, bolstering its effectiveness. Largely inaccurate past fifteen yards, he would switch to the sidearm when, and if, the draugen drew close enough.

His unique sword completed the loadout. It was an iron khopesh from the sandy plains of Egypt; a multi-purpose weapon with a wicked curve, sharpened on only one side. Capable of slicing, bludgeoning, and even hooking opponents. Where modern bladed weapons were made of steel, which enhanced their strength and flexibility, iron and silver were the most effective metal against the undead. But silver was far too soft to be used with bladed weaponry. The precious metal was better suited for filigree and charms. Accents against otherworldly aggression.

As he had mentioned to the deputies, the khopesh could be used to finish a draugr off, if needed. But Garrett doubted it would come to that. Plus, he would prefer that the sword stay in reserve until their true foe manifested.

Garrett felt a slight charge in the air, a familiar sensation. His spectral companion had sensed something within her own realm and was reacting to it. Things were about to get ugly, and his heartbeat sped up in response. Whoever said that waiting was the hardest part of any engagement had surely never faced the supernatural.

Moira stirred as if on cue, head raising slowly. She lifted a single arm and pointed down the street. Southward. The stillness of earlier was gone—strands of spectral-blue hair were lifting into the air, the hem of her dress undulating without sound. *"Ware the dead. The beasts draw near. Three, as you predicted."*

"Lucky guess," Garrett replied, shrugging his shoulders.

"Self-deprecate as per your preference, Garrett Kayce, but do not expect me to play along. It is luck until it isn't, as you very well know. Such modesty is unbecoming."

Rarely one to speak any more than was necessary, there were times when Moira would impart some truism that struck him as profound. Perhaps the afterlife granted a certain amount of philosophical introspection. He looked at her sideways, one eyebrow raised ironically.

"Now who's being theatrical?"

"Just playing the part," she retorted, her deadpan delivery a fair facsimile of his own voice. *"Adding to the mystique."*

Garrett could count the number of times that Moira had cracked a joke on one hand and still have a couple of fingers remaining. Her behavior since reaching Harper's Hollow could only be referred to as unusual, but he hadn't yet sussed out why. She was also unlikely to tell him unless queried directly. Never in his life had he known a more taciturn woman, living or dead.

But those were thoughts for later, after the ghouls and gun smoke had disappeared. He needed to focus on the task in front of him.

Garrett gave Epona one final pat and then stood, stretching his arms and loosening his fingers. Getting his body ready for the fight to come. He adjusted his holster and sword to their most comfortable locations and gave the rifle one final glance-over. He was as ready as he could be.

Moira had not moved from her spot, situated almost directly between him and the approaching threat. Her head tracked from side to side with slow precision, focused on something he could not see.

"The other two have split off. One to the left, the other right."

"Looking to flank us, as expected."

Letting out a low whistle, Garrett signaled to his backup, advising them of the shift in strategy. His own gaze remained fixed ahead, waiting for the third draugr to arrive. It took only a few moments before it materialized from the gloom, loping gait making it appear almost simian. The moment that the creature caught sight of him, and the prone horse at his feet, it let out an inhuman howl, a primeval sound of hunger that echoed off the storefronts with merciless resonance. Garrett raised the rifle to his shoulder, thumbing back the hammer with the ease of familiarity. As he peered down the sight, the draugr leaned forward, breaking into a scampering run. It was making a beeline straight for him, just as he knew it would.

It was do or die time—the moment of truth. He rested his finger upon the trigger, the curve of the metal as familiar as a longtime lover. Everything around him seemed to move in slow motion.

The draugr drew ever closer. Seventy yards, then sixty. Hitting anything past fifty yards was a gamble. Garrett focused on his breathing, forcing himself to take measured breaths, even and slow. Calmness was vital. A steady hand paramount to his survival. All he could hear was the beating of his heart, thrumming firmly.

As soon as the creature was within fifty yards, he gently squeezed the trigger. The rifle slammed against his shoulder, muzzle rising with the recoil, gunshot breaking the quiet of the night like a nearby thunderclap. The draugr was knocked backwards and into the dirt a split-second later, arms pinwheeling almost comically, a gaping hole where its throat used to be. The New Model's .56 caliber rounds were deadly to the living at any range, but a single shot was not enough to kill the undead creature. It sprang back up with a growl and continued advancing, dead eyes locked onto his own.

More deathly howls called out into the night, coming from behind. From atop the balconies and rooftops came the sounds of weapons being readied, satisfying clicks as hammers were cocked and rounds fed into chambers, his posse preparing to add their own thunder to the mix.

"Headshots if you can land them," he had told the assembled shooters less than an hour earlier. "Otherwise, aim for center mass." Hidden behind sturdy cover, barrels of various length rested on wooden supports and railings for added accuracy. Anything that reduced muzzle sway was a good thing. Another howl pierced the night, much closer this time, and then all hell broke loose as every gun in the junction opened up, spitting fire and lead from on high in a deafening chorus.

Garrett left them to it—he had his own target to focus on. The center draugr was close now, within twenty yards, body pockmarked and torn. Garrett expended the remaining rounds in the cylinder, each shot finding its mark. The last bullet caught the creature on the bridge of its nose, snapping its head back with a resounding thwack. The draugr's legs flew out from under it, spilling it into the dirt once more. This time it stayed down.

He laid the empty rifle across Epona's saddle and drew his pistol, spinning around to face the remaining enemies. The one on the left was on the ground as well, twitching in defiant defeat. While Garrett watched, Lucinda put one final round through its temple, ensuring that the creature was out of the fight for good. It was a mighty fine shot over such a distance. She gave him a nod over the sights of her rifle, and he touched the brim of his hat in respect. The high priestess had spoken true.

To Garrett's right, the remaining draugr had fared better, appearing relatively unscathed. The barrage from above redoubled, every firearm now pointed at the last remaining foe and raining withering fire its way. Missed rounds sent plumes of dust into the air, while the creature jolted and jerked with each successful impact. But it was not enough damage to halt it. From less than ten yards away he could hear its ragged breathing over the din. It was only an illusion, an artifice of life, as no air would be found in those dead lungs. At five yards he could smell the decay that still clung to its desiccated body, a rotten odor that nearly made him gag. No more shots came from above, the draugr far too close to Garrett for the posse to risk friendly fire. Once it got within striking distance, it lunged forward, reaching for him with death-gray fingers. If those hands grabbed him, he was a dead man.

But Garrett sidestepped at the last second, jagged fingernails missing him by inches. As the creature sailed past, clawed feet a hair's breadth from Epona's haunches, he tracked it with the revolver and let six rounds fly in rapid succession. The .44 caliber bullets hit with the force of a freight train, pushing the draugr further along its trajectory, while the archaic runes carved into the pistol lent their invisible power as well, siphoning the curse of the creature's reanimation with each impact. It hit the ground like a boneless fish, rolling to a stop more than twenty feet away.

Unwilling to take any chances, Garrett reloaded as he approached the insensate beast, putting five more rounds into its spine, walking them upwards at regular intervals, a savage game of connect the dots. The last bullet went into the back of its misshapen skull, just for good measure.

And then, just as quickly as it had begun, the firefight was over. Silence swept back into town with the gusto of a grassland gale, impermanent but invigorating. A haze of blue gun smoke hung in the air like a fog, filling his nostrils with the acrid tang of expended ammunition. Garrett could almost taste it on his tongue. He helped Epona to her feet, gave her a comforting pat, and then shooed her off to a side street, rifle placed back in its leather sling. Long range weaponry would be of no use against what was coming next.

Moira stood over the corpse of the nearby draugr, gazing down at it in silent contempt. His companion harbored an unbridled hatred for the risen dead that could be felt across the veil. She had tried to explain it once, the established hierarchy within her spectral realm, the unspoken ranks and echelons automatically assigned to each type of entity, but Garrett had only come away more perplexed. It had been as though she was speaking a foreign language. As best he could tell, reanimated corpses were on lower end of the scale. Barely tolerated at best, and downright shunned or enslaved at worst. Or so it seemed.

"Back inside!" he yelled to the posse, thoughts returning to the situation at hand.

As per the plan, they were to disperse back to their own households and hunker down. To be as far away from the center of town as they could get. Unlike the draugen, who were beholden to the same laws of gravity as the living, a wraith could manifest wherever it chose, regardless of height or physical barriers. The lawmen would be particularly exposed on the rooftops, easy pickings for a vengeful spirit. Far too tempting a distraction. Garrett needed its attention firmly fixed in his direction.

The stomping of their boots receded into the night. Only one person remained, still in her same spot on the rooftop of the general store. Lucinda's Winchester rifle had been replaced by two stones, though he was unable to identify them in the gloom. These she held in her palms, rubbing her pale thumbs along them in circular motions, the movement as measured as a metronome.

Garrett gripped Callie's hair charm in his left hand, squeezing with intent, willing the wraith to appear. Flinging mental taunts out into the ether. Most undead were predictable in their behaviors. Easy to goad, easy to anticipate. Such was the hope that the Hollow's wraith would be no different—the object of his desire was ensconced behind a latticework of protective spells, his minions had been dispatched with alacrity, and another man held a talisman begat from Callie's body. Any one of them would be enough to anger a spirit; all three should put it into a furor. Garrett had a feeling he wouldn't be waiting very long.

"He comes," Moira declared a few seconds later, fading from sight like a desert mirage, fully slipping into her own realm. He could feel only the barest suggestion of her presence. Whether his cohort had any fear of the wraith or not, Garrett couldn't say. She was beyond aloof when it came to such matters. All he knew was that if she chose that moment to abandon him, his life would be measured in a handful of seconds. And very painful seconds at that. Not even Lucinda would be able to stop such a monster on her own.

With a shriek of pure hatred, the wraith made its presence known, materializing from the gloam halfway up the main street, visible but immaterial. A phantom reaper come to collect. No time was wasted on intimidation or threats—it simply came straight for him with mutinous rage. Where the draugen could only manage a moderate speed, the wraith moved like greased lightning, rocketing towards Garrett so fast as to be nearly a blur. Ghostly blue vortices were left in its wake, much like the afterimages of lighting superimposed onto awestruck retinas. It would be on him in seconds.

He could feel the aura of evil preceding its arrival, a grim herald for the commencement of immoral grandeur. Unbidden thoughts formed in Garrett's head, visions of rape and sadistic torment, the preemptive psychic attack assailing his mental defenses, searching for vulnerabilities to be exploited. Only, there were none to be found. The wraith's skull-like face twisted into a snarl of frustration, its already fearsome features suddenly more so, a vision of hell itself. Garrett resisted the urge to draw his sword. It was better if he appeared defenseless, giving the wraith no reason to suspect that it might be in danger. But he couldn't prevent his muscles from tensing up in apprehension.

His foe emerged fully into the physical realm with a scintillating flash, attenuating the aether's power as one would hone a blade, confident in its victory. However, for all of its speed and fury, the wraith came to an immediate stop less than two feet from Garrett, as though reaching the end of an unbreakable tether. Which was not far from the truth. Moira had reappeared behind it, snapping back into existence in the blink of an eye, one hand gripping its shoulder, the other buried in its patchy hair. The wraith's dreadful eyes widened in shock, realizing, far too late, the trap it had waded into. It struggled and twisted, desperate to break free. But Moira's hold could not be overcome.

The question of who the stronger spirit was had been answered in the most spectacular of ways.

Knowing its doom was near, the wraith tried to return to incorporeality. To flee back into the spirit realm. But there was no escape—whatever magic Lucinda was invoking held it fast, denying its metaphysical shift. Moira pulled hard on the apparition's hair, exposing its jugular, while Garrett drew and swung the khopesh with one smooth motion. The iron passed through the wraith's neck like a warm knife through butter, decapitating it with a metallic rasp.

As its body crumpled to the dust, Moira kept ahold of the head. Turning it with almost delicate motions, she brought the wraith's face to within a few inches of her own, scrutinizing its features with soundless intensity. A minute went by, followed by another. Garrett could only watch and wait.

After what felt like an interminable delay, Moira tossed the head aside contemptuously, apparently dissatisfied, a look of scorn flashing across her visage. The gristly trophy dissipated into nothingness along with the rest of the remains.

"Not the one who did you in?" Garrett asked, although the answer was plain to see.

"No," she replied, sadness overtaking her voice in a rare display of emotion. *"It wasn't him. This one has not been astir for long. Months, at most. We have rid your world of a monster, to be certain, but our hunt is not over."*

"Still, it was nice to have a bit of help for a change."

"Was it? Do not be distracted by a comely face and ivory skin. Their aid was steeped in culpability, with nary an altruistic thread to be plucked. You know this as well as I."

"I do," he admitted, nodding his head in agreement. "Most wraiths were practitioners of black magic in life. It is very likely that he was a Harper, or perhaps one of their enemies. Either way, I am certain they created him, although I doubt it was intentional."

"Inadvertent or not, blame is blame. Intent does not exonerate guilt."

"No, I suppose it doesn't," Garrett acknowledged, trying not to focus on how angry Moira sounded. For all his bluster, he was far from prepared for the possibility of her turning against him. In all honesty, he was not so sure which one of them would survive such a collision, should that time ever come.

And that was a sobering thought indeed.

Part 06 — A Maelstrom of Magic

Callie had decided that, once she was old enough to make such decisions, she would set out to acquire her own snowflake Appaloosa. She might even borrow the name as well. Epona was like no horse she had ever met, even-tempered and majestic. Nothing like the big stallions that roamed the prairie, but intrepid in her own understated way. As constant as the North star.

She had just affixed a feed bag to the mare's bridle, allowing her to graze with leisurely contentment. Not quite ready to return home, Callie was allowing herself to be distracted by minor considerations. Stalling for time with improvised excuses. It was a tactic with which she had plenty of experience.

"It's nice to see your smile returning, even if it's just for an animal," Lucinda said, a hint of jest in her voice. Though the wraith had been vanquished and the all-clear given, the older girl was always nearby, an adjacency that seemed to stem more from sisterly affection than any actual worry.

"I just like horses," Callie replied, stroking Epona's muzzle with gentle fingers, breath frosting in the crisp morning air. It was cold enough to bring a rosy glow to her cheeks, but she didn't mind. The chill reminded her that she was alive. "They're strong but loving, smarter than we admit, and loyal to a fault. Brave, too. I think people could learn a thing or two from their beasts of burden."

"And what about the men who ride them?"

Callie could tell that the older girl was toying with her, testing her boundaries. Callie accepted it as a matter of course. She had come to know the girl well enough to not take things personally. It was just Lucinda's way.

"I think I will steer clear of such distractions for a while yet."

Lucinda's laugh was a gregarious thing, loud and genuine. As magnificent as a melody. "That is for the best, little one. It never goes like you want, and only halfway as well as you need."

Unsure of what the witch was referring to, Callie left the comment alone. She knew that silence was sometimes the best policy when it came to adult concerns.

"I suppose I should be getting on home soon," she remarked after a few minutes, leaving Epona to her meal. She exited the Harper's barn, Lucinda at her side, nearly in lockstep. A storm was brewing to the southwest, dark clouds forming on the horizon. Her home was not far, and Callie was quick enough on her feet—she could beat the inclement weather if she hurried.

"If that is your wish."

"Maybe it is. I don't know. I miss my family, naturally. But it will be hard, I think, returning to the area where all that bad transpired. I already feel the constant need to look over my shoulder, and I'm still on your property."

"For a short while, perhaps. But time will weather those rough edges, smoothing them out so they are not so painful to the touch. 'This too shall pass', as the Persians say."

"Sunshine all the time makes a desert," called a voice. Garrett Kayce rounded the corner of the house a few seconds later, arms laden with sundries for the trail, cigarette hanging from his lips. He stopped in front of the girls, adjusting his miscellany with practiced precision. "If we are slinging proverbs, let us not forget that one. It's an Arabic saying, and it means that a little adversity isn't a bad thing, since life's trials make us stronger in the end. Speaking of which, are you holding up alright?"

The last words were directed at Callie, but she couldn't seem to find the right words and had to settle for a nod instead. Garrett took it in stride, flint-colored eyes sparkling with amusement, a wry smile tugging at his lips. Fortunately, her newfound friend was willing to come to her aid.

"Have you been to Arabia?" inquired Lucinda with palpable curiosity. She seemed rather intrigued by the ghost hunter, and Callie thought she could understand why. Maybe. Garrett Kayce was a little strange, and a little dangerous, but there was a goodness to him as well, buried deep like hidden gold.

"I have," he acknowledged, giving the witch a single nod. "And the other sandy nations as well. My sword is from Egypt. Several of my charms were found in Morocco. It's breathtaking country over there. Harsh, but beautiful. You look up, and you see the exact same stars, but in an entirely different sky. Amazing."

"Are you heading off, Mr. Kayce?" Callie asked, nodding to his supplies. She was not entirely unhappy to see him packing up. While she had no personal qualms with the man, indebted to him as she was for the elimination of her ghostly pursuer, his presence still made her nervous. As though he was sticking around due to unfinished business. Ghost hunters went where the spirits were, after all. And if he was still in town...

"I am," Garrett affirmed, arranging his parcels once more. "Heading south. There's rumor of another specter causing trouble, and it's going to be a long, cold journey. This is where I bid you ladies farewell."

They watched him leave from the comfort of the wrap-around porch, neither woman speaking, content to share the moment in companionable silence. Garrett packed up his saddlebags with the ease of practiced repetition. If the cold bothered him in any way, he took great pains to keep the fact hidden. It wasn't until horse and rider disappeared down the lane that the ladies returned to the warmth of the house.

Theirs was a busy residence, the Harpers, full of incessant comings and goings, some mundane, others esoteric and mystical in nature. The kitchen was never empty, the hearth never cold. Songs were sung frequently, and with much fervor, though not every voice was on key. Callie didn't understand a tenth of what she saw, and even less of what she heard. But there was something enchanting about their lifestyle, and the ways in which they abetted each other. Not that her own family wanted for cordiality—the Ferguson residence was a largely benign environment, where the children were, for the most part, treated like young adults instead of infantile servants. And yet it was nothing like nearly the telepathic compassion which manifested from each and every resident within the Harper manse.

She couldn't put it into words, but there was a sense of purpose beyond the usual imperatives of physical necessity. An unspoken harmony, not only within the house itself, but beyond its walls as well. A transcendental existence the likes of which she had never before imagined. Her thoughts funneled into a vortex of what-ifs, spiraling across a multitude of scenarios. Some were dark—most were poignant. One or two held a gravitas that lay far beyond her teenaged comprehension. Answers to questions she didn't even know to ask and wouldn't for some time.

Callie hadn't realized that she'd been daydreaming until Lucinda nudged her shoulder. "Where did your mind go just then, sweetling?"

"Nowhere, really. I was just thinking about this house. Your family. The future. There's something about this place. A congruency that's almost..."

"Magical?" the other girl asked with a smile, pulling the word straight from Callie's lips.

Callie nodded, embarrassed. "Yeah. Which is like saying water is wet. But you know what I mean."

"I do, indeed. It's as though the answer to everything is just on the other side of the door. And all you need to do is turn the knob, fling it wide open, and then you'll learn all the secrets that ever were, and all the secrets that ever will be."

"Something like that, yeah. I kind of wish I could stay here forever. Be a Harper, even by proxy."

Lucinda leaned over, resting her head on Callie's shoulders. It was such a casual gesture, innocuous even, but the act seemed to speak volumes. A sudden charge filled the air, as though lightning was fixing to strike all around them.

"It's funny you should mention that," the witch said, dulcet tones as smooth as velvet. "My family and I have been saying much the same thing."

With hopefulness and disbelief struggling for dominance, Callie could only whisper a response. "You have? But I can't do what you do. I'm just an ordinary girl."

"Oh, darling, is that what you think? Ordinary? An ordinary girl could not have broken free from the wraith's embrace. You're a handsome young lady, possessed of a strong disposition and a big heart. But those are not the only reasons why he was drawn to you. Not the only reasons by far. You can fly without wings, Caledonia Ferguson, you just haven't been shown the actual sky yet. That firmament is bigger than you can possibly imagine. Let's have a chat with the high priestess, you and I, and she can tell you all about it."

"All about what?"

Was it just Callie's imagination, or did she detect the slightest bit of reverence in Lucinda's voice. "Why, your latent power, of course."

Fin

SEE NO EVIL (FINALE)

Wherein all of the disparate narratives converge towards a final, nightmarish confrontation.

Dramatis Personae

James Guthrie

An inspector with the London constabulary

Constance Wright

A prostitute in London's Poplar district

R.M. Müller

An unscrupulous man of science and medicine

Constable Higgins

A young policeman

Schaffer

A metalworker and tradesman

The Director

A mysterious figure with an agenda

Charles Purcell

JACK WELLS

An inspector with the London constabulary

CHAPTER XXV

Rather than return directly to the precinct, I instruct the driver to take me home. I need time to contemplate everything Lady Ellington said, as well as all the things she did not. I am also desperate to change attire—my suit is growing more uncomfortable with each passing minute. The sooner I am back in my uniform, the sooner I will feel like myself again.

My house is a modest two-story affair, unceremoniously sandwiched between a plenitude of indistinguishable structures. It is of orthodox design, wood atop brick, with an austere parlor, single upstairs bedroom, and tiny galley-style kitchen. A cramped space even with only a single occupant. In need of repair and woefully under-decorated, the only amenity worth mentioning is the pump-operated indoor lavatory. Considering there are open sewers only a few streets over, having a functioning toilet makes me feel almost cosmopolitan.

I grab the post on the way in, mostly unsolicited pamphlets and circulars, and a handful of garbage mass-mailers, all of which I will save for use as cut-price kindling. The advent of cheap postage has clogged London mailboxes with a never-ending supply of wasted paper. Considering there can be up to twelve postal deliveries per day, I have grown accustomed to the dross. Today, however, I have also received a thick letter from Purcell, nestled inside one of his bespoke forest-green envelopes.

The penny stamp hasn't only given rise to junk mailings; it is not unheard of for scattered families throughout greater London to carry on an entire conversation through hourly correspondence, the closest thing to real-time dialogue over long distances other than the telegraph. Newspapers and broadsheets are mailed almost as frequently, a way for children to fill their parents in on the happenings in their district, or vice versa. With over 150,000 employees, London's postal service is arguably the busiest workforce within the city. Busier even than the constabulary (which I acknowledge grudgingly).

Purcell and I have traded epistles since our separate postings three years ago. It started as a simple way to keep in touch but has morphed into a mixture of friendly dialogue and detailed case studies. I have helped him on a few of his more challenging assignments, and he has done the same in return. Because we employ such dissimilar methods, we frequently stumble upon clues or concepts the other has overlooked. Not that Purcell overlooks much—my friend is very nearly the living embodiment of Sherlock, though without all the damnable social ticks. In fact, if I didn't know any better, I would assume Doyle had shadowed my friend whilst writing his novel, only adding in the excessively bizarre mannerisms to avoid creating a complete facsimile.

My last letter to Purcell included a smidgen of tangential information surrounding the Blackwall murders: a few of my suppositions and theories, several sketches I made of the different burns (of thoroughly amateur quality, admittedly), and the official byline coming down from my superiors. I am quite eager to see what he has to say in response.

Refreshed and in uniform once more, I settle into my frayed but serviceable blue velvet wingback chair. It was a hand-me-down from my father, formerly used in the printing press office. The fabric still smells faintly of industrial grease and the imported tobacco he favours. Although I have no regrets about joining the constabulary, the aromas instill in me a certain sense of comfort, transporting me back to my formative years, when I would sit next to him as he worked, an attentive and heedful lad, desperate to earn his approval and affection. But try as I might, I was never able to find interest in typefaces, paper density, or conventional versus aqueous inks.

Such divertissements, however, keep me from the task at hand, and I push them from my mind. Purcell's reply deserves my undivided attention. The envelope is thicker than usual, practically bursting at the edges, and stamped with extra postage as a result. My curiosity is piqued—I doubt I've ever received so laden an envelope from him before. It very nearly pops open like a spring with the barest nick of a letter opener.

Standing in stark relief against the cream-coloured paper he prefers, Purcell's large, looping script is as familiar as a favorite novel, comfortable and easy to get lost in.

James,

Greetings, dear fellow.

Can you believe that autumn is very nearly spent? I swear it was Christmas only a few weeks prior, yet here we are, waltzing into winter again with nary a pause to catch our breaths. I, for one, am not looking forward to the first snow. It always seems to exacerbate the dormant lunacy in those individuals prone to such behavior.

My parents and siblings are well, I will have you know. They all ask about you and inquire at regular intervals about why we must both remain so occupied. As if they expect crimes to simply solve themselves. Diligence is the price of safety, and there are no two ways about it, though this is a tough concept for the wealthy to grasp.

In the interest of keeping you fully apprised of my activities, I must inform you that my courtship of Pauline Craft seems to have run its course. Though our liaison ended on an amicable note, and despite the intermittent pang of her absence, it is difficult not to speak of the demise of romance without a tone of brittle apathy. I wanted her close, yet such intimacy engendered within me a feeling of confinement. I found myself at an emotional impasse with no easy answers in sight. I suppose it is one of life's great ironies that, out of all the phenomena of this world, it is the workings of love which I find completely incomprehensible. A riddle that even the most analphabetic of people can solve, yet it is nothing more than gibberish to my heart. Ultimately, I am content to return to bachelorhood. In this, I know you can commiserate. We are both wedded to our work, you and I, which leaves precious little time for wooing members of the fairer sex. Even those of bounteous curves.

As far as the job is concerned, two interesting cases have come across my blotter.

The first is the more urgent: A nanny of immoral disposition has been poisoning the children of several influential Mayfair families and has caused, at the time of this letter, two deaths and five hospitalizations. Her method is bizarre, albeit ingenious: she gains employment within the household by means of falsified references, giving her name as either Meredith, Marian, or Marisol, and then utilizes dollops of sugar laced with some form of lethal compound to harm the adolescents, after which she makes good her escape. As you know, there isn't a child in Britain who would refuse a helping of sugar, no matter the taste or appearance. I am still attempting to discern both a motive and a pattern, though she is purportedly a fetching young lass; therefore, I cannot discount the possibility of extramarital dalliances with the fathers. No ransoms have been asked, no taunting letters sent anonymously, and none of the families have reported any theft. I cannot even be confident whether death or merely sickness is the desired outcome. There are even rumours, as of yet unsubstantiated, that the children were ensorcelled through some manner of invocation or limerick. And yes, I know how improbable that sounds. But melodies or tones which can induce a trancelike state are not unheard of (pun intended)—perhaps she employs some rhyme or metre which subconsciously encourages compliance? I have sent along supporting documentation and copies of my current notes. Please review at your earliest convenience, as I would value your thoughts on the matter.

Second, it would seem the Harper coven is once again causing mischief in Westminster. Whilst the vast majority of the coterie emigrated to America over a century ago amidst a flurry of persecution, a small number of them remained behind, not quite willing to abandon their native soil so easily. They have kept themselves hidden, rarely interfering with the affairs of their neighbours. But something is stirring them up, and over the coming days, I will likely have a very real, and very literal witch-hunt on my hands. Should prove a worthwhile distraction, if nothing else.

I realize I have not yet brought you into my confidence regarding England's most rancorous yet enigmatic spellcasting coterie. Nor have I shared the story of my harrowing experience with a blind member of said coven—you may scoff, but I am not pulling your leg. I shall resolve both of these omissions the next time we are vis-à-vis. And yes, I have considered that Mary, the murderous minder, could, in fact, be a Harper. It seems unlikely, but I won't discount the possibility.

Now, let us turn to the concerns in your bailiwick.

Yes, the eyes are the primary motive. There can be no doubt about that. Also, like you, my initial assumption was that your murderers (I agree that there are two, likely working in tandem) were simply disposing of the corpses in the general vicinity of wherever the killings had taken place. Seemed the most logical course of action. However, I have since learned that we were way off the mark. At least one of the perpetrators is a literate man, though his choice of periodicals leaves much to be desired. For insight as to why the bodies were placed as they were, I would direct you to a couple of penny dreadfuls currently in circulation. The first, *Butchery in the Berths, tells of* victims stowed inside shipping crates in nearly identical fashion to one of your doxies. Broken bones and all. The other one you need to peruse is titled *Sacrificial Lambs,* wherein victims of a demonic cult are hung upside down for their blood to be drained and harvested. I cannot vouch for the quality of said publications; I have not read them myself, merely mentioned gruesome deaths to a local bookseller, at which point he listed off more examples than he had fingers and toes. But it would appear at least one of your murderers is borrowing liberally from these types of stories. Sorry to say, but since penny dreadfuls can be purchased on nearly every street corner, locating a suspect through such transactions will be next to impossible.

As for the burns, I offer my apologies. I have never come across the like and could not begin to guess their origin.

But all is not lost. One of my more reliable informants within the criminal element has notified me about a shipment of medical implements he delivered to the Isle of Dogs several weeks ago. Now, he is very cagey about who hired him and did not provide an exact address, merely a general location within Blackwall, a backstreet called Drogue Row, where the items exchanged hands. He mentioned being greeted by two men: a large, brutish chap, and an older fellow with a limp. This informant is a miscreant through and through, from top hat to tap shoes, but he has proven reliable more often than not. His story had the ring of truth.

Furthermore, eyeless doxies and medical tools in the same general location and timeframe cannot be coincidental. Whether your murderers operate out of Drogue's Row or simply arranged for the delivery in that spot due to its seclusion, I would advise caution as you proceed. That section of Blackwall is known to be more perilous than most (not that I need to tell you this).

I must also mention that we have had a string of unusual deaths in my district as well. Corpses missing their limbs, which have been removed with surgical precision: mostly arms, but several sets of legs as well. Regrettably, one of the victims was a young constable from my precinct. Citizens have also led us to few bodies without heads. These are clean, singular cuts, James. The meticulous work of professionals. Or maybe even a guillotine. Either way, I am beginning to suspect that your eyeless doxies and my limbless corpses are somehow related. And that, my friend, is a worrying thought. I sincerely hope you still have the Webley I gifted you—I have a feeling you may want to start carrying it.

On that dreadful note, however, I must bid you adieu. The hour grows late, and I have yet another busy day on the morrow. I eagerly await your response.

Stay safe, old friend.

C.P.

I sink even further into my chair, thoroughly stunned. Limbless corpses, witch covens, and nefarious nannies... were these annotations and theories not written in Purcell's own hand, I would assume they were the musings of a madman. But the fact that they originate from my colleague, whose mental fortitude has never been in doubt, is worrisome. Purcell is not one to entertain trivial conjectures or flights of fancy.

That there are other deaths with a surgical bent to them is the most alarming piece of information. Some prominent members of the medical community have expressed concerns that, due to the rapid improvements in surgical procedures, we will soon experience an increase in back-alley organ harvesting. A black market for body parts, as it were. Perhaps the "soon" has already arrived. As for the people willing to engage in such appalling practices, I cannot say if we will every truly understand what makes them so cold. So clinical. The mind is a labyrinth, after all. A puzzle box of extraordinary complexity and unknowable avenues. What hope do we have of ever unravelling such a knot of heterogeneity?

There are moments, when I give myself over to contemplations of the future, in which I think that perhaps by understanding these villains, we could better catch them when they go loony. Perhaps even head them off at the pass. But there is an opposite side to that coin, as well. Perhaps it is better if we never comprehend the reasonings and rationalizations of the demented. Nietzschc's theory about those who fight monsters potentially becoming monsters themselves has proven true in the past. Despite my best efforts to the contrary, it is a consideration which is never far from my mind.

After all, I have spent a great many moons staring into an abyss—what are the unforeseen consequences of the abyss staring back?

CHAPTER XXVI

R.M. Müller
Undisclosed Location
Sept 14th, 1892
Research Journal Entry # 127
5:18 PM

The creature is gone!

In hindsight, it almost had to happen. Whatever remains of its brain still possesses enough basic cognitive functions, including retention of information, for it to not only learn but to make new memories based on those discoveries. Whereas the initial containment cage had several locking mechanisms and redundancies, the carriage was not so equipped. Only a single padlock held the loading door secure. Given the creature's immense strength, that single, tiny piece of metal had no hope of keeping it confined. I'm not terribly surprised that it escaped, to be honest. I very nearly expected it. But not in this way. How could something so simple and yet so important get overlooked?

{I feel very fortunate to have had no involvement with the transportation side of our project. I would not want that particular stain upon my pedigree nor to face the inevitable wrath yet to come. Of course, this is one of the dangers I warned the director about. The unknown quantity when variables are introduced to the control. But it would be most unwise to remind her of that fact, so I shall remain silent.}

It is only in these most dire of circumstances that I have seen the director lose her composure. She is not ranting and raving like a lunatic, nor is she pacing the floor in a fret, biting her nails down to the quick. But, when held against her usual detached stoicism, I can sense the flux of her emotions—she is screaming on the inside. As fuming as a kitchen fire.

To say that our operation is suddenly in jeopardy is a gross understatement. Discovery was always a distant risk, a what-if scenario that seemed wholly improbable. But that time has passed. Whitechapel is by no means sparsely populated, and the surrounding districts are just as inhabited. Even without the extra limbs, our creation is impossible to miss. Its size. Its pallor. Its rotten flesh. And we certainly did not clothe it or hide it under a shroud!

{Why did I not think of some manner of covering, even if just for added secrecy, whilst it was within our facility? I cannot help but feel to blame for that particular oversight. But my lips will remain sealed on this matter as well. I rather enjoy being alive and would hate to wind up strapped to my own operating table.}

We have but two factors working in our favor.

One – night is already descending, and the skies are cloudy. Illumination from the heavens will be minimal at best. On top of this, there are nowhere near enough streetlamps to keep the darkness at bay.

Two – there is an exceptionally thick fog this evening, reducing visibility even further. One could not ask for a more effective concealment.

However, even with those considerations, unless the creature has somehow learned to move stealthily and sticks close to the shadows at all times, someone is bound to catch sight of it. And if that happens, the jig could very well be up for the director's insurrection. And, by proxy, those who participated in it.

{A vision comes to my mind, vivid and visceral, of a mob of Londoners descending upon this very location, torches and pitchforks held aloft, angrily chanting for our demise with such vociferousness that they siphon away the very air itself, leaving me gasping like a landed fish. A comical thought in any other circumstance, but thoroughly terrifying given my current frame of mind.}

Of course, only one real question remains: Where would the creature go? Being a logical man and given that it only visited one location during the field test (an assumption on my part, but one made with confidence), it is likely that it has returned to that same place, guided towards the familiar by instinct. I have said as much to the director, and she is in agreement. I volunteered to be part of the search party, but she bid me to finish packing my belongings for the new location, especially now with the added danger of discovery. She will handle the search herself, along with three handpicked underlings.

{Secretly, I am relieved not to be accompanying her. Meeting the creature in a darkened alley, with the director nowhere near enough to control it, is a fate I am keen to avoid. Getting snatched up by the constabulary is also something I would rather not experience. If discretion is the better part of valour, I will be even more discreet than the fabled silent monks of the Carthusian Order.}

The carriage clatters away once more, thunderous hoofbeats resounding like the snappish beat of war drums. The hammering horseshoes mirror the thrumming of my heart, urgency evinced both within and without.

{I've never had much use for luck, considering it to be nothing more than a delusion of gamblers and thieves, but I find myself hoping for a little slice of providence. We are all going to need it.}

CHAPTER XXVII

A peculiar hush hangs over the precinct when I return, the diffident gazes of my colleagues hounding my every step. As though I have come back a sideshow oddity, somehow transformed by my brush with the aristocracy. That they assume I could be so easily influenced is more bothersome than hurtful. There is not a single sycophantic bone in my body, but some people, even law-enforcing constables, will only ever see what they want to see.

My peers who know me better, the ones I get on with, are undoubtedly hungry for the particulars of my meeting yet possess far too much decorum to ask. That English stodginess shines through in all places, but especially at work. I do my best to remain insouciant, feigning serenity, but my mind is anything but calm.

Part of my unease stems from the Webley revolver tucked beneath my coat. Its cold metal frame weighs heavily upon my conscience, if not my body. Gun ownership is perfectly legal in London, and citizens can even carry shooting irons outside of their homes as long as they have procured the appropriate license. But I am not overly fond of firearms and only kept the Webley because it was a gift. Investigating gun-related crimes and injuries assails my fortitude every time—such incidents are unilaterally gruesome and needlessly vicious. Firearms are also superfluous to the execution of my duties. I have never required more than my baton, which is standard issue for all policemen. Though it can serve as a weapon, and an effective one at that, the constable's wooden truncheon, a handheld rod roughly fifteen inches in length, is more a symbol of station than anything. A casual reminder instead of an overt threat. They are implements of last resort, only to be employed in the most dire of circumstances. I have only had cause to wield mine twice.

Typing my report for Lady Ellington is proving difficult, as my thoughts continually coil back to Purcell's imparted revelations. Almost before I can say knife, the shadow cast by old Jack the Ripper doesn't seem quite so long, having been supplanted by circumstances far more puzzling in nature. But, even more worrying than the killings themselves is the timing, not to mention the varied locations. One person committing a crime, heinous or otherwise, is an occurrence. An isolated incident. Two people is a partnership. Or possibly even a fluke, though our murders are far too aberrant to be coincidental. But three or more? Three or more people performing calculated murder, with body parts as the *modus operandi*, is a conspiracy, as sure as eggs is eggs. To what end, I cannot say. But I am certain that there is some grand design at work, an overarching motive suspended just beyond my comprehension.

That Lady Ellington is also investigating the Blackwall deaths, albeit from the Special Sciences perspective, is a slight comfort. At least the constabulary is not alone in this predicament. And with my unique position of being party to both organizations, I should be privy to all developments. Provided she is willing to share what she learns, of course.

With as cagey as Amelia's been so far, I should probably hedge my bets on such a likelihood.

I am very nearly finished with the confounded typewriter when Higgins approaches my desk with hesitant steps. Having grown tired of the whispers and stares surrounding me, I am but a heartbeat away from berating him for being so pussyfooted. But then I notice the constable at his side, a young lad I am only passingly familiar with, and the admonition dies in my throat. The expression on the newcomer's face causes a pit to form in my gut. Beet red and wheezing from exertion, the poor lad looks positively spent.

"Sorry to interrupt, sir," Higgins says, as sincere an apology as he has ever uttered. "Young Mr. Allen here has just reported in from Blackwall, and I think you need to hear what he has to say."

The pit becomes a chasm, my stomach seeming to twist into nothingness. I am so certain that the lad will inform me of another dead doxie that my mind practically invents the words, causing me to miss what he actually says.

I hold up my hand, stopping him cold. "I apologize, Mr. Allen. My mind was elsewhere. Could you please repeat that?"

"Certainly, sir." Allen swallows hard, and I realize he assumes I am going to mock him in some way. Or possibly give him a dressing down in front of the entire precinct. The man is positively dripping sweat, and it takes him a few moments to catch his breath. He must have run all the way back to the precinct. "I was just finishing up my stint in Blackwall, making my way north, when I heard a scream of terror. Several other shouts of astonishment immediately followed, and I rushed towards their source. When I arrived, there were maybe six or seven people gathered about, swearing upon their mother's maiden names that they had just glimpsed the most hideous creature loping along through the mist. Blackwallers may be keen on looking after their own, but they'll cry foul right quick when something is truly amiss. More shouts and screams arose further up the street, and I got the same story when I went to investigate. They all mentioned a creature of considerable size, misshapen and odorous, moving with a strange gait through the fog."

The constable lowers his voice, leaning towards me conspiratorially. I cannot help but mimic the motion.

"They, uh, they said it must have been the werewolf, sir." Allen swallows a big gulp of air, visibly preparing to receive my scorn.

But today has been a day for the fantastic, and I am not willing to discount anything. Whilst I may not believe in monsters or mythology, the fog has a way of distorting and warping proportions, and the man I am looking for is most certainly large. Easy enough to attribute a fiendish mien to something only tangentially glimpsed. People see what they expect to see, after all. In addition, if he has been hiding out or laying low, his hygiene has undoubtedly been neglected, which would account for the stink. He might have even been in the process of transporting another body, hence the strange movements.

Behind my eyes, all the accumulated bits and pieces of supposition and evidence slide together seamlessly, the weight of certainty settling upon my shoulders like a yoke. The apparition in the fog has to be the Blackwall killer. It *has* to be. And, if he left any sort of trail, this could very well be my best chance to find and collar him.

Nevertheless, Purcell's warning reverberates between my ears like thunder, and I cannot help but touch the Webley, verifying it is still in place. It may just come in handy after all. However, I have one final assumption to verify before I can act.

"Relax, constable. I believe you. Did any of the witnesses happen to mention where it was going, perchance?"

The lad nods, relief etched across his face. "It was headed straight for Drogue's Row, sir. That's the last place it was spotted."

Drogue's Row. I can't even say I'm surprised, for it is the very name I expected. Weeks later, and the killers are still in the same location where they received their shipment of medical provisions. The place where they perform their foul deeds upon the dead. Their idleness is nothing more than a lucky break, to be sure, but I will take whatever advantage I can get. Constable Allen's confirmation spurs me to action, my heartrate quickening in anticipation. After weeks of near-fruitless investigation, not to mention the emotional toll of handling the corpses of four young women, I am more than ready to bring those responsible to justice. To put this nightmare behind me. I mustn't tarry—the trail grows colder with each passing moment.

"Mr. Allen, I thank you. Get some rest, lad. You've earned it." I turn towards Higgins, affixing him with my most forceful stare. At that moment, the fact that I despise equine transportation isn't even a consideration. "And you, saddle me a horse. I don't care where it comes from, nor do I give a damn to whom it belongs. But get one here straightaway!"

CHAPTER XXVIII

Constance awakens as if from a drunken stupor—head full of cobwebs, vision swimming in and out of focus, the coppery tang of blood slick on her tongue, unpleasant but not unfamiliar. As though she had picked a fight with a gaggle of country cousins and lost badly. Time advances languidly, her bruised face counting the measure with every heartbeat, an internal metronome of involuntary malaise. The last thing she remembers is Schaffer grabbing her arm... the rest is elusive and fragmented, unwilling to coalesce into congruous thought. She is still not quite sure how he managed to get the drop on her. Such a large man should not have been able to move so silently.

Even the slightest effort to raise her head brings a wave of nauseated anguish roiling throughout her body, an endeavor she abandons without a second attempt. Instead, she remains perfectly still, allowing herself only the shallowest of breaths, attempting to stave off panic through sheer force of will. Looking around can wait; a wealth of particulars can still be gathered in the interim, beginning with her immediate well-being.

She is sitting upright on a cold floor, back pressed against the wall, her body leaning against a cold iron stanchion. Hands rest limply in her lap, wrists bound together by a thick leather cord knotted taut enough to cause her fingers to tingle. She is unable to find any slack in the ligature. None of her bones seem to be broken, though several teeth wiggle worryingly as her tongue passes over them. She is, surprisingly, still clothed, yet one shoulder of her dress is torn, hanging in tatters just below her clavicle. The most important detail of all, however, is that the stiletto remains secured against her inner thigh.

That Constance still has the blade gives her hope, tenuous though it may be. But even fleeting hope is better than none at all, and she'll need to hold onto that poise if she is to make good her escape. For the moment, however, she needs to focus solely on her own fortitude. This is not the first time she has been knocked about—abusive clients are part and parcel of prostitution, and her boyish figure has prompted more than a few bouts of maltreatment. She has also been in plenty of streetside scraps—tussles of varying levels of pugnacity. But the big man hits with all the force of a bucking Breton horse, and she'll need time before her senses fully revive. Her best bet is to remain at ease and take stock of her surroundings, at least for the short term.

With her head mostly clear and her stomach settled, Constance casts her gaze about gingerly, eyes adjusting to the gloom with a somnambulant sluggishness. What she sees is hardly encouraging.

Her proximate concern, the restraints binding her hands, is also the least encouraging. The ligature around her wrists is expertly knotted with a sturdy hide cord crisscrossing over itself multiple times. A long strip, three inches wide at least, leads up to the ceiling, tied around a cross beam well out of reach. The leather appears to be horse tack, blackened with age, well-oiled and as unyielding as cast iron.

The room gives the impression of a workshop of some kind, utilitarian and cramped. Whatever miscellanies would be fabricated here is beyond her ken—though she recognizes a few tools, like a blacksmith's hammer and assorted grinding stones, she cannot discern the purpose of any of the larger machines. Their design is unlike anything she has seen before—all sharp angles and gleaming finish, bedecked with cranks and swivels, dials and rulers.

Flames from a centrally located hooded forge crackle and curl, the flickering light casting malformed shadows... umbral outlines which caper and undulate across the factory's many surfaces. The light fails to illuminate the far corners of the workshop, including what might be a relaxation nook, leaving their contents undetermined.

A foul odour taints the air, tempered only slightly by the charcoal smouldering in the unattended forge. Constance cannot place the scent; it is both elementary and exotic in equal measure. Regardless of the vestigial constituents, there is something about the pervasive corrosion that births a primal fear behind her sternum, a reflex undiluted from generations long past, when the first homo sapiens walked the earth. A time when instinct ruled and mortality was balanced upon the edge of a purulent blade.

Beyond the fecund smell of decay, another residue clings to the air like a ghost, refusing to fade into nothingness. A filtrate that has nothing to do with physical elements. It is the lingering impression of terrible deeds and abhorrent remorselessness. Of lives cut short. Women have died here, and horribly at that. Possibly, probably, Fiona as well. Somehow, Constance just knows, as if a trace of their pain and suffering has fused with the walls and equipment, leaving an indelible stain of brutality. One that manifests at a subliminal level, reverberating like an evanescent echo, felt instead of heard.

Then again, the odour is not the only horrible spectacle to be found.

The withered remains of a corpse lie near the shop's entrance, lurid specifics nearly lost in the penumbral gloom. Or, at least, Constance assumes it's a corpse. Owing to her living conditions and hazardous profession, she has seen more than a few cadavers up close, usually beggars done in by the elements or fellow doxies fallen prey to disease or molestation. Death was no stranger to the destitute. But the sheer level of violence which has been visited upon this body, which she believes to have been male, takes her breath away. Only a few constituent pieces are readily identifiable. A foot here, half of a hand there. The rest is a discoloured mishmash of sinew, bone fragments, and chunks of what she assumes to be internal organs. As though the body was put through a thresher.

What she does not see, however, is anything resembling a head or face. It is entirely possible that the finer details are lost amidst the carnage, especially since looking at the tableau for longer than a few seconds causes her stomach to twist like an angry snake, and she must avert her eyes. Regardless, she espies neither hair nor teeth in the assorted heaps of gore.

Just what in God's name had happened here?

From the corner of her eye, she catches furtive movement, a lighter shade of darkness shifting gradually in the deepest recess of the room, the motion nearly imperceptible in the murk. Once again, that feeling of creeping death skulks along her spine. It's large, whatever it is, and its head much closer to the ceiling than her own. Anthropoidal in an abstract way, albeit bastardized and exaggerated. A cloud of menace seems to radiate towards her, a pall of danger she cannot characterize. As before, Constance's world tilts, and she feels as though some part of her soul, still intimate and innocent in spite of her sins, is being torn apart, ripping away like dry burlap.

The thing—and it is most assuredly a thing, not a person—halts the moment she peers straight at it, like a child caught in the cupboards after bedtime. A succession of clicks and moans emanate from it, as muffled as murmurs. They are anything but kind, those sounds, akin to the discordant tone of a battered jack-in-the-box. The dissonance before the startling reveal.

She knows not what it is, but one point is certain—whatever observes her from across the veil of shadows is something that should not exist. That cannot, by all laws of the universe, be extant. All at once, her belief in the supernatural is substantiated, even though she firmly wishes for the contrary. Her idealized version of the afterlife crumbles into so much dust. This is no Dickensian spirit. No cautionary spectre or helpful apparition sent across the mantle of death to aid the living. This is evil unearthed. The unmaker of life.

Constance rises on unsteady legs, the urge to flee alighting her senses, flooding her body with sudden vitality. The knife seems a paltry defense against something so inexplicable, but she reaches for it all the same. Before her fingers have traveled far, the large door swings open with a bang, loud enough that she nearly jumps out of her skin.

Schaffer enters the center of the room, crimson light cast from the charcoal fire lending him a devilish appearance. His arms are laden with metal canisters of various sizes, more than she can count, all of which bear the word *KEROSENE* in as many different motifs. He hardly appears to be fazed by the encumbrance.

Any lingering doubts about him being Fiona's killer have fallen by the wayside, recent circumstances aligning too flawlessly to be coincidental. The leather straps entwined around her wrists. His lecherous temperament. The residual suffering permeating the workshop. There is no sheep's clothing in sight, only a wolf amongst wolves. Just being in the same room with him makes her skin crawl. Even so, that discomfort is quickly subsumed by rage, a fiery mote that grows exponentially, the latticework of hatred searing her from within. She longs to charge at him, hissing and kicking and spitting like a feral animal, leather strap be damned. Any which way she can cause him harm.

And yet, despite her repugnance for Schaffer, the unknown entity remains the larger concern. Speaking to the villain is anathema, and she is loath to give him even an ounce of satisfaction, but Constance has no other alternatives. When trapped between two monsters, appealing to the one who is still human seems the only recourse. Desperate times, desperate measures.

She does, however, attempt to feign ignorance. "Please, good sir, untie me. There's something hideous over there, lurking in the dark. Some kind of miscreation." She tries to point to the corner, forgetting that her wrists are bound together, and drops them back down in front of her.

"Well, looks who's come 'round, then." Schaffer's voice grinds like stones in a lapidary's tumbler, any trace of pity long since worn away by the burnishing process, leaving only a smooth husk of apathy behind. He doesn't even spare a glance to where she indicated. "I thought maybe I hit you too hard, and you wasn't gonna wake back up."

"Just look!" she cries, frustration and fear threatening to boil over.

"Wot, you mean the tall bloke behind me?" he asks, hooking a thumb over his shoulder in the direction of the creature. He does not sound the least bit worried. "A mite shy, that one. Prefers to stay hidden, he does, wary as a burglar. An' who can blame him? Flesh fallin' off like mouldy bread, enough hands to finger four cunnys at once, slinkin' about with his pecker exposed. Well, if he still had one, that is. I reckon them worms went straight for the dangly bits first, yeah?"

"But... but what is it?"

Schaffer shrugs, not the least bit concerned. "I dunno. Showed up 'ere before you did. I imagine it's wot kilt my associate, though I wanted that honour for meself. But I recognized its nature, I did. And it recognized mine. Birds of a feather, I say." Whilst he speaks, Schaffer unstoppers each of the kerosene tins, spilling their contents about the room in a haphazard fashion. Noxious fumes fill the air, coaxing tears from Constance's eyes. Her body feels flushed, feverish with the realization of Schaffer's intentions. "It be wearin' that contraption what Milt made, and them eyeballs floatin' in the solution, them come from whores. Just like you. Mayhap you even knew some of 'em. Twas splendid work, puttin' them green eyes up front like that. The bitch they came from, a red-headed filly, she was my favorite of the bunch. Gave it her all, she did. Fucked like a proper tart and then fought to the bitter end."

Hearing Fiona referred to so flippantly, with so much invidiousness, transforms Constance's demeanor as though she were Jekyll and Hyde. The heat within her shrivels instantaneously, replaced by a bitter chill. While his attention is diverted, she reaches under the hem of her dress, pulling the stiletto free with one smooth motion. Cutting through the long strap is certainly feasible but will take some effort. Instead, she turns the blade around, point facing upwards, concealing it behind her arms. The motion has caused her dress to slip further, exposing a pale-skinned breast. Schaffer, occupied by his impending arson, has yet to notice.

"She came to me, the boss lady did. Telled me them bobbies was gettin' too close to the truth, and to raze the place to the ground. A purgative fire, she called it. *Tabula rasa.* And then you showed up, straight outta the blue like a bleedin' miracle, and it got me thinkin'... I ain't never burnt nobody up before. Leastways not when they was still breathin'. Yet here you are, all wrapped up like a yuletide present—maybe it's true that e'ry dog 'as his day. Oh, and by the by, that dame didn't say nuffin' about needin' yer eyes, so I spose you get to watch as them flames start creepin' in, nippin' at your dress all hungry like."

He finally turns to face her, only a couple of canisters left unemptied. Only then does he notice her partial nudity, mouth parting slightly, and she watches as his expression goes slack, as though all of the blood has emptied from his head. Which, in a roundabout sort of way, is entirely accurate.

"But ain't no reason we can't have a bit of fun afore the end, yeah?" he says, ambling towards her, his eyes affixed to her bosom as if by a string.

Constance shies away, playacting at fear, body angled defensively. He likes them meagre, she recalls. Small and helpless. She folds in upon herself, exaggerating her vulnerability. The most pitiable of prey. Her arms twist at an awkward flexure, keeping the knife just out of sight. Schaffer stops mere inches away, mammoth hand engulfing her breast, squeezing painfully. Revulsion threatens to overpower her; she has to swallow the urge to vomit.

Tongue darting across cracked lips, Schaffer leans closer, pungent breath hot on her cheek. His exhilaration is obvious, pressing against her belly with lustful promise. That his gaze never rises above her chest is hardly surprising—he is too enraptured with his ravishment to notice anything else. "Tis truly a shame that you..."

He never gets a chance to finish the sentence. With a shriek of pure vitriol, Constance raises her hands as far to the side as she can, blade nearly horizontal. Before Schaffer can even react, she stabs at the side of his head with all her might. One single, mighty thrust. Fiona's rusty stiletto, all six inches of it, slides into Schaffer's ear with almost no resistance whatsoever.

The pained look of surprise on his face is the most beautiful sight she has ever witnessed. For the span of a single heartbeat, one perfect moment of righteous reprisal, he stands motionless. Uncomprehending. Ochre eyes wide with shock and denial. But the injury cannot be ignored, and Schaffer releases his hold, staggering backwards on tremulous legs, the blade sliding free with a wet scrape. Constance brandishes her weapon triumphantly, a cheapjack David having bested the lubricious Goliath. A penny dreadful heroine brought to bloody life.

Triumph turns to alarm, however, as Schaffer's runaway bulk caroms against the hooded forge, knocking it over with a resounding crash. Enflamed charcoal briquets scatter every which way, igniting the kerosene with a deafening whoosh. A blast of heat rushes outwards, throwing her bodily against the wall, joyous tears evaporating in a superheated flash. The workshop becomes bright as day, shadows expelled by the rapidly expanding inferno.

Hidden no longer, the creature looms in all its ghastly glory, undaunted by the flames, commanding her attention like some ancient, disremembered titan. Afloat in cloudy liquid, green eyes regard her dispassionately behind a layer of glass. Fiona's eyes, stolen and profaned. The creature begins to move towards her, exuding menace with every stride. Were it not for the threat of impending immolation, she would be frozen in fear, awestruck into inaction. That such an abomination could be birthed into the world seems an affront to God himself. Heresy of the highest order, wrought by the hands of man. Despite the chaos surrounding her, an impulse takes root in Constance's mind, inchoate and nebulous. A desire to bring ruin to all such creations, in whichever form they might take.

But, in order to do that, she must first survive.

Tearing her gaze away from the monstrosity, she lays into the strap with reckless abandon. Intuition guides her, conscious thought slipping away, the roar of the blaze fading to a low hum. Back and forth with the knife, leather fetters hindering her motions. The effort feels like it takes hours, though mere seconds have passed. The creature is closer now, less than ten feet away. Constance doubles her efforts, sawing frantically. As the strap separates and her arms pull free, she has but one principal impetus.

Run. Run! RUN!

CHAPTER XXIX

Londonʼs sky has opened up with everything it possesses, heavy rain coming down in veritable sheets. Lightning flashes in the distance, quick bursts of brilliant ghostlight, the accompanying rumble of thunder lost amidst the clatter of hooves.

My appropriated horse and I fly through the fog at breakneck speed, navigating more by memory and presentiment than actual visibility. On such a dark and stormy night, soaked to the bone and halfway terrified, I cannot help but feel as though I am racing towards disaster. Hurling headlong into an unsavory fate. Nevertheless, I hold fast the reins and press into the stirrups as though I am one of King Arthurʼs knights, galloping into the fray atop a loyal destrier, sworn to defend the realm at any cost. Bound for honour and eternal glory. Except, in my case, the warhorse is an ill-tempered nag, as put upon as an after-hours solicitor, punctuating his disdain with frequent snorts of misery. Having been worked into a lather owing to our mad dash, I fully expect him to buck me off at his earliest convenience.

I, of course, am no knight. No *personae exemplar*. No jingoistic martyr gladdened to serve as fodder for Queen and country. I am just a man sworn to uphold the law by solemn vow. Leave the heroics to the young and foolhardy—I simply wish to execute my duties to the best of my ability. To be worthy of the inspector's badge.

My first concern, naturally, is to apprehend the Blackwall murderer. His reign of terror must be stopped before another young lady is harmed. Moreover, doxies or not, the four dead women are owed a measure of justice, and I shall see it delivered. Sentimentality may not matter much to the dead, but those left behind in the wake of tragedy require some manner of closure. I would like to knock upon Connor's door, hat in hand, informing him that Fiona's killer was safely behind bars, there to rot for the rest of his natural life. Cold comfort when held against such an unbearable loss, but life is rarely anything other than uncharitable.

On the opposite side of the coin, if there is a twisted conspiracy brewing in London's underbelly, its orchestrators must be rooted out at all costs. These dismemberments cannot be allowed to continue.

Of course, having the best of intentions is not enough on its own. Confronting a deranged individual (or possibly two) on their turf without a plan or backup is a risky venture. Dealing with the big man alone would be a tribulation, but with similar crimes taking place in other parts of the city, there could be a whole host of accomplices waiting for me. A veritable army of ruffians. That Higgins will send additional constables to Drogue's Row is only a matter of course. He's a quick study, sharp and hardworking, unafraid to take the initiative when warranted. He will ensure that someone comes to my aid. The only drawback will be the time it takes to get additional bobbies mobilized, as well as their travel distance from Limehouse.

In the interim, I am on my own.

Despite our mutual disfavour, the steed and I make it to Drogue's Row, suffering neither accident nor incident, relieved that our frantic flight has concluded. Unwilling to inflict further torment upon the poor animal, I dismount with as much grace as I can muster. Which, as it turns out, might as well be none at all, for I practically tumble straight into the gutter. Thankfully, there is nobody around to witness my equestrian ineptitude. Obligation fulfilled, the horse turns tail and heads back the way we came, vanishing from sight almost instantly.

Little more than a serpentine alleyway, Drogue's Row is devoid of distinguishing characteristics. There are dozens of lonesome lanes like it in Blackwall. With the rain and fog blotting out even the most rudimentary details, it could be any street in London. Nevertheless, whatever apprehension I might have had in finding the correct venue turns out to be moot—fire rages within one of the buildings, black smoke billowing out of its open door like a beacon.

A conflagration in the very location I am investigating cannot be a coincidence, and I approach with caution, truncheon at the ready. What's more, there is something else in the air. A charge of frightful premonition, though I am unable to identify the source of my unease. Perhaps my quarry had a lookout who saw me approach, and the fire is a trap or possibly even a distraction, as unlikely as those options seem. But unlikely doesn't mean impossible. These criminals have proven as canny as cats already. I mustn't make the mistake of underestimating them.

I am less than ten feet from the building, close enough to feel the heat, when a half-naked woman bursts through the doorway as if shot from a cannon, feet scarcely touching the cobblestones in her haste. Between her bound wrists and panicked expression, I feel that my hunch was correct—that I have stumbled upon another would-be victim of the Blackwall killer. The girl's features are familiar; I feel certain I have seen her before, possibly even more than once. She darts behind me like a hare to its burrow, and I grip the truncheon tightly, bracing myself for a face-to-face confrontation with the Blackwall killer.

But what emerges through the doorway is nothing I could have expected—neither man nor beast of legend, but something else entirely. Something far worse. A brutish aberration which could conceivably pass as human, but only when the light was low and shadows long. My baffled mind struggles to make sense of what I am witnessing: multiple appendages, a metal-and-glass contraption affixed to its head like a visor, the gray complexion as pallid and withered as a corpse. An appropriate observation, as the creature is undeniably a cadaver, freshly disinterred, though what has bestowed upon it the power of locomotion is anyone's guess. A pall of doom emanates from it like a bow wave before a ship, crashing over me with near physical force. At least I now know how the missing arms that Purcell mentioned are being employed. The science of such a feat eludes me, yet I am beholding incontrovertible proof. Some of my colleagues, fellows older than myself, have mentioned moments in their careers when, suddenly facing long odds, they felt as though someone had walked over their graves. It is a feeling I have never experienced until this very moment. Nor have I ever felt so defenseless. So vulnerable.

The truncheon drops from my fingers with a clatter, and I draw aside my coat in a panic, clawing for the Webley. If the creature recognizes the weapon or has any fear of it whatsoever, there is no visible sign. It takes a single step forward, all four arms raised threateningly. Fear grips me like a vice, hesitation freezing my muscles in place.

"Shoot it, Guthrie!" the girl cries, the terror in her voice mirroring my own sentiments. Her scream breaks through my yoke of inaction, and I require no further coaxing, firing off a single round at the thing's sternum, adding manmade thunder to the storm raging around us. Though unfond of firearms, I know my way around them well enough. The Webley Mk I service pistol, a break-action short-barrel revolver chambered in .455 calibre, may not be a battlefield powerhouse, but the 265-grain cartridge is still robust enough to bring most men to their knees. I hit the thing square in the chest, roughly where its heart should be, bullet passing straight through its torso with a puff of grave dust. Not a bad shot for a journeyman.

Lamentably, "not bad" is still nowhere near enough when one's target appears unshaken by a gunshot. I can't even be sure if it felt the impact, for it didn't react in any way. Not even so much as a gasp. The silent creature takes another step, not deterred in the slightest, closing the distance with implacable persistence. Having no other recourse, I fire four more times in rapid succession. I cling to the hope that a salvo will succeed where the single shot failed. In for a penny, in for a pound, metaphorically speaking.

Much to my dismay, the additional bullets prove just as impotent as the first. The brute is close enough now that I can see eyes suspended in the visor, green irises contrasted against a mauve fluid, unveiled glower fixated upon me with murderous intent. Behind me, my newfound ally is mumbling to herself. She might be praying, or perhaps she is cursing my inability to cause any damage. I would be sympathetic to either instance.

A brave man would tell her to flee, to save herself whilst I meet the beast head-on. But words fail, my mouth having gone dry. Even more terrifying than the creature itself is the thought of facing it alone. It must be a shared sentiment, for she stays with me, gripping my coat with shivering hands. Whatever fate is to befall us, we shall endure it together.

I have but one cartridge left. An inkling of an idea forms in my mind, and I grasp at it like a drowning man straining for a lifeline. Raising the Webley at the brute's face, I take aim at the visor, right between those lidless eyes. The one feature that is different than the rest—wrought instead of risen. If I can blind it, the girl and I just might stand a chance. A frangible hope born from pure desperation, but it is all that remains.

I allow the creature one more step to maximize my accuracy, and then pull the trigger. Beyond the recoiling muzzle, I watch fluid fountain outwards, my bullet having struck true. The visor splits apart, glass and metal shattering as it falls away. Staggering backwards into the smoke-filled doorway, the brute grabs at the wound as if surprised, all four hands covering its face in belated defense. It arrests its faltering mere feet from the blaze, dazed but not defeated. Seizing the opportunity, I spring forward with all my might, planting a shoulder directly into its stomach, the impact sending it reeling straight into the inferno. Flames rip at its dead flesh like hyenas, heedlessly ravenous. Within seconds, the creature is completely enflamed, disappearing from view as the blaze flares ever brighter. A low moan issues from within the building, a woebegone lamentation cast into the night. It nearly stops my heart, that dirge of the dying, though I am uncertain whether the sound promulgated from the brute or is simply the structure protesting as flames gut it from within.

For the briefest of moments, time halts its eternal progress. Even the rain holds steady, suspended mid-plummet, though I am certain that is merely a phantasmic illusion conjured by my disquieted mind. That I am in shock is without question, but even in my distress, I swear that the entire world is balanced upon the precipice of disaggregation. It is as if the night is holding its breath, expecting the other shoe to drop. Hesitant and tremulous.

The moment passes as if a dream upon waking, a broken spell robbed of endowment. No longer held thrall by the creature's terrible presence, I break open the revolver and reload it, pulling spare cartridges from my coat pocket. I cannot say with absolute certainty that the brute will succumb to fire. Given the events of the past several minutes, it is not a risk I am willing to accept. Taking aim at the doorway, I cock the hammer back and wait, hand trembling as the excitement begins to vacate my muscles.

It is only when the girl appears next to me, lowering my hand with hers, frayed bindings falling away from her wrists, that I allow myself a moment of shaken repose, releasing a breath I hadn't known I was holding. Now that we are safe, I am able to survey her countenance without distraction. She accepts my scrutiny with a glimmer of bashfulness, but I am no closer to discerning her identity. Just how do we know each other? My absentee manners return soon thereafter, and I cover her nakedness with my coat whilst also placing my cap upon her head. It is more a chivalrous gesture than a practical one—we are both completely sodden, and no headpiece is going to change that fact.

It turns out to be a most fortuitous propriety, however, for now that her face is no longer partially concealed by a cascade of hair, recognition blooms. I *have* seen this woman before, and I have also seen her as a young man instead, pulling a wain whilst Higgins and I conferred mere feet away. She had disguised herself almost flawlessly.

My surprise must be evident, for she cuts me off before I can utter a word. "I'm sorry you had to find out this way, Guthrie. It's not quite how I imagined it would transpire. My real name is Constance Wright. Fiona and I didn't just share a residence, we also shared the same occupation."

I nod, not knowing what to say in response. Another astonishment in the span of a handful of minutes has rendered me inarticulate. I simply hope that my laconic demeanor is not misinterpreted as virulence. There is no anger regarding her deception, only a rueful self-recrimination at my misjudgment. In hindsight, I should have uncovered Constance's true gender right off, as many of the signs were present. Her effete mannerisms. Her high voice. The odd way in which she pulled the cart, adjusting her clothing almost self-consciously. It was all so patently obvious, yet I remained oblivious, looking no deeper than surface level.

Standing in the middle of a rain-soaked alley, we make for quite an incongruous pair. The inspector and the prostitute. Not that I care one whit for her background or chosen profession, for what right have I to dictate how a woman employs her body? Times are hard for all, and even the most basic of necessities won't pay for themselves.

"It's a pleasure to meet you, Constance," I stammer, tongue-tied once again in the presence of a woman. "Even in circumstances such as these. I am assuming you know the whereabouts of Fiona's killer?"

She nods in the direction of the smouldering building, eyes flashing dangerously. "Aye. He had every intention of adding me to his tally, after a quick bout of pre-murder fornication, I might add, but failed in both attempts."

"Self-defense it is, then."

"This isn't over, though, is it?" she asks, turning to face me again. There is something almost anticipatory about her expression, though everyone copes with survival differently. Perhaps I am misreading her affectations. When it comes to the fairer sex, it would hardly be the first time.

"No," I reply, hoping that my tone conveys reassurance. The immediate mystery may be solved, and the Blackwall killer stopped, but an even greater enigma has been laid upon our doorstep. "I believe we have only scratched the surface. Judging by the appliance the creature wore, this conspiracy surely runs deeper than we can possibly imagine. Dark days are looming, I fear."

"Very well," Constance rejoins, looking northwards. She does not seem displeased in the slightest. "Troubles for the future, I suppose. As for concerns of a more immediate nature... care to walk a defenseless girl home?"

A part of me cannot help but feel dismayed. With both the Black-wall killer and the risen corpse burnt to ash, no proof remains of what transpired tonight. Nothing for me to present to Lady Ellington or my superiors. Without evidence, and only the testimony of a doxie for corroboration, I would be made a laughingstock at best, or branded a lunatic at worst. Much like Aberline with his werewolf sightings in and around the Talbot estate. But, as Constance said, those are worries for another day.

For now, I must take solace from the small victories we have achieved.

I hold out my arm, which she takes in a ladylike fashion. I know little of Miss Wright, other than that she is plenty capable. However, I am willing to playact the part of the valiant protector, at least for the time being.

"It would be my pleasure, my lady."

End Finale

ACKNOWLEDGEMENTS

Bottom line up front—this collection would not exist without the love and support of the authors, publishers, and readers of the indie writing and reading community. Never in my wildest dreams would I have imagined being so welcomed, respected, encouraged, and celebrated by so many wonderful people. Thank you all so much!

To my beta readers who had various levels of involvement with these tales, keeping me honest and on track, I offer my sincerest gratitude. Daemon, Esther, Hayley, James, LeeAnne, Karen, Kelly, other Kelly, Marie, Patti, and Sam—you guys are the very bestest.

Much love for James G. Carlson of , a truly peerless horror homie, for combing through my tangle of words with a critical eye and helping to keep imposter syndrome at bay.

My hat is off to Christy Aldridge, , for the absolutely stunning book cover. With just the barest of guidelines, she absolutely nailed the aesthetic of the tales, delivering the perfect artwork in the process. Thank you for allowing me to wrap these stories in something so lovely!

To Last Waltz Publishing, , for allowing me to spaz out on the dance floor from time to time, I am eternally grateful to be a part of this family.

ABOUT THE AUTHOR

Jack Wells is an unassuming, introverted author of various types of fiction, ranging from thrillers to mysteries, from horror to historical. Favoring smaller-stakes tales with ordinary people in extraordinary situations, Jack prefers to focus on character-driven narratives and modest, more intimate plot twists.

When not putting pen to paper, Jack can be found spending time with his sweet but quirky family, kayaking, fixing up his 1960s home, shooting, and sipping whiskey by the fire pit. One can often catch Jack taking spontaneous late night road trips throughout northern Utah with the latest retro synth music providing a surreal soundtrack. Outside of all the fun activities, Jack spends much of his time herding cats as a beleaguered government employee..

LAST WALTZ PUBLISHING

Visit our website for a list of titles and authors

FREE STORY FROM LWP

Grab a free copy of The Dead Girl. Subscribe to the Last Waltz/ Daemon Manx newsletter for discounts and info on new releases.